A Ghost at the Door

MICHAEL DOBBS

**SIMON &
SCHUSTER**

London · New York · Sydney · Toronto · New Delhi

A CBS COMPANY

First published in Great Britain in 2013 by Simon & Schuster UK Ltd
A CBS COMPANY

Copyright © 2013 by Michael Dobbs

1 3 5 7 9 10 8 6 4 2

Simon & Schuster UK Ltd
1st Floor
222 Gray's Inn Road
London
WC1X 8HB

www.simonandschuster.co.uk

Simon & Schuster Australia, Sydney
Simon & Schuster India, New Delhi

A CIP catalogue record for this book
is available from the British Library.

Hardback: 978-1-47111-151-8
Trade Paperback: 978-1-47111-152-5
eBook ISBN: 978-1-47111-154-9

This book is a work of fiction. Names, characters, places and
incidents are either a product of the author's imagination or are
used fictitiously. Any resemblance to actual people, living
or dead, events or locales, is entirely coincidental.

Typeset by M Rules
Printed and bound by CPI Group (UK) Ltd, Croydon, CR0 4YY

A Ghost
at the Door

To the memory of
Timothy Hadcock-Mackay,
a very special friend.

PRELUDE

Through the double sash of the window she could see
the light beginning to redden as an evening breeze
blew across the embers of the day. When she'd arrived
a few hours earlier, the wind had been blowing impatiently, stirring the waters of the lake, but now the
elements were at peace, rocking gently, like a childhood
lullaby bringing the day to its close. Her last day. In the
corner of her line of sight she could glimpse the ivy-
covered ruins of the Victorian boathouse that stood
sharp against the glistening water, brown on mottled
silver, its hollowed eyes staring, its open mouth mocking. The sun was sinking behind the distant scribble of
hills and by the time it was gone, she realized, she
would be dead.

He had poisoned her. Stupid, it was the drink, of

course, a final whisky, he'd said, and suddenly she couldn't feel a thing. She was wiggling her toes, so she told herself, as though buried in the sand of her beloved island, but nothing happened. She was paralysed, couldn't move, except for her eyes. She felt no sense of panic, not yet, not for a few seconds at least; there was little more than a tremor of incomprehension that she could hear his breathing but not her own. For a moment she wondered whether this was another of his mind games, a test of her devotion, even though she'd never given him cause to doubt, not once, not in all the years since she'd turned up at the lecture rooms off St Giles and found him staring at her from the podium. Two enquiring minds of exceptional talent, two bodies of youthful needs, soon to be thrown at and upon each other.

Theirs hadn't been much of an affair, not in terms of weeks, little more than a medley of urgent couplings that had trussed her Catholic soul in knots, until he'd declared that he couldn't both supervise her doctorate and take her to bed, not at the same time. He'd made his choice clear and she had followed it, without ever losing hope that he might change his mind. Ever. Even now.

Strange, she could almost taste it once more, that breathless moment of orgasm when the body locks up,

2

refuses to breathe, a moment that seems to last for ever before it releases everything.

The mounds of her once youthful breasts were barely moving now; she struggled to speak but could find only one final word: 'What . . .?' She had meant to ask, 'What is it? What have you done?' But the words wouldn't form. A coldness was stealing through her, she couldn't feel her feet, no movement in her arms, fingers, no breath. Stuck in that moment.

'It's experimental, a derivative of snake venom. Filled with what's called mambalgins, so no pain,' he said, as though offering comfort. Then, 'Forgive me.'

Her lips trembled once more but she couldn't make sound any longer. The sun was no more than a rim of fire, its light breaking up in anger as it forced a way through the thickening peel of atmosphere. Her eyes seized upon it, trying to drag it back into the sky.

He watched her struggle, knowing what she was thinking; he'd always been able to read her mind. 'Why?' he said, posing the question for her.

Her eyes stopped their wild flickering as she concentrated, desperate to hear the answer, to understand.

'Harry,' he said.

The word came as a hoarse whisper, like air escaping from a long-sealed box in which so many secrets had been hidden. And now she began to panic, to scream about injustice, but only in the silence of her mind. Harry Jones wasn't her fault! She'd done nothing she hadn't been asked to do! This wasn't right, wasn't fair!

She tried to drag her heavy eyes back to her killer, in this crowded room of memories, to plead with him, but she couldn't find him, only greyness, and his picture, in the silvered frame, with his wife, the wife she had always hoped he would put by for her, but never had, not even after the wife had died.

Only then did she understand what a fool she'd been, had always been. There had never been any point. To those years. To her.

And, with a final snatch of air, the panic gave way to appalling fear. It rushed through her body, closing down every synapse, snapping every sinew, until it had consumed her completely.

He sat and watched for a few moments, finishing his drink, until he was sure.

The sun had gone, and had taken her with it.

CHAPTER ONE

Two months earlier

It took no more than five short words to shake the world of Harry Jones to pieces. They turned out to be malevolent, sharp-edged little words, yet were intended to be an expression of love. And the day had been going so well for a change.

Harry was driving to Henley on Thames and the traffic, swollen by those who were flocking to the local festival, had ground to a crawl. The fields by the river used for festival parking were sodden after weeks of summer rain and had turned into a biblical mire of misery that left some drivers impatient. That included Harry. He'd ducked onto a minor road that cut through the back lanes, only to discover that half of humanity had grabbed the same idea. Progress was rotten, getting worse, a world turned to aggravation and exhaust fumes. That's when he saw the halfwit in his wing mirror, wrong side of the road, flashing his headlights, drawing closer, jumping the line of cars behind. It was a canary-coloured Porsche Boxter with hood down and sound system at a level set to stun. As Harry watched, it pulled in only three cars back.

Harry's fingers drummed on the worn black leather of his steering wheel. In the passenger seat sat Jemma Laing, his . . . What was the word they used nowadays? 'Lover' was accurate but gave rise to giggles, while the description of 'girlfriend' seemed too quaint. Many people used terms like 'partner' or 'soulmate' but Harry didn't give a damn for many people. Jemma was what she was. Achingly cute, understanding, irreverent, sometimes even patient, very Scottish, great complexion. And unpredictable in bed, there was that, too. A woman who had remained at his side through everything recent months had thrown at him.

They were approaching a blind corner, the lane squeezed between the hedgerows. The Porsche driver was laughing with his passenger, a young woman whose oversized designer sunshades were pulled firmly over her eyes as she pretended not to notice the stares of disapproval being thrown at them. Harry's hand hovered over the gear stick of his old Volvo estate. He and Jemma were out for an elegant evening, a black-tie-and-pretty-frock affair; she didn't deserve confrontation and road rage. Trouble was, the irritating Porsche man with bollocks for brains knew it, too, and was intent on taking advantage. As the traffic began to crawl slowly forward once more, he revved up and pulled out to overtake. Harry lifted his foot gently off the clutch, knowing he wouldn't have a prayer of beating the Porsche for straight-line speed. But Harry didn't do straight lines. Instead he swerved into the middle of the road, into the path of the yellow sports car as it leapt forward.

A collision seemed inevitable. Harry gave the wheel another decisive twitch to force him wider.

Porsche Man had little choice. He had no room and a huge excess on his insurance. He blinked, flipped the wheel and swerved into the only gap still available to him. It turned out to be an open gate leading into a ploughed field. The Porsche bounced, the engine revved, the tyres spun as its driver struggled to regain control. The wheels plastered the paintwork with mud as they dug themselves little graves. The driver had time for no more than a single unimaginative expletive before he found himself hopelessly stuck.

Harry pulled nonchalantly back into the queue of traffic. Jemma pretended not to notice.

'Sorry about that,' he said as eventually they found a place to park that didn't require them to wade.

'No, you're not,' Jemma replied.

'You're right. Must be a syndrome or something. I just hate yellow Porsches.'

'Good job you saw that open gate.'

'I didn't.'

'Oh, Jones,' she sighed, shaking her head as she swapped her high heels for more practical slip-ons until she could find firmer ground. 'Try and remember that we're here to have a good time. Don't go killing anyone before I've had something to eat.' The freckled tip of her nose waggled in rebuke. Then she burst out laughing. She'd long ago realized there was no point in trying to change him. Live with it or move on.

Which was precisely the choice presented to her later that evening. The setting of the festival was sublime: a floating stage on the river with marquees along the bank where the audience could eat and watch the performance. It featured the Military Wives Choir and a sensational young American tenor whose voice made the night air crackle with excitement. The ripples of the stream began throwing back a mixture of candle flame and lasers with ever greater intensity as the natural light began to fade and the cares of the day were set aside. Men dressed in a manner that rekindled the elegance of an earlier age, women decorated their breasts with jewellery and, for a few hours, the gathering darkness kept the rest of the world at bay. Harry and Jemma had been invited by Costas, a friend of so many years that Harry had been best man at his first wedding and helped him sober up after his second. Costas was Anglo-Greek, heavily into shipping, and had organized dinner on a small and beautifully restored Edwardian launch named *Persephone*, whose wooden hull had plied the waters of the Thames for more than a hundred years. Seafood. Rare wines. Music. Moving gently on the river current. Just the four of them, Costas had said.

Except that Costas hadn't brought his wife, who was apparently summering in Greece, and instead was accompanied by a disgracefully young Estonian with a tongue-twisting name that even the polymath Costas had trouble with; he shortened it to Annie. She was all clinging silk and cleavage, and Costas was as bald as she was blonde. He greeted his guests from the prow of the launch with a glass of vintage Pol Roger in one hand and the other on the shoulder of his new friend. He explained that she was the niece of a business partner and was participating in some sort of work-experience programme. Her English was as limited as her eyes were wide and they all sat on deck at a fine table decorated with crisp linen and crystal. Harry tried to make conversation.

'What do you do?' he asked.

'I am ... independent business consultant,' she replied in a thick Baltic accent, spitting out each word. 'Self-employed,' she added, as if it were a badge of honour.

'What sort of business?'

Harry watched as the lips parted, formed shapes, but words came there none. Instead, she arched an eyebrow, shook her head to send her blonde hair cascading around her bare shoulders and offered nothing more than a smile to feed his imagination while Costas fed her titbits of seafood from his own fork.

Harry felt awkward. The Greek had got it wrong. It wasn't that Harry was a moralist or had led a life of particular purity himself, but he knew Costas's wife and liked her; he found himself struck by a case of divided loyalty, so, when they had finished eating and Costas dutifully suggested a stroll along the riverbank, Harry and Jemma declined. Costas assumed they were being tactful and gave them a wink of gratitude, grabbing his business consultant and disappearing into the throng.

Harry and Jemma fell silent, lost in the embrace of the night. Gentle wisps of mist were rising from the river, twisting in the eddies, and Harry found himself taken back, lost in memories, old pains, failures, the times he'd let down those he loved and been cheated upon himself, and a few reminders of good times, too. Not recently, of course, particularly not this last year, a bottomless pit of time in which he'd sunk almost without trace, lost his seat in Parliament, lost his fortune, almost lost his life. He'd have sunk completely without Jemma. She'd held him tight, dragged him back onto dry land. Hell of a woman. His dark memories tugged at the corner of his eyes; she noticed, as she always did, and once again rescued him from himself.

'I've got a better arse than she has,' she said.

'I beg your pardon?'

'You were lost in thought. A dangerous habit in a man like you. Not thinking of hiring your own independent business consultant, were you, Jones?'

Harry shook his head. 'No, Jem, I wasn't there, wasn't thinking of that at all.'

'What, then?'

'Just ... To hell with it, I don't know. You. And me.'

'Sounds pretty profound.'

He leaned forward, took a deep breath, catching the scents of the summer night. He reached slowly across

11

the linen-covered table, took both of her hands in his; her deep-hazel eyes turned to gold with the light of many candles. 'I was just thinking . . .'

'What were you thinking?'

His thumbs were brushing the backs of her hands but suddenly they held her tightly. 'That it's about time. You and me. Isn't it?'

She knew precisely what he meant, didn't react immediately, searching his eyes. 'You really have to ask? Damn, but I still have work to do on you, Harry. Could take me some time.' Her nose twitched, almost aggressively, then her face broke into the gentlest of shy smiles. 'A lifetime, I hope.'

'Thank you,' he whispered.

It was later that evening when, unwittingly yet with extraordinary precision, she destroyed all the contentment that had taken hold of him with those five short words. She was in his arms, head on his chest, listening to the beat of his heart, when she lifted her eyes. They were filled with a new sense of curiosity.

'Tell me about your father.'

—⚯—

Johnson Eric Maltravers-Jones, Harry's father, better known as Johnnie, had been both part icon and part enigma for his son. In translation, it meant he'd had the propensity to be an unremitting bastard, although in his defence he would probably have said he'd needed to be. Johnnie's own father had blown the family's modest inheritance during the Great Depression by following the advice of others, a weakness that Johnnie had sworn never to follow. By contrast and in deliberate contradiction to his father, the son was never likely to be orthodox. His parents had fled to Cardiff to hide from the shame of bankruptcy and it was there, during an air raid and in an Anderson shelter dug deep into the back garden, that Johnnie had been conceived. It was his father's one moment of inspiration for, in almost all the other stretches of his life, he left behind little but grinding disappointment. He had hovered around the margins of the advertising industry and, while others had found celebrity, he had encountered little but calamity, sliding ever backwards, to the point where at school Johnnie had been known as Jones the Broke. That left scars, and had instilled in him a determination never to be as poor or as pathetic as his father. Money mattered. And, if that meant having little time to worry about those who were being trodden on in the process, it was a price he paid without losing much sleep. Johnnie Jones didn't do victim support.

He was bright. Won a scholarship. Got to Oxford, made his mark, then got married, and, by the time

Harry came along, they lived in some style in one of those tree-lined avenues of Holland Park, not the best avenue but still pretty damned in-your-face. Harry remembered an eddying autumn day when he was seven, answering a knock on the door. Standing in the rain on the York-stone doorstep he found a nervous woman with pale face and red rims to her eyes begging to talk with his father. A little later, from behind his bedroom door, Harry heard them arguing. She was the widow of his father's business partner, recently buried, and now she wanted her share, for the children. Johnnie explained that he had a family of his own, that their business was in cash, no records, no formal partnership agreement. Anyway, he had added, her husband had spent months dying and had contributed nothing. At that point Harry had quietly locked his bedroom door and buried his head in a book. He knew how the conversation would end. It was a lesson he was to see repeated more than once during the next few years.

And yet ... And yet, despite it all, despite the unreliability, the rows with his mother and the times he simply disappeared from their lives, his father had offered moments that Harry had cherished. Like the Christmas Day when Harry had woken to find the streets covered in snow. He'd been so excited until he found his mother in tears. The Aga had broken down, the fire gone out, their day destroyed. Harry remembered her being almost fearful of his father's reaction, yet Johnnie hadn't even raised his voice. He'd hauled an old wooden sledge from the attic, placed Harry on top wrapped in his overcoat and favourite football scarf, and they had walked through the park to the Dorchester Hotel for their dinner, his father pulling Harry all the while. The snow had fallen around them every step of the way, laying down memories that would last a lifetime but that would never quite manage to swallow up the darker moments.

Harry had never been able to get to grips with how his father earned his living – the term 'financial adviser' covered so much ground. The family had covered a fair amount of ground, too, spent their holidays in Val d'Isère, Cannes, Antigua and Australia, and Harry's life had lacked for nothing in a material sense. His father had taught him to drive in the South of France in a green, three-litre, 1924 Bentley with a leather strap across its bonnet and a wicker hamper in the boot. He'd been barely sixteen when he'd first sat behind that wheel, another sparkling father–son moment that, as so often, Johnnie had soon contrived to ruin. It was on that same trip that Harry had slept with his first woman – something else his father had arranged. Yet, for Harry, in hindsight, it was too much. Surely that moment of all moments should have been a private matter, not something for his father's holiday album or banter in the yacht club. Anyway, Harry suspected that his father had screwed the girl, too, but it was the 1980s and the word 'excess' seemed to have been banned from the language.

Other women had always been a feature of his father's world. After his mother had died, alone in her large bed in her empty house in Holland Park, one woman in particular had, for a while, become a part of Johnnie's life. Harry thought for a while she had driven them apart. It was about the time that Harry had applied for a place at Cambridge – he had no intention of following in his father's footsteps to the other place, Oxford, as Johnnie had tried to insist upon. The son could be stubborn, too. So, when the crested letter of acceptance had arrived, his father stared at him across the kitchen and said Harry was now on his own, that the fountain of money would be switched off, that he had to learn to stand on his own feet – 'just as I did'. A barrier was built between them. At first Harry blamed the new woman, but she eventually disappeared, was replaced, but nothing changed. His father still spent vacations in exotic places but no longer with his son. Harry paid his way through college by working nights at McDonald's and weekends at a call centre. Communication with his father diminished. In his final year at Cambridge, Harry waited for his father to call him. He waited six months. Then he deleted Johnnie's number from his contact list.

'Tell me about your father,' Jemma had said. Harry didn't even want to tell himself, yet she stirred something inside him that for several days had distracted him, made him seem distant. He was soaking in his bath, remembering too much, when Jemma walked in. She hadn't a stitch of clothing on her. He appeared not to notice.

'Seems I need to pay a hell of a lot more than a penny for them,' she laughed – she always laughed so easily.

'What?' he said, raising his eyes in confusion.

'Your thoughts.'

He went back to staring at his water-wrinkled toes. 'Sorry, Jem. But you got me thinking about my father.'

'I'd like you to tell me more.'

'I don't even know where to start.'

She wrapped a towel around herself and perched on the end of the bath. 'OK, let's start at the end and work backwards. When did he die?'

'Oh, back in 2001. Early summer,' he replied reluctantly.

'I'm sorry.'

'I'm not. Left me a fortune.' The comment was uncharacteristically callous. His father seemed to bring out a dark side in him, yet in Harry's eyes Jemma could see a rare sheen of vulnerability.

'Where did he die?'

'On a yacht. Off Missolonghi in Greece. It was where Byron died.'

'Poetic.'

'Not really.'

'I don't understand.'

'You wouldn't believe me if I told you.'

'I do sometimes.'

Hell, she was persistent but she had a right to know. He sighed. 'My father was sixty and screwing one of his women. In her twenties, apparently. Didn't pace himself, never could. Heart attack.'

'You Joneses, you always rush things. Still, he died in bed.'

'On the sun deck, I'm told.'

'I really am sorry, Harry.'

'No need. He and I, we . . .' He seemed about to add something, but trailed off. 'It doesn't matter any more.'

It didn't matter? He had lied to her before, of course, as all couples do, but nothing more than modest white lies, usually to protect her. This was the first time he had lied to protect himself.

'Where's he buried?' she encouraged softly.

'In Greece.'

'Not here?'

'It all got a little complicated. You see, the boat was owned by a Russian and registered in Panama. Flag of convenience, fewer rules, lower taxes, that sort of thing. And it was sailing off the Corinth Canal in international waters. So when it happened no one wanted the responsibility, not the Greeks, the Panamanians, certainly not the British consul in Patras, and least of all a man from Moscow who was on the make. Even when he was dead my father proved he could be a very accomplished pain in the arse.'

'But what about you? You were next of kin.'

'Didn't hear about it for a while. No one could find me. It was the time when I was finishing off my days in the Army, in West Africa and very officially out of contact, doing a little job that even our own Prime Minister wasn't supposed to know about.'

There had been quite a few of those, during his military career. He'd told Jemma about them, even though she wasn't supposed to know, either; he'd had to find some way of explaining the collection of scars that decorated his body. Anyway, there were little things like a Military Cross and Distinguished Service Medal that rather gave the game away.

19

'No one wanted an unclaimed body hanging around,' he said, hoping to finish with the story, 'so someone decided to deal with it.'

'But who?'

'I've no idea. And frankly I didn't particularly care. What the hell does it matter, anyway? My father didn't deserve a state funeral.' This was said in a tone that betrayed his discomfort. Harry hauled himself up from the cooling bathwater, suds meandering in sluggish streams down his body. He'd had enough of this conversation, but Jemma wasn't so easily put aside.

'You should care what happened to your father,' she said, gently but insistent.

'For God's sake, why?'

To bring closure, to cut the emotional dependency, to set old ghosts to rest, all those things that counsellors urged on the bereaved, but Jemma knew that a little cod psychotherapy would never be enough with Harry. So she stared at him, not letting him escape. 'Because, Harry,' she whispered in a way that seemed to ring an entire peal of bells, 'our children will want to know.'

—∿—

A manila documents folder. Neglected, blue, scruffy, its corners battered, its second-hand status betrayed by the felt-tipped scrawling across its cover that declared it had once been used for Harry's old tax papers. That was it, all he had left to record the death of his father, and it wasn't even half full. A passport, its corner clipped. A copy of a death certificate, in Greek. A brief and tautly formal note from the Foreign & Commonwealth Office expressing regret, alongside a handful of notes of condolence, mostly from people Harry had never met. His father always had peculiar friends – no, not friends, wrong word, but colleagues, associates in business, whatever damned business that was. Not true friends.

And a single photograph, of Harry when he was perhaps thirteen, smiling coyly, in swimming trunks, with his father's arm around his shoulders. They were on a beach of a distant shore, the photo probably taken by some unsuitable female friend of his father's, though Harry couldn't remember for sure. It was wrapped in a single folded sheet of notepaper from his father's lawyer and executor, Robert Tallon, a senior partner in an exclusive London legal firm. The letter was dated August 2001. It summarized previous correspondence and recorded the fact that, due to the complexity of his father's estate, it would take considerable time and in all probability several years before matters regarding the estate could be finalized and that, in the meantime, he was transferring the sum of £8,376,482.04 to Harry's account as an initial instalment. Tallon was a punctilious ferret of a man, right down to the last four pence.

It was in the riverside offices of the same Robert Tallon that Harry and Jemma were now sitting, the file and its contents spilling uncomfortably onto the glass-topped conference table. Tallon, elderly, experienced, probably close to retirement, sat peering down a red and slightly damp nose on which were perched his rimless glasses. His hands were clasped in front of him, his silk tie spilling above the waistcoat of his tailored chalk-stripe suit, his overcombed hair was greying, his complexion pale, but the eyes were sharp.

'Mr Jones,' the lawyer began – even after all these years and so many millions, he still clung to the formalities – 'you ask about your father.' There was a hint of Edinburgh in the slow vowels. 'I'm afraid there's not much I can give you. I met him only rarely – he spent so little time in this country in his last years. Your father always told me, with some pride, I should add, that he was a citizen of the world.'

'No wonder he was never home,' Harry muttered.

The lawyer dabbed at his nose with a handkerchief he kept tucked up the sleeve of his suit. 'He was cautious about his affairs. Which were, as you know, complicated.'

Harry's fingers brushed across the manila folder.

'This is all I have. A ridiculously simple file for such a complicated man, isn't it?' Jemma thought she noticed an edge of both regret and self-rebuke in his voice. He turned to her. 'Seems he didn't own a home anywhere, just postboxes in various dusty places and a financial operation so impenetrable that it's kept Mr Tallon here busy ever since.'

'Well, not busy, not any longer. We wait patiently. For developments.'

Outside the window the Thames wound reluctantly through the piers of Waterloo Bridge. In the distance the towers of the City stood beneath a glowering ozone sky of purples and browns like skittles waiting for the clout of the next financial onslaught.

'Developments? I'm sorry, what developments?' Jemma asked.

Tallon turned towards her with a suggestion of reluctance: he didn't welcome the presence of amateurs. 'I think we have to conclude that the senior Mr Jones's arrangements were deliberately obscure. He lived in several countries but didn't have title to a residence, at least not for tax purposes. He had many investments but didn't own a single share.'

'Oh, I see. You mean he was a tax evader.'

The lawyer arched an eyebrow in displeasure. 'Not an evader as such, but he was undoubtedly efficient.

He broke no laws, otherwise I would never have acted for him.'

Jemma offered a smile of understanding, wondering if a diet of prunes might help the lawyer relax.

'It seems my father buried his money so deep that taxmen would need a degree in deep-shaft mining in order to get anywhere near it,' Harry said.

'I'm sure your father had nothing but your best interests at heart, Mr Jones,' the lawyer said in a tone that suggested he cared little for Harry's description.

'You'll forgive me but I'm sure that was the last thing on his mind.'

'You were the sole beneficiary,' Tallon said, staring over the rim of his glasses in rebuke. 'To this point his estate has been able to remit to you a total of fifteen million, three hundred and eighty-eight thousand, five hundred and twelve pounds. And eighteen pence,' he added, peering at a neat file in front of him. 'In time, I hope we shall disentangle more. Your father's share in the landholding in Brazil could prove particularly beneficial once the authorities understand the rather complex nature of his investment trust and lift their embargo on its sale.'

'It's been more than ten years.'

'Matters move somewhat slowly through the rainforest.'

'Let's hope it's still there in another ten.'

Jemma gazed at the thin blue file with its curled edges and scrawlings on the cover. Recycled crap. It was all Harry seemed to think his father was worth, despite the millions. She began to understand how angry Harry was, and had always been.

Tallon's lips moved slowly as he searched for the right words. 'Mr Jones, I understand, I sympathize. I know how *challenging* this past year has been for you.' He paused for some expression, some indication of what Harry felt, but got none. 'I assure you I shall continue to do my very best to release whatever money is left in the estate.'

'But it's not really the money, you see, Mr Tallon,' Jemma said. 'That's not why we're here. We simply want to know more about Harry's father. You seemed the obvious place to start.'

'I can't help you.'

'How he died, what happened,' she continued.

'You have all I know.'

'There must be something.'

'You said . . .' Harry interrupted them both. 'When you and I first met, Mr Tallon, you spoke of a young woman. The cause of his heart attack.'

The lawyer took off his glasses and began polishing them with his handkerchief while he blinked rapidly

25

in evident discomfort. 'It was no more than a rumour.'

'Whose rumour? Where did you hear it?' Inside, Harry felt a flicker of shame that it was the first time he'd even bothered to ask. There was so much about his father he hadn't wanted to know, at least until now.

The lawyer said nothing. He got up from his chair and moved to the window, gazing down to the dark cupola of St Paul's. 'I apologize, Mr Jones, I should never have mentioned the matter. Unprofessional of me. It was only to explain any reticence you might have detected in my handling of your father's affairs. I haven't mentioned it to another soul. I thought it right that I should try to protect not just his estate but also his reputation.'

'So how did you come across this exquisite piece of gossip?' Harry persisted.

Tallon turned to face him. 'It was a phone call. I can't remember from whom – the ship's captain, the local consul, perhaps. It was a long time ago.'

'You made no note?'

'It's not my habit to record gossip.'

'Just to pass it on.' The accusation sat between them before Harry apologized. 'Sorry.'

'My fault entirely. As I said, with hindsight it was

unprofessional. But I saw no point in pursuing the matter: sometimes it doesn't pay to stir up the mud at the bottom of the pond. In any event, it made no material difference to your father's estate.' From the pocket of his waistcoat he pulled an ancient gold-cased watch that hung from a fob chain. He had already given them an hour. 'Forgive me, is there any other way I can be of assistance?'

Harry stared out through the window at the sulking sky. It had been a waste of time. 'No, thank you. Just send me your bill.'

'I wouldn't dream of doing such a thing. Not for the son of Johnnie Maltravers-Jones.' He stood up and extended a hand. For the first time the lawyer's smile seemed comfortable. 'I shall continue to do everything I can for you, as always.'

'I hope you'll forgive my testiness, Mr Tallon,' Harry said. 'My father and I never had a comfortable relationship. It doesn't seem to get any easier, even though he's dead.'

'I understand, of course I do. I only wish there was more I could do to help.'

The lawyer sat quietly once his visitors had left, staring after them. Then he grew agitated, rose and returned to his spot at the window, moving stiffly, his limbs suddenly feeling their age. He stood there for many minutes, gazing out but not seeing, struggling with his thoughts. It took those thoughts some time to batter him into submission, but when they had done so he turned and reached for the phone on his desk, only to recoil, cursing. 'No, you fool!' he snapped at himself. Every call made from that phone was recorded, its trace left on some log. So he reached for his personal mobile, buried in an inner pocket of his suit. Then he made his call.

CHAPTER TWO

It was always said of him that Harry Jones was single-minded, far more than most; at times it made him appear almost obsessive. It was both a strength and character flaw, inspiration and potential entanglement. Ruthless, some said, and not unfairly, while others saw it as arrogance and disrespect, to a degree that it had cost him the Sword of Honour at Sandhurst and always managed to get the nostrils of commanding officers twitching in dismay. Yet that same trait made him a scarily effective soldier, which was why they'd given Harry so many of the dirty jobs: Iraq, Colombia, Armagh of course, and that one in West Africa. 'His exceptional leadership in extracting his patrol and its casualties from the chaos behind the Iraqi lines merits a high gallantry decoration,' trilled one report after he'd dragged back the body of one of his buddies across desert and through several nights, 'but his intemperate criticism of the personalities involved in the operation makes it unlikely that Capt. Jones will be asked to return to Special Forces.' There were plenty more appraisals along those lines. They did, however, ask him back because Harry was the sort of bloody-minded bastard even *they* couldn't ignore.

Always rushing ahead of others, that was Harry. One day it would kill him. But not today, thanks to Jemma.

'Harry!' she screamed, lunging after him, dragging him back just in time from the path of the taxi bearing down on him as he tried to cross Temple Avenue not far from Tallon's office. He was somewhere else in his head. The wing mirror brushed Harry's shirtsleeve, leaving a graze of dirt. The taxi driver waved a fist of rebuke through the open window. 'Arsehole!' Harry barked, but not so much at the cab driver as at himself. Damn it, this wouldn't have happened ten years ago. Just that morning he'd noticed that the strand of summer-bleached hair on his head had been joined by others. The conclusion was inevitable: it wasn't so much sun-scorch as middle age. No denying it, no matter how stubborn he got. *Tempus fugit*, waits for no man, all that shit. Perhaps that was why he was in so much of a screaming hurry. He brushed at his bruised arm and pushed ahead.

The heat of the day was rising, the crawl of traffic thickening the air. Harry headed into the cobbled alleyways and cloisters of the Inner Temple that made up the heart of legal London. Barristers occupied shady corners, stripped to their white shirts, sweltering in their starched collars, mobile phones clamped to their ears, while around them tourists wandered and motorcycle couriers weaved. Harry ignored it all, his heels smacking into the old paving stones as he strode on.

Jemma struggled to keep pace. She was beginning to wonder what she had unleashed. She'd been the one to push him into this chase, yet she was no longer sure it was sensible: she'd watched him tossing in his sleep, his lips moving but making no sound as he tussled with his dreams. The previous night they'd made love – except, unusually, there had been little sign of affection about it. Harry was an experienced lover, a man of many previous berths, but that side of his past didn't bother her – use it, enjoy it, she'd always told herself – and they'd developed an especially intense physical relationship that sometimes didn't make it to the bedroom but instead upturned tables and flooded the bathroom floor. Yet last night wasn't Harry. It was as though someone else had thrown himself on her, demanding, impatient, intensely inconsiderate. Punishing her. Bruising her, too.

When he'd finished he'd rolled over on his side, hadn't said a word. A stranger.

'Slow down, you idiot!' she found herself shouting once again as he paced ahead, head down, leaving her behind.

He turned, surprised, shocked at himself. There was sweat on his forehead. They were in a small courtyard outside a pub that claimed on its frontage to have been built in 1615 but was clearly Victorian. Old metal-hooped beer barrels stood on the pavement serving as tables. 'Stay!' she commanded, and he did so while she went inside and soon reappeared with two beers.

'Why not let's forget it?' she suggested, putting a glass down in front of him and throwing two packets of dry-roasted onto the barrel top.

He took a sip of his beer, pulled a face at the sourness and slowly shook his head. 'Can't,' he said quietly. 'Not now.'

He'd spent his life leaving people in his wake: his first wife, Julia, swept away as she tried to follow him through off-piste snow; Mel, the second, lost along with a considerable chunk of his fortune way back in some divorce court; Martha, the American woman who'd taken the emotional wreckage that had been Harry Jones and blown the spark back to life. Martha had saved his life; in return he'd left her buried back on an ice-smothered mountainside in central Asia. Not his fault, but it kept happening. 'I love you, Harry, I so do, it's just that I can't keep up with you,' one of his lovers had said. He didn't want to remember which one: it hurt too much to look back. But in the case of his father he couldn't avoid it. He leaned on the barrel, sipping, not tasting, his father's file in front of him.

'OK, Batman, what's our next move?' Jemma asked.

He flipped open the file and slowly extracted his father's death certificate. It was in Greek, but he knew enough of the script to decipher it. 'We start digging,' he said, a cold light in his eye. He reached for his phone.

'Taps, you busy?' Harry asked when his call was answered. Simon St John Tappersley had been a fellow officer in the Parachute Regiment and was now a maritime insurance broker at Lloyd's.

'Of course,' came the dry reply.

'Good. You always operated better under a little pressure. There's something I need you to do. Kapetanios Marios Kouropoulos. Master of the SS *Adriana* back in 2001.' It was the name on the death certificate, the man who had reported his father's death. 'I need to know where he is. Want to talk to him.'

'How quickly?'

'By the time I've finished my beer.'

'You're kidding.'

'Never.'

'You haven't changed, Harry.'

'I'm hoping you haven't, either.'

'Screw you.' Tappersley hung up.

Twenty minutes later the screen on Harry's phone flashed into life.

'What kept you, Taps? I've had to go get a second beer.'

'Perhaps that's because you called in the middle of my lunch.'

'I owe you.'

'You most certainly bloody do. Your Captain Crapulous. According to the records of the Greek Masters and Mates Union, he was born in some place called Mastichochoria in Chios in 1952. Earned his Master's Certificate in 1980. Left the service in 2004.'

'You mean he retired?'

'In a manner of speaking, yes.'

'What sort of manner?'

'He died, didn't he? On his ship.'

'In his sleep or on the sun deck?'

'Neither. His propeller got snared in some old fishing net, so he went over the side to cut it away. Some idiot restarted the engine just as he'd finished and was still

34

underwater. Like a scene from *Jaws*, so the chap at the Masters and Mates said. Cleaved in two. I can think of better ways to go.'

'So could my father,' Harry muttered, before adding, 'Thanks, Taps. I owe you that lunch.'

Tappersley sighed in resignation. 'In all honesty, it was nothing but a little lobster salad. I suspect it will have kept.'

Harry's lips twitched as he put his phone away. It was his father who had shown him how to dive for lobster in the Med, how to cook and shell them, too. Suddenly everything in his life seemed to be coming back to the same point: Johnnie. That morning, as Harry had shaved, he'd wiped the mirror with a towel only to find the bloody man staring back at him through the porthole of mist. He was everywhere. A man walks in his father's footsteps knowing that at some point he will overtake the father and leave him behind, that was the given order. But even though Johnnie was dead, Harry had never caught up with him.

'Harry?'

His eyes came back to her. Gentle lines of concern were scribbled above Jemma's nose.

'You seem angry,' she said.

He crushed the empty packet of nuts in his fist. 'Just

thinking that lobster salad sounds a hell of a lot better than a packet of dry-roasted for lunch.'

'Yes, you sure know how to treat a girl.'

'Don't worry, I'll make it up to you.'

'How?'

Before he could reply, his phone beeped again. A text message. Details of an address from the electoral register. Harry brushed the screen to examine it and began to smile in satisfaction.

'Can I suggest a little trip?'

'Where?' she asked, intrigued.

He checked the screen once more. 'How about the Lake District?' he said, gathering up the file and setting off once more.

—m—

They found the cottage up a short, grass-tufted lane that cut off from the road leading into Braithwaite, an unpretentious Cumbrian village in the lee of Barrow fell. Harry parked the Volvo beside an uncertain stone wall that seemed to be held together by little more than lichen and moss. They had found their man and it was clear why he wanted to live here: on a clear day the view from this spot would stretch all the way to the peaks of Catbells. But this was the Lakes, and clear days came at a premium. Harry turned off the windscreen wipers and they clambered out. The cottage was small, with a roof of old slate and faded whitewashed walls. The garden gate swung in the breeze, creaking on a lazy, unoiled hinge. The paintwork was peeling, the garden unkempt; so was the ruddy-cheeked man in a crumpled shirt who answered the door. The rims of the eyes were of much the same hue as the cheeks, and he had a lick of thinning grey hair stuck to his forehead.

'Hello, Mr Smith? My name's Harry Jones. I telephoned yesterday.'

'I remember. I also remember telling you to go to hell.' The man had opened the door but a fraction, using his body to hide the clutter that was spilling from inside. 'How did you find me?'

'Does it matter?'

'Yes, it bloody does,' he snapped, staring defiantly though his one good eye; the other was clouded, full of cataract, and downcast, like the rest of him.

'OK, you tell me how many other Euripides Smiths I'm likely to find on the electoral register.'

Harry kept a straight face but he wasn't being entirely honest. He'd also called the former honorary consul in Bari, a man with whom he'd got enjoyably hammered during an official afternoon that drifted into an alcohol-fuelled evening until they'd found themselves watching the sun come up across the Adriatic.

'Smithie? Our man in Patras?' the former honorary consul had responded when Harry telephoned to enquire about his colleague. 'Scarcely knew him. Ran across him on a training course in Malta a while back, rather a waste of time – the course, not Smithie. Seem to remember he left not long after that under a bit of a cloud – well, plenty of us did back then. Cuts, of course. But it was more than just a cloud: in his case he left with a distinct clap of thunder, too. Yes, the brain re-engages, it's coming back to me ... That's right, some whining backbencher had sailed into port and expected a ten-gun salute. Not old Smithie's style. Gave him nothing but a ripe raspberry. Good for him, too. We were volunteers, not slave labour. But I guess Smithie had been in post just a little too long, took things for granted, perhaps. Took an occasional liberty, too.'

'What sort of liberty?'

'Oh, of the alcoholic kind. Nothing many of us didn't do occasionally.'

'As I remember.'

'Yes, that was a good evening, wasn't it? But Smithie didn't choose his timing well. The politician complained, made a hell of a fuss, so, when the great god Austerity struck, Smithie had already laid himself out on the altar. Sacrificial lamb – or goat in his case. Made

it easy for them. There was a wondrously rude vale-
dictory e-mail to his bosses in which he kept
misspelling the word "cuts", and off he went into the
wide blue yonder.'

'In which direction?'

'God knows, it's not like we were close. But, hang on,
something stirs. There's a weasel running round inside
my head whispering – Lake District. Can't be positive,
mind . . .'

'Thanks, old friend.'

And now, as Euripides Smith defended his
doorstep, Harry reckoned that the suspicions about the
man were right. He could see the wash of alcohol as
well as anger in the other man's eyes.

'Do I know you?' Smith demanded.

'In a way, yes. You once wrote to me. Look, er, can we
discuss it?'

'You can't come in,' Smith snapped, suddenly defen-
sive. 'I'm in the middle of clearing up.'

That was the moment Jemma chose to step forward.
She was wearing tight-waisted jeans and a thin cotton
blouse that, in the cool drizzle, was leaving less than
usual to a man's imagination. She allowed Smith's
good eye a second or so to grow distracted. 'Over a
drink, perhaps, Mr Smith? We passed a pub a mile or
so back. I'll drive while you two chat.' She guessed that

was why the lane had so much grass on it: there was no sign of a car, Smith didn't drive, had probably lost his licence to the local magistrate and got most of his exercise walking to the nearest pub.

Smith eyed Jemma for every second she allowed before making up his mind. 'Well, I suppose, seeing as you've driven all this way . . .' he muttered, closing his front door behind him.

Smith said almost nothing in the car, trying to smarten himself up, buttoning his shirt a little higher, rerolling his sleeves more neatly, scratching away at a glob of breakfast that had stuck to the lap of his trousers. Harry reckoned he was late fifties but looked older, greyer. A few minutes later they were sitting around an old varnished table beneath the low beams and brass bric-a-brac at the Royal Oak. The beer was local, better than in London. When they had taken the head off it, Harry produced the letter of regret about Johnnie's death that the former consul had written all those years ago.

'Oh, so it's you, is it?' Smith said, looking more keenly at Harry.

'Can you tell me about what happened to my father?'

'Yes, remember it. Didn't get too many bodies to deal with,' Smith began, reflecting into his glass, 'not that I really dealt with your father's body at all.'

'You didn't see it?'

'Good God, no. Honorary vice consuls have no power, no authority. We're little more than glorified messenger boys. Corpses are way above our pay grade. Not that we got paid, of course. Did you know that, Mr Jones?' His tone betrayed an edge of bitterness. 'Got no expenses, no training, either, absolutely nothing, apart from a manual of procedures with an oversized crest on its front, and it took them two years before they even gave me one of those. I had to make much of it up as I went along.'

'How wonderfully reassuring.'

The other man shrugged and drank.

'So you didn't arrange for my father's burial?'

Smith shook his head. 'All I could have done was suggest the names of a couple of funeral directors. But nobody asked. It's usually the family, but apart from you there didn't seem to be any family. And you didn't ask.'

'You were satisfied that everything was ...' Harry suddenly hesitated. A note of discord began to flutter through his thoughts. 'You satisfied yourself that every-thing was in order. Due process, or whatever they call it.'

'Satisfied myself? To be honest, not particularly. Wasn't my job. As I said, I was a messenger boy. Inform the embassy in Athens and the next of kin, that was all. The rest was up to others.'

'Who, precisely?'

'The Greek authorities. And you know what they can be like, particularly in a place like Patras.'

'Not really.'

'Well, you know where your father is buried.'

The statement was left hanging, as a question. Harry didn't respond, seemed suddenly embarrassed. He hadn't even visited the grave. Not once.

The old consul sighed, recognized Harry's guilt, and a layer of aggression seemed to peel away from him. He understood the pain that raking the embers of a past life could bring. 'I lived there twelve years, should love the place but . . . Patras is what it is. A port, a crossroads, it's sprawling, sometimes mucky, not particularly glamorous. I remember your father – his case, I mean. Yachts like that have their autopilots stuck on places like Venice and Cannes and Santorini. They didn't stop off in Patras, and certainly not with bodies on board.'

'So what happened?' Jemma encouraged.

'Well . . . Mrs Jones?' he enquired, raising his eyes at Jemma.

'No, not quite yet.'

He nodded softly. 'Wish you well, young lady. As much luck as I had with my wife. She died in Patras, too.'

'Oh, I'm so sorry.'

He blinked in gratitude, was elsewhere for a moment before he returned to his tale. 'Anyway, I got a call from the chief of the port police. About your father, Mr Jones. Courtesy call, nothing for me to do, but I wandered down nonetheless.'

'Why?'

'Dunno. No need, not as a consul. But my wife ... Anyway, it was a fine day. I needed the exercise.'

'The consulate is near the port?'

'The consulate? What sort of operation do you think Her Majesty still runs? The consulate didn't exist, not beyond me and my mobile phone. I'm half Greek, Mr Jones, named Euripides after my grandfather. We'd been living in Patras for a few years, my wife and I, living off a bit of business here and a bit more there – you know what it's like in the Med. One of those bits was a restaurant; I ran the consulate from one of its back rooms. Suited me, you see. Brought in the punters. Did some of the consulate stuff up at the bar, encouraged them to buy a round of drinks for my pains; often they'd hang on for a meal, too. Yes, suited me well, right up to the time some pompous little prick of a politician turned up and started throwing his weight around. Don't you just hate politicians?'

'What was his name, this politician?' Harry asked, ducking the question.

'Madrigan. Peter Madrigan.' He spat out the name, but as quickly as his anger burst forth it was overtaken by bewilderment and a fresh row of furrows erupted across his brow as fragments began to coalesce. He picked up the letter once again, studied it. 'Henry Jones,' he read out, then looked up. 'Are you the . . .?'

Harry nodded.

'Ah, well done, Smith,' he said in mock self-congratulation. 'Perhaps I wasn't meant to be a diplomat after all.' He chewed his bottom lip. 'A good friend of yours, is he, this Madrigan?'

Harry smiled and shook his head. 'You're spot on about him – although the description of pompous little prick scarcely does him justice. In private he's much worse.'

'It's folk like him that's given me an aversion to people knocking on my door.' It was as close as the other man would get to an apology.

'So what happened to my father? I don't even know that.'

'It's another reason why I remember the case. I got a right bollocking for it.'

'Why?'

'The Foreign Office gave us nothing, no pay, no

44

facilities, but they made up for it in grief when they thought their backsides were exposed. Your father was a British citizen, to be sure, but he died on a foreign-registered ship—'

'Panamanian.'

'That's right. Owned by some scummy Russian and sailing off Greece. Frankly, it was a job for the United Nations to sort, not some part-time dosser stuck on his bar stool. So I did what I was supposed to do, informed the embassy in Athens, and they were supposed to find the next of kin. You.'

'I was out of contact.'

'And your father, well … there's no better way of explaining it. Your father slipped between the gaps. By the time the embassy got back to me his body had already been taken care of. The ship's captain made the arrangements, I think. Nice man, rather distressed by it all. You really should get in touch with him.'

'I've tried.'

'Look, there was nothing illegal about what happened. It just wasn't due process, as you called it. Hell, when has there ever been due process in a place like Greece? But the goat chasers at the Athens embassy started slurping in their soup, claiming I hadn't paid sufficient attention, wasn't being sufficiently servile, some such crap. Bastards never forgave me. Blocked my MBE. Then encouraged your Mr Madrigan to screw me.' His tone was acid and he drowned the memory in the last of his drink.

Without being asked, Jemma got up to fetch another round. A group of young people burst noisily into the pub sheltering from the rain, shaking damp hair and clothing. 'Hi there, Euripides,' one of them called from the scrum at the bar. 'Haven't seen you around in a while. You keeping well?'

'I'm keeping.'

'Missed you at the last darts match.'

'No, you didn't. I couldn't hit the board, let alone the bull.'

'Yeah, you were rubbish. But you're still the only one who can keep score without a calculator.'

The young man laughed and made a gentle shaking sign with his hand to enquire if he wanted a drink, but Smith shook his head as Jemma turned from the bar, her hands filled with new glasses. Harry noticed that the young man's appreciative eyes stuck to her every step of the way until she'd sat down. Harry didn't know whether to feel flattered or furious before he realized he simply felt old – old enough to be challenged by a young stranger at the bar. In his Army days he'd seen chairs smashed and bars wrecked for much less, but this wasn't the time, and perhaps those times were past. He returned his attentions to the diplomat. 'So, Mr Smith, when you went to the yacht, did the captain tell you anything – about what had happened to my father?'

'No, not much.' Smith reached for his fresh beer, as though anxious to find something else to deal with.

'My father's lawyer says he died having sex with a young woman. Did you tell him that?'

Smith replaced his untouched beer carefully on the table. 'That's what the captain told me, yes.' He sighed, as though in an act of confession. 'It's why I didn't feel the need to go poking too deeply into the matter. A dead man should be left with his dignity. I think perhaps the captain thought so, too.'

'Which was why – how should I put this? – he took care of things.'

Smith nodded and, confession extracted, reached for his drink once again.

'And did you meet the young woman, too?'

'No. I didn't get to the yacht until a couple of days after the boat had docked. I think most of those on board had left. Didn't meet anyone, apart from the captain and one of the passengers. Female, but not the woman in question.'

'How can you be sure?'

'Too old. About the same age as your father would have been.'

'So you never met the woman. And you never saw my father's body ...'

Harry sat staring silently into the past. Too many unanswered questions. Jemma picked up the death certificate and began studying it. She knew where Harry's mind was leading him and didn't care for it. 'But your father's death was certified by a doctor,' she said, holding out the piece of paper, pointing to the doctor's details.

'And somehow, Mr Smith, I feel certain you never met the doctor, either,' Harry added drily.

'There was absolutely no need. I was a messenger, not a mortuary attendant.'

'Just humour me on this. You're a man of the world, you with your bar in the middle of Patras and the whole world coming to your door. Tell me, if I had a little money in such a place, cash in hand, how far would it go? Would it go as far as ... well, let's say finding a dodgy doctor? Even persuading a port official or policeman to look the other way?'

'What are you suggesting?'

'I'm not sure. But I think I know places like Patras. So, hypothetically, could such a thing happen?'

Harry was hoping the other man would dismiss the idea out of hand: he didn't want to charge through all those doors that were opening in his mind. But, instead, and for the first time, Smith held Harry's gaze. 'I'm not a young man any more, Mr Jones. Not gullible. Gave up believing in most things long ago. The tranquillity of old age. The transience of income tax. The gratitude of children. But what you say, what you suggest ... As I told you, Patras is a crossroads. There's Europe in one direction, the vast stretches of Asia and Africa and the Middle East in the others. Every kind of cargo passes through that place and much of that cargo is human. Patras is one of the main centres in Greece for drug dealers, illegal immigrants, smugglers, every type of human sewage. Does Patras have the best police force in the world? No. Can you buy your way in and out? For sure. Could I find you a dodgy doctor there? Well, if you were able to give me ten minutes it wouldn't be too much of a problem so long as it wasn't Easter Sunday. And I suspect you could even find a dodgy diplomat there, too, if that's what you're implying.'

'No, that's not what we're implying at all,' Jemma interrupted, casting a dark look of rebuke at Harry. 'This is difficult territory. We're not finding this easy.'

'The tide flows in, then it flows out again. There's no telling what it leaves behind. That's why we have our little consulate there. So many other outposts have been closed down but there, in Patras, it's still needed. Take care of Patras for us, Euripides, old boy, they said, those Foreign Office shirtlifters, it's one of the most wicked places in Europe. So I did. And still I wasn't good enough for them.'

He banged his empty glass down on the table.

'I'll get you another,' Jemma said immediately.

'Young lady,' he snapped, 'I know what you think of me. You look at me and see alcohol. An old soak. And, yes, I ran a bar, and it's true I enjoy a drink – two, indeed. That's the limit my doctors allow me. The drugs they're giving me to treat my cancer don't mix with alcohol, they tell me, but as it's going to kill me anyway they reckon a couple shouldn't do too much harm.'

'I'm so sorry,' Jemma whispered, aghast. Instinctively she reached out and placed her hand on his. It was as though it were the first form of human intimacy the man had had in months. He stared at Jemma's hand, so freely offered, and something inside him melted. He didn't want to fight any longer. He fashioned a weak smile. 'It's why the roses don't get pruned or the windows repainted. There's not much point, you see.'

Suddenly, both Jemma and Harry saw different things in his aching eyes.

'I'm the one who should be apologizing, young lady,'

Smith continued. 'I'm sorry I couldn't be more help to you. Or Mr Jones's father.'

Some years before, Harry had lost an ear, carved off while he was strapped to a chair by a central Asian security official who'd intended it as an appetizer to the pleasure of slitting Harry's throat, yet who had tarried too long and found himself just another body Harry had left somewhere along the way. The ear had been replaced by a first-class surgeon but it had left scars, which was why Harry grew his blond hair a little longer these days and why, when his peculiar inner sense for trouble was engaged, his ear gave him warning, began to throb. Right now it felt as though the Devil were dancing on it, cloven hooves clattering. He heard none of the gentle words that Jemma and the other man exchanged as they drove back to the cottage, only managed to blurt out perfunctory thanks as they parted. Jemma was already at the car, preparing to leave, when he turned at the squeaking gate. 'One last thing, Mr Smith. Silly question after all this time, but the woman you met with the captain. I don't suppose you can remember.'

'Remember what?'

'Anything. Absolutely anything.'

'You're right, very silly indeed,' the other man said, closing his door.

—⁂—

She nestled up to him as he lay in bed, breathing on his neck, but he seemed not to notice. Harry lay on his back, naked, his body tense, his hands clenched instead of reaching out to her. He was staring, and Jemma followed his line of sight through the open door of the bedroom to the sitting room beyond, where on the bookshelf in the light of the street lamps he had propped the photograph of his father with him on the beach.

'Harry?' Jemma's voice was plaintive, edged with concern.

Eventually he stirred. 'Sorry.'

'For what?'

'Being a prick. Last night. Then today with Smith.'

'He was only trying to help.'

'I know but . . .' He paused, she could feel the tension in his muscles suddenly disappear, as though he was no longer fighting. 'I'm finding this difficult to deal with.'

'What, exactly?'

'I'm angry about not knowing my father; even more angry when I find out more about him.'

'It's my fault, I should never—'

'No, Jem, it's *him*. And my bloody ear.'

'What about your ear?'

'Hasn't stopped burning, not since we met with that horse's arse of a lawyer.'

'What's it saying?'

'Not saying anything, nothing I can make any sense of, anyway. Just stirring. Stirring up all the old . . .' And his fists had clenched tight once more.

Her fingers slid slowly down through the hair on his chest. 'Come on, let's try Plan B.'

But he shook his head and turned away.

CHAPTER THREE

It was a couple of days later that two envelopes dropped on the mat for Harry. One was crisp and cream, the weight of the vellum paper almost making it creak, and sent first class. It had taken no more than three days to arrive. The other was recycled manila, clumsily resealed in brown tape, with Harry's name scrawled across the fresh address label in uncertain biro. Every corner curled like the ear of an old dog; it gave the impression of having fought many battles and lost more than a few. The letters arrived hidden among the usual avalanche of mail and magazines but found their way to the top of the pile. Harry made himself a mug of coffee before settling down on Jemma's sofa to open them.

He no longer had his own sofa. After his old friend

and financial adviser 'Sloppy' Sopwith-Dane had flushed out his brains with alcohol and prescription painkillers and succeeded in bringing Harry to the verge of bankruptcy, many things had changed in Harry's life. The ready money was gone, along with the parliamentary seat and his political career, the Audi S5, the best of the paintings, the collection of rare first editions, the holidays and almost everything else he'd lived with for so long. Somehow he'd managed to keep hold of the house in Mayfair but it, and the sofas, were now rented out. He'd been told by many that it would be far simpler to declare himself bankrupt, simpler still to shop his old friend, but 'Sloppy' had killed himself in remorse and dancing on his grave would have destroyed Sloppy's widow and two young daughters. Harry didn't do stuff like that. Anyway, he'd survived, not been declared bankrupt. Just. Now he spent his time with Jemma, living off a modest parliamentary pension and his rental income while he searched for new meaning in his life. And something more reliable to live on.

He sipped at his overheated coffee and opened the first envelope, using the spoon handle as a letter opener. For all the intensity of the paper on which it was printed, the corporate letterhead itself was almost nouvelle cuisine, minimalist, leaving much to the imagination.

'My dear Mr Jones,' the letter began, written with a fountain pen, as was the signature at the bottom of the single page, although the rest was printed.

You may remember that our paths have crossed on a couple of occasions [Harry didn't] and I trust you will forgive this intrusion. As CEO of this company, I have it in mind to expand our board of directors and am therefore engaged in a search for suitable non-executive candidates with the appropriate formidable talents and qualifications. I would be honoured if you would be willing to consider such a position.

Harry put his mug of coffee cautiously to one side.

As you are probably aware, we are a non-quoted company and have always taken the quality of our governance very seriously. I need hardly mention that your experience in international affairs, your level of personal contacts and your reputation for integrity are assets that my company would value very highly.

Level of contacts? Once, for sure, but since he'd lost his seat he'd found that doors had a habit of closing quietly on him. And, as for his reputation, it was true he hadn't been charged after his arrest on suspicion of murder, but the smell hung around him like an old kipper.

We have ambitious expansion plans for the future, and we expect our board members to share in that success. Your commitment would consist of attending between six and eight board meetings a year, three or four of which would be abroad as a result of the global nature of our operations. The remuneration would reflect your exceptional background and what we believe would be your ability to make a unique contribution, and I would expect it to be towards the top end of the usual scale for non-executives, plus share options and other benefits.

Top end of the usual scale meant the best part of a hundred thou. He read on: 'I am anxious to move forward quickly on this matter, and must ask for an early indication of your interest . . .'

Harry fell back into the soft cushions, clutching the letter. He stared into space, into his past, into what this might mean for his future. The plight of many former MPs is extreme: they wake up one cold, colourless morning to a world in which they have neither place nor profession. Sure, the system provides a comfort blanket in the form of a winding-up allowance and a limited pension, but it's rather like a guy's manhood after he's spent the night in a cold ditch: it's never quite what it once seemed. How do you compensate for the loss of self-confidence and the sense of humiliation that can gnaw away like a cancer? Some discarded politicians find it all unbearable. Harry knew of broken marriages, of former colleagues who were drowning in a sea of alcohol or drugs or depression, one colleague who'd been driven to suicide, parked his car in the middle of his former constituency with a bottle of whisky in one hand, a hosepipe from his exhaust in the other and a pathetic note on the dashboard that simply said 'Sorry. Forgive'. Not much of an epitaph to cover twenty-eight years. Yesterday's man.

My direct line and mobile numbers are at the top of this page. Since this is a matter of considerable urgency to us, please feel free to contact me at any time to discuss.

There are turning points in lives when a switch is thrown, the tracks changed, a new direction found. This could be one of them. A chance to crush the doubts. Get things back together. Give Jemma what she deserved.

The front door slammed and she was standing in the doorway, a bag of groceries in her hand, staring at him collapsed into the sofa. 'You look as if someone's just given you a damned good shagging. I hope you're not cheating on me already, Jones.'

In feeble response he waved the letter at her. She dropped the shopping and sat down beside him. He could feel her excitement rising as she read.

'Who are these people?' she asked.

'Good question. I'm not entirely sure.'

'The address looks like one of those holding companies in Mayfair, all front and not much furniture. Just round the corner from your old place.'

'Has links with the aircraft and defence industries, I think.'

'We'll have to find out.' And already she was interrogating her laptop. Typical. She was a research queen. Perhaps it was because of the endless questions she was asked by the children in the primary school where she taught that she was always driven to unearth the answers; she was relentless.

As Jemma tapped away at the keyboard, throwing out frequent exclamations of surprise along with nuggets of information, Harry remembered the other letter. It had almost got lost down the side of a cushion and peered at him like a cat in the dark. He retrieved it, inserted the spoon handle once more and struck. The flimsy envelope burst apart, tipping its contents into his lap.

It was a handwritten letter from Euripides Smith. 'Sorry if I seemed a bit off-colour,' he apologized,

but I don't get many visitors nowadays. Truth is, I got shafted by the FCO, don't care to be reminded of those days, but that wasn't your fault and I shouldn't have taken it out on you and your lovely friend. Anyway, after you left I thought more about the incident of your father and went into the loft to look through my old papers. Eventually I found a couple of boxes from my time as consul. Not much, I'm afraid, nothing that I haven't already told you, but I did discover this photograph. One of my hobbies at the time. I see I scribbled some details on the back. I enclose it, in case it helps.

For a moment Harry almost panicked – he couldn't find the photograph; he scrabbled around and found it lurking even further down the side of the cushion.

The photograph was unloved, its colours a little faded, and it had been bent in two in order to get it into the envelope. It was taken from the dockside, looking up at a large, white-hulled luxury yacht of around forty metres, Harry reckoned, whose sleek lines disappeared into the distance. Standing in front of his yacht was the captain, in uniform with bare forearms and dark glasses. Beside him, on the other side of the crease, dressed in a white blouse and bright cotton floral print, was a woman. She was thin-faced, greying, a little scrawny and defiantly old-fashioned to Harry's eye, distinctly pale in comparison with the captain, squinting awkwardly in the fierce light. Not the type to be slipping and sliding on his father's sun deck. He flipped the photograph and found scratchy writing on the back: 'SS *Adriana*'. Beneath that, a name: 'Capt. Kouropoulos'. And still another: 'Sue Ranelagh'.

At his side Jemma was erupting with excitement and corporate highlights, but he was no longer listening.

—⋙—

They sat side by side on the sofa, bent over their respective laptops.

'Their website's full of smiles and expensive orthodontics,' Jemma said, with a hint of suspicion. 'Its parent company's based in Andorra.'

'Tax haven.'

'Not too much about it. No negative stuff. You're right, it's deep into military bits. Fancy end. Software rather than bayonets.' She turned, her nose wrinkled in concern. 'Is that a problem for us, darling?'

Without looking up he arched an eyebrow. His career in the British Army had included the Paras, the Pathfinders, the 22 Special Air Service Regiment and mortal combat on four different continents. Occasional visits to an office in Mayfair was unlikely to cause him sleepless nights.

'There are bits here about new ventures into what they call cleantech industries,' she added, more enthusiastically.

'Sounds almost charitable.'

'Er . . .' – she hammered away at the keyboard – 'one of the big accountancy firms does their audits. That's important, too, isn't it?'

'Enron thought so.'

'Harry, what's your problem?' she snapped, slamming down the lid of her laptop. 'They offer you a way out of jail and you don't seem to give a damn!'

'This is the problem,' he said, holding up the creased photograph. 'Sue Ranelagh. She was on the boat when my father died. But who the hell is she?'

'You've Googled?'

'Of course.'

'I suppose there are hundreds on the Internet.'

'Many thousands.'

'So we know nothing about her.'

'Well, we do. This photo was taken in 2001, so she's – what – in her sixties by now?'

'If she's still alive.'

'We know she's rather conservative in her dress sense and probably her outlook. North European, at a guess. And probably had money.'

'How do you know that?'

'She wasn't on board because she was all teeth and tits. She was a passenger, a guest. One who could mix with the likes of oligarchs and other wealthy arseholes. Like my father.'

'Still doesn't help us very much.'

'Oh, but I think it does. I couldn't wade through the tide of Sue Ranelaghs that the computer threw up, or even those that call themselves Susan. But I thought: money, traditional, bit posh. So for the hell of it I tried the name Susannah.' He swivelled the laptop so it was facing her. 'And there she is.'

Jemma examined the page on the screen. Just one entry, but enough. A photograph of a Miss Susannah Ranelagh, President and Patron of the Bermuda Arts and Cultural Foundation, pictured making an award to three black music students. A couple of years old. A short caption, no supporting text.

'But you can't be—' She was about to suggest he

couldn't be certain, until he expanded the photograph. The same face, somewhat greyer hair, and identical dress sense.

'I need to go and see Miss Ranelagh,' he said in a voice that seemed strange, as though it had been sieved through filters somewhere inside.

'No rush,' she said, opening up her laptop once more.

'I think there is.'

'You've waited this long, what difference—'

'As you said, she's old.'

'But you can't.'

'Why not?'

'You've got this to deal with.' She waved the letter.

'It can wait.'

'No, he explicitly says this is a matter of urgency.'

'If he wants me that much, he'll wait. A few days.'

'But bloody Bermuda? You can't afford it. Why not call her?'

'Because I need to see her. She was one of the last people to see my father alive.'

'Harry!' Jemma pounded the cushions in frustration. 'This ...' She grabbed the letter once more, threw it angrily into his lap. It was growing into an argument, a big one, their first. 'Accept this and many more could follow. You become flavour of the month once again –

Harry Jones, the man everyone admires and wants a piece of. Oh, perhaps you don't want to become a corporate creature, not for ever, but this is a chance for you to get back on your feet. For us to move forward, Harry. I love you, I've hated watching you suffer. This could be our future. We don't need the past.'

'That's not what you said before.'

'Please?'

She was pleading, but he wouldn't respond. He stared, not just defiantly but in raw and rough-edged anger; it was a passion that bubbled up from somewhere so deep within and so up close that it frightened her. Suddenly she was looking at a part of him she scarcely knew. This was a man who couldn't be stopped, not just because he was simply determined but because the stupid bastard didn't know when to stop. That could be dangerous. And it terrified her.

—〰—

Robert Tallon's golfing partner was lining up his second putt on the decisive seventeenth when the lawyer's mobile began to vibrate. He glanced at the caller's number. 'Sorry, it's an emergency,' he declared.

'Christ, Robert, it had better be,' his playing partner growled, waving his hand at the six and a half feet of manicured lawn that lay between him and bragging rights in the bar.

Tallon wandered down from the tee to the shelter of a nearby rhododendron shrub, trying to find a little privacy and protection from the wind that had shanked his last drive thirty yards into the sand trap. 'Couldn't it wait?' he said, instinctively covering the mouthpiece with his free hand.

'I've just spoken to Jones,' the caller said.

'Ah, good.'

'Nothing good about it. He's not biting.'

'But he must!'

'Says he's got too much on his plate at the moment. Wondered if we could give him more time.'

'You told him that wasn't possible, of course?'

'Of course. I was very clear.'

'And you also made it clear that you were prepared to be generous?'

'Exceptionally.'

'Damn it! He can't have more bloody time.' Tallon glanced over his shoulder to where his partner was standing, leaning impatiently on his putter. 'So go back and offer him more money. Add something to the benefit package, more share options or something. I feel sure my client and your key investor will approve.'

'And, since it's his money, I shall do my best. I'll let you know. But I'd better get my skates on.'

'Why?'

'He said he had a plane to catch.'

The phone went dead, leaving Tallon with the feeling that all was not well in his world. But he was a lawyer, an Edinburgh soul in exile who permitted his emotions to range freely only on rare occasions, such as the run-up to the sale of Victorian watercolours at Christie's or those wind-swept afternoons spent in his debenture seat at Hampden Park. Now he watched impassively as his partner sank the winning putt and gave a little jig of jubilation.

CHAPTER FOUR

'Don't come looking for me, Harry. Not behind doors that I've closed.'

He remembered his father's words, but how could he forget? Shortly after his mother had died, when Harry was around fourteen, he'd spent a few days with his father in the apartment he was renting on one of the elegant tree-encrusted squares of Bloomsbury. Harry had taken himself off to the British Museum for a new exhibition but it had failed to capture his imagination and he'd returned much earlier than expected to his father's place. He knew his father was at home because the latch hadn't been double-locked. He'd marched naïvely, innocently, through the living room and then through the bedroom door to discover his father. He was naked. So was the woman beneath him. 'Your turn soon, eh, Harry, old boy?' his father had muttered, but the embarrassment was as impossible to hide as his father's wrinkled arse. The woman had been bundled rapidly away and, as the front door closed behind her, the light-heartedness of his father had turned to stone. The words were thrust at him like a steaming poker. 'Don't come looking for me, Harry. Not behind doors that I've closed.'

Then his father had struck him, across his face. There had been clips and taps before, even a gentle backhander or two, but this had been the first serious assault. One man marking out his ground against another. Even at fourteen Harry had wanted to hit back and had no thought of running, but instead he simply stood there and took it. And the second blow. He wouldn't hit his father. But that was when the blame began in earnest. He saw his father in a bleaker, more desolate light, no longer knowing him, and Harry began taking sides in his parents' busted marriage. The awe and loyalty of childhood began to sink almost without trace beneath the doubts that come with adolescence and endure far longer than any bruise.

His broken memories were disturbed as the pilot gave his aircraft the lightest touch of thrust and the Boeing 777 banked over the ocean for its final approach to L. F. Wade International airport. This was one of the finest approach runs anywhere in the world, into the islands of Bermuda that hung like a string of pearls in the empty Atlantic, and it was early evening, the sky shaded with gentle hues as the aircraft passed above St George's. It would be a couple of hours yet before the lights of the old township were switched on and began to light up its narrow and picturesque streets. Beneath him Harry could see the microscopic outlines of people strolling about their business. This was subtropical paradise; nothing happened in a hurry.

The island was a remnant of empire – what was in the official script described as a British Overseas Territory. It still doffed its banana leaf to the Queen but in almost all other respects it went its own way with its own government, its own laws and, most importantly for the tribe of wealthy expats who claimed residence there, its own tax regime. Despite the ever-present threats of hurricane and social incest, so many flocked to its shores that it was rumoured to have the highest per capita wealth in the world, but no one knew for certain. And that was the magic of the place. No one knew, not for certain.

Harry had nothing but hand luggage, an old leather shoulder bag he'd picked up in Colombia when his luggage had been stolen, and he was soon at the front of the line for passport control. 'Business or pleasure,

Mr … Jones,' the black official in a crisp blue shirt asked, glancing at the proffered passport.

'Entirely personal pleasure,' Harry replied, and was waved through.

The airport was barely six tree-lined miles from the capital, Hamilton; Harry took a bus. He jumped out at Front Street by the harbour, not knowing for sure where he was headed, but it didn't prove to be a major inconvenience. Hamilton was small, a population of barely two thousand; nothing was more than a cat's cry away. He tarried only to fill his lungs with air that had last touched land somewhere off the Gulf of Mexico, before asking a passer-by for directions, then walking as he'd been directed through the colonial backstreets with their verandahs and pastel-painted galleries and taverns, weaving through slow-moving traffic, climbing steps, until he had found the B&B he'd booked on the Internet. By the time he'd registered, been shown his room and thrown his shoulder bag on the bed, he was ready for a drink.

It was still early evening but he was five hours ahead; he retraced his footsteps and found himself in the bar of the Pickled Onion on Fore Street. He had beaten even the early crowd and sat at the long frost-coloured bar. He ordered a local beer, then almost gagged on its lack of conviction but stuck with it as he ran through his options. He'd rushed, hadn't made much of a plan, which was unlike him, but then he didn't normally have heated rows that included a cracked mug of coffee and tears with Jemma. She'd thought Bermuda was a bad idea, had got passionate about it, couldn't go with him, not in the middle of the school term, said that anyway he couldn't afford it and that maybe, just maybe, he had other priorities. Like? he'd asked, very stupidly. Making a few plans, she'd suggested, very tartly. And maybe even finding her an engagement ring, although she'd been too proud to make any direct reference to that. It hadn't been a great farewell. So Harry sat, swallowed the last of the insipid beer and ordered a bourbon on the rocks; in a hot climate he preferred it to malt whisky.

He had come in search of one woman, knew nothing except for her name. Jemma had reckoned the whole idea was like looking for nuts in a nunnery – that was when she'd smacked the mug of coffee down so hard she'd been left holding nothing but the handle – but to Harry it seemed a reasonable bet. The island contained barely sixty thousand people. Only a third of them were white and many fewer would be female and elderly. And probably only one would be named Susannah Ranelagh. An hour in the National Library should be enough; he'd passed its canopy-covered

73

door on the stroll to the bar and it would be open at ten in the morning. Anyway, as he'd reminded Jemma, nuts stood out in a nunnery. That was when the tears had started.

He didn't need to wait for the National Library to open. 'Miss Ranelagh?' the bartender said as he splashed the dark spirit over a mountain of ice. He was young, mixed-race, subtle earring, late twenties, full of cheer and named Vince. 'Sure I know her. Everybody knows everybody here – and everything,' he chuckled. 'That's why it's so quiet. You wanna misbehave you spend the weekend in New York and hope you're not gonna meet your neighbour at the check-in.' Vince laughed again. 'But somehow I don't think you'll be finding Miss Ranelagh playing away. No, sir, not she.'

'Tell me about her.'

A thread of suspicion rippled though the bartender's eyes.

'Don't worry. She's an old friend of my father but I've never met her. Thought I might go and say hello.'

Vince began polishing a glass as he considered. Harry had paid for the bourbon with a twenty and left the change on the counter. Vince cast the towel aside and leaned over the bar. 'It's not like I get invited to dinner, you understand. She's one of the Stay-Ons. Most of them only come to visit for a while, count their money and make sure it's hidden somewhere safe, but she seems to genuinely like it here. Does a lot. Arts and stuff. A patron of the governor's favourite charity.'

Harry finished his drink and ordered another. He paid for it with a fresh twenty, once again leaving the change on the bar, smiling at the young man. 'This is a spur-of-the-moment thing for me, Vince. I'm not even entirely sure where she lives.'

Vince polished the bar with a fresh towel, carefully, not rushing, sweeping up the change as he did so. 'Oh, Miss Ranelagh, she lives out in Flatt's on Harrington Sound. Everyone knows that, don't they, now?'

'She ever been married that you know of?'

Vince scrunched up his face. 'Nah. Not that I know. No way, not her. She's not a – you know, what d'you call them? – a woman's woman. That's not what I mean. She just seems a little old-fashioned. Catholic. From Ireland, I guess.'

'I think she may have been a business partner of my father's.'

'What does he say?'

'Not much. He's dead.'

Vince spent a moment digesting the information. It seemed clear that Harry wouldn't be making just a social call. 'Not really sure what business she's into,' he said, 'but no one's ever really sure what other people are into here, unless you're a bartender. And even I have a few other irons in the fire.' He stared hard at Harry, drew closer. 'How long you staying, mister? You're on your own, right? You interested in a little action, maybe?'

'What sort of action?'

'Whatever. Golf, if that's your thing. Sailing. Fishing.' A gentle pause, a raised eyebrow. 'A little local culture, maybe.'

Harry smiled but shook his head. 'No, thanks, Vince. I've got a brand-new fiancée and she's all tucked up at home waiting for me.'

Except Harry was entirely wrong. She wasn't.

—⁓—

Jemma wasn't the sort to sit idle at home. In any case, she was deeply hacked off with Harry, but that wasn't the end of the story: her exasperation masked an even deeper concern. She could put up with being left behind on his trip to Bermuda, and there was no way she could wangle the time away from teaching, but in his determination to get to the truth about his father's death she had also seen and sensed a side of Harry that she didn't recognize and didn't much care for. He'd convinced himself there was some funny business about it – he said his burning ear told him so –

and he was deaf to every word of caution and reason she threw at him. It was beginning to seem like an obsession. She'd glimpsed that in him before, of course, but had never had to confront it. The cold deliberation, the lack of flexibility, a machine that was programmed for a single purpose and seemed to have no off switch. He was going to find Susannah Ranelagh and that was it. Even as she fretted she realized it was partly her own fault – she was the one who'd pushed him off on his search for his father in the first place, so she wouldn't wail and whine. She'd started the whole affair; she decided she might as well help finish it. Get the old Harry back. So, even as he was being pimped by the bartender she was sitting on their sofa, wearing his slippers and one of his old shirts, finding comfort in his smell and going through the file about his father.

She read every scrap of paper in it, the bits she had seen before and those that were new to her, particularly the small bundle of letters of condolence. There weren't many of them, fewer than a dozen, bound up with a rubber band, and some so perfunctory and formal that they were addressed only to 'The Family of Mr Johnson E. Maltravers-Jones'. Professional advisers, in the main. A pathetic epitaph for any man's life. Yet there was one letter that was different and took her interest. It was addressed directly to Harry and began,

I hope you will remember me. As an old friend and business associate of your father's, our paths have crossed on a few occasions when you were younger and your mother was alive. Although I haven't seen you for many years, your father kept me abreast of your progress on a regular basis. He took great pride in your achievements. You must miss him terribly.

Jemma noticed that the letter bore the marks of so many creases that it must at some point have been screwed up and thrown away, only later to be retrieved and smoothed, not entirely successfully.

Now he is gone [the letter continued], I can do little other than to offer my profound sympathies. The passing of a father is a moment of huge significance in any man's life, and my thoughts are with you.

If I can be of assistance or support to you at any point, I hope you will feel free to get in touch. In the meantime, my renewed condolences.

The letter was written in a bold if occasionally illegible hand wielding a thick, expensive nib. The name at the top of the letter was Alexander McQuarrel. It had no postal address or phone number but at the bottom of the page, in small type, there was an e-mail address.

Jemma reached for her computer and began typing.

—⁓—

Harry woke early to the sound of birdsong being carried through the open window on a warm salt breeze. He lay for a while, struggling to disentangle his thoughts, before they were disturbed by the gentle clattering of preparations in the kitchen, soon followed by the sweet rush of brewing coffee. He rolled out of bed to check his e-mails – nothing from Jemma, she was still mad with him – then he stood with his back against the wall to begin his stretching exercises. The abuse he'd given his body over the years was beginning to take its toll – 'A little morning stiffness?' Jemma had once joked as he'd woken with a back tied in knots. The seven-hour flight in economy hadn't much helped. Neither did the heavy pancakes and solid eggs that appeared for breakfast. He pushed them aside and got stuck into the fruit bowl.

A little later he was waiting outside the tiny garage that offered moped rentals even before the owner opened the shutters. Car hire was forbidden to visitors in Bermuda, so they jumped onto small Japanese bikes that buzzed like sewing machines and travelled around the island's narrow roads at the top speed limit of 22 m.p.h. Even at a crawl and with nothing more to guide him than a tourist map, it took Harry only twenty minutes until he found himself on the road that hugged the northern shoreline and turning along the inland bay of Harrington Sound at a place called Flatt's Village. As he slowed, knowing he must be somewhere near his goal, up ahead he spotted a group of black kids playing football in a wayside park. He switched off the engine and coasted to a stop just as the ball attempted earth orbit and bounced into his arms.

'Sorry, mister.' A bright face smiled and two hands stretched out to reclaim the ball. The boy seemed no more than eight or nine and had jewels of sweat on his brow.

'I could confiscate it,' Harry said, returning the smile but holding onto the ball.

'And your bike vanish while you wasn't looking.'

'What, you'd steal it?'

'Steal? No, not me. But this here's the Bermuda Triangle, right? You hear 'bout that thing? Everything disappears.' The boy's eyes grew huge with exaggeration.

Harry burst into laughter. 'What's your name, kid?'

'Kenny, maybe. Depends.'

'Tell you what, Kenny. Maybe, I have to visit some-one who lives somewhere around here. Why don't I pay you a couple of dollars so you can look after my bike for a while. Make sure it doesn't disappear. Sound like a deal?'

'Couple of dollars? But there is five of us, mister.' Kenny waved in the direction of his friends.

'OK, five dollars.'

'How long?'

'Well, I'm going to see Miss Ranelagh. You know where she lives?'

'Sure do.'

'You show me.'

'Directions? Better make it ten.'

'I ought to give you a bloody good hiding for extor-tion.'

'But then you end up wandering around lost all day,' Kenny chirruped.

'Hah! Know something, young Kenny, you remind me of myself.'

'What does that mean?' the kid asked, his nose wrin-kling in suspicion.

'It means you win.' Harry reached inside his wallet and pulled out two notes. 'Here we are. Five now when you tell me her address. Five more when I pick up my bike.'

'That's fair,' the boy declared, reaching for the note and inspecting it as though he might be dealing with a high-class money launderer. 'And my ball, mister.'

'So where is Miss Ranelagh?'

'Miss Ranelagh? Why, that's right there, ain't it?' Kenny exclaimed as though he were dealing with a dimwit. He pointed. They were standing almost directly outside the house. The boy grabbed his ball back from Harry and scampered off to join his playmates.

The clapboard house was probably a four-bedroom, Harry reckoned, scrupulously neat and pastel pink with shutters on its sash windows and an elegant porch above its front door. The roof was startlingly white, the front garden small but manicured with just enough room for a couple of graceful palm trees. The property was approached from the road by a short semicircular drive. Far from ostentatious but impressive. As his hand wrapped around the brass cloverleaf knocker he still had no clear idea of what he should say. In the event it proved not to be a problem. Susannah Ranelagh opened the front door, took one long look at Harry, went several shades of grey and fainted into his arms.

CHAPTER FIVE

Susannah Ranelagh recovered her senses but had yet to recover her wits. Harry had taken her through to her sitting room and fetched a glass of water. 'Come on, take a sip,' he encouraged, kneeling beside her. She opened her eyes and stared; they were still swollen with torment.

'I'm sorry if I startled you, Miss Ranelagh.' He drew back to give her some space.

'No, no,' she protested, brushing strands of grey hair back from her forehead, 'it's not your fault. At my age you get moments like this. Should've had a proper breakfast.' Her voice retained an Irish lilt, the words rushing forth like waves brushing against the sandstone rocks of the Kerry shoreline where she had been raised.

'My name is Harry Jones,' he announced.

And who else could he be? she thought, with those deep eyes, the broad forehead and that mouth with its downturned, determined corners? There was an inner energy, too, like his father had possessed and which this younger version exuded with every breath.

'I'm sorry. What did you say your name was?' she said, finishing the glass of water and sitting back into her armchair, trying to affect the look of a woman once more at her ease despite the trembling in her hand.

'Harry Jones. I think you knew my father.'

'Oh, really?' she replied.

'Johnnie Maltravers-Jones. I think you were on the yacht when he died in Greece. Two thousand and one.'

Dear God, he knew – but how much? She felt the flood of panic rising inside her once again and trying to drown her senses. She willed herself to be strong, not to let everyone down.

'Ah, yes, of course. He was your father, you say. Such a tragedy. My condolences, Mr Jones.'

'Thank you. That's kind. I wonder, did you know my father well?'

As well as your mother did, she screamed silently. The panic was beginning to gain ground. Was this a trick question? But there was a steadiness in his eye

84

and an openness in his face that suggested nothing but genuine concern.

'I was simply a fellow passenger,' she replied, spreading her hands in apology.

'I know so little about the circumstances of his death, even why he was on board.'

'I'm sorry, Mr Jones, I don't think I can help you. I was little more than a hitchhiker cadging a lift.'

'From whom?'

'I beg your pardon?'

'I mean, who offered you the lift? Who else was on board?'

'But it was such a long time ago.'

'Please, anything you can remember. Names, descriptions. There was a younger woman on board, wasn't there? Where was the boat sailing from, going to? Can you tell me that?'

He leaned forward, eager, but in Miss Ranelagh's eyes he was like a mugger preparing to pounce.

'I'm an old lady,' she wailed.

'What can you remember of my father? Anything. Any recollection, no matter how small. You must surely remember something,' he pressed.

By this point the flutter of despair she placed on parade was entirely genuine. 'Stop! We must stop. I feel ...' She waved a forlorn hand in front of her face

85

that was flushing more deeply with every breath. 'I need to rest.'

'Miss Ranelagh, I've come such a long way to see you. Please.'

'No!'

Her sudden forcefulness startled them both. He dragged his eyes away from her and gazed around the room in frustration. It was meticulously tidy with expensive prints and oils hung on the wall, a collection of fine Irish crystal glass in a corner cabinet, the bookcases filled with hardbacks of some of the finest novels of the last fifty years, many of which Harry recognized as collectors' items, and a long and intricately carved piece of whalebone portraying the world of ancient sailors rested on a stand of polished cedar. Everything about this woman was old-fashioned but tasteful and expensive. It was also more than a little lonely. Every corner, every cranny of free space, was filled with old photos and mementoes, every inch of this place was hers yet hers alone, rarely shown and never shared with anyone else. It suggested stubbornness, that she did things her way, and he knew he wasn't going to be able to shift her. And, as he stared back into her darting, anxious eyes, he knew she was lying.

She, too, knew that she couldn't simply dismiss him, send him away empty-handed, for he was his father's son and he would only return. Anyway, a curt dismissal would do nothing but antagonize him and raise his suspicions. Play for time, Susannah, play for time! And get some help.

'I'm sorry, Mr Jones, truly I am,' she began again in a far more emollient tone. 'I would like to help you, of course I would, but . . .' – she shook her head, the grey hair falling across her face once again – 'now isn't the time. I'll tell you everything I know about your father' – there was more! – 'so why not come back around this same time tomorrow? I'll collect my thoughts. And make sure I have a proper breakfast.' A little joke. She was regaining control. The thin bones of her fingers brushed at the stray fronds of hair, putting everything back in order. 'You will come back tomorrow, won't you?'

'I promise I will.'

She smiled weakly as he got up. This man had come crawling through her past and now threatened everything she had set out for her future. His bloody father, he'd been a nightmare, too. Tell the son all she knew about Johnnie? Never. Anything but that.

—⚒—

Alexander McQuarrel had responded immediately, if a little stuffily, to Jemma's e-mail. 'It would be an honour to meet the fiancée of Harry Jones,' he had replied. 'As it happens, I shall be in London tomorrow with a diary that is not overly full and is flexible. I would be delighted to meet with you ...'

Jemma was allowed an hour's lunch break from the primary school where she taught. There was no wiggle room, so they agreed to meet on a bench overlooking the Thames in Battersea Park. When she arrived the river was low, leaving banks of glistening mud. A common shag perched on a navigation sign and preened itself while hooligan pigeons scuttled around her feet and hopped in impatience. McQuarrel, when he arrived shortly after her, was tall, upright, elegant, his stride long and confident despite the fact that by her reckoning he was well the other side of seventy. He wore an expensively tailored blue suit that clung to his lean frame and his complexion talked of fresh air and country living. The eyes were blue and bright, the hair like a blanket of snow and parted carefully with a comb. He seemed to recognize her and extended a hand in greeting.

'How did you know it was me?' she asked, curious, as he sat beside her.

'If you'll allow me the indiscretion of age,' he said, and paused as though not to take her for granted, 'you're the most naturally beautiful woman I've seen all morning.'

'I'm in a tracksuit,' she protested.

'There's also the dab of bright-green paint on the side of your cheek.' Her fingers flew instinctively to her face and began rubbing. 'And you said you were a teacher of very young children.'

Jemma laughed in congratulation. Far from being stuffy, he seemed charming.

'Please don't let me keep you from your lunch.' He nodded towards the plastic bowl of homemade salad sitting on the bench beside her.

'Oh, yes,' she stumbled as yet again he caught her off guard. 'I'd offer to share it but . . . somehow I just know you've got a far more splendid lunch waiting for you.'

'And you've only one fork.'

She smiled. She was going to find it easy to talk to a man like this. 'So,' she began, chewing a mouthful of rocket as more pigeons hovered at her feet, 'you knew Harry's father.'

'Most certainly. At one time he was a man of some importance in my life.'

'Harry wants to know a little more about him. I wonder whether you might help us.'

An unmistakable shadow passed behind the old man's eyes. 'You must understand, Miss Laing—'

'Please. Call me Jemma.'

'Johnnie was a *turbulent* sort.' He pursed his lips,

choosing his words with care. 'I don't want to be unkind, but I have to warn you – Jemma – you're likely to discover things about Harry's father you will both find uncomfortable. Distasteful, even.'

'I understand. But Harry can be painfully persistent.'

'Oh, as was his father.' His silver head seemed to be weighed down with the memory.

Suddenly the sun disappeared; the shadow of a man fell across their path. He was standing in front of them, dressed in a long overcoat despite the weather. He stank of sweet-stale urine and cheap alcohol and held out a filthy hand. 'Spare some change,' he blurted through cracked lips. Jemma flustered, did nothing. 'Change,' the tramp demanded in a more hectoring tone. He swayed, his hand moved from Jemma to McQuarrel, who said not a word, did nothing but stare, yet something was exchanged between the two men, something in the eyes that Jemma couldn't see but had the same effect on the tramp as a stick shoved up his backside.

'Yeah, you, too!' the tramp shouted as he leapt back, glaring. He wiped his mucus-crusted nose on the back of his coat sleeve and roared incoherently at them both before turning and shuffling away, kicking out at the pigeons as he went.

'I'm so sorry,' McQuarrel said quietly.

'It's scarcely your fault.'

He sighed. 'When you get to my age somehow everything seems your fault.' He seemed elsewhere for a moment before turning back to Jemma. 'I was rather hoping Harry would be with you.'

'He's abroad.'

'Somewhere nice?'

'Bermuda. But it's no holiday. He's gone there to talk to someone else about his father. A Miss Ranelagh. You don't happen to know her, I suppose.'

'It's not a name that means anything to me. But, when he gets back, can I suggest we all meet up?'

'That would be kind, Mr McQuarrel.'

'Alexander, please. And I hope you'll allow me to find somewhere a little more comfortable than a park bench. After all, I'm an old friend of the family – you're about to become a member of that family; we should celebrate. You know I haven't seen Harry since he was . . . oh, no more than a boy. He wouldn't remember me, I dare say, but I've followed his career. You're marrying an extraordinary man.'

'I know.'

He smiled and placed his hand on hers. 'I'm afraid I must ask you to forgive me. You've almost finished your lunch and I must attend to mine. Will you give me a call as soon as Harry gets back?'

'Of course. You've been very kind, Alexander.'

'I haven't been the slightest bit of help.'

'I know you will be.'

Her hand was warm within his; he squeezed it, held it firmly. 'Jemma, will you take a little advice from an old man? All too often in my experience the past comes back to haunt you. So you and Harry look forward to your future. Don't waste too much time raking over bad times that have long since been buried. Be happy. And be careful.'

—⁓—

Harry tossed around his bed like a ferret in a sack, wrapping his sheet into impossible knots. Something was chasing him through the shallows of the night, screaming at him so loud he could barely hear, let alone sleep. It wasn't simply that Susannah Ranelagh was lying, nor that his presence alone had been enough to make her swoon with fright. There was something else, something nagging at him with ferocious persistence, something about her, or about her house, he couldn't be sure which, yet it was setting him on edge like the sound of a dentist's drill. His intelligence training in Northern Ireland had taught him how to observe, to soak up images and information even when there wasn't time to analyse it all, to make sense of it later.

He had half seen something and he pursued it until sweat was running down his back.

Then he knew. Hit him so hard that he sat up in bed as though a grenade had been thrown through the window. In her house of many memories the old girl had many photos. Relatives, perhaps, or close friends, those who had clearly left a mark in her life. It was one of those photos that had been screaming at Harry, in a silver frame among the crowd that filled the top of the bookcase. Of a young Susannah Ranelagh, before her hair had lost its life and her features had been stretched by disappointment, at a time in her life when her smile suggested not simply the pleasures of the moment but also the expectation of more ahead. She was at a dinner table at which sat six others, four men and two other young women, in formal evening wear. A student ball, Harry guessed. Black-and-white, a little grainy. And perhaps it was the utter impossibility of what he now saw that had delayed his understanding and fought so hard with his wits, because one of the men at the table was Harry himself. No, not Harry, that was absurd: it was years before he'd been born. But, if not Harry, then someone who looked so like him that it left Harry gasping in amazement.

His father. It was Johnnie.

Harry didn't wait for the smell of coffee or the

clattering of breakfast bowls. He dragged himself down the hotel stairs three at a time, lashing out at doors and charging past the astonished receptionist. Soon he was gunning his bike past the upmarket haunts of Pitts Bay Road and way past the local speed limit. A few early-morning walkers shook their heads in disgust. Harry bent low over the handlebars to squeeze out the last breath of speed. It was only minutes before he was on the coast road, heading east, the sun playing games with him, bouncing off the water and into his eyes as he took the gentle curves and low rises of the North Shore Road. He held his head down, the sea wind whipping tears from his eyes. It was as he came to the junction that led to the Sound, barely a few hundred yards from Susannah Ranelagh's house, that he was forced to pause as other traffic crossed his path. He raised his eyes, looked both ways, then ahead. That was when he caught a sight that made him scream loud with frustration and fear. Up ahead he could see a spiral of evil, insistent smoke punching through the clear morning air.

By the time Harry's moped had slithered to a halt, the tyres sliding out on the sand-strewn tarmac, dumping the bike to the ground, the front of the house was already disappearing behind a curtain of smoke and fire. The front door was a sheet of flame, the porch beginning to scatter droplets of burning confetti that were scorching the grass. The lower windows were gone and already smoke was gathering behind the windows on the first floor and seeping out through the eaves. A group of neighbours had gathered across the street, powerless, pathetic; Kenny was there, too, his football held protectively under his arm. Harry ran to the rear of the house, where he found a swimming pool and beyond that another garden. He was alarmed to see that the garage at the side of the house was already throwing out quantities of vile, acrid smoke; an explosion sent an arrow of brilliant orange flame bursting through the window – a can of petrol, he suspected, and nothing to what would happen very shortly if there were a car inside.

He rattled at the back door and the French windows that led to the patio; both were locked. It took three of his best shoulder shots before one of the locks gave way and he was sent sprawling onto the floor of the kitchen amid splinters of glass and wood. He picked himself up and shouted for Miss Ranelagh; there was no reply, nothing but the flames that crackled like gunfire. The rear of the house was as yet relatively undisturbed, but as he found his way to the stairs he could see nothing but arms of fire and suffocating smoke waiting for him at the top. He screamed out her name once more. Nothing. In the kitchen he found a housecoat and thrust it beneath a tap to soak it, wrapped two wet kitchen towels around his hands, and, with the housecoat over his head and shoulders dripping water down him, he stood at the bottom of the stairs, afraid. Christ, he was well beyond forty; the years of youthful ignorance were way behind him; he knew exactly what he could expect.

Even as he returned from the kitchen he could see that the flames had already taken hold more firmly of the top floor and were waiting for him. 'Oh, shit!' he cried. He'd always hoped he might find something more inspiring as his epitaph, final words to carve on his gravestone, but the last time he'd been caught in a fire he'd watched a friend burn to death. He still saw the man's face in his dreams. He hated fires. But still he ran up the stairs.

The heat soared with every step. He knew the fire was reaching the temperature at which it would take control and explode, grabbing everything in its path. From a front room he heard windows exploding, feeding more oxygen to the flames. He didn't have much time. He fell to his knees and crawled.

She wasn't in the first two bedrooms he checked, nor the bathroom. The third bedroom had been converted to a study; the ceiling was already burning, setting the tops of the bookshelves alight, the floor rug already smouldering from cascading embers. Even as he watched, it burst into flame. Then there was only one bedroom left, at the front, where the fire was most fierce. Smoke was ripping at his throat, blinding him, screaming at him to go back, but he crawled forward, cowering beneath his damp rags until he had reached the door. Smoke was already squeezing beneath it, searching for him. He reached up for the handle. Even through soaking towels it was so hot it scorched through to his fingers. A volley of what sounded like rifle fire exploded on the other side of the door. He knew what was waiting for him; he very much wished he didn't.

Lying on his back, covering his face, he kicked at the door. Once, twice. It flew open. The noise and menace of the flame that rushed to fill the space above his head was like the passing of an express train. Then, for the moment, it was gone. He couldn't call out for her: he no longer had breath and he daren't fill his lungs. His brain was befuddled and his wits drowning in fear. With the last of his strength he forced his way inside.

Every part of the room was breathing fire. The windows were gone, the curtains billowing in the onrush of wind sucked in by the fire and burning like Roman candles. The carpet beneath his hands was smouldering, melting. And there, at the far end of the room, was the bed with its brass ends, its covers like a funeral pyre. But she wasn't there. The bed was made. The bloody house was empty.

Miss Ranelagh's home was built of wood and offered no resistance. The fire dragon that had taken hold of it groaned, twisted, belched; part of the roof collapsed, filling the room with a swarm of super-heated fireflies. Harry had to retreat, while he could. The stairs he'd climbed were now a river of flame. He crawled to the rear of the house, his mind filled with the darkness of smoke, the blanket of heat trying to force him down. Often it is easier to accept than to struggle, but Harry had the genes of a mule. It was little more than brutish anger that kept him going until he found himself beneath a window at the rear of the house. With what seemed like the last of his strength, he opened it, crawled onto its ledge and threw himself onto the lawn. He landed heavily, cried out in pain, then rejoiced: the pain meant he was still alive. He lay on his back, gasping for air, gagging, trying to clear his lungs of treacle. Through the fog of confusion and starved senses he could hear the siren of a fire engine. Someone was at his side, trying to help him. Harry struggled to his feet, looked around, took a breath of clean air. Then he dashed back into the house once again.

Every corner of the ground floor was now dancing in the flames, but Harry knew his purpose. He staggered and skipped over burning timbers as he forced his way into the sitting room, where on the previous day he had talked with the old woman. He saw what he wanted. He stumbled over the chair in which Miss Ranelagh had sat, sent himself sprawling, but he refused to be deflected. He grabbed the photo. Then he was gone, back out through the kitchen door that was spitting smoke like a chimney.

There were more people out on the lawn now, firemen taking control of the situation but not the fire. It was too late for that.

'Are you hurt, sir?' a fire officer asked, his voice muffled by his helmet. He was black, huge across the shoulders and belly, and dragged Harry almost nonchalantly a safer distance from the fire.

'I'll survive,' Harry replied in a voice that didn't sound anything like his own.

Harry began retching but it cleared his lungs. The fireman sat him in the shade of a jacaranda tree that marked the boundary of Miss Ranelagh's property; another fireman offered an oxygen mask that Harry clamped to his face until the sweet gas began blowing away the clouds of confusion.

'What's your name?' the fireman demanded.

'Harry. It's Harry,' he said, still coughing.

'OK, Harry, this is important. Is there anyone else inside?'

Harry shook his head. 'No. I had a good look round.'

'Almost too damned good, I'd say.'

'Yeah.'

'You sure there's no one? What about Miss Ranelagh? Is she there?'

'No,' Harry replied, now very clear in his mind. 'The lady's gone.'

CHAPTER SIX

They were almost indecently polite, the police and the fire officials, treated him like a hero once they were clear he'd arrived only after the fire had started, a man who'd dashed heedlessly into the flames in search of Miss Ranelagh. It was a good story that, if not entirely accurate, had the advantage of being pretty damned close to the truth. Yet still there were answers to be given. Harry was shaken, wanted time to think and point-blank refused hospital treatment, but agreed to come in for an interview later in the day at Hamilton police station. One over-eager policeman tried to pester him on the spot but came to a sudden halt as the car in the garage blew up, taking the roof of the garage with it and sending debris flying like fireworks. After that, every hand was bent to ensuring the fire didn't spread to neighbouring properties. So they let him go, for the moment. They could afford to be relaxed. This was Bermuda – there was nowhere for Harry to go without their knowing.

'OK, this afternoon. The police headquarters on Victoria Street. You know it?' the policeman asked. 'Three blocks back from the harbour front.'

'I'll find it.'

The crowd was larger now, but silent, gathered in awe to watch the last rites being pronounced over the mass of charred timbers and still-erupting ash that until an hour before had been their neighbour's house. Harry found his moped lying in the dust where he'd abandoned it. Kenny was standing guard.

'I wouldn't let no one touch it, mister,' the kid said.

'Thanks, Kenny.'

'I knew you was coming back.'

'Did you?'

'Sure, won a bet on it. They all thought you was a lunatic.'

'They may be right. See you around, Kenny.'

The bike had leaked a puddle of fuel that had stained the dust, but it coughed and kicked over after a couple of jabs at the starter button. Harry settled gingerly into the saddle, gripping the handlebars, trying to pretend his hands weren't shaking. He turned his wrist and set off much more steadily than he'd arrived, wondering why the stench of the fire still filled his nostrils even as he left it well behind. It was only after he'd run his hand across his face that he realized he had scorched his eyebrows and hair; it was he who stank. His eyes were still protesting from the hot ash, tears trickled down his cheeks, his shoulder ached from its encounter with Miss Ranelagh's rear door, his back was protesting at being thrown out of a first-floor window and his knee was bruised after coming off second best in its tussle with the overstuffed armchair. Still, he'd been worse, but the older he got the less comfort that over-used excuse seemed to give him. He had little idea where he was going, had no desire to return straight to the hotel, so he lost himself on a road that meandered down towards the south of the narrow island, past beaches and clubs and isolated strips of clean, elegant sand. Soon the sea air was filling his lungs and brushing his soul clean once more. The road twisted and turned along the shore, like a ribbon that had been thrown down in a gentle Atlantic breeze. For much of its length it had neither footpath nor hard shoulder, was simply edged by grass or scrub or bare sand, or overlooked gentle cliffs that dropped to the sea below. He passed a fire engine, lights flashing, horn blaring, headed in the opposite direction; Miss Ranelagh's house was evidently still putting up a fight. As he rode on, the houses became more isolated and the shoreline more insistent; he relaxed as he leaned the bike into the road's gentle corners, disturbing the gulls that had taken up squatters' rights along this increasingly empty stretch of roadway. They gave a raucous cry as he approached, lifting away on the currents of salt air that welled up from the breaking sea below.

It was as their cries of protest were carried away and died on the breeze that Harry realized he was no longer alone. He sensed before he saw the approach of another vehicle behind him, a flatbed delivery truck with a white driver's cabin, and as he stared in his mirrors he saw yet another, a red Toyota hatchback typical of the neat and modest cars on an island that had only 130 miles of public roads and a ferocious vehicle import tax. He hugged the side of the single-lane road to give them plenty of passing room and opened the throttle a little as the route began to lift above the sea. The other vehicles closed, then seemed to hesitate, reluctant. In his mirror Harry could see the driver of the truck, eyes staring from a dark and shaven head with an expression that suggested this wasn't a casual morning delivery run, nor did it suggest he was the type who spent his life driving in the slow lane. Beneath him and to one side he could see the waves beating against rocks that formed the face of a modest cliff. Harry eased off, allowing the moped to slow as it tackled the increased elevation of the road. The truck and car slowed with him. Harry squeezed out a little extra speed; the others kept their place. And suddenly Harry's ear was screaming at him.

He searched ahead for some form of cover, some means of escape, a side road, a place to run where they couldn't follow, but to his left the road fell away to the rocks below while on his right the front of the truck had pulled alongside him. He could see the driver directly now, through the truck's open window, was looking straight into his eyes. They were cold eyes, yet filled with excitement. Intent on doing Harry great harm.

Behind him the red Toyota had drawn up close, revving its engine like the pant of a pursuing animal, almost brushing into his rear wheel, falling back a few feet, then accelerating close again. They were running him down. And now, to his horror, Harry could see another man kneeling in the back of the flatbed, dread-locks dangling from beneath a multicoloured Rasta hat, clinging to the truck with one hand while his other massive fist was closed around the handle of a baseball bat. The bastard was grinning with enthusiasm.

The truck edged still closer. Harry couldn't brake:

he'd be mown down by the car behind. Neither could he outrun them. Below him the rocks snarled like angry teeth. He was trapped. They would beat him senseless with the bat or break his leg or ribs, or force him off the road and onto the rocks without leaving a mark on either truck or car to suggest they had any involvement in what would be classed as a tragic accident. They'd timed it well, for the road was reaching its highest point above the rocks. Harry was toast. Damp, dismembered toast.

The truck drew ever nearer; the bastard with the bat gave a practise swipe, getting his eye in, grinning so hard his face threatened to crack in two. The solid ash club whistled inches past Harry's head. A second swipe. Closer still. Ready for the final blow. The Toyota's engine roared in triumph, the truck driver hit his horn in anticipation of victory. Then for an instant the truck veered away. Only a fraction and only for a second as it bounced into a pothole and the driver wrestled with the wheel, but it was all Harry needed. He had nowhere else to go. He drove straight off the cliff.

—⁓—

Harry knew he was still alive, but only because he hurt too much to be dead. He remembered falling off the cliff, tumbling past screaming seagulls, twisting, trying to find a sliver of clear water between the gnashing teeth of rock, and failing. The last thing he remembered before slamming into the side of an outcrop of volcanic limestone was the blue-ringed eye of a gannet staring at him in disbelief. Then nothing, until now. He took a breath. Almost choked. He'd done enough to survive but the pain told him it had been a close-run thing.

Slowly he opened his eyes, struggled to gain some sort of focus, found a dark face staring at him. It wasn't grinning, thank God. And the eyes were generous, if clouded with concern.

'Where am I?'

'Hospital,' the nurse said, taking his wrist to check his pulse. 'The King Edward Memorial Hospital to be precise.' She let go his wrist; Harry became aware that his other arm was held captive by a swathe of plaster that stretched from biceps to hand.

'What's the damage?'

'Oh, considering what you been up to, you got off light. You have a pretty bad concussion, then there's a dislocated shoulder, and you made a bit of a mess of your right elbow.' She shook her head in exasperation; Harry could see her more clearly now. 'We had to operate and put a pin in it for you. You hurting?'

Harry slowly tested the various parts of his body. He was. Everywhere.

'You gotta hurt a bit to heal. And you seem to have got yourself a prize collection of scrapes and scratches and scorch marks and stuff, but, judging by the old scars we found, you be well used to that. So you ache, maybe have a bit of trouble with your right arm, but you'll live. This time.' Her tone smacked of matronly disapproval. Her face, with its frizzy grey-ing hair, disappeared from his line of sight. He could hear her fussing over a few more observations, then he heard the door close. He stretched a little, tested the muscles in his neck, looked around and found another black female face staring at him. This too, had disapproval written firm across it. The shape of the face was oval with a prominent chin, the skin smooth and several shades lighter than that of the nurse. She was also wearing a different uniform, a starched white shirt, epaulettes and black shoulder lanyard that identified her as an inspector in the Bermuda Police Service. She was studying him with eyes that were sharp and expressive. The lips were equally animated.

'You up to a few questions, Mr Jones?'

'Depends how many.'

'Quite a few in your case.'

'And I suspect none of them is what I want for breakfast.'

'Breakfast? It'll soon be time for tea.'

Harry blinked, focused more sharply. 'Who are you?'

'I'm Inspector Hope. Inspector Delicious Hope.'

He began to splutter; her eyes flashed in warning.

'You and me, we've got some talking to do, Mr Jones.'

'About?'

'Accidents. Maybe arson.'

He was about to protest that it wasn't any sort of bloody accident when some instinctive hand held him back. He had no idea what sort of hole he'd jumped into, except for the fact that it had almost got him killed. He trod with caution. 'You said arson?'

'That's what it looks like. Too early to be sure but there are signs an accelerant was used.'

'And Miss Ranelagh?'

'Yes, that's something else we're rather keen to ask you about.'

'She's . . .?'

'Disappeared. We haven't finished searching, haven't been able to touch the basement. It was sure one mother of a fire.' A significant pause. 'We'd like to know what you were doing there.'

109

'Me? A family friend. Called on her yesterday, she invited me back today.'

'Can you prove that?'

'Why should I need to?'

'Because we have a suspicious fire and a little old lady who's suddenly gone missing.'

'And I'm helping you with your enquiries.'

She bit her bottom lip and exposed startling white teeth. 'Let me put it this way, Mr Jones, you're right at the top of my list. I'm just not sure about you. You're either a hero or some mean arsonist and maybe even a murderer. I'd like to know which.'

'Somewhere in between, I guess.'

'You up to this?'

He nodded. He concentrated on her shirt and after a momentary struggle the sharp creases on her breast pocket came into focus. He decided that was a good sign, even though it caused the inspector's eyes to narrow in irritation.

'How do you know Miss Ranelagh?' she asked.

'I didn't say I knew her.'

'You said—'

'A family friend. Of my father.' He stirred, managed a wiggle of his legs and groaned as they transformed into a river of fire. He twisted his neck stiffly to look around him. 'I had a photograph . . .'

110

'This one?' She held it up gently by its corners. It showed every mark of its ordeal by fire and water yet it was still clearly recognizable. 'I'm afraid the frame didn't make it. I'm told they took pieces of it out from between your ribs.'

'You've been through my things,' he sighed.

'Of course. We needed to ID you. And, when we had, I made you my prime suspect. In fact, at this stage you're my only suspect.'

'Inspector, I think you need a little more imagination.'

'And you perhaps have a little too much of it, Mr Jones,' she said, holding his eye as it threatened to wander back towards her breasts.

'That's Miss Ranelagh in the middle,' he said, getting back to business. 'And my father sitting next to her.'

'This one?' She pointed at Johnnie. 'Guess I can buy that. The family resemblance. Stubborn chin.' She sniffed. 'So explain the fire.'

'I can't. It was already like Guy Fawkes by the time I arrived.'

Her face remained serious, a furrow of suspicion digging in between the eyes; he decided it didn't suit her, wasn't her natural pose.

'How do I know that?' she demanded.

'Look, Inspector, if I started the bloody thing, what was I doing hanging around?'

111

'Making sure, perhaps.'

'Dashing in and out? Lighting more matches?'

'OK, so what were you doing?'

'Looking for Miss Ranelagh, of course.'

She sucked at her lips as she considered what he'd said and slowly the official mask began to slip. His story wasn't too difficult to accept, several witnesses had said much the same but she still had to check, particularly with the old woman missing. 'Hero, then.'

He shook his head, delighted to discover that to do so no longer left him in agony. 'No,' he said sadly. 'It was just the wrong place, wrong bloody time.'

Her chest heaved as she seemed to exhale the last of her doubts. 'Been checking up on you, Harry Jones. Right Hon. George Cross. Military Cross. Quite a few other bits of ribbon, too.'

'That's me. I keep forgetting to run away. Bloody idiot.'

'So what made you go off the road?'

His torn ear was still screaming caution. Three total strangers had tried to murder him and they'd come prepared with a plan and a bloody great baseball bat. Professionals, he guessed, so who had paid them? Miss Ranelagh, maybe? She'd been almost the only person who knew he was on the island and there had been no doubting her fear of him. But why? Why was she so afraid? And where was she? The questions tumbled round in his mind until his head hurt even more, but he was functioning again. He knew if he admitted any of this to the inspector it would tie him up for days. Attempted murder? Could even be weeks. 'Go off the road? I got dizzy, I guess. The smoke, shock, maybe.'

'Perhaps you just got careless,' she suggested, her tone dripping incredulity.

'If you say so.'

'What I do say is that you'll have to hang around a while.'

There it was. His instincts had been right. 'No, thanks,' he said. It slipped out too bluntly, like a challenge.

'Don't think you get much choice in the matter, Harry. I'm no doctor but your body looks like it could do with a little downtime.'

She was staring at him and for the first time he became aware he was naked from the waist up. He also saw that her eye wasn't entirely professional. They had at last established some common ground.

'And we got to get into that basement, be certain Miss Ranelagh's not there,' she continued. 'This could still be a murder case.'

Suddenly, Harry sat up with a jerk that made him

gasp, but the pain he felt was dulled by the onrush of insight. Miss Ranelagh wasn't dead. She'd been terrified of him, put him off for a day, but now he saw she'd never had any intention of meeting with him again. 'I don't think she's in the basement,' he declared.

'So where?'

'Check to see if she got on a plane today, will you?'

'What, you suggesting she flew out and left breakfast burning on the stove?'

'That she started the fire?' He couldn't imagine why, except that terrified old ladies can do strange things. 'Just humour a beaten-up old hero, will you?'

'You want to play policeman, Harry?'

'Just let's say that I'd be happy to help you with your enquiries.'

She puckered her lips as she tried to make up her mind about him, aware of the ambiguous undertones in his invitation, then reached for her phone. While she gave instructions to someone on the other end, Harry tried to clear his mind, glad that some of the numbing effect of the painkillers was wearing off. No, Susannah Ranelagh would never have burned the house that held all her memories. What would be the point? And he doubted she knew enough about murder to arrange for his. But what he did know was that something had happened between Miss Ranelagh and his father to

114

leave her fainting in terror simply because she'd found Harry standing outside her door.

Delicious was finished and was tapping the tips of her fingers together as though in applause. 'Harry, you can join my team any time. Nail and head. Seems Miss Ranelagh left our island this morning, went through Wade International on the early flight to London via New York.'

He took a deep breath of satisfaction and with every breath found his strength being slowly restored. 'So, what do you reckon, Delicious? That I may not be an arsonist and murderer after all?'

She smiled, nodded. 'It's possible.'

'Then I'm free to leave Bermuda.'

An ember of provocation flickered behind her eyes. 'Don't be in such a damned hurry, Harry. This is a great island we have. Do a little healing here.' Then the slightest but most meaningful of pauses. 'Be happy to show you some of it.'

'That would be great, Delicious, in another life.'

He spoke softly, and the ember in her eyes died as she realized he wasn't a sole agent. 'Some other life, then, Harry. But don't go rushing into it, OK?'

'What flight did you say Miss Ranelagh caught?'

'Early one.'

'How early?'

'Nine-thirty. As I said, she changed in New York. Didn't wait for the direct flight. Must have been in a hurry.'

'I'm sure she was. Do me a favour, will you, Delicious – no, two?'

'Tempt me.'

'Call the nurse. I need to get myself sorted.'

He bit his lip to stifle the pain as he hauled himself into a sitting position on the side of the bed. There wasn't much to hide his modesty; she had noticed. He challenged her with his eyes; she threw it straight back at him. 'And that second favour, Mr Jones?'

'Call those nice guys and gals at British Airways. I need to change my ticket, fly home before the weekend. Without any penalty. You could pull a little rank, ask them to do that, couldn't you?'

'I suppose you'll be wanting an upgrade next.'

'Make that three favours.'

She burst into laughter. 'You and I would make a good team, Harry. You ever come back on the island, you let me know. Spend a little time. Play good cop, bad cop.'

'And I bet you can be a very, very bad cop, Delicious.'

'Seems you're never going to find out.'

Their eyes held and tangled, their imaginations dancing in another life.

'What plane you want to catch, Harry?'

'First thing tomorrow.'

'Hot damn, she must be really worth getting back to.'

'She is.'

But, even as he raised her, it wasn't Jemma he had so much on his mind as Susannah Ranelagh. If she had caught the nine-thirty flight there was no way she could have set the fire herself. She had neither the time nor the motivation. No, there was someone else in all this, someone who wanted him dead. It wasn't Susannah Ranelagh, but she would surely be able to point him in the right direction.

CHAPTER SEVEN

It had been a long flight, stretched by the need to change at JFK, every moment filled with the cackling of demons. Susannah Ranelagh was familiar with demons: they'd been an integral part of her Irish upbringing in the hills around Lough Leane, instructed by the priest and exaggerated still more by her own narrow-minded mother. At one point in her younger days she'd even considered escaping from the fires of Hell by retreating to a convent but that had never been a realistic option. She'd never been able to open her heart or close her mind sufficiently to accept God. It was the same with men. When she'd arrived at Oxford she'd been determined to lose her pent-up innocence and had set about it as much out of intellectual curiosity as physical need, and had quickly identified a Classics scholar in his final year for the purpose, but the experience had left her desperately unfulfilled. Too little finesse, too much thrashing of limbs, and all that inevitable Catholic guilt. Susannah Ranelagh wasn't by any means a prude but she was intensely private and self-contained. She was also stubborn and had persevered through a succession of sweated encounters only to find her heart broken on every occasion, just as her mother had warned her it would. Revel and regret, until eventually her life had been devoted simply to regret.

Except for one man. He had been a constant part of her life ever since they'd met at Oxford, along with Johnnie Maltravers-Jones and the others. She'd slept with him all too fleetingly, and only in those early days, but theirs had been the one relationship that she'd convinced herself might succeed. She'd held to that through all the ensuing years, through all the other men, even after Oxford, even after he had married. Marriage didn't always last for ever, even her pious mother had been forced to admit that, and so Susannah had waited. Patience had become her faith.

And, as she walked through Heathrow's Terminal Five dragging her small suitcase, there he was, waiting. She was in her sixties yet still she felt herself flustering, the colour beginning to rise and stain her pale cheeks. Why, he could have sent a driver, or met her at the station, but no, he had insisted! 'I'll be there for you, Susie,' he'd said. 'You always have been,' she'd whispered in reply. Now he stepped forward from the crowd and she thought she would trip over the tangle of her emotions that surrounded her. Ever since she'd found Johnnie's son on her doorstep her fears had been pursuing her like a headless horseman, but here he was to take her in his arms and sweep all the terrors away. He held a large bunch of fresh roses in his hand and, if they were of assorted colours rather than the blood red of devotion, what did it matter? And what did it matter if, in the process of throwing herself too eagerly into his arms, just like all those years ago, she crushed them? She was never going to leave him again, not till the day she died.

—⁘—

Harry's welcome at Heathrow two days later turned out to be considerably less enthusiastic. Jemma was waiting. She'd rushed, got there early, driven by excitement and his early return, was jumping from sneaker to sneaker to catch first sight of him, but when he emerged through the throng she was appalled. He was hobbling, his body bent, his right arm in a cast and sling. The skin on his forehead was scorched and raw while his right cheek had a revolting bruise that had spread to his eyes to a degree that even the sunglasses couldn't hide. She gave a yelp of dismay and rushed towards him, only to discover that getting up close was even less reassuring.

'Damn you, Jones!'

'Sorry, Jem. Didn't want to upset you by telling you on the phone. Fell off my bike.'

She swore once again, unsure whether she should try to hug him or break his neck. Despite his reassurances, there was no way she could be casual about it and during the next hour she discovered that he was anything but relaxed either. It wasn't just the pain that was still making him wince or the after-effects of the anaesthetic: he seemed distant, distracted, elsewhere. He told her little except to say that he had met Susannah Ranelagh, pushed away all her other questions until she came to the conclusion he was avoiding her.

'I don't believe you, Harry,' she said when at last she had settled him at home on the sofa.

'Believe what?'

'That you fell off your bike.'

He didn't dispute the point.

'I deserve more than bullshit, Harry.'

'Fair enough,' he sighed in exhaustion, and sank back into the pillows.

'And if you ever want to sleep in the same bed as me you'd better get on with it.'

'Don't think I can sleep with you, not with this.' He stared at his plastered arm, which was resting on a pile of pillows, in an attempt to deflect her, but Jemma was having none of it. She stared with a mixture of torment and fear that was so ferocious it could be rooted in nothing but love. It was why she was so blind with anger. He sighed and surrendered, and for the next few minutes took her on a canter around the course of his last few days, sparing her nothing: the fire, the fall, the cars that caused him to swerve, everything except for admitting to the deliberate attempt to kill him. She didn't deserve that. 'So she's in Britain,' he concluded. 'Susannah Ranelagh's here. I've got to find her.'

'No, you haven't. This has got to stop, Harry.'

'I can't. Sorry, Jem, but ... I can't.'

She'd always known there was a darker side to Harry, that his past had led him to alleyways down which no ordinary man would ever willingly wander. He had killed, in the Army and since, and put his own life on the line. She'd heard him muttering through his dreams, sometimes crying out, calling names. He'd never be conventional or often even comfortable; that was part of his appeal, the mystique of Harry Jones, and she was sensible enough to know she couldn't change him. Yet she couldn't deny her hope that she might help him move on, to a future they both could share. But this wasn't it. It was one thing for a woman to know that the man she loved had hidden depths, quite another to watch him drowning in them.

'We're supposed to be getting married, Harry. Stop this – please. For my sake.'

'You must understand, I have to find this woman. To know what happened to my father.'

'Forget your father. He's dead.'

'Jem . . .' He was about to protest that she'd been the one who had set him on the trail but the pain in her eyes told him there was no point in trying to win the argument with logic.

'Harry, it's you and me. The present. Our future. Damn the past.'

'You don't understand, Jem.'

She stood up. 'Correct. Full marks. Top of the class. I don't. First fucking thing you've got right since you got back!' She disappeared into the bathroom and made a point of slamming the door behind her.

—⟋⟍—

There had been a further surprise for Susannah Ranelagh in addition to the arms full of roses.

'You're staying with me, Susannah,' he had announced.

'I'd thought . . . a hotel. As always.'

'I wouldn't hear of it,' he said as he placed her bag in the back of his Mercedes. She'd arrived with her life teetering on the brink of damnation and yet within minutes he had brushed the clouds away. As, some-how, he always had.

She had tried to talk of Harry while he was driving the several hours to his home but his hand reached out for hers, squeezing it in comfort. 'No, all that later,' he instructed and, as ever, she had done as he had asked. Instead, they caught up on old times – so many of them and too old, perhaps, but, with every mile along the motorway and through the winding hedgerows of the country lanes, she felt the years slip away and she was young once more.

As the Mercedes bit into the gravel of the long drive she gazed on the ancient house in awe. His home, set in the cupped hands of the hills behind. It was her first time. She wondered how long it would take her to climb to the highest point, just as she had used to, at home in the hills of Kerry. He left her suitcase sitting on the tiles of his wonderful, echoing hallway. 'I'll take it to my room,' she suggested but he shook his head. 'No. Later. Eat. Relax.'

She stretched up to kiss him, on the cheek, nervously, and his eyes filled with surprise, just as they had that first time in his rooms at Oxford after she had dropped her blouse and advanced upon him.

'A glass of champagne before we eat,' he suggested. It had been sherry back then. But he clicked his fingers in correction. 'No, of course. Forgive me, Susie. You prefer Pinot Grigio.' She always had. And the glass was there, with a simple meal not far behind. Smoked salmon. Salad. Prepared by his own hand. She felt sure that a man who lived on his own in a house of this size would have a cook and a housekeeper but there was no sign of either. Of course, he'd sent them away, so she could be alone with him. Private. Intimate. In the wonderful oak-filled library he had created. He gave her his antique New England armchair clad in tobacco leather with its view down to the lake. And whiskey in a thick crystal tumbler.

'Irish,' he said.

'The whiskey or the glass?'

'Both.'

They had always drunk the same, the whole group. One would decide on the drink of the moment and the rest would follow, even the girls. It had been the sixties, no place for feminine weakness. Drink together, learn together, love together, five young men and three women joined in a conceit and a conspiracy that would last so long as they lived. They hadn't thought of themselves as pretentious, just better than the rest, sitting around each other's rooms in college, propped on window seats or in overstuffed armchairs, honing their minds, scraping away convention while their less talented contemporaries got drunk on cheap port and threw up in the corner of the quad. They were an elite, dedicated to intellectual outrage. The drink wasn't the reason why they had all ended up sleeping with each other but it hadn't stood in the way, either, oiling the wheels that had taken them along a new and liberating path away from the confines of convention, and in her case from the Catholic Church – or so she had thought. It was only later that, somehow, her upbringing had reclaimed a goodly chunk of her, dragged her back, made her feel guilty. And lonely. Not even the wealth she'd gained could prevent that. Mrs Nun, they called her on the island – or was it Mrs None? But only behind her back. Didn't stop them accepting her money. Yet sitting here, with him, for the first time in her life she felt that everything could be reconciled.

She raised her glass in silent toast, drank. He was telling her some amusing tale about poor Findlay, one of their group from Oxford, when she began to feel the jetlag kick in. A sudden lethargy made her mind wander. No surprise, at her age. Bone weary, as only old bones can be, but she thought nothing of it, drifting along on the sound of his voice until she realized she wasn't simply drained but couldn't move. Beginning to find it difficult to breathe. A stroke, perhaps? But she could feel no pain. And still he was smiling.

It was only then that things began to fit into place. At first she refused to believe. Why he had picked her up at the airport. Brought her here. Dismissed the staff. Not allowed her to be recognized by a single other soul since she'd set foot back in Britain. 'Why?' she gasped, but already she knew. 'Harry . . .'

—⁓—

He remembered – how could he ever forget? – that first time in his rooms overlooking Christ Church meadow when she'd arrived for her tutorial wearing a tight little frown and a still tighter blouse tucked into her waist that didn't even pretend to hide the body beneath. She'd 'sported his oak', locked the outside door behind her as she'd come in so they wouldn't be disturbed. A stifling day of the Trinity term, the ivy around the old sash window rattling in exhaustion from an unseasonably dry summer that left him sweating inside his woollen suit. He'd asked her if she would like a glass of sherry and she had slipped off the blouse. Desperately earnest, no gentle allure, no foreplay, no real idea. He'd suspected, and later confirmed, that he'd been almost her first.

The sex had been an academic exercise. It was never going to be sustained: he had too much to lose. So, instead, he led her up another path, where they quickly slipped into a sharing of minds rather than bodies, flirted with ideas, fondled fantasies and shared these fantasies with the others in the little group he formed. They shared their bodies, too, although she'd made it clear to him that she slept with the others only because it was what she knew he wanted. Finding oneself through others, he'd called it. Which was precisely what he was doing now.

Killing her was inevitable. The Darwinian conclusion of it all. Survival. His, not hers, of course. She was an irrelevance – a useful irrelevance over the years, he had to admit, but her purpose had long since faded, like her grey, forlorn hair and skin dried by exposure to too much sun, although the eyes were still bright, full of marmalade and chestnuts, those same eyes he remembered looking up at him from the front row of the lecture hall, leaning forward, eager. Even then she'd been just that little bit too enthusiastic, like a sheepdog that followed a step too close. Inevitable she should be trampled.

Like Findlay. He'd killed Fat Finn, too, plied the blancmange of a man with drink to the point of oblivion, then taken him to a point beyond. That had been four months ago and still no one had found the body. In another while the brambles would have overgrown the path and the cottage would disappear

In his mind he'd almost managed to persuade himself he'd done Findlay a favour, put him out of his misery. No fear, no blood. He hadn't truly killed Findlay at all in one sense, merely hastened the process. But now, with Susannah, this was different. There was no escaping his responsibility as he sat watching the woman die, her eyes twitching, widening in alarm as she began to realize what was happening to her. He was surprised at how calm he felt. He wondered if he would still feel the same in the morning.

CHAPTER EIGHT

Harry had slipped into a world he found impossible to share and it seemed as though Jemma had followed his example. Breakfast had proved desultory; she'd not slept and it showed.

'What's next?' she asked as she watched him make a mess of buttering his toast with his left hand.

'Help me?'

She did as he asked and with meticulous care, buttering every corner of the toast before covering it with a blanket of her mother's homemade marmalade. She did it without either complaint or conversation, then pushed the plate in front of him. 'And?' she whispered, wanting to know whether he had changed his mind.

'Try to find Susannah Ranelagh.'

He hadn't. Harry Jones. Always determined. Driven.

And, it was beginning to seem to her, inexcusably selfish.

'I'll leave you to it, then,' she said. Couldn't butter his own bloody toast yet still he wouldn't back off. 'Mustn't be late for school. Clean up the breakfast things. If you can.' And, before he could finish chewing, she was gone.

—⁄⁄⁄—

The lake. One of his ancestors had built it, shortly after returning from Waterloo when labour was dirt cheap. Took them almost three years. Two centuries later he knew every bit of bank, every stand of bulrush, every blind spot, and the depth of every reach of the water to the nearest foot. Useful, when you want to dispose of a body.

He stared out from his living room, cup of tea in hand, retracing his footsteps. She'd been light, almost gaunt after all those lonely years, and even at his age he could still manage a wheelbarrow. It left traces in the dew-damp grass but they would already have disappeared with the rising sun. The spot just along from the willow, with nothing but owls and a foraging vixen as mourners. She was wrapped in a heavy, rusted chain that he'd found in the old stable block, secured with two heavy padlocks, and that had made

132

it hard physical work. He'd almost lost his grip as he'd heaved at the handles of the barrow, but he'd managed; not so much survival of the fittest, he'd thought, not at his age, but at least the most determined. Susannah had cooperated – hadn't she always? – slipping beneath the dark waters with scarcely a ripple and nothing but a startled moorhen to offer the eulogy. Then it was done.

He thought he'd avoid that spot by the willow for a while. Go about the rest of his business. He had so much still to do. And his tea had already gone cold.

—◊—

For the next three days Harry and Jemma stumbled around each other, glad of the excuse that it was Harry's arm and bruised body that kept them from sharing a bed. They didn't share much else, either; he continued worrying away at things she no longer wanted to know about; he didn't offer, she didn't ask. It couldn't last, something had to give, and it was Jemma who made the first move. She came back from school and discovered him staring at the photograph of Susannah Ranelagh that he'd propped up on the bookshelf in place of the one of his father on the beach. She sighed. It was time to build a few bridges.

'I like your father's long hair,' she suggested,

dropping her bag and heading for the bottle of Sauvignon in the fridge.

'You recognize it's him?'

'No mistaking him,' she said, returning from the kitchen with a generous glass. She waved it in his direction, enquiring if he wanted one himself, but he shook his head. Painkillers. And confusion. She'd spotted his father, done instantly what had taken him hours to figure out. 'I got trained by the best in British Intelligence to analyse faces but you're just way ahead,' he lamented.

'I'm a woman, Harry. We do faces. We're a congregation that spends half our lives praying before our mirrors.'

They exchanged a smile, their first in days.

'Who are the others?'

'I wish I knew. Susannah Ranelagh's the one in the middle. As for the rest . . .'

Jemma picked up the photo and studied it. Eight by eleven, or thereabouts. Four men and three women, which made for five strangers. Circular dining table, formal black tie, young faces laughing at the camera, relaxed, casual arms on receptive shoulders, one pair of spectacles slightly askew, the scene awash with alcohol and half-eaten puddings. Friends, probably very close. 'Early sixties, judging by the awful fashions. Those frills look like they're designed to throttle the girls and you could hide an army beneath those petticoats. University chums, were they?'

'Why do you say that?'

'Pay attention, Jones. You told me your father was at Oxford in the early sixties.'

'Yes. That's right.' He felt sheepish. Now he could see it, of course: the photo screamed of youthful indulgence. So his father and Susannah Ranelagh went back that far . . . Damn, he needed to sharpen up. Shove the painkillers. 'I'll have that glass of wine after all,' he said.

'So?' she said as she handed over his drink.

'Indulge me in this. Please, Jem?'

'I've got schoolwork to prepare,' she responded, heading off to the bedroom. At least she hadn't thrown it back in his face.

The wine seemed to mark a turning point in Harry's recovery. The painkillers went in the bin and with them the dullness that seemed to have filled his mind with fog. Harry began making calls. The first was to Cecil Pisani, a Cabinet minister when Harry had first entered Parliament and who was now in graceful semi-retirement as an emeritus professor at Johnnie's old college. He readily returned Harry's call and extended an invitation to dinner on the college's sumptuous High Table. 'You'll have to bear with me, Cecil,' Harry pleaded. 'I'm afraid I'm a bit crocked.'

'The entire wretched country is crocked, old boy,' Sir Cecil Pisani replied in the comic patrician accent that had probably cost him any preferment higher than Culture Secretary. 'Better do some damage to what's left of the college cellar before we have to sell it to the Chinese.'

He tried to make a call to the photographer whose details were printed on the back of the image, only to discover that the telephone number was no longer valid. The company had long gone out of business but it had been taken over by another Oxford photographic firm who understood the value locked up in old images. 'We don't throw nothing away, Mr Jones,' the helpful young woman on the other end of the phone told him. 'Trouble is, all that old stuff arrived on the back of a truck and got dumped in our warehouse. Photos, negatives, unpaid bills. Quite a few rats, too. All jumbled up, and for a while the rats were winning. I tell you, trying to find anything in that warehouse is like going down a coal mine without a lamp.'

Yet she promised to try. Harry gave her the reference number on the back of the photo and waited. At the very end of the week she called back. 'I've got something, not much. Are you ready?' she asked. 'Hilary term 1964, it was. Can't tell you more, no names or nothing, except there's a scribbled note on the negative sleeve that suggests they were members of the university's Junior Croquet Club. Does that ring any bells?'

His father indulging in the genteel summer sport of croquet? Pimm's among the petunias? About as likely as a tax rebate. His father had always embraced any excuse for a drink but this connection seemed far-fetched, although he suspected it might have suited Miss Ranelagh down to her cotton socks.

Harry had less success when he tried to call Tallon, his father's lawyer. He left a telephone message with his secretary asking him to return his call urgently. He got a text message from him in reply, explaining he was away from London. Harry texted him back asking if he'd ever heard of Susannah Ranelagh. Simple. Yes or no. He was to hear nothing for a week; eventually he got a curt message stating there was no mention of any Susannah Ranelagh in his father's papers.

He had to track her down, yet she remained obstinately elusive. She had arrived at Heathrow. And she had vanished. Harry had an extraordinarily wide circle of friends from his days in the Army and at Westminster and he began putting them to use. He spoke to retired policemen, old Army chums now working in the private security field; he even spoke to a couple of investigative journalists who owed him a favour and asked them to help trace her whereabouts. It all came to nothing, so he made one last call.

'Very formally, Harry, old chap, I have to tell you to go screw yourself.' The lilting Welsh tones of Detective Chief Inspector Hughie Edwards travelled down the phone. 'Good God, man, you know the Metropolitan Police can't go peddling information like that. Right to privacy and all that bollocks. And you should know: it was your lot what passed the bloody legislation.'

Harry sighed. No one was willing to take the risk, not after the phone-hacking scandal had taken down an ill-assorted collection of journalists, policemen and private investigators, leaving politicians who had stood too close covered in all sorts of collateral shit.

'But you know all that,' the Welshman sighed, 'so I have the sneaking suspicion that this is important to you.'

'Very. She may have tried to kill me.'

'Then make an official complaint.'

'It was in Bermuda.'

'Ah. I see.' The Welshman sucked his teeth. 'Then all I can suggest is that the next time someone tries to kill you, you arrange for it to happen on my patch. Then I can be of some assistance, you see. But for now, old chap, you're buggered.' More sucking of teeth. 'So, having got all that official cobblers out of the way, isn't it about time we caught up with each other, you and me? Been a while, hasn't it? Why don't you buy me a drink tomorrow? About midday? Red Lion? And don't be bloody late.'

The Red Lion pub is something of a Westminster institution. Sandwiched between Parliament and Downing Street, it claims to have served beer to every prime minister for more than five hundred years right up to Edward Heath, who refused to enter the place. It was one of many fine old traditions the curmudgeonly Heath broke. Yet the Red Lion survived with its reputation intact, which was rather more than could be said for its antagonist. Harry was a few minutes early, lingering outside its black-gloss door, when he spotted a former colleague, an ambitious backbench politician, one of the upwardly servile who had survived the last election cull and whose ear was now firmly screwed to his phone. He was walking towards the pub and gazing quizzically at Harry, as though chasing a faint memory. He almost stopped, then suddenly quickened his step and scurried by.

At least the policeman recognized him, just. His arm was still clad in its sling and plaster cast, his face still scarred. 'Sweet Jesus, Harry, who did that to you?' the man blurted out as he took in the signs of disaster. 'No, don't tell me, not that little old lady of yours in Bermuda?' Edwards began laughing. 'The entire Iraqi Republican Guard couldn't nail that ugly arse of yours, and now this.'

'Fell off my bike,' Harry replied doggedly.

'You're slowing down.'

'Thanks. Makes me feel so much better.'

And again Edwards laughed. 'I'll buy the drinks. Looks like I'll bloody well have to carry them, too. You wait here, we'll drink outside.' And soon he had returned with two froth-spilling pints. Edwards was in his civvies, a man a few years older than Harry and of considerably bigger girth, front-row stock, with a large broken nose, stormy eyes and two Cox's pippins for cheeks. 'Still, look on the bright side,' he said, setting Harry's drink down on the brass windowsill. 'At least you're safe for now.'

'Meaning?' Harry said, sipping clumsily. He'd bitten deep into his lip during the accident and it was swollen and sore.

Edwards drew a little closer, lowered his voice a notch. 'That *missing-person* case you brought to our attention,' he said, his eyebrow arching cryptically, his accent adding further emphasis. 'I can't tell you where she is.'

'I understand that, Hughie, but I was hoping for maybe a hint—'

'No, you don't understand. I can't tell you where she is because I don't bloody know, do I? Can't find her. Not a ruddy trace. Oh, she landed at Heathrow all right, like you said, but since then your Miss Ranelagh seems to have vanished as effectively as my overdue promotion. Not used her credit card, her Internet account, her mobile phone. Nothing. Not a dicky.'

'Isn't that a little odd?'

'Too damn right it's odd. Not supposed to happen nowadays, no matter how many right-to-privacy laws you politicians pass.' He paused. 'Oh, I was forgetting, you're not a politician any longer. Thinking of going back into that den of iniquity, are you?' he asked, nodding towards the Parliament building.

Harry shrugged; the effort made him wince. 'Got other things on my plate.'

'Politics. Like pneumoconiosis, so it is: no shifting it, not once it gets into the lungs. Never been my game. Thankless sodding task. Like my old dad used to say, it might seem like a rich seam of coal to you, boyo, but it's just a few bags of nutty slack to them out there.' The policeman's tired eyes betrayed a tired soul; he was closing in on retirement and the constant compromises of his job had ground away at his enthusiasm.

'So what can we do, Hughie?' Harry asked, bringing him back to the business in hand.

The policeman shook his head. 'There's nothing more I can do, not without someone making a formal request. I've already dangled my manhood over a meat grinder on this. I can't push it any further.'

'Damn.'

'My old copper's nose tells me something's up with your Miss Ranelagh. When little old ladies disappear from the face of the earth it often means they're under it. But that's instinct. We need hard information and there is none.' He glanced at his watch and placed his glass back on the windowsill. 'I better be disappearing myself.'

'You've hardly made a dent in your drink.'

'Well, at least no one can accuse you of touching me up for information, then, can they? Can't be too careful nowadays.' He laughed his deep baritone laugh once more, but the red eyes didn't join in and the trace of humour died quickly beneath the noise of passing traffic from Parliament Street. His expression was dark. 'I know you, Harry Jones. You're a mad bastard, so you are. Look at the state of you already. Tread safely. You mark my words, there be dragons out there.'

CHAPTER NINE

Dragons. He felt he'd been living with one since his return from Bermuda. His fault. Both he and Jemma were angry, but trying to make the best of it.

'You'll need some physio once that comes off,' she'd remarked across the breakfast table, waving a knife smeared with Dundee thick-cut in his general direction. 'I've got a friend, Tanya, she can sort you out. We did our teacher training together. Blonde. Excellent hands.'

'Thanks!' he said, perhaps a little too enthusiastically.

'Just make sure it's only your shirt you take off.'

Was it a joke? Or a test, a sign she didn't entirely trust him? He'd given her no cause to doubt him since they'd been together but a man with a hands-on past like his was always liable to conviction rather than be given the benefit of reasonable doubt. But Harry loved her, owed her, and not simply for all the things he couldn't do for himself with only one arm. This was just a bad patch. So he decided to surprise her, fix dinner, even with only one arm. Couldn't be too difficult, not for a man whose extreme survival training at Hereford had included killing and cooking a chicken with one arm strapped behind his back to simulate a battle injury. Simple enough. Pick up the chicken. Place teeth around head. And pull. It was astonishing how easily a chicken's head came away from its body, although it did tend to flap around in protest for a while after. Anyway, a bowl of penne wasn't going to put up too much of a struggle, didn't even cluck.

Even so, there was a price to pay. Every time he stretched or stirred, he hurt, and every time he hurt, his thoughts came back to Susannah Ranelagh. He knew he couldn't drop it. He was standing in the small galley kitchen of Jemma's apartment trying to chop herbs and growing increasingly frustrated. Why did women never keep their knives sharp enough? He reached for the phone.

'Hi, Delicious.'

'Harry, is that you? Harry Hero?' she responded, recognizing his voice and sounding glad of it. 'How's the arm? The head? The rest of you?'

'Suffering.'

'You need to be back in Bermuda, not in that cold climate of yours. I did so tell you.' She laughed.

'Any news?'

'Well, I went out with this new guy last weekend, but I don't reckon on him becoming my life partner. Seems like he was more interested in getting off a speeding ticket than getting off with me.' She laughed again, a rich, throaty sound that hinted of candlelight and long tropical nights.

'He must be mad.'

'Why, thank you, Mr Jones. I'm so glad you approve. And, er, how are things at your end?'

'A little local turbulence.'

'I'm not surprised, the mess you made of yourself.'

'Now I guess that's why I called, to hear your sympathy.'

'Then you obviously hit your head harder than I thought. So what can I do for you, Harry?'

'Miss Ranelagh.'

'Great. I take second place to an old spinster with grey hair.'

'The fire, can you tell me? Was it arson?'

A short pause before: 'Well, that's what we normally call it when a jerrycan of unleaded is poured through a broken window. Unimaginative but surely effective. Is there a particular reason you ask?'

'I think she's gone missing. Not just in Bermuda but in Britain, too.'

There was a short silence. 'Time to level with me, Harry. Why are you taking such an interest in a woman you barely know?'

'There's something I may have omitted to tell you.'

'Somehow I am not surprised.'

'That traffic accident. It wasn't. I got some considerable encouragement from three of your local hoods. They deliberately rode me over the cliff.'

'You serious?' The humour in her voice had vanished. 'Why you been holding out on me?'

He sighed. Another angry woman. Right now he wished he hadn't thrown away all those painkillers. 'It must have been the concussion.'

'Hot damn, Harry. I'll give you concussion. You stop playing with me now, you hear? You tell me why they tried to kill you. Right now I want to kill you myself.'

'It's just that I think it may all be mixed up with Miss Ranelagh.'

'Explain.'

'It's not much more than coincidence. And instinct. And a broken arm.'

'You still got one more arm to break.'

'And there was me thinking we were partners.'

'So you playing good cop or bad cop, Harry?'

146

'Just wounded cop, I guess. So I was wondering, could you file a formal request with British police to try and locate her.'

'And why should I do that?'

'As a favour?'

'Now I really feel the urge to break your other arm.'

'You wouldn't do that: I'm a hero.'

Suddenly she lightened up and laughed, and Harry knew he was in the clear.

'OK, on one condition. You're going to have to make a statement. No way I'm going to have goons running round my island pushing people off cliffs. That's my prerogative. You realize, of course, you may have to come back to Bermuda to give evidence.'

'That would be my pleasure.'

'I would do my personal best to ensure you got a warmer welcome than last time.'

'The way you put it, I can hardly wait.'

'Then I'd better get on with the paperwork.'

'You're a special lady, Delicious.'

'By name and nature.'

'I owe you.'

'Look forward to paying off your debts, Mr Jones.'

'Can't wait.'

It was only a little innocent flirting, never did any harm, simply oiled the wheels, they both knew that. At least, that was the theory, until Harry turned and discovered Jemma standing in the doorway. He didn't need to be any sort of detective to deduce that, from the look on her face, she'd been there some considerable time.

—⦿—

Some women would have stormed out. Jemma stood her ground and punched low. 'Who was that woman?'

'How do you know it was a woman?'

'That grin on your face and the strain on your zip.'

'She's a police inspector in Bermuda. Her name's Delicious.'

'You're kidding.'

'Yes, a little whimsical, isn't it?' He turned back to the stove and resumed stirring, struggling to recall precisely what he had said, what she might have overheard. 'She's just a decent cop going the extra mile.'

'So I see.'

'No, you don't. Look, Jem ...' He turned, exasperated, spoon held high, the sauce beginning to creep down the handle. 'What's with this suspicion? It's like you don't believe me.'

'Not a word, not since you told me this latest neardeath experience of yours was nothing but an accident.'

Damn, she'd heard that much. The sauce glooped onto his wrist and began crawling down his sleeve. 'I wanted to spare you that.'

'So spare me. Drop this whole thing before it gets out of hand.'

'I . . .' He threw the spoon in the sink. 'It's not as simple as that.'

'Why not?'

'Precisely because they tried to kill me.'

'Harry, entire armies have tried to kill you,' she spat, her voice climbing through several octaves of despair, 'yet you managed to put all that behind you.'

He shook his head.

'Why, Harry?'

'My father. He's in the middle of all this. Somewhere.' He took a towel and began trying to wipe his arm. 'I need to know, to get to the bottom of it so I can move forward.'

'It's the past, Harry, for God's sake! *I'm* forward. You and me. The future. Remember?'

That was when he lost it. Frustration. Over everything. With the stubborn, sticky mess on his sleeve. With life beating him up at every turn. With Jemma for refusing to understand that this was really about her. With the pain that hit him from inside and out. He threw the towel onto the floor, his jaw moving, about to spit out his fear. 'That's easy for you to say with your nice suburban parents in their neat little semi, curtains drawn, slippers by the fire.' Oh, dear God, he'd gone too far, let it all get to him, but he knew that when you're dragged out in front of a firing squad you should never stand still. 'I didn't have that. I'm not sure what it is I had but I really need to know, to touch the places I came from, otherwise I'll be fucked up like my father and you'll end up just like my mother, never knowing when I walk out the door if I'll ever be coming back.' He was panting with emotion. 'So don't ask me to stop, no, don't you dare. I can't brush my father aside. I need to find out who he was so I can know who the hell *I* am. I didn't just happen, I was made and I hate some of the bits that got mixed up in there.' He was staring at the mess on his hand as though it were eating away at him. 'Sometimes I think I shall never be clean. Never.'

There were tears in his eyes when he looked up at her. His voice had grown thick and hoarse. 'You know, while you were still toddling off to Sunday school in a clean little frock and singing hymns, I was slitting Iraqi throats. And sometimes I wonder, where was your God when I needed him, Jem? Didn't see much of him, not where I was sent, not when I was having to decide how many Provies or ragheads or dark-skinned motherfuckers I needed to kill in order to save my own miserable life. And do you know what? The whole world said I did good, gave me medals for it, but when the band stops playing and the Queen goes back inside the palace for her tea you're left on your own. All on your own. With nothing but the faces of the men you've killed and the noises they make when they're dying. And no matter how many times you wash, you just can't get rid of the smell of blood.'

His hand was shaking; he began to wipe it feverishly on his trousers. 'The only way you can live with that is by being able to live with yourself. And for me to know, in the middle of those quiet nights when you stir and then go back to sleep while I lie awake, that the noise I just heard was a car backfiring, the shadow moving on the wall is nothing more than a curtain blowing in the breeze, the noise at the window is only the scratching of rain and not the last sound I'm ever going to hear. So don't lecture me about the past, Jem, or tell me to put it behind me, because I can't. The past is what we are, what made us; the future is nothing more than maybe.'

—⁜—

She had fled, in tears. She hadn't come back until the early hours of the morning. She showered, changed,

151

left for school. Not a word. He blamed himself. He was like a loaded gun, bullet in the breech, not knowing in which direction he was pointed.

Later that morning he found his way by foot and bursting Underground to Holland Park, glad to be anonymous in a crowd. Three minutes from the mouth of the Tube he found his old family home, a four-floor Victorian brick terrace with draughty sash windows looking out onto the Campden Hill Square. The area had gone up in the world since Harry lived there, had become an exclusive enclave, and the old house itself had been tarted up, too, with security lighting, marble where the York stone doorstep had been and new windows all round, yet this was still the place where he had lived and his mother had died. His bedroom had been on the top floor, at the rear, away from his parents'. He hadn't minded. His mother and father weren't good people to be near, not when they were together. No carpet in his room, just bare floorboards. Pity about that: the floorboards had leaked sound, his parents' rows.

It started to rain, a haphazard shower, and Harry had no jacket, he'd come unprepared. Not like him. He stood on the sloping pavement beneath the sprawling arms of an old beech tree dressed in all its summer splendour.

His mother. Jessie. Her image in his mind was like a childhood dream, with no clear edges. His father had thrown all the photographs of her away, so that every time he reached for her she was already gone. But some memories never die. When he had reached the age of around ten, started to grow and no longer needed her, she had shrunk within herself to a place of dark and corrosive thoughts that had ended up eating her away. She'd made a private world for herself in her bedroom, on the first floor overlooking the rear garden, spent the final two years there, not ever leaving the home, so far as Harry could remember, until at the age of thirteen he'd been summoned back from boarding school to discover a large black sedan parked outside, a concerned neighbour looking on and a bundle of something being loaded in the back. 'Too late, Harry,' his father had said. 'Perhaps for the best.'

His mother had died of a broken heart, so Harry liked to think, although the death certificate had declared otherwise. No bloody imagination, those doctors. And by the time the school term had finished the house had been sold; in any event, his father hadn't slept there for the best part of a year, had his own place, the apartment in Bloomsbury. When Harry had come to take a last look around, to say goodbye, it was nothing but empty rooms. He had sat in his mother's bedroom, his back up against the wall, and tried to remember her. He'd felt something with his fingertips, wedged between the fitted carpet and the skirting board – a wristwatch. No strap, anonymous Swiss, not particularly valuable, not even gold, one Harry remembered his father complaining about because it lost time, a minute a day. 'Timing is everything,' he had said in another of his phrases. 'A minute ahead of the pack and you're boss. A minute late and you're bust.' Yet, surprisingly, Johnnie had made a fuss about its loss, searched high and low before reluctantly buying himself a replacement, far more valuable piece. When Harry found the old watch he discovered an inscription on the back: 'To JMJ. From his father.'

It was raining more steadily now, the tree was no longer giving much protection. Harry still had that wristwatch. He'd put a new leather strap on it and had begun wearing it again. It still lost time but what the hell! It was all he had left of his father. He rubbed his fingers across its face, like a charm, pressing his body into the trunk of the tree as he'd done so many times while waiting for his parents to come home.

There had been better times, of course, before Harry had been forced to take sides. Kicking autumn leaves on their way to Sunday morning coffee in Holland

Park, when Johnnie had ransacked the newspapers while Harry fed his currant bun to the sparrows. Summer drives to a pub on Hampstead Heath so that Johnnie could meet his business contacts while Harry waited outside in the car, guzzling Coke and crisps. And that football. It had been a birthday present, and the best part of it had been when Johnnie had stolen a couple of hours to play with Harry, Harry in goal and Johnnie allowing him to make a few glorious sprawling saves. Harry could still recall the thud of the ball on his burning palms, the thump of his shoulder against the ground, the triumphant smear of mud on his cheek. He even imagined a post-battle mug of hot chocolate, although he was never entirely sure it had happened. There were many things in those days he wished had happened, like Johnnie being around to help fix his bike, take him for a swim, buy him a dog, but Johnnie wasn't like other fathers. Harry had hated listening to the family gossip that other boys brought back to school. It made him at first isolated, then self-reliant, sometimes angry and ill-disciplined, but usually with his teachers and only once with another boy, who had asked Harry why his father never brought him back to school, never watched matches or came to school plays. 'Are your parents divorced?' he'd asked sneeringly. For want of a better reply Harry had thumped him, loosened a tooth. Harry had been sent home in disgrace and his mother had burst into wails of embarrassment. Johnnie had laughed his socks off.

It was all gone now. The home. His mother. Johnnie. Left him standing outside, his face wet, the rain trickling down his collar as his fingers searched once more for the comforting touch of the wristwatch. He was glad it was raining. Only he could be sure they were tears.

According to Jemma's devout and much-disparaged parents, God had a plan for everything, although they had failed to pass their strength of belief in a divine planning authority down to their daughter. The world had never seemed far short of chaos to Jemma and never more so than now. Bloody Harry. The kids didn't help, either. That morning she'd taken Year 3 off in the school bus to the municipal swimming pool and even her well-practised ears were hurting as they screamed and splashed in the water while she stood on the side of the pool and made sure none of them drowned. The din was so great she almost missed the quiet words whispered in her ear.

'Hiya, stranger. You look great.'

She turned, her eyes widening in surprise. Oh,

bugger. Steve Kaminski. 'I don't,' she said, almost snapped, in contradiction. 'I'm harassed and I barely got any sleep last night.'

'That's the way I remember it.'

How long had it been? Three years? Her affair with Steve Kaminski hadn't been prolonged but it had been passionate and he knew all about what she looked like without enough sleep. Now he was gazing at her in his way that said she was both desirable and desired. He did that for all the girls, of course, which was why it had always been clear to Jemma that they were never going to grow old together, but the realization hadn't got in the way of a few healthy and drawn-out nights and a weekend in Amsterdam.

'Hello, Steve. What are you doing here?'

'Much the same as when we first met.' He taught at another local school that shared this pool.

'I heard you'd got engaged,' she said.

'Yes. That's right. Then I got myself disengaged. Wasn't sure I was over you, J.'

'Bollocks.'

He began laughing in that natural, infectious manner he had. 'Hey, why not come back for a swim later? Catch up with each other.'

'No.'

'Why not?'

'You know bloody well why not, Steve.' There had been that moment in the changing rooms those years ago that might have got both of them sacked. 'Anyway, unlike you, I am engaged.'

'Great. Congratulations. I'm really pleased for you. He's a lucky man, I hope he appreciates that.'

And there was something in her eye that she feared might have betrayed her.

'A drink. For old times' sake, J.'

She looked at him, suddenly felt weak, and turned.

'I'll give you a call,' he said to her back as she made herself walk away.

CHAPTER TEN

Christ Church, Oxford. Once known as Cardinal
College in honour of its founder, Thomas Wolsey, until
he fell foul of the king and was stripped of his
reputation. Despite the downfall of its founder, it continued to thrive in both treasure and reputation. Over
the centuries it had provided thirteen prime ministers
along with any number of imperial viceroys and gov-
ernors-general, and yet for all its pomp had still found
room for a poor Welsh brat. Perhaps that was why
Johnnie had clung so tenaciously to the double barrel,
as cover for being conceived in an air-raid shelter.
Harry entered his father's college through the gate
beneath Sir Christopher Wren's pepper pot of a tower
and, in a few paces, the bustle of St Aldate's and the
High had been left behind. He found himself in a great

Tudor quadrangle, known simply as Tom. The sun was splashing across the weathered limestone walls, sending shadows reaching out across the meticulously manicured lawns, while at the centre of the quad the fountain spilled out a careless fanfare of water music beneath the feet of the bronze figure of Mercury. Overfed carp with petulant mouths peered up through the lilies. The bell from the tower struck noon, as it had done on every day for more than four hundred years. All seemed well and safe with this world.

'Ah, Sir Cecil's guest,' the elderly porter announced with a distinct Oxford burr as Harry presented himself at the lodge. The porter looked up, staring over his glasses as he stuck a tentative thumb in his waistcoat pocket. 'Begging your pardon, zur, but didn't you used to be ...?'

'That's right. Harry Jones.'

'Yes, of course. Welcome to Christ Church, Mr Jones. Were you one of our young gentlemen in your time?'

'No, but my father was an undergraduate here.'

'Well, you'll find that nothing much has changed. We've put you in the Meadows Building, if that's in order with you, zur. Staircase Seven.' He pushed a key across the counter. 'It's supposed to be haunted, like, is that staircase. Not a bother to you, I hope.'

'That's why I'm here. To look up a few old ghosts.'

'Come to the right place, then, so you have.' The porter's crumpled face cracked into a broad smile.

Harry dragged his overnight case through the quad. A group of students dressed in their formal *subfusc* academic gowns and white bow ties were in high spirits, spilling over the grass, drinking champagne and exchanging tearful embraces as they celebrated the end of their Finals. He'd done that once, he remembered, when it seemed as if there was no limit to what lay ahead. For a brief moment Harry felt a pang of jealousy at the seeming simplicity of their world. As he stared, one of the young women danced towards him.

'You looking for your son?' she asked.

He was taken aback. 'No, my father . . .'

She laughed, all high spirits and alcohol, having no idea what he was talking about. She reached up and kissed his cheek, then laughed once again and scampered back to her friends.

He dropped his bag in the guest room and sought out the Steward's Office, which he found in the lee of the college chapel, which also doubled as the city's cathedral. Nothing here was done by halves, not even dealing with God. 'Hello, my name's Harry Jones,' he announced to the attractive young blonde who sat at a large and cluttered desk in the outer office.

'And I'm Helen,' she said, smiling and squinting at the same time, as though she was using the wrong prescription in her glasses. 'How can I help you?'

'I'm dining on High Table this evening with Sir Cecil Pisani but, before that, I was wondering ... My father was here. Johnnie Maltravers-Jones.'

'Oh, yes. Of course.' A ripple of curiosity ran across her brow.

'What? You couldn't have known him?' Harry spluttered in surprise.

'Not knew him, exactly, but I'm sure I know *of* him. I think he was one of our regular donors until he ...'

'Yes, he died.'

She nodded and squinted a little more.

'He was a donor,' Harry said softly, his voice rising in surprise. 'I had no idea.'

'Very reliable he was. Every year.'

'How ...' Harry was about to say how bloody uncharacteristic but choked it back down, making do with, 'How good to know. So maybe you might be able to help me after all. I know it's a long shot, Helen, but I was wondering whether you had any information about him, perhaps some old photos with his classmates. He came up here in 1962.'

'Oh, dear, it was a long time ago and we weren't very good with records then.' She sucked the tip of her forefinger in concentration. 'I think the only thing we're likely to've kept is the formal Freshers photo – the one we take of every new class. It would simply be one of him with about a hundred or so others.'

'That's fine – it's some of his friends I'm trying to track down.' He pulled out the photo set around the dining table.

'Well, they wouldn't all have been at Christ Church, of course, not the women, not in those days.' Her squint grew more pronounced. 'What year was it, did you say?'

And soon Harry was seated at a desk beside a window overlooking the Dean's garden, where once a young mathematician named Charles Dodgson, better known as Lewis Carroll, had spotted an earlier dean's daughter whose name was Alice and turned her into one of the most formidable literary creations of all time. On the desk in front of him was a wide card-mounted image of around a hundred and twenty young men ranged in six long rows, all in formal academic dress and paraded before the Library; beside this he propped up his own rather more crumpled photo. The images of the Freshers photo were small, grainy, black and white, and there was plenty of youthful hair to help mask the facial features. Harry borrowed a magnifying glass and stared.

It took him several moments before he found him. Third row near the middle. Johnnie, youthful confidence shining from every pore, with even the suggestion of a moustache struggling to make an appearance on his upper lip. And looking to one side, not straight ahead. Bloody typical. A shiver ran down Harry's back and through his plastered arm until his fingers tingled; there was no denying the fact that it looked so much like his own Freshers photo when he was at Cambridge. Now Harry began ransacking the other faces, desperate to find one he might recognise. 'Jemma, where the devil are you when I need you?' he muttered.

'Can I help?' Helen enquired from the other side of the room.

'I was just trying to spot a connection,' he said, rather pathetically.

She came over, squinted at the faces in his photo, then screwed up her face some more as she bent over the formal photo. 'Why, there, of course. Sort of cute, don't you think?' She pointed to a face at the end of the rear row. It was one of only three non-white faces in the group, not black but certainly of darker hue than the rest, burned by some foreign sun with its features almost lost in the depths of the ancient window behind it. He kicked himself. It was the face of the young man seated on the other side of Susannah to his father. He stared through the magnifying glass, then back at the dining scene. No mistake. Even he could see it now. 'And who are you?' he whispered.

Helen simply turned the photo over; on its back, secured by yellowed tape that was cracking with age, was a list of names, its letters punched from an old electric typewriter. Her finger ran along the line.

Ali Abu al-Masri.

'I think he was a good friend of your father's,' Helen announced. 'He also used to give to the college.'

'Do you know where I can find him?'

'Oh, dear, Mr Jones, I scarcely know how to tell you this, but he died, too. Shortly before your father.'

The world seemed to be slowing down, almost to a standstill. Harry could hear himself breathing. He also heard himself asking how al-Masri had died.

Helen grew visibly distressed.

'It's all right,' Harry said, trying to reassure her.

'No, it's not, Mr Jones, not at all. It was awful. You see, he was assassinated. Blown up. A car bomb. It took him and his entire family.'

—ɷ—

'Do you believe in coincidence, Cecil?'

The politician-turned-academic puckered his expressive, rather damp lips in thought. 'There are times when I find it a convenience, Harry. A useful excuse. But I fear Lady Rachel was a social worker before I married her and still does good works at Her Majesty's places of incarceration, and as a result has developed a hard carapace of cynicism. The defence of coincidence in our family is rather over-quarried, I fear. And in my case utterly depleted.' The Pickwickian figure of Sir Cecil Pisani stared over his sherry glass with eyes like old oysters and smiled. He might have influence in the college and at one point have ruled over half the kingdom, but on the home front his servitude to Lady Rachel was legendary. 'Why d'you ask, dear boy?'

They were taking preprandial drinks in the Senior Common Room, where the walls were covered with panelling and portraits of old members and would have been recognized without hesitation by Charles Dodgson. A steward helped Harry into the academic gown that was still worn for dinner, threading his cast through the folds of heavy black cotton.

'There was a friend of my father. They matriculated in the same year and died within months of each other.'

'Not such a coincidence after all, then. Little more than the depredations of age, I fear.'

'No, not quite. His name was Ali Abu al-Masri. He was murdered, blown up in his car.'

'Ah.' His position outflanked, Sir Cecil sighed and shook his wattles. 'I've heard his name mentioned. Let us make enquiries. Kathy!' He turned to the busy room and summoned a colleague who was part of a group that had gathered around the mantelpiece above an unlit grate. 'Katherine is the money man around here, knows where everything is buried – Kathy, my dear, Ali Abu al-Masri. What can you tell us?'

Katherine Pontefract was no more than five foot four, even in heels, which caused her to bounce on the balls of her feet as she spoke as if to gain height and look the others in the eye. Her eyes were dark and intense, and a little weary, her hair cropped short and a surprising shade of claret. 'Ali was a great loss to this college,' she declared in a voice cut from the working face of a Yorkshire coal pit, and stroking the bridge of her nose with a forefinger as though inspecting for dust. 'A regular donor and a great authority on Middle Eastern matters. Perhaps too great an authority, mind, flew too close to the flame. Got himself assassinated, in Beirut, I think it was, about ten years ago, perhaps a little more. One of those interminable political feuds.'

'He was a politician?' Harry asked.

'Who isn't in the desert?' she replied, bobbing. 'But he wasn't exactly a politician, not officially. More of

167

a . . . a facilitator, a constructor of networks, a man who pitched his tent in many places.'

'Not all of them very welcoming, apparently,' Harry added drily.

'It was most distressing.'

'He was a friend of my father's. I was wondering if they might have been in business together. Tell me, what business was Mr al-Masri in?'

Pontefract leveraged herself to her full extent with an expression that suggested Harry might have trodden on the most sensitive of corns. 'I have absolutely no idea. Not the slightest.' Her voice was firm, brooking no contradiction, even though Harry didn't believe a word. 'It's enough, don't you think, that he was an alumnus of this college and willing to help educate a new generation of young men and women?'

'As was my father, I believe.'

'Your father?'

'Johnnie Maltravers-Jones.'

At the mention of Johnnie's name she relaxed a little, stopped bobbing. 'Who was also a generous benefactor. Great pity he's no longer with us.'

Harry suspected she was talking about his money rather than any social loss. While Kathy Pontefract wittered away, the door of the Common Room opened once more and an elderly man entered. He was tall,

stood out among the crowd, with a long, finely chis-
elled face and high cheekbones that bore the blush of a
life spent facing into the wind. His hair was thick for
his age, well cut and remarkably white; his manner was
confident and his blue eyes were alert, taking in everything around him. A colleague reached for his sleeve
but the man merely dipped his head politely, moved
on, intent on discovering more challenging game. He
was threading his way elegantly through the throng
when he saw Harry and his face clouded in bewilderment. Then, with barely half a pause of hesitation, he
crossed directly to him.

'Harry? Harry Jones? Why, what a coincidence.'

'No, we don't believe in such things,' Sir Cecil
declared.

'I'm sorry, do we know each other?' Harry asked,
mystified.

The other man extended his hand and smiled
generously. The grip was firm. 'My name's Alexander
McQuarrel. I knew your father. And you, too, when
you were much younger – about eight, I think you
were, the last time. And recently I met your lovely partner, Miss Laing. Didn't she mention it?'

Something else he and Jemma hadn't got round to
discussing, it seemed. 'No. I've been away.'

'Yes, she said.'

And before they could take the matter further they were distracted as the steward summoned them to dinner.

'Perhaps we can talk afterwards,' McQuarrel suggested.

'If you've got time.'

'For you, Harry – if I may call you Harry – I'll make the time. We have much to discuss.'

CHAPTER ELEVEN

'Is Tamanna coming?'

'She left a message. She'll be half an hour late.'

'And Laurie?'

'He's always half an hour late.'

'Then I suppose we'd better get started,' the convener, Hayley, said with an air of resignation as she opened her folder.

The small group was seated around an over-varnished bar table in a corner of a South London pub, all teachers from neighbouring schools gathered to form the coordinating committee tasked with agreeing the arrangements for the Annual Inter-School Water and Waves Festival. There was a time when it had simply been called a swimming competition until some razor mind had decided that sounded all too judgemental.

'Hi, J,' a voice said.

Jemma looked up, startled, as a bottle of Mexican beer with a lime in its mouth was put in front of her and Steve Kaminski slipped into the seat beside her. 'Steve, I didn't know ...'

'What, that I'm on the coordinating committee? Would you have returned my phone calls if you'd known?'

'I've been busy. You know what it's like in a summer term.' It sounded pathetic, they both knew it, and she reached for the beer. Her favourite brand. 'You remembered.'

'Of course.'

'That's spooky. You keep a file or something?'

'Of course.'

'You're kidding!' she cried in alarm.

He burst into laughter. 'Oh, J,' he said, shaking his head. 'Anyway, I wouldn't need a file to remember everything about you.'

She couldn't stop herself from blushing. She bent her head pretending to study the papers in front of her, hoping he hadn't noticed, knowing he had.

—w—

The diners, about twenty in number and all in their gowns, wound their way up a narrow stone staircase until in a single step they had burst upon what to Harry seemed like the stage of an awesome theatre. The High Table on which they were about to dine stood on a raised platform overlooking a Tudor hall with soaring roof timbers cut from dark oak, ornate ancient windows that glittered in the evening light and, in the heart of the hall, three rows of age-polished tables. Chattering undergraduates were already seated. It was like a scene from Hogwarts, which even Sir Cecil would admit was no mere coincidence: this was where the set designers had found their inspiration. The ancient walls of Hogwarts had been covered with portraits of wizards; here there were monarchs and prime ministers and imperial viceroys and bishops. Despite its pageantry, this place had seen its own share of dark practices. It was where the deluded Charles I had convened his parliament after being forced to flee London. It was also where, a little later, Cromwell's victorious troops had stabled their horses as an act of contempt. Yet the ancient customs survived. The grace, a lengthy one, was delivered in Latin.

Sir Cecil sniffed cautiously at the claret. 'Your father would have supped better, Harry,' he declared. 'In his day the college cellars were renowned. Source it, lay it down, wait for the right moment. Time was meaningless – until we discovered one of the undergraduates was selling large quantities of our vintage port outside college at one helluva markup. We encourage enterprise, of course, but there are limits.'

'What became of him?'

'The young man? Governor of the Bank of England.' He shook his head in sorrow. 'Our fault, of course. We became too indulgent. Too set in our ancient ways. We should have swept places like this away when we were in government, Harry, don't you think? After all, how are we to justify it? Oh, a fine history, that I grant, but what has this place achieved recently?' He sipped at his claret, seeming still uncertain.

'Apart from Albert Einstein, of course,' Katherine Pontefract chipped in, almost as an afterthought.

'And John Gurdon. The biologist chap. Won a Nobel Prize the other year, didn't he?' McQuarrel added.

Sir Cecil waved a languid hand. 'Auberon Waugh, W. H. Auden, William Walton – but I don't suppose they count.'

'The last Archbishop of Canterbury, he was one of ours.'

'And that Indian fellow who runs Tata Steel.'

'Going to rack and ruin,' Sir Cecil concluded.

'Except for a few Olympic athletes, I suppose. And the chap who worked out the connection between smoking and cancer,' Pontefract said.

'Yes, damn him.'

'Enough!' Harry acknowledged, waving his fork and smiling. This was clearly a routine they enjoyed. 'I get the point.'

'And there was your father, of course,' McQuarrel interjected, more softly.

'This place would have fallen down like rotten Cheddar on our heads long ago without people like him,' Pontefract said. 'Raise young minds and repair old buildings, that's what he helped us do.'

'I'd never seen him in that light,' Harry said, struggling with his food; he still hadn't mastered the art of eating with his arm in a cast.

'There was something special about those who came here in the sixties,' Sir Cecil said. 'What made them different, I wonder? Something to do with the rejection of dreary postwar conformity, perhaps, the embracing of new ideas.'

'And each other,' Pontefract added, arching an over-plucked eyebrow.

'But it was more than that,' McQuarrel said. 'I was a junior research fellow at Brasenose at the time and those friendships weren't simply struck, they also stuck, had a habit of enduring.'

'I don't think my father had any close friendships,' Harry said.

175

'But you're wrong, Harry,' McQuarrel replied. 'I like to think that I was his friend, and there were many closer than me.'

It was after they were done with dinner and back in the Senior Common Room that Harry produced the photo from his pocket. He laid it on the coffee table around which they had gathered and tried with less than total success to smooth out the conspicuous central fold. 'These were some of his friends. I wonder if you can help me.'

'Damn, but you look just like him,' Pisani said.

Harry frowned. He was fed up with hearing that. 'I know who three of these are' – he pointed to his father, Susannah Ranelagh and al-Masri – 'but as for the other four . . .'

'Why, that's surely Christine Leclerc,' Pisani interrupted, stabbing at one of the women in the photo with his finger. 'Christine Berserk, we used to call her. Hell of a woman, even in her fifties. Fine features, look at those cheekbones. Unmistakable. Didn't you ever meet her, Harry?'

He shook his head.

'The most senior woman in the European Commission, she was. Immensely powerful. Could cut a budget proposal in half at fifty paces.'

'And now?'

'Oh, dead and gone.'

Harry's coffee suddenly tasted intensely bitter. Another one who hadn't made it. 'How?'

'Plane crash. Private jet on her way back from the Sudan on some aid mission. Came down in a freak storm. Don't you remember? Perhaps not, it was probably before you got into politics.'

'And this rather righteous-looking specimen' – McQuarrel indicated the figure on the far right – 'is surely another of our old boys, Randall Wickham, the Bishop of Burton. Yes, give him a haircut and a mitre and a few decades and that's Randy. See, he's lost the top of his little finger, bitten off by a Yorkshire terrier when he was a kid. Always notice that when I see him giving the benediction.'

'You know him?'

'Not desperately. He delivers a sermon in the cathedral here occasionally. Enjoys his college port.'

'Still alive and kicking?'

'Well, preaching, at least. Retired by now, I suspect.'

'My father – and a bishop?' Harry shook his head in disbelief.

'Forgiveness on tap,' McQuarrel said, in a tone that suggested he wasn't being flippant.

—ɯ—

'A final drink, J?' Kaminski asked as Jemma shuffled together her papers at the end of the meeting.

'For old times' sake?'

'Something like that.'

She hesitated. 'OK.'

He had been full of humour and insight as Hayley the convener had sniffled her way through the agenda and her latest allergy. Steve didn't deserve unnecessary grief. And he seemed in excellent shape, the thigh that in the crush had nestled up against hers still rock-hard from his rugby and squash. She remembered everything about his body being gratifyingly solid. That played no part in her decision, of course, and no part at all in her barely noticing that their final drink had been followed by another. She was relaxing, having a good time. Too good a time. His eyes were full of music, and mischief. Typical bloody Steve.

'So what about the man you're dating?' he asked.

'Engaged to, remember.'

'Oh, that's right. Sorry. But you're not wearing a ring.'

'No.'

'I hope he knows how lucky he is. Name?'

'Harry.'

'Reliable sort?'

'Next question.'

'So where is he?'

'Off getting stuck up his family tree, I think.'

'Whoops. Choppy water?'

'We're in a relationship, stupid.'

'Ah, I see.' And he had. Very deliberately his hand reached out and went to hers. 'You're a special lady, J, deserve nothing but the best. I so hope you get it.'

Her own hand was growing warm beneath his; she didn't move it, not even when it closed around hers, and that wasn't the only part of her that was beginning to react.

'And, J, if ever you feel like getting a second opinion . . .'

Without thinking, she sprang to her feet, knocking over her beer in her haste to get away. She didn't bother to make excuses or say goodbye, simply ran for the door. She was confused, and not just from the beers. She knew what he was going to suggest next. For old times' sake. That was why she panicked, because, right at that moment, she hadn't any idea what she would say in reply.

CHAPTER TWELVE

Harry and Alexander McQuarrel sat on the steps of the Old Library, where, more than fifty years before, his father had stood among his friends to have his Freshers photograph taken. It was late, the towering Corinthian columns staring down upon a Peckwater Quad that had fallen almost silent as the last of the summer evening faded from the sky and the hour nudged midnight. Lights were still blazing from the windows of students' rooms, splashing across the grass, just as Johnnie would have remembered.

'Why are you chasing your father so hard, Harry?' McQuarrel asked, rolling the tumbler of port he had brought between the palms of his hands. The tumbler was excessive, but so was the atmosphere, deep, cloistered by the walls of the quad, almost conspiratorial.

Harry clung onto his own tumbler with his one free hand and took a while before he replied. 'It's not easy to put into words, Alex. I never knew him well. And I know it sounds like a pathetic cliché but I need to know more about him in order to know myself.'

'You don't know yourself?'

'You think you do, until you get to see yourself through the eyes of others.' Particularly Jemma, of course. 'Sometimes you discover you're not the answer to every prayer.'

'I've kept track of you over the years.'

'Why?'

'Natural interest, knowing your father. Anyway, it hasn't been too difficult. I can't remember a year when you weren't somewhere in the headlines. I even read that you get a personal Christmas card from the Queen.'

'Then you know more about me than I know about my father.'

'Johnnie was . . .' McQuarrel eased his elderly frame on the hard stone as he stretched for the right phrase. 'A complicated man.'

'He seemed to have had many different lives.'

'He was full of imagination. Quite brilliant with it.'

'He drank.'

'Made a fortune, of course.'

Harry swivelled so that he could confront his new friend. 'How, Alex? How did he make all that money?'

'He was – what's the term? – a financial consultant.'

'And what the hell did that mean?'

'He gambled. Bet against the system. Spotted winners before anyone else and sold short those that were headed for a fall.'

'But how?'

'I told you, he was brilliant. Not only instinctively but intellectually. He came back here often, and you know what the Senior Common Room is like, stuffed full of men and women who are the brightest in their field yet who are strangely and sometimes deliberately cut off from reality. You can't dine off college silver every night and still claim to have the common touch. And we do so love a gossip. So when your father arrived with a glass in hand and laughter in his eyes, and with all his tales of the outside world, we'd fall into his arms.'

'But what would he get from a professor of Ancient Greek?'

'Not a lot, perhaps. But I'm a biochemist, a Senior Fellow – all but retired now, of course, very much Emeritus, but alongside the academic work I was involved with various research companies. Cutting-edge stuff. Trying to find out how we can live for ever. The graveyards are full of my failures.' He seemed to find it a wry joke. 'But eternal life is what we're promised and what many will pay a fortune for in their vain attempt to achieve it. Johnnie understood all that and had an inexhaustible capacity for turning people's hopes and fears into money. So he would come here, and many other places like this, and listen. And he had a very good ear. Soaked up all our braggadocio and intellectual conceits, grabbed every morsel of information. Biochemistry, aerospace engineering, quantitative finance, computer science, we've got the lot. And the very best. People who advise corporations and governments around the world, who start revolutions not from behind barricades but in boardrooms and labs and from computer silos. Johnnie knew that. He would stand beside the fire in the Senior Common Room and make love to us all.'

'No one minded?'

'Oh, a few, but he handled us so gently, and we're vain, we do so love to lift our skirts. Particularly when we've had a drink, and, by God, did Johnnie know how to hammer the drink.' He raised his glass in silent salute. 'Anyway, he made sure we shared in his success. He would always come back with a large cheque. We're dreamers here, Harry, but dreams cost money and you'd be surprised what people will do to pursue their dreams.'

'His dream was money,' Harry whispered.

'He was a man with many facets.'

'A rough diamond.'

'I found him rather polished.'

'Alex, you said you knew me when I was eight.'

'Around that age.'

'So ...' There was a slight glitch in Harry's voice. 'You must have known my mother.'

McQuarrel paused, then nodded, slowly, as though it took a considerable effort, and stared deep into his glass. 'She had a hard road to walk.' He looked up, his eyes almost pleading for Harry not to press him. 'I didn't know her well. I'm sorry.' A heavy silence stretched between them in the darkness. 'Don't judge too harshly, Harry. No one can know the truth of such circumstances, even those who are involved in it.'

As he stared forlornly into the darkness two men and a young woman burst from a staircase on the far side of the quad, spilling onto the lawn in post- or pre-coital exuberance. From somewhere near at hand a clock bell chimed midnight. Harry glanced at his father's wrist-watch: six minutes slow. He advanced it seven.

'I must go, Harry. Dammit, I've spent so long sitting here I feel like Methuselah. Are you coming?'

Harry shook his head. 'This is where he sat. Got drunk.' He stared into the past. 'I think I'll stay awhile.'

McQuarrel rose stiffly, testing his legs. 'Don't be too hard on your father, Harry. It never does to disinter the dead – you'll find nothing but corruption. Better to move on.'

'Jemma told me much the same, too.'

'Then make it unanimous. I'll see you in the morning.' The old man began to walk away.

'Oh, one last thing, Alex. Does the name Susannah Ranelagh mean anything to you?'

McQuarrel stopped, turned slowly. 'No, nothing,' he said from the darkness, and disappeared.

—m—

Jemma woke, warm, damp, her breasts cupped in his hands. 'Oh, fuck!' she muttered.

Beside her Steve stirred. 'Morning,' he whispered, and kissed her shoulder. Then he began nibbling her neck.

She pushed him away. 'Fuck!' she said again, more loudly. She wanted to blame him but she couldn't: it was all her fault. She'd felt so childish about fleeing from the pub, so when he had caught up with her on the pavement outside she'd apologized.

'Why did you run?' he'd asked.

That was when she burst into tears. She didn't know why, not for sure. She was confused, in need, wanted a shoulder to cry on and hands that would smooth away all her creases and cares. She wanted Harry, the old Harry, not this new one who'd come back broken and harsh from Bermuda, but neither Harry had been there on the pavement when she'd needed him. So she'd made do with Steve. Distraction. And it had worked, for a few hours. He had brought her back to his place and slipped off her clothes, touched her so softly she scarcely knew which part of his own body he was using, finding those hidden places, reminding her of all the reasons why she'd been with him in the first place. It was only as she woke the following morning that she remembered all the reasons she'd decided she should stop. She knew she would go to his bathroom, reach for his brush and find another woman's hair embedded in it. Discover spare toothbrushes hidden away. Yet she wasn't angry with Steve, not as angry as she was with Harry. Steve hadn't promised her anything other than a great time, and he'd delivered, while Harry . . .

Getting laid by Steve wasn't the answer to anything, she knew that, but she wasn't any longer sure that Harry was, either. At least Steve wasn't complicated. His hands were back on her breasts and something was digging into the small of her back.

'So here's the deal, J. You can have breakfast in bed. Or breakfast in the kitchen.'

She turned, felt his body against hers. 'After last night I'm surprised you've still got an appetite.'

'I've got an appetite. I need an answer.'

'Then both,' she said. 'I'll take both.'

—◆—

Summer was spilling across the great quad, with fingers of early-morning sunlight weaving rainbows through the spray thrown from the fountain. Harry let it settle on his cheeks. He remembered tales his father had told about late nights that ended with his being thrown into this fountain, dressed in his dinner jacket, to swim among the spotted carp with their bulging bellies that lurked beneath the tangled carpet of lily leaves.

'Maybe the fish remember Johnnie,' a voice said at Harry's ear. He turned to find McQuarrel at his shoulder. 'Carp can live to be seventy, apparently,' McQuarrel added.

'The bloody fish know more than I do,' Harry muttered.

'What do they say, Harry? "The evil that men do lives after them; the good is oft interred with their bones". Mark Antony's oration over Caesar's body. I'm not the greatest fan of Shakespeare – overwritten, too many words – but there are moments when he gets it. I wonder what any of our lives will look like in

188

hindsight. Flaws are cut in stone while our merits are like footprints in the sand.'

'So let it be with Johnnie, is that it?' Harry said, echoing the play's lines.

'He never much seemed to worry about death, not that I remember. He was all about the moment and living it to the full. "Die happy," he used to say. "It's a once-in-a-lifetime thing." He did so like his *bons mots*. I hope he meant it.'

'About what?'

'Dying happy. It's a rare privilege. Harry, I'm not in much of a position to preach but as a friend ...'

'Tell me, Alex.'

'You should think of Jemma. A remarkable girl. I got the impression – how can I put it? – she was ...'

'Deeply and most sincerely pissed off with me.'

'As you say.'

Harry's shoulders sagged. He was having trouble carrying all this weight.

'I hope the two of you will be spectacularly happy together,' McQuarrel said.

'Do you have a wife, Alex?'

The older man smiled forlornly. 'She died.'

'I'm sorry.'

A brush of summer breeze ruffled his hair, causing a silver lock to fall across his forehead, and his eyes seemed damp. 'Some would say it was a blessing.' The words came softly and were filled with hurt.

'But not you.'

'She committed suicide. Been frail for many years. Not mentally feeble, you understand, far from it. Agnetta was the most determined woman I've ever met, but she found no joy in life. There's a certain type who draws the curtains on a Sunday in case Death walks by, but for her Death wasn't a distant rumour: he was a constant companion. Like I suspect he has been for you, for much of your life.'

Harry nodded.

'And eventually he became her friend. Her closest friend.'

'It must have been difficult for you.'

'She was a scientist, Harry, like me. When the time came for her, Death was an adventure, something to explore. She met him face to face and embraced him.'

'I've always preferred to kick the bastard in the balls and run like hell.'

McQuarrel's tone and eyes suddenly hardened. 'Then do the same again, Harry. Don't go trying to dig up Johnnie. He's dead, well buried. Get back to the better things in life. To Jemma.'

Harry had to admit that McQuarrel had a point. He'd found it difficult to sleep, and not just because of the excess of port. Jemma kept dancing through his dreams, enticing him, then running away as he reached for her, disappearing. Perhaps it was time to get back to the happy stuff. As he thought about what McQuarrel had said, he was distracted by the vibrating of his phone. He clamped it to his ear.

'Hi, there, Harry Hero,' a familiar voice warbled.

'Inspector Hope. I guess that just has to be you.'

'Anyone else think you're a hero?'

'Come to think of it, right now I don't believe there's another soul on the planet.'

'I thought you'd like to know that I'm still chasing our girl.'

'Susannah Ranelagh? Me, too.'

'And I'm getting nowhere. No trace of her in Bermuda. So I thought I'd come and give my colleagues in the Metropolitan Police a gentle kicking. See if they'll get off their pampered rumps and take a look-see for themselves. Just like you suggested.'

'Great idea.'

'And while I'm about it I believe you and I need a conversation.'

'Over drinks or breakfast?'

'Across an interview desk. You got trashed in Bermuda and it's about time you told me the details. All of them, Harry.'

'I owe you that, I guess. When are you arriving?'

'I'm here. Just landed at Heathrow.'

Harry could hear the buzz of the arrivals lounge in the background.

'I'm staying at the Soho Hotel. Meet me there.'

'When?'

'Six o'clock.'

'For an interrogation?'

'Let's make it a drink. The thumbscrews come later.'

'Soho Hotel. Six o'clock. Do I need to bring a lawyer?'

'Only if you forget to pay for the drinks,' she declared, ringing off with laughter in her voice.

Harry looked up at the clock on Tom Tower; as he did so it began to strike nine. He turned to his companion. 'I must be going. Summoned by the Bermuda Police.'

McQuarrel's brow creased with concern.

'No, nothing too harsh. A couple of drinks. I think I can handle that.'

'Your father's son.'

'Thank you, Alex.'

'For what?'

'For ... being here. You're about the only link I've got.'

'Call me any time. Let me know how it all goes.'

'I will. Don't have much choice. Right now you're the only one who wants to listen.'

—⁓—

When he got back to Jemma's, she was scrubbing saucepans, her hands covered in suds. She turned to greet him but the combination of her damp arms and his stiff cast seemed to get in the way and the welcoming kiss was perfunctory. The attempt at a warm homecoming fell flat.

'Just fixing something special for supper,' she said. It had been intended as a peace offering.

'Thanks, Jem. But, er, I've got to go out.'

Her face flushed in dismay.

'I can be back by eight, though,' he added hurriedly. 'Latest.'

She was chewing at the inside of her cheek.

'How was yesterday evening?' he asked, looking to change the subject.

'I'm more interested in yours.'

'I met Alex McQuarrel.'

'Ah.'

'Something you forgot to mention.' He hadn't intended it as an accusation but somehow, as they crossed the kitchen, the words found sharp edges.

She turned back to the sink, seeking distraction. 'Sorry. Nothing deliberate. It's just that . . .'

'What?'

'Well, we haven't been communicating much recently. Never get to finish what we've started.'

'Even the arguments.'

'I think we can do better than that.' She threw the dishcloth aside and turned to face him once more. She was wearing a thin T-shirt with a motto across it that said GIRLS DO IT IN THE KITCHEN. No bra, and she was glad he'd noticed. It was time to make up. And cover her guilt. 'Hey, Jones, before you rush out, how about some really sordid, spontaneous, bend-over-backwards, up-against-the-wall, across-the-kitchen-table, any-way-you-want-it, window-rattling sex?' Before he could answer she was in his arms once again and this time she stayed, letting him feel the softness of her body until she could feel the firmness of his.

He was breathing hard when at last their lips parted. 'Stay here, Jem. Give me a nanosecond to get a rubber.'

But she held him with surprising determination, refused to let him go. 'There's no need,' she whispered, 'not any more, not if we're getting married. Let's start now.'

'Kids?'

'You bet.' And she was kissing him, but this time his mind was elsewhere. 'What's the matter, Harry?'

'It's just ... You mentioned kids.'

'You have a problem with that? It's simple. We have

insane sex, I get pregnant, nine months later we have a kid and for the next twenty years we pay through the nose. Correction, I guess it's nearer thirty years nowadays.'

'It's just that—'

'And I want a whole troop of them.'

He pulled back from her. 'Jem, I've got to tell you. I already have a son.'

She stopped panting, all but stopped breathing, her face frozen in astonishment. Then she took one faltering step backwards until she hit the sink and couldn't back away any further. 'But . . .' she whispered in protest. She couldn't finish the thought, her mind was frozen, too.

Harry scowled as he concentrated. How the hell could he get this all so wrong? His first wife, Julia, had been killed when she was pregnant; he'd lost his wife and child in a single beat of fate. Then his second wife, Mel, had trashed their relationship with an abortion. With Jemma it should have been so much easier.

'But . . .'

'His name is Ruari. Almost twenty now, lives with his mother and her husband in the States. Great kid, great family.'

'I'm so pleased for them.'

'I didn't even know of his existence until a couple of

years ago. He didn't know about me, either, still doesn't. We decided to tell him when he was twenty-one.'

'Why twenty-one? What's so bloody special about twenty-one?'

'They'll be back in this country, we can tell him all together. Something like that. It's what his mother wanted.'

'His mother?'

'Terri. Her name's Terri.'

'And what about what I want, Harry?'

'When you mentioned kids I felt I needed to tell you—'

'And, if I hadn't mentioned kids, when precisely were you planning to produce this little nugget?'

'You said yourself we haven't been talking much—'

'Let me get this straight. You complain about me forgetting to tell you about some old man, yet your own son seems to slip completely from your memory.'

'Jem, this is silly. It doesn't make any difference.'

But Jemma wasn't listening. She was drowning in her own guilt. She pushed past him. 'I'm going out. I might be a hell of a while.' She gathered her coat, her bag, pausing only at the door to turn and say, 'Fuck you, Harry.'

When the door slammed behind her it rattled not only the windows but shook the entire floor.

CHAPTER THIRTEEN

The Soho Hotel was a remarkable place, built in the heart of one of London's most crowded and creative quarters from the remnants of an old multistorey car park – quirky, colourful and nestling alongside the Italian restaurants and advertising outlets of Dean Street, where Karl Marx had lived while writing *Das Kapital* in what had then been described as one of the worst and therefore one of the cheapest quarters of London. The place had come a long way since those days, and the restaurant above which he had lived now bore a Michelin star and a price tag to suit. Harry made his way along the bustling street, forced to step into the gutter to avoid the happy-hour crowds that were spilling onto the pavements. The gentle pleasures of the early Oxford morning were now a forgotten memory;

this was central London, sweltering, an armpit of an evening.

When Harry walked through the doorway of the hotel he found Delicious already in the book-lined lobby, chatting with a young receptionist in a brightly coloured waistcoat. She was leaning over his desk, her back end in tailored trousers and parked prominently. For a woman in her mid-thirties such delights weren't down to the casual good fortune of youth. She clearly worked hard at it. Harry couldn't help but take note.

'Hello, Delicious.'

She turned. 'Harry! Meet Pablo. Pablo, as you can tell, is the cutest and most helpful concierge I think I've ever met. And Pablo' – she turned to the young man who flashed a smile full of naturally white teeth – 'this is Harry who's a good cop, assault victim and criminal suspect all rolled into one. Hell of a guy.'

She was firing live shot and already Harry's dark mood was being tickled into submission. They made their way to the drawing room, which was full of colour and wooden furniture with oversized butterfly joints, settled on a sofa in a quiet corner and ordered beers.

'It's great to see you,' he said, taking the head off the glass. 'Really great, Delicious. I could do with some good news.'

'Then I guess I'm not your girl, Harry. I come empty-handed. Our Miss Ranelagh's disappeared, nowhere to be found, like a taxi in the rain. That's why I'm here: got a meeting with the Met tomorrow morning to see if they can pick up her trail from Heathrow. But so far as we can tell she's not spent a cent or made a single call since she arrived.'

'My old man's friends seem to have an unfortunate habit of disappearing,' Harry said, producing his iPhone and bringing up the photograph of the young diners. He went along the row of smiling faces. 'My father's dead, Susannah Ranelagh's missing, that one got murdered in a car bomb and she was killed in a plane crash. Four out of seven. Bloody awful odds, even for people in their seventies.'

'The other three?'

'One's a bishop. The other two unknown.'

'Let me have a copy, Harry.'

With a touch of the screen it was done. They both sat bent over their phones, staring at the image, seeking inspiration.

'I've been doing a little digging into Miss Ranelagh's background,' Delicious announced.

'She played croquet.'

She threw a glance full of fire at him. 'How d'you know? Damn, you holding out on me, Harry?'

'I guess I have an eye for these things.'

'I've seen what you have an eye for, Harry,' she said provocatively.

'No, seriously. Our Miss Ranelagh, she has the ankles of a croquet player.'

'You're winding me up.'

'And it's a photo of an Oxford Junior Croquet Club dinner.'

'Harry, you're an idiot. But you're right. She was a keen member of the Bermuda croquet crowd down at Somerset.'

'Any good?'

'Lucky. Very lucky, apparently. Had a good eye, and not just on the grass. Our Miss Ranelagh had a charmed life, it seems.'

'Had?'

'Past tense. My instinct says her luck's run out. But while it lasted it was truly remarkable. Luck of the Irish – and then some. Her family had no great wealth but she came to Bermuda thirty years ago and seems to have done little else except play croquet, join charities and move her money around. She plays with her money like Tiger Woods plays with his balls.'

'And how did she do that? Was it respectable money?'

'Harry, it's Bermuda. Who cares if it's respectable? You want respectable, you buy it. And Miss Ranelagh bought a good deal of respect. At least twelve million dollars' worth and still counting.'

Harry went back to staring at the photo. 'No one knew where my father got his money, but he had a small mountain of it, too. As did he, as did she,' he added, pointing once more to the faces of al-Masri and Leclerc. 'Now that's something else they have in common. Rich. And dead.'

'Not so lucky after all.'

'You thinking what I'm thinking, Delicious?'

'You're a man: I always know what you're thinking.'

'If it wasn't for the bloody bishop who is still alive and preaching we might even have a full house.'

'And there was me feeling deeply pissed that I've never had the time to take up croquet.' She drained her beer and set the glass back down. 'So how the hell did they all make their money?'

The room was filling, the noise level rising. A couple came to sit uncomfortably close on an adjoining sofa and began to rehearse the details of a forthcoming client pitch.

Delicious shook her head. 'Come on, Harry, let's seek a little peace and go raid my minibar.' She scribbled a signature on the bill and led the way.

Her room on the second floor was light, designer-clad and expensive. 'A bit like Bermuda,' she quipped as she led him in. It had a bed the size of a tennis court clad in cushions and contemporary fabric, but there was plenty of other furniture in the room, mirrors scattered across the walls and a designer mannequin in the corner. She dropped her bag onto the sofa and headed for the minibar. 'What's your poison, Harry?'

'Whatever you're having.'

'Don't call me chicken if I grab some tea. Jetlag sure dries me out. But you—'

'No. Tea will be fine.'

'Then would you mind calling for a tray? Give me time to jump in the shower. God knows what you Brits do to sunshine to make it stick like glue.'

As she disappeared into a separate part of the room hidden behind a half-wall, he picked up the phone, jabbed buttons and tried to scratch at the skin beneath the cast that was beginning to itch like an army of fire ants. Six weeks of healing, they'd said at the hospital in Bermuda. Six weeks of purgatory, fighting an enemy he couldn't even see.

The tray of tea arrived and Harry set about it. 'You take sugar?' he called out as he rattled the cups. No reply. She couldn't hear him through the shower and behind the door. He tried again, but nothing, so Harry went to the corner of the room where she had disappeared, preparing to press his question more forcefully.

That was the point when he discovered there was no door. The bathroom area was not only *en suite* but also *alfresco* and behind the half-wall the shower was in full view. So was Delicious. Only the curtain of water that was cascading down the glass wall concealed her finer details. He prepared to turn from the embarrassment but before he could drag himself away she stepped from the shower and was standing in full and glorious view.

'I . . . I . . .' What the hell was he supposed to say? 'I was wondering whether you took sugar in your tea.'

'How very English.'

His mouth suddenly felt like the bottom of a parrot's cage. 'I'm sorry, I never meant . . .'

Water was dripping down her skin, little streams that moved around the contours of her body. She didn't move; time ceased to exist.

Harry stood rooted. He suspected his lower jaw had sagged and was making a fool of him. A million years of evolution was being crushed into a fragment of time – this time – and against that the veneer of conventional morality that stretched back not even as far as his father seemed to count for nothing. What was he supposed to think? Men in such circumstances are rarely given to intensive analytical processes, yet he couldn't fail to remember Terri, and their affair, and the hurt it had done to Julia. Instinct was taking over, firmly pressing its point. Delicious was perfection on a plate, every man's lingering dream. Harry took an enormous breath, preparing to both speak and act, although he still wasn't certain how.

Then his phone began burbling in his pocket. The moment was broken.

'Are you going to answer that, Harry?'

He smiled sheepishly. 'Not right now. I need … a moment to myself. I'll just go and sit quietly next door.'

Their eyes wrestled in disappointment and sympathy and understanding and all the things that told her Harry belonged to another woman. 'By the way, the answer is two.'

'What?'

'Sugars.'

Only then did Harry retreat, released from the spell. He went back to the tea, ripped open a packet of sugar, sent it scattering everywhere but into the cup. Delicious appeared, clad in a towelling robe of brilliant white, and settled in a chair with her feet curled up beneath her. He couldn't stop the cup rattling in its saucer as he handed it to her.

'To our meeting in the next life, Harry,' she said, raising the tea to her lips in salute. 'And I wish you and your lady good luck in this.' The eyes said she meant it. Then she threw her head back and let forth a laugh that sounded like a peal of church bells on an Easter morning.

Harry, his dignity retrieved but tattered, proceeded to tell her what he had discovered about his father's money.

'Insider trading?' she asked.

'I'm not sure. Nothing that could be proved, perhaps. Just good gossip.'

'And useful friends.'

'In Bermuda, Brussels. The Middle East.'

'Stretching all the way back to Oxford.'

'And worth killing for, maybe?'

'In which case those remaining three are right there in the frame.'

'The bloody bishop?'

'When you have excluded what is probable, then what is merely possible . . .'

Suddenly he glanced at his watch. 'Bugger, I'm late.'

'Hot date?'

'I doubt it. Jem – that's her name, Jemma – just walked out on me. I need to go see if she's come back. I have this dull male instinct that it wouldn't be the brightest move since the Creation to keep her waiting.'

205

He got to his feet; so did she. 'Harry, we're not finished. I need to know more of what went on in Bermuda.'

'Tomorrow.'

'And we're not quite finished with today. Can't leave things as they are, not with a cup of tea.' And like an evangelical preacher she looped one arm over his shoulder and the other around his waist and held him close, in friendship. 'I'll call you. After I've been to the Met.'

He was at the door when she touched his arm, held him back once more. 'Harry, if you're right about things there are corpses scattered everywhere. Someone out there sure won't take too kindly to you kicking over their kennel. Don't be a hero. Just be careful.'

'Careful? Like a nun. Nothing but cold showers from now on.'

'Stay safe, Harry. I'll see you tomorrow.'

—✺—

As the lift doors opened and he stepped into the lobby, Harry glanced again at his watch. He would have difficulty getting back by eight, as he'd promised Jemma. He scurried down the steps and out into the street. He didn't look back, didn't spot the figure tucked away in the corner hiding behind a copy of the *Evening Standard*. The man watched Harry disappear in the distance. Then he reached for his phone.

CHAPTER FOURTEEN

It was eight thirty-two as Harry stepped into the apartment, and it took him only a breath to know something was wrong. It stank of burned food. 'Bugger!' His dinner was charcoal. It also meant Jemma hadn't returned. He spent the best part of an hour distractedly scraping at the casserole. Then he waited some more. Ten. Eleven. Jemma didn't come home, not all night.

—⁓—

It took Delicious little more than ten minutes the following day to walk to St James's Park once her meeting at Charing Cross police station on Agar Street had finished. Her British colleagues had been welcoming but cautious: there was only so much time and manpower they could give to a missing-person case from another jurisdiction, no matter how attractively the request was packaged. Cuts. Priorities. Paperwork, they explained. But they would do their damnedest, for her – she had that sort of effect on people, and particularly on middle-aged coppers. It was as good as she could hope for, but no sooner had the promises been issued than the cost-saving computer system they relied on had crashed. Promises had given way to pandemonium. Without eyes, without screens, they couldn't catch a cat. She agreed to come back the following morning.

Trafalgar Square was abustle with tourists and tour leaders with flags raised high above their heads as they led their flock of foreign ducklings. Delicious listened as one of them described how the smallest police station in the country had once been housed in the base of one of the square's corner lanterns, but no longer. Closed decades ago, of course. Cuts, even in those days, even though it was barely large enough for the swing of a truncheon. She dodged through the crawl of traffic that struggled around the square and found herself in the Mall pointing towards the squat outline of Buckingham Palace in the distance. It took only a few more steps before she was in the park and walking through the avenue of ancient plane trees, past carefully tended flower beds and to the lake that had originally been dug out by Charles II for his revelries and duck meat. She hurried on, not wanting to be late, uncertain of what lay in store for her.

The phone call that had summoned her here had been made to her hotel room shortly after Harry had left.

'Inspector Hope?' a man's voice had said.

'That's correct. And who's this?'

'If you don't mind, I'd prefer to introduce myself properly when we meet. I believe you're looking for Susannah Ranelagh.'

'Yes, but how do you—'

'Please, I must ask you to bear with me. I'm in a somewhat delicate position, you see, and I need your word that you'll treat anything I have to tell you in the strictest confidence. That includes my identity.'

'An anonymous informant?'

'Only until tomorrow. Can we meet? There's a restaurant and coffee shop just behind Downing Street called Inn the Park. That's two N's. Would that be convenient?'

'How will I recognize you?'

'Oh, no need. I'll find you.'

'But how?'

'The Bermuda Police Force website. Very fetching photo, if you'll allow me to say so.'

She paused, made up her mind. 'Two thirty?'

'I'll be there. Tell you everything you need to know.'

She was formulating more questions, wanting to know how he had found out she was staying at the Soho, what was his connection with Susannah Ranelagh, but he had already rung off.

She found the restaurant with its views over the lake. It had a grass roof, a glass frontage and a long, curving terrace at its front. She stepped tentatively inside, peered around the busy interior, but no one caught her eye. She moved to the terrace, glancing in both directions, and there at the very end, at the table nearest the lake, a man was sitting on his own. As she stared he raised his head from the book he was reading and nodded, then stood. 'Inspector Hope,' he declared as she approached. He held out his hand in greeting. 'It's good of you to make the time.'

'It was an invitation I couldn't easily refuse.'

'I suppose so. Susannah must be something of a mystery for you.'

'So are you. Who are you?'

But he held up the palms of his hands to deflect her question. 'All in good time, Inspector. I've a lot to tell you. But, first, have you had lunch?'

'A sandwich. A cheese-and-lettuce sandwich. A very stale cheese-and-lettuce sandwich.'

'Then a drink of some sort. In honour of the heat,

how about a glass of Pimm's? It's our version of a rum fruit cocktail but without the rum.'

She nodded her head. 'Love one.'

'Two minutes.'

While he was fetching the drinks she looked around her. The book he had been reading was Dickens with a bookmark from something called the Folio Society protruding from its pages. Much thumbed, not the first time of reading, and well chosen, as was the table he had commandeered, as private as any on the crowded terrace. It was at the end of the row with a view over the tranquil lake with its wildlife and fountains. On the pathway beneath the terrace, tourists ignored the signs that warned them not to feed the waterfowl and were besieged by an army of squirrels and several flotillas of ducks. Beyond the precincts of the park she could see the roofscape of Whitehall with its towers and cupolas, and beyond it the London Eye peered down like a multi-eyed mechanical Hydra. She began to relax: her mystery man had taste.

When he returned, clutching two glasses, he placed her drink on the table in front of her and raised his own. 'To your good health and successful visit, Inspector.'

'Thanks but—'

There seemed to be so many unanswered questions

in their dialogue. She was growing impatient and he tried to reassure her.

'I've known Susannah for many years, since long before she came to Bermuda. Since she was a student. Always a very private woman.'

His stare was bold, direct, so much so that she felt it slightly disconcerting, as though he was studying her. She pushed around the cucumber in her drink.

'She had few friends,' he continued. 'I was one of them. We, a small group of us from university, would meet once a year to catch up, to exchange news.'

They were interrupted as her phone buzzed. She apologized and pulled the phone from her bag. It was a text from Harry, confirming their arrangement to meet a little later in Westminster, telling her he was on his way.

'I'm so sorry,' she said, looking up, 'where were we?'

'I was telling you how Susannah made her money.'

'Were you?'

'Yes. The news we exchanged. Because of our positions, much of it was commercially sensitive. Over the years it's turned out to be worth a small fortune – several small fortunes, in fact.'

'The Oxford University Junior Croquet Club!' she exclaimed in surprise.

'Precisely. Although that sounds a little too formal.

We used to call ourselves the Aunt Emmas. It's a technical term suggesting that we took the game rather less seriously than some others.'

'Croquet has technical terms?'

'You'd be surprised.'

So Harry had been right. Good cop, Harry, right down to the scar on his left buttock she'd seen peering out at her from beneath his hospital gown. But in the same flash of understanding she grew confused: no way was this man anyone in the photograph, not for all the fifty years that had passed since it had been taken.

'So the members of the Aunt Emmas were in some sort of insider-trading ring? A cartel?'

'It was an intellectual cartel, if you want to give it a label. It's important that you understand the nature of elites, Inspector, for these people were undoubtedly an elite, the very best and brightest whose parents had betrayed the world, then condemned it to stultifying postwar mediocrity. They knew things could be different and set out to prove it. They met to exchange views and opinions, as old friends would, but they were also highly competitive. And in a competitive world money seems always to become the final arbiter, the measure of success. They were all in positions where they were recipients of confidences – that's the nature of elites – but it got to the point where those confidences were broken by being shared with each other.'

'Even Susannah Ranelagh?' she asked in surprise.

'Even Susannah Ranelagh. Oh, yes, a tiny shrew of a woman in so many ways but quite exceptionally bright. People underestimated her. She arrived in Bermuda with a respectable tranche of money, passed around a little of that money to establish herself as a paragon of all the maidenly virtues, then confirmed her saintliness by helping raise money for high-profile charities. In the course of all those good works she would meet most of the biggest players on the island. It was a favourite saying of hers that the biggest dicks always like to expose themselves. So she tripped over an enormous amount of useful information.'

'*Inside* information,' Delicious insisted.

'Well, I suppose some might call it that, but nothing you'd ever be able to prosecute in a court of law. I don't have to tell you that Bermuda is a place of quiet money. Nobody likes to make a fuss. But listen carefully and you could hear the whispers, the bragging, who's on the way up and who's heading for the fall. She was like the Miss Marple of the money game and in her own quiet way would see things more clearly than almost anyone. She had a close friend who worked in a senior position in one of the banks and who advised her on likely charitable targets, clients who were about to receive a windfall of some sort. And she'd be invited to the governor's mansion, take tea with the island's high and mighty. There are always those who want some sort of medal, some trinket or other in the Queen's Birthday Honours, and she had a reputation for having the ear of the governor on such nonsense. So they would confide in her. Tell her things they'd never tell another soul. She said there was more horseshit deposited around the governor's roses than in any other garden in the kingdom.'

Delicious sat in the afternoon sunshine transfixed. She was a police officer, she dealt with car crashes and drug dealers and the occasional gang fight. She'd never had tea with the governor.

'What she and her old university friends did didn't seem illegal, not at first. It was nothing more than a game of intellectual arrogance. But almost without their knowing a line was crossed and by then it was too late to turn back. Anyway, elites don't turn back. You press the logic of success to its conclusion and don't give a damn for the morality of the masses.'

'Susannah Ranelagh?' she whispered in astonishment.

He sighed. 'There was a price to be paid, of course. You don't understand that when you're young, you think you're immortal. But none of us are.'

'So she's dead.' There was something in his tone as well as his words that made Delicious certain.

'It all started with one of the group – her name was Christine Leclerc. A stellar woman, there was nothing she couldn't have achieved in life, anything from president of Renault to president of the French Republic, but she was brought up in the French bureaucratic tradition and ended up in the European Commission. Now, there's an insider-trading deal if ever there was. Not since the Triumvirate in Ancient Rome divided the spoils after Caesar's murder have so few made so much from so many. But when she was killed – entirely accidentally, I should add – the rest of the group panicked. Realized they were vulnerable. Had she left behind anything that might incriminate them? They needn't have worried, of course: Brussels doesn't wash its underwear in public. But it raised the question. Who would be next? What might they leave behind? Old age is odd, particularly for elites. Makes them impatient, with rules and, in this case, with each other. And Susannah became a liability.'

Delicious sat, her mind reeling, breathless as the world floated past. A curious sparrow hopped onto the table in search of crumbs. She tried to brush it away but somehow all her energies were focused on what he was saying and what it all could mean.

'An endangered species, the sparrow,' he said, observing. 'More than half of London's sparrows have disappeared. But so are we all, all endangered.'

There was hidden meaning wrapped up in his words that she was struggling to decode.

'That's why Susannah was killed. She was weak, couldn't take the pressure, the questions. Would have let everyone down. And perhaps you've already worked out that's why her house was burned, in case she'd left anything behind.'

Delicious felt almost overwhelmed by what was being thrown at her. She struggled to form the words, knowing she was about to understand everything. 'How? How was she killed?'

He paused, held her stare, for what seemed like forever. The words, when they came, were delivered individually, with precision, like the sound of distant cannons. 'In the same way I have killed you.'

She jumped as she heard his words but only inside. Nothing moved, she tried to shout but produced no more than a croak, she screamed but it echoed endlessly inside.

'You shouldn't have come here, Inspector, stirring things up. No good was to come of it.'

She fought, with all the strength she had, in fury, in fear.

'Don't worry, it's entirely painless,' he said softly.

Painless? You motherfucker! I'm drowning in here!

He was talking but she was no longer paying much heed, catching only snippets. He was leaning forward, staring, examining her, like a doctor, but her mind was elsewhere, reacting to the signals that were flashing in alarm from her body. She was paralysed, sitting in the chair, her hand on her phone, her back towards anyone who might help her. As she returned his stare she found she could no longer even blink. And slowly her eyes were drying in the heat, the shapes they saw growing confused, the colours cracking, the world breaking into fragments of searing sunlight. The tear ducts were drying. She could feel one final teardrop trickling down the flesh of her cheek.

That was the point when she knew, for certain, that she was dying. Her first reaction was one of desperate anger. No, this wasn't right! Not yet! There was still too much left for her. She was only thirty-four. She fought, as she had done all her life, tried to kick out in fury, but nothing moved, tried to focus all her strength and coor-dination into her hands, but it produced only the smallest tremor that faded as soon as it emerged. Then she grew afraid.

She began to beg for help, for a chance of life. She still had a twelve-year-old son to raise, Marley, by herself. He came first, as he had done ever since his father had walked out and left them on their own. Please, whoever you are, whatever I've done to offend you, change your mind, take pity. Please, take pity on me . . .

He was no longer staring at her. His attentions were focused on wiping her glass to remove all traces of his fingerprints, just as he would take his own glass away with him to destroy every trace of his presence. He seemed calm, methodical, like a butler cleaning up after a successful dinner party. Then the sun destroyed the last fragments of her eyesight. She could take in only sounds, final moments: the last trickle of breath escaping her body, the frantic yammering of her panicking heart, the imploding of lungs drowning in fear, the laughter of children at play in the park and the scraping of a chair as he got up and left.

CHAPTER FIFTEEN

No one bothered Delicious. The terrace was busy, the staff scurrying after other customers, the tourists on the pathway below passing by, oblivious. If they looked up and saw anything it was no more than a woman resting in the sun. Lucky girl. Only the sparrow seemed to take an interest, hopping onto the table, fluttering its feathers in hope of attracting interest and crumbs. It was a considerable time before the waitress, a shy girl recently arrived from Estonia, approached Delicious to reclaim the table. Something wasn't right. The sparrow had left a fresh blob of guano beside her hand, yet she hadn't moved. Fast asleep, perhaps. Then the young waitress saw the sticky, sightless eyes gazing into nowhere, dropped the tray with all its crockery and fled screaming. Afternoon tea in the park was cancelled.

It was only minutes before two constables in a patrol car pulled up on the pathway. Very quickly they called for backup. It wasn't simply that the body was so young that aroused their suspicions, nor even the Bermudan Police ID they found in her handbag. The main problem was that her lifeless hand was on her phone and it seemed she'd been trying to dial 999 but managed only the first two digits. Anyway, Downing Street was only a dog bark distant, far too close to take anything for granted, so, before the geese had time to honk in protest a Murder Investigation Team had arrived, the onlookers had been pushed back and the restaurant cordoned off behind police tape.

The phone became a crucial piece of evidence. It showed its last contact as being with a man the call log identified only as Harry. He was on his way to meet up with her. It showed he'd been in touch almost since the moment she'd arrived in Britain.

Police coverage of the Westminster area is handled out of Charing Cross police station, the stucco-fronted building on Agar Street that Delicious had left less than two hours previously. It didn't take long for the names of Inspector Hope and a man named Harry to circulate and reach the ears of DCI Hughie Edwards. The name of Susannah Ranelagh followed only moments behind. It was a perfect storm for the DCI, a combination of events that threatened to turn his world upside down and drown him. Yet on the other hand, if he played it right, it might just mean that promotion to superintendent that the arse-wipers had denied him twice already. He'd always reckoned he deserved a super's job. His papers were in for it again, one last throw of the dice. It would mean a much better pension, a bigger lump sum. It would also mean taking a few risks but that's what good coppers did – at least the ones who pulled in the results. He swore most colourfully, sat at his desk with his head in his hands impugning Harry's parentage for several minutes. Then he went to see his boss, the chief superintendent.

It took only a few more minutes after that for Harry's phone to spring into life.

'Harry, where are you?'

'Hi, Hughie. I'm sitting beneath a plane tree in Dean's Yard ogling a couple of Italian tourists.'

'Stay there. You sodding stay there. Don't you dare bloody move.'

Then the phone went dead.

—⚘—

Dean's Yard is an unexpected corner of Westminster, a secluded quadrangle in the lee of the twin towers at the western end of the Abbey. It was once a medieval monastery and now forms part of the estate of West-minster School. The boys play football on the grass and even claim to have invented the game, while in summer when they've packed their trunks and bug-gered off to Benidorm the area turns a profit by offering tea and cake to weary travellers. Dean's Yard is no stranger to lawlessness. In medieval times the area around the Abbey was renowned for a noisome mix of debauchery and rampant criminality – it contained countless brothels, was the site of murders and insur-rection and near at hand was a quarter named Thieving Lane, rumoured to be the site on which HM Treasury is now built. Dean's Yard was used to claim the ancient right of sanctuary from arrest and was ideal for the purpose. It has restricted access and so proved ideal to repel attack from bailiffs. By the same token it made it a bloody difficult place from which to escape.

Even from within the Yard Harry could hear the commotion, the sound of sirens wailing back and forth outside the walls. Then the sirens stopped their rush-ing and instead were parked insistently close at hand. Harry was sitting at a table beneath the shade of the trees when he saw policemen beginning to pour through the gates at both ends of the Yard. They were in a hurry, like eels swarming between the reeds; a table was knocked over, a woman screamed, a child began to cry. It took

Harry a second before he realized that every single one of the policemen was headed for him. As he sipped from his mug of tea he found that a forest of dark-blue bulletproof jackets and helmets had sprung up around him, sprouting Heckler & Koch muzzles. Nine-millimetre cartridges. He'd seen what one of those could do. A neat and subdued hole in the chest that could blast through the spine and leave a hole like a whale bite in the back. An angry whale. The mug of tea froze to his lips as he tried to figure out what the hell was going on. Then the forest parted and the substantial form of DCI Hughie Edwards emerged.

'Hello, Harry,' he said, yet with no welcome in his voice.

'What the hell's going on, Hughie?'

'You're coming to help us with our enquiries.'

'Into what?'

'The sudden and very unexpected death of your friend, Inspector Hope.'

There were more words, about his being arrested, about his not having to say anything, about what he did say being used in evidence, but Harry heard none of it. He was frozen. What was left of his tea was slowly trickling onto his trouser leg, but he didn't move, didn't even notice. He didn't flex a muscle until he was hauled to his feet by two oversized policemen clad in body armour. They tried to handcuff him but it wouldn't work, not with his cast. Edwards shook his head in resignation and Harry was bundled into a waiting patrol car.

—∙∙∙—

'How the hell can you think I had anything to do with her death?' Harry spat.

'Which of the dozen compelling reasons do you want me to get to first?' Edwards replied. His eyes were full of storm and suspicion, like a gale blowing off Swansea Bay, and it had taken all trace of their friendship with it.

They were facing each other in an interview room at Charing Cross. The atmosphere was recycled, the floor worn, the walls painted in two different shades of ageing magnolia. A sergeant sat beside the DCI while Theo van Buren, Harry's solicitor, was next to his client. Harry's clothes had been taken from him for forensics and replaced by a one-piece white romper suit manufactured from recycled bottle tops. The two sides were separated by a table whose veneer was distinctly chipped. So was the civility.

'We'd like to know what grounds you have for holding my client,' van Buren insisted.

Edwards began counting off on his thick fingers.

'Your client knew the deceased. He was involved in a serious ongoing investigation that had brought Inspector Hope to Britain. He met the inspector at her hotel within hours of her arriving in this country. He was the last person to make contact with her on her phone. They had arranged to meet. He was in the area at the time she died.' He'd run out of fingers. 'You think that's enough for us to be getting on with?'

'You don't know for a fact she was murdered,' the solicitor replied.

'And I don't know there's not a Santa Claus but I'm working on the assumption that it's a pretty safe bet.'

'Hughie, I want to help you as much as I can.' Harry interrupted the professional jousting. 'Delicious was a friend. A close friend, I think. And I'll save you the trouble by betting every bottle in the brewery that she was murdered.'

'So why d'you suppose the lady was murdered, Mr Jones?'

'She was looking for Susannah Ranelagh. Both of us were. And we both believed Miss Ranelagh is dead.'

'Another body? Just drags you in deeper.'

'I believe she was here this morning, discussing the case.'

'I know she was. With me.'

'Then you know what I'm saying is true.'

'What I know, Harry' – it was the first time he'd used his Christian name or deigned to accept that there was anything other than formal hostility between the two of them – 'is there's something deeply unpleasant going on here. Smells like a sewer, so it does, and you're right in it up to your neck. So why don't you tell us all about it?'

'You know my interest in Susannah Ranelagh.'

'Do I?' An eyebrow arched in warning. Ah, of course, that was the reason for the edge in Edwards's tone. The DCI was in this mess, too, if not up to his neck then at least up to the hole in his trouser pocket. They both knew that with hindsight he should never have shared anything with Harry privately, yet there was nothing to be gained for either of them by admitting to it. So it had never happened. 'Why don't you start from the beginning?' Edwards suggested, leading the witness onto safer ground.

So they sat and spoke, for more than an hour, about Susannah Ranelagh, and about Bermuda, although Harry decided to talk only in the gentlest terms concerning his father. The more complicated this got, the longer it would take him to dig his way out from beneath the avalanche of circumstance and suspicion that was threatening to bury him.

—ɷ—

Search squads don't knock, not in murder cases. Their task is to secure evidence that might be flushed away in seconds, so protecting feelings comes way down the list. Often they will simply batter down the door but there was no need for that in Harry's case: they had his keys. Even so, they didn't hang around or waste time on common courtesies. They were investigating a probable murder, of a police colleague; anyway, they had no idea someone else was in the apartment. They swarmed through the front door and into the living room to find the windows open, a fan pushing around the thick evening air, and Jemma sitting at the table wearing nothing but a thin cotton crop-top and knickers. Some women would have screamed, others fled to the bathroom, a fair few fainted, but Jemma had her own ways. She sprang to her feet and started shouting at them to get out of her fucking home before she called the *Daily Mail*. The leader of the search team, a detective inspector, wilted beneath the broadside, taking a step back and ushering forward a female colleague.

'What the bloody hell do you think you're doing?' Jemma stormed, climbing into a T-shirt that was hanging from the back of a chair, any awkwardness entirely swept aside by her anger.

'Harry Jones lives here,' the DI declared, a trace of uncertainty in his voice. His last bust had got entirely the wrong address and left him drowning in paper-work for a month.

'This is my apartment,' Jemma spat in return.

'But . . . he lives here.'

'So what?'

He waved his warrant card at her. 'So we're going to look around.'

'You got a search warrant?'

'Don't need one.'

'I've got cockroaches with better manners than you.'

'We tried to call.'

'You didn't even ring the bloody bell!'

'The Police and Criminal Evidence Act allows us to search the premises of an arrested person.'

'Arrested?' The flame inside Jemma began to flicker in uncertainty. The DI held out a sheet of paper spelling out her rights but she ignored it. 'What's he done now?' she asked, sinking back into her chair.

'Mr Jones has been arrested on suspicion of murder.'

And the flame was gone. 'Murder? You can't be seri-ous. Who?'

'A female officer of the Bermuda Police Force. Delicious Hope. An inspector. You know her, by any chance?'

'I need to go to the bathroom.'

'Not until we've checked it.' The DI nodded to his colleagues and seconds later she could hear the banging of bathroom cupboards and the rattling of bottles and containers. The cistern lid was lifted, the system flushed, the rubbish bin rifled. Through the open door she watched them poking through her box of tampons.

They moved to the bedroom, where they pulled back the duvet, examined the sheets for God knew what, poked around in the cupboards, took some of Harry's clothes and all the dirty linen, including her own. When one of the uniformed policemen pulled at the top drawer in the chest it slid straight out and emptied her underwear over his shoes. He retrieved it with a glance of embarrassment and apology.

They spent a lot of time in the spare bedroom, which was used as an office. They took the computer hard drive, his laptop, her laptop, too, despite her protests. 'That's mine.'

'Not for the moment it's not.'

An exhibits officer made a record of everything.

Then they asked for her mobile phone. She found it in the bottom of her bag and handed it across. It was switched off, had been all day, and perhaps that had been a mistake. She always switched it off while at school, then after work she'd shared a glass of wine with a girlfriend as she tried to make sense of the emotional jumble of her life. Hadn't wanted distractions from anyone, and particularly Harry.

A constable switched the phone on. 'No sign of any details for Inspector Hope, Guv,' he announced, scanning the records. 'But there's voicemail.' Without asking permission he played the messages over the speaker. Three were from Theo van Buren, asking her to call him urgently. One was a lengthy monologue from her mother complaining about a vet's bill for the cat. A message from the police proving they had tried to call. And there was Steve's voice, low, soft, a little cautious, thanking her for the previous night, his ingratiating tone leaving little doubt as to what he was grateful for and expressing the hope they could do it all again. 'Again. And again!' he said, chuckling as he rang off.

It left an uncomfortable silence in the room.

'Erm, Mr Jones, is he going through any emotional turmoil, perhaps?' the DI asked.

If eyes threw spears he knew he'd have been pinned halfway up the wall and bleeding through his socks. She said nothing.

After they had left, carrying computers and clothes and other pieces in plastic evidence bags, Jemma was left to sit, alone, a sweat of fury trickling beneath her shoulder blades and down her spine. She felt humiliated but, even more than that, she felt violated. By the police. Because of Harry. She wondered if she could ever again feel clean in this apartment, or in their relationship. 'Why, Harry? Why?' she muttered as she tore off her T-shirt and headed for the shower.

—⁓—

Alcatraz must have been more fun than this, he thought, when he stirred the following morning, stiff from a night of restlessness on an inadequate mattress covered in heavy-duty plastic. The custody cell at Charing Cross was totally charmless, stripped of any comforts. Four solid walls covered in scratches of graffiti, a bare and easily scrubbable floor, a high window and a concrete plinth just wide enough to take the plastic mattress. The door was steel and when it closed made the sound of a falling guillotine. Yet the cell seemed the least of his troubles. He hoped he wouldn't be kept here long – Hughie Edwards would surely establish he couldn't be involved – but the death of Delicious had left him twisting in agony. He was the reason she'd come to Britain, him and his father and Susannah Ranelagh. He liked her, they made sparks together, could have become lifelong friends in this life, let alone the next. Now she was dead. His fault.

And he hadn't seen Jemma in days, hadn't talked with her in weeks. That was probably his fault, too. But where the hell had she been these last couple of nights? Staying over at a friend's, punishing him, making him sweat, it was that sort of passion and unpredictability that he loved, but even so . . .

Would he have had sex with Delicious if his phone hadn't begun to ring? He'd never know, not now. But as he considered his own shortcomings he began to realize that his early release might not be as easy as he'd anticipated. If he'd had sex with her his DNA would've been all over the place, but even so it wouldn't take Hughie's men long to discover that he'd visited her hotel and spent some time in her room. Men in plaster casts tend to attract attention. And then there had been their long and final embrace. Her DNA over his clothes, with Hughie Edwards jumping to all the wrong conclusions. Jemma would jump to the wrong conclusion, too; damn it, in her current mood he might have to ask the DCI to keep him locked up for his own protection.

He soon found out he was right. Wrong conclusions were piling up so high he'd need a rope and oxygen to climb over them.

'OK, Harry, let's go over your story one more time, shall we?' Edwards said as a little later they gathered

once again in the interview room, van Buren in atten-
dance. He opened a blue case file in front of him and
made a point of studying it, even though he knew precisely what it said. He had to make the suspect believe
he knew the answers. He looked up with grey, enquiring eyes that were red at the rims with doubt. 'Let's
start with this, shall we? The victim's DNA all over
your clothes.' He threw an evidence bag onto the table
between them. It was Harry's shirt. 'Why don't we
have a go at explaining that?'

'She was just saying goodbye.'

'You weren't shaking her hand, that's for certain.
Forensics reckon it was more of a clinch, a close
encounter of the old-fashioned kind. You make a habit
of kissing police inspectors, do you?'

'In your case I'll make an exception.'

'Detective *Chief* Inspector,' Edwards reminded him
pointedly, as though it might give him some advantage. 'You spent some time in her room. The hotel
receptionist remembers you going up there and then
leaving, roughly an hour later. He was very sure it was
you.'

'Give Pablo my best when you next see him.'

'You getting your leg over, were you?'

'Chief Inspector,' van Buren interrupted, 'you must
have pathology reports by now. Is there any evidence

that Inspector Hope and my client had engaged in any form of sex?'

Edwards sucked his teeth. 'Not that we can confirm. Yet.'

'And do you have any evidence that my client or anyone else in a plaster cast and sling was at the scene where the inspector died?'

The DCI stopped sucking his teeth and instead chewed his cheek. 'We're still pursuing our enquiries. There was a lot of people in the park that afternoon.'

'But presumably you've established the time of death.'

'There, or thereabouts. The path-lab people are still working on that.'

'What? Still?'

'There are some unusual circumstances surrounding this death that we're trying to get to the bottom of.'

'Let me get this straight,' the solicitor said, sensing a weakness. 'You can establish no motive for my client being involved in the death. And you can't even show he was at the scene and so establish he had opportunity.'

'We've got a hell of a lot of circumstantial and even more questions that need answering.'

'But it's up to you to answer the questions. You can't

keep my client on the grounds that he was having a cup of tea half a mile away.'

'A mug. It was a mug of tea.'

Suddenly van Buren understood. Edwards was flapping like a torn sail. 'Chief Inspector, can you confirm the cause of death?'

There was a pause. His face was frozen, no more chewing. He glanced sideways at his sergeant, then looked slowly back at the solicitor, trying to muster every ounce of authority that twenty-eight years in the police service had given him. 'I can tell you that she didn't die of natural causes.'

'Come on, you can do better than that. Was she murdered?'

'Our tests aren't finished.'

'You don't know? Then you can't even be sure that a crime's been committed.'

The DCI flushed in discomfort. 'The initial autopsy suggested that Inspector Hope died from snake poison.'

Van Buren threw his hands up in disbelief. 'Snake poison?' he said, every syllable soaked in ridicule. 'You can't be serious.'

'A cobra,' the policeman replied doggedly.

The absurdity of the statement stunned them all into silence.

'That's why we're still doing tests,' Edwards eventually said. 'And, until they're done, your client is going nowhere.' He glanced across at Harry for the first time in a while, his eyes fixed and determined, yet flecked with discomfort.

'You said there were dragons out there, Hughie,' Harry said. 'You didn't mention anything about bloody snakes.'

CHAPTER SIXTEEN

It was the first mutterings of Saturday evening, a full thirty hours after Harry had been arrested. In a few more hours the police either had to ask a magistrate for more time and give him good reason, or let their prisoner go. This way, by releasing him early, they could drag Harry back in and still get a few more hours at him before any magistrate started getting sticky. Keys jangled, the lock moved back with a dull thud and the cell door swung open. Edwards was standing in the doorway, the custody sergeant at his shoulder.

'You're out of here, Harry.'

Harry rubbed his eyes; they were sore from staring at walls. 'I'm free to fly?' he asked.

'Police bail,' Edwards said. 'We're going to want you

back in. A few more questions,' he added with emphasis. He didn't appear happy with the situation.

'Hughie?' Harry's voice was loaded with exasperation, leaning on their past acquaintance.

The DCI glanced over his shoulder and the custody sergeant clanked his keys and withdrew, leaving them alone.

'We believe she was probably murdered,' the policeman said, 'and you're the closest thing I've got to a suspect.'

'You know me, you can't think I did it.'

'No one else in my book right now. And it's because I know you that I've got to do this by the bloody book.' The DCI came and sat his large frame beside Harry. His body language said he was tired. The plastic mattress didn't even flinch. 'We cell-traced your phone, Harry. Now I'm not telling you anything your solicitor won't find out inside five minutes. But your phone says you were never in the park. Says you were checking the cricket scores at the time the inspector died.'

'Second day of a test match, what the hell do you expect a man to be doing?'

'That's not proof,' the policeman snapped. 'Only shows what your phone was doing, and we don't have any current plans to press charges against your sodding phone.' Then he heaved a sigh, seemed to relent, just a little. 'But.'

'That sounds like a big bloody "but", Hughie.'

'The waitress is Polish, accent you can slice with a spade. She was busy, run off her feet. Distracted. Says she can't remember anyone in a sling.' He sniffed. 'That doesn't mean a damned thing, of course.'

'Of course.'

'I did warn you, Harry!' The policeman's mood had swung once again, his patience had disappeared and he levered himself wearily back to his feet. 'I told you there were dragons out there but you had to go and poke a stick in its eye, didn't you? Always were an awkward Welsh sod.'

'Half-Welsh. An awkward half-Welsh sod.'

Edwards shook his head. 'Puts us both in a difficult position.'

'You know something, Hughie? From this side of the bars it hasn't looked like that.'

'I'm that close to making superintendent,' Edwards said, holding up a thumb and forefinger with barely room for a cigarette paper between them. 'Then I can finish my thirty years and bog off with a pension. But now this. I should never have talked to you about Susannah Ranelagh.'

'She's connected, I know she is,' Harry insisted,

growing irritated with a man he realized he could no longer consider his friend.

'You'll need a better alibi than that.'

'I don't need any sort of alibi! I didn't kill Delicious, for Christ's sake. She was a friend. You're screwing with me, Hughie.'

'You want a complaint form?'

'No. But for old times' sake maybe a favour.'

'It was doing you a bloody favour what got us started on all this in the first place, remember?'

'Look, I've got a photograph of Susannah Ranelagh. She's with my father and some others. I can't prove it's connected to anything, but there's a large number of people who knew Miss Ranelagh and who somehow ended up dead. Now Delicious. It's an old photo, taken fifty years ago, and there are two people in it I can't identify. I don't know, there might be something in it and I was wondering, with your facial-recognition software, could you—'

'Not a bloody chance.'

'Come on, Hughie, don't disappear up your own arse.'

'Listen. The software requires high-resolution images, something like sixty pixels between the eyes. Your image is fifty years old, you say. Waste of time. Bit like trying to read my own bloody handwriting.'

Harry's head fell in disappointment. He knew the policeman's handwriting. It resembled iron railings hit by a car.

'So you can go and play with the fairies,' the policeman said, turning towards the door. 'For the moment.'

—⚒—

Harry suspected it was going to be tempestuous, an evening that both of them would prefer had never happened. When his key turned in the lock it felt stiff, reluctant to let him in. He found Jemma in a T-shirt and shorts. She had turned the apartment into a laundry: everywhere there were freshly washed sheets, pillowcases, duvet covers, but most of all underwear. It seemed as though every item she owned was being set out to dry, spreading from the bathroom across the rest of the apartment, where it sat like a fall of fresh snow down the back and on the seat of every available chair. When he walked in she stood near an open window testing a pair of knickers, holding them to her cheek to see if they were dry. She looked up but it was almost as though it had been seconds rather than three days since they'd last seen each other.

'They made me feel dirty,' she said slowly.

'Who?'

'Your friends. The police.'

A silence.

'I tried to call,' he said.

'I know. My phone was off.'

'Why?'

'I didn't want to speak to you.'

He entered the apartment cautiously, uncertain of what was waiting for him. 'I got myself arrested. They thought I'd murdered someone.' He tried to make light of it.

'Another good reason for turning my phone off.'

Battle lines were being drawn.

'They made me feel violated, Harry. My home, ransacked by the bloody police. They went through everything. Bathroom, bedroom, my underwear drawer. Everything that was private. To me. They even know what brand of tampon I use. Thanks for that.'

'It was a mistake,' he protested. 'I was in the wrong place at the wrong time.'

'Who?'

'What?'

'Who were you supposed to have murdered?'

Another silence before, 'Delicious. Delicious Hope. The Bermudan—'

'Yes. I remember.' The knickers she was holding were now crumpled into a tight ball inside her fist. 'So she was in London?'

'Yes.'

'That I didn't know. Perhaps because you didn't tell me, Harry. Like you forgot to tell me about your son, Ruari.'

'You're reading too much into it.'

'You and her? I wonder.'

'I had a cup of tea with her. That's all.'

'And now she's dead.'

Christ, she was as suspicious as the police. It was still almost eighty outside; the air inside was stifling.

'There was nothing between us, Jem.'

'And yet.'

More silence. Their eyes tangled, told of pain, sadness, mixed with wisps of suspicion.

She bit her lip, took a deep breath, her T-shirt heaved as she came to the main and most difficult point. 'I want this to stop, Harry.'

'What exactly?'

'What you're doing. With your father. It's got completely out of hand; it isn't reasonable any more. You're pushing me away.'

'I love you, Jem.'

'But there are other things that are even more important to you than love.'

'No, nothing.'

'Then give this up.'

'I can't.'

Her bottom lip was trembling now, no matter how hard she bit on it. 'I know you can't. But I had to try.' There was an air of finality about her words that made him feel suddenly scared.

'He's my father, Jem. I can't just forget him.'

'You managed to do that perfectly well for twenty-odd years.'

They were still standing feet apart, where they had started, on opposite sides of the apartment, like gunslingers. He was covered in beads of sweat, and so was she, or were they tears?

'There are too many questions,' he said. 'There's something wrong about it all. My father. Susannah Ranelagh. Now Delicious. Somehow I feel like it's all my fault.'

'Don't give me this childhood guilt crap. It's not your fault. And it's certainly not and in no way ever been bloody mine!' She flinched in pain, her fingers flexed, her underwear fluttered to the floor like a dead bird falling from the sky.

'Nothing has been your fault, Jem.'

He took a step forward but she recoiled, in guilt. It had been only a couple of hours since she'd showered off the last traces of Steve Kaminski.

'Jem, I want to spend the rest of our lives together,

246

you and me. But we're all prisoners of our pasts, no one starts with a clean sheet. You understand that, don't you?'

'And how!' she whispered.

'I have to find some way of breaking away from that, from my father. I need time. Give me a little time. Please, Jem, that's all I ask.'

She turned away, looking blindly out of the window, trying to hide the turmoil inside. When she turned back, her face was a picture of misery. 'Don't you want to know where I've been these last couple of days?'

'Not particularly,' he said, very slowly.

'Why not?'

For the first time he began to sense that this wasn't just about him, or Ruari, or Delicious, that she'd done something he desperately wouldn't like. He didn't want to think what. But he couldn't forget that Delicious had died and it was his fault. That choked his soul, so that right now he didn't have any room left inside to be angry with Jem, too.

'Why not?' he said, repeating her question. 'You know why, stupid.'

There were tears now, of that he was in no doubt.

'Neither of us are teenagers, Jem. We've both got enough previous to ask for any number of additional offences to be taken into consideration, but so what?

We both know we can live without each other. I just don't want to. Ever.'

She didn't reply. Her lips trembled as though trying to speak but not a word emerged. Instead she stripped off her T-shirt and dropped it alongside the discarded laundry. Her body swayed as she crossed to him, naked from the waist up. She took him in her arms, made sure he felt both her body and her tongue against his. Then she led him to the sofa. He was wearing a shirt that was sticking to him in the heat; her fingers tugged and twisted until they had undone every button, not hurried, as if they had all the time in the world. She stripped the shirt from his back like the peel of an orange, pulling it over the cast on his arm, then kissed him again. A breeze had begun to waft through the window, spilling over their bodies, joining in with them, and he could feel that her breasts had caught fire. She stripped him of the rest of his clothes, her fingers deftly manipulating every belt and button, falling to her knees in order to free his feet from the tangle of clothes and leave him naked. She looked up, wide-eyed, like a penitent. She kissed both his knees, then worked her way up, slowly, deliberately, lingering at every stopping place, until their eyes met once again. She pushed him down onto the sofa. She had taken complete control.

When he was stretched out there, his head cushioned, she discarded what was left of her own clothes, throwing them carelessly to one side. She knelt beside his head, kissed his brow, each eye, very softly, the merest brush of her lips, then the tip of his nose, his cheeks, chin, in a ritual that finally led once more to his lips.

Many months before, when they had first started sleeping with each other, they had spent an evening when she had gone over every inch of his body, examining the scars, the marks of his previous life, and he had told her a little of their history. The severed ear, the scars of bullets, and knife blades, and burns, the stitch marks left after a tumble from a motorbike in the Indian Himalayas had opened up a six-inch wound on his outer thigh, the creases of skin left by the passage of shrapnel, and some marks he simply couldn't remember how they had been caused. She had marvelled how they had healed in different ways, the surgical scars that had faded almost to memory, the new flap of ear that was totally without sensation, the wicked purple mound of flesh on his back left by a bullet of the Iraqi Republican Guard that would have killed him had it been a finger's width closer to his spine. The flesh around that wound still seemed angry, refusing to settle. These marks were Harry – not all of him of course, but she had realized from the very start that he was not and never could be like any other man she had known. Now she went to every one of his old wounds, brushing them with the gentlest of touches, smoothing away their creases with her lips and her fingertips, as though to heal them and chase away any lingering pain.

Then she climbed astride him. Settled herself on him, and made love to him with a tenderness they hadn't shared for months. Not a single word. A rivulet of sweat trickled down between her breasts, through the blonde downy hair of her navel and onto his, binding them as one. Then she brought her feet forward alongside his chest, leaned her own body back, rocked to and fro, and moments later gave a small cry. They were done.

They didn't hurry, not even their parting. But as soon as she got to her feet she scooped up her clothes and began climbing back into them, struggling with the damp, clinging T-shirt. When she spoke the tenderness was gone, the voice very practical, stripped of emotion.

'I'd like you to pack a bag, Harry.'

'What?'

'I want you to go.'

'I don't understand.'

'Like you, I need some time.'

'Come on, Jem, what for?'

'To think.'

'About what?'

'Us, of course.'

'And how long do you think this might take?'

'I don't know!' she shouted, her composure slipping. Then she added, very softly, 'Fuck you, Harry.'

'But we just—'

'That ...' She waved an animated finger at the wreckage of the sofa. 'That was to see if we still had it, if we had something to build on. It's been so long, I needed to be reminded. I was. And now I need to be by myself. You can phone me, if you like. But not too often.'

'Are you sure about this?'

'Very.'

He felt cheated, almost deceived, but he didn't argue. He knew it would have no purpose, that he could never badger her into changing her mind. He'd asked for time, so now she demanded her share of it, too. He took a shower, trying to scrub away his feelings of resentment along with the lingering reminders of sex, then packed a few things while Jemma began tidying her apartment, filling the time with mindless activity, retrieving underwear and bed linen and folding them into neat piles. There was no anger, no hostility on her part, just emotional blankness as she struggled to keep her knees from shaking.

Harry was being thrown out. Yet, as much as he might want to rage against the powerlessness of it all, there was also a considerable chunk of sense in it. He knew what he was doing was hurting Jemma. He also knew he couldn't stop. He had to carry on. That was what Harry Jones always did, which was why he had so many bloody holes in him. He couldn't stop now. He owed that not only to himself but even more to Delicious. His fault, no one could tell him otherwise. Yet too many people connected to Susannah Ranelagh had died and he knew there was every chance he might be next in line, which meant that anybody standing beside him was in danger, too, let alone anyone sleeping with him. Jemma. It was right to get away. For her sake.

'I love you,' he said, hovering at the door.

'Bye, Harry,' she said, not daring to look up.

He turned away and the door closed behind him.

CHAPTER SEVENTEEN

Temporary accommodation was never going to be much of a challenge for a man like Harry. His years in the military and in politics had left him with a wide network of friends. And the timing was right at the start of the summer: Parliament had just gone into recess and many of the boltholes used by politicians as their London bases were now empty. It took him only a couple of phone calls to find somewhere, and it proved to be exceptional – a houseboat moored on the river at Chelsea just off Cheyne Walk. It belonged to a Scottish hereditary peer, Lord Glenmartin. 'Make yourself at home, dear boy. No maid service, no milk in the fridge and the claret's pretty disgusting, but it's yours until October, if you want.'

'You're a pal, Angus.'

'But what is it, Harry, woman trouble?' The Scotsman sighed. 'Not again. I'd lend you my sister but, well, you're a friend and she has this terrible habit of wanting to marry every man she sleeps with.'

'The keys and the claret are more than enough.'

'I'll give the security chaps a call, let them know you're coming. Ah, spare key. Unimaginative, I know, but it's in one of the flowerpots. Third on left.'

The houseboat turned out to be forty-six feet of old pine panels, book cases, narrow beds and Spartan cooking facilities, with an old solid-fuel stove in the middle of the main cabin and the paperwork that marked the paraphernalia of a parliamentary life piled on almost every conceivable surface. It was south-facing, almost stifling in the sun, and he threw open all the windows and hatches to catch the breeze. He found the claret, a case of ageing Saint-Julien that only Angus would dare call disgusting but which was in dire need of rescue from the heat before it turned into cooking wine. The faint aroma of cigars hung in the air and dying stags stared at him from every wall. He found fresh linen in the closet, where Glenmartin had directed him, restocked the fridge and tidied the papers into orderly piles. When he had finished he took himself up to the sun deck at the bow, overlooking the river, and started on the first bottle of claret. The cork crumbled but he dug it out patiently. Beside him was a large flower pot that had been commandeered during the spring as a nesting site by a family of ducks. On the river swam bobbing moorhens; along it flew cormorants in search of elvers. His iPhone sat beside him for company and he kept staring at it, wondering if she would call, and debating whether *he* should. The light was beginning to fade, the noise of the water fading to a gentle murmur of the ebbing river. Still she hadn't called, and he knew she wouldn't. He sighed. He knew he shouldn't bother her but picked up his phone anyway.

'Hello, Alex. You said I should call.'

'But of course, Harry,' the now familiar voice replied. 'How are things? How's Jemma?'

'I guess we've been better. Taking a bit of a holiday, truth be told.'

'I'm so sorry.'

'Things have got a little confused, what with my father, Susannah Ranelagh. I even managed to get myself arrested.'

It took McQuarrel a moment to take in this news. 'You ran a red light or something?'

'There's a Bermudan police officer, came over here to investigate the Ranelagh disappearance. Somehow she got herself murdered.'

'Good grief!'

'For a moment they thought I'd done it. I think they still do.'

'But, Harry, this is appalling.'

'Jem agrees with you.'

'Harry, please, tell me, how can I help? Anything. I have a few good friends in the law, or if it's money—'

'No, just the bishop. The Bishop of Burton. I'd like to have a word with him, see if he has any insights. Can you help?'

'I'm not sure I can, Harry. I'm not sure he's even a bishop any longer. They have mandatory retirement at seventy, don't they? And he must be all of that?'

'Oh, I thought that you and he ...' Harry couldn't hide the disappointment in his voice.

'Randall Wickham and I pass like ferries in a fog, no more than that. Had a bit of a falling-out, actually, some years ago. Over the bloody Arabs. Typical Senior Common Room banter, you know what these things are like. He wanted to bomb them with bibles. I thought it a rather silly idea and he took offence. Well, you know, High Table should be a bit of a battlefield, there ought to be casualties. After that we rather avoided each other, opposite sides of the fireplace in the Senior Common Room.'

'That's a pity.'

'I suppose I'll bump into the man at some point, pon-
tificating at High Table, but at the very earliest that
won't be until the start of Michaelmas term in October.'

'Bugger.'

'But if you don't mind my asking, what do you need
him for?'

'He knew my father and Susannah Ranelagh so I
was, you know, sort of hoping he might . . .' It sounded
confused, and was. The claret wasn't helping.

'Harry, it's not for me to interfere.'

'I called you, remember? That makes it a sort of
invitation.'

'Where's all this taking you? With the police. Your
relationship with Jemma.'

'It's become a pain in the butt, hasn't it?'

'So why bother? Why carry on?'

'The Father Thing, I guess. Chasing ghosts.' Harry
looked deep into his glass as though he might find
the answer there, but it was no help. He sighed. 'You
know, Alex, I've been struggling to remember the last
thing we said to each other. I can't. Some unkind word,
some intended slight, I suppose. I keep wondering if
it was about my mother. I was barely a teenager when
she died. I never really knew her.' He was growing
maudlin.

'Oh, Harry, but I knew her! And one day I'll sit with you and it will be my pleasure to tell you everything I knew of her. But don't damn your father simply because she was unhappy in her final years. I know he tried.'

Harry struggled in silence with the idea as a wisp of breeze off the river tussled his hair.

'I know you want to take sides, Harry, but that's not a good idea. They are both dead, you can't change a thing. Better to let it lie.'

'I suspect that's good advice.'

'Then take it.'

'I can't, Alex. I'm their son. When they made me I think they forgot to include a pause switch.'

'I hope you won't live to regret that.'

'You know, there's something I do remember him telling me,' Harry said, dredging the memory up from deep within his glass. 'He always had a saying of some sort, eternal wisdom, like a bloody Christmas cracker. "Regret only what you don't do." That's what he said. Perhaps that's why he died never regretting a thing – he left that to everyone else. Johnnie the Chancer, Johnnie the Cheat, Johnnie the Cynic, the Irreverent, the Utterly Irresponsible,' he said caustically. Something else Harry remembered his saying: 'Never fall in love with anyone but yourself: it only leads to disappointment.' And, as he remembered, Harry reached once again for the bottle.

—⁂—

As DCI Edwards had warned, they summoned Harry back in for another session. Arrested him all over again, cautioned him once more, bundled him into a car. Same interview room, same veneer, except there was no veneer left on Hughie Edwards. He walked in, grim-faced, clutching a file that was considerably thicker than the last time Harry had seen it. The DCI dropped it on the table, there was much scraping of chairs, the sergeant switched on the tape recorder and read out the formalities. It began.

'Morning,' Edwards began. His voice was as dull and as flat as an iron. It wasn't a greeting, merely a statement of fact.

'I want the record to show,' Theo van Buren began, anxious to land the first blow, 'that my client has always been willing to attend on the police voluntarily and to help them with your investigation in every way he can. There wasn't any need to arrest him or to harass him.'

Edwards's gaze didn't flicker; his eyes fixed upon Harry's face were like thin slices of pomegranate, bleeding from exhaustion. He ignored the solicitor. 'She was murdered. There were no bite marks, see. Couldn't have been a bloody snake after all. Poisoned. That thick-as-treacle waitress was certain they were drinking, Inspector Hope and her murderer. The till receipts suggest that someone bought two glasses of Pimm's at around half past noon. In cash, of course. We think whatever killed her was in the drink.'

The solicitor was about to intervene once more but held back, wanting to hear more.

'She was murdered, Harry,' Edwards continued. 'The woman you say was your friend was murdered. After you arranged to meet her. Then she was gone. Hell of a coincidence, that, don't you think? Or no coincidence at all. You want to tell me how you poisoned her?' He held up a palm to silence the inevitable objection from van Buren. 'A young woman has been murdered in broad daylight, a young policewoman at that, and for doing nothing but her job. And your client's got his fingerprints and name all over that case file, so, yes, I'll harass your client, Mr van Buren, I'll hassle the entire population of London in order to get to the bottom of this one.' He opened his file. 'She had a young boy – did you know that, Harry?'

Harry's expression turned to one of intense pain.

'Twelve years old, he is. That's all. Brilliant sprinter,

so I'm told, plenty of prospects. An education. Income. Now he's on his own. Totally buggered.'

'Chief Inspector, I must—'

But the policeman cut him off. 'It's a technical expression, Mr van Buren. You understand, don't you, Harry?'

Harry nodded sadly.

'You say she was poisoned,' the solicitor began again.

'In a drink.'

'You've checked the glasses for fingerprints?'

'There were no glasses.'

'But you said—'

'The murderer removed them, didn't he, so we couldn't find any fingerprints. Isn't that right, Harry?'

'So what evidence did you find at the table?'

'Nothing but bird crap. And Inspector Hope's body.'

'No CCTV?'

'Not in the restaurant. We're still checking the cameras around the park but it was crawling with tourists. That's what gets me, Harry. Hundreds of people watched Inspector Hope die. She was sitting right there in front of the crowds, yet nobody remembers seeing a damned thing.'

'So what evidence do you have against my client?' the solicitor demanded, his voice rising in exasperation.

'That's what we're here to find out, isn't it?'

'But there's something I don't understand,' Harry intervened. 'You said earlier that it was snake poison.'

'And so it was, as good as. Synthetic. Made in a lab. That's what took forensics so much time, they couldn't identify it at first. Don't ask me to explain all the molecular bollocks but it's based on cobra venom.' He sniffed. 'You travelled a bit, didn't you, Harry, in your earlier life? Even spent some time in Africa.'

'Sierra Leone.'

'They have cobras in Africa.'

'They also had cobras in Afghanistan when I was there.'

'I've got snakes in my compost heap in Sussex,' the lawyer said scornfully.

'And in Colombia. You can add that to the list, too, Chief Inspector. I served there.'

'Doesn't show up on your military record,' Edwards muttered, glancing at the file.

'That's because it wasn't supposed to.'

'Just checking.' He was playing a game. He might sound clumsy at times but that was only to encourage the witness into being equally so. It was astonishing what suspects would blurt out when they took you for granted.

'This is ridiculous,' van Buren snorted in contempt. 'You said it was synthetic. Made in a lab.'

'What was the nature of your relationship with the deceased?' Edwards asked, keen to change course.

'I first met her when I was in hospital a couple of weeks ago in Bermuda. And, before you ask, I have no idea whether there are cobras in Bermuda.'

Edwards smiled thinly at the sarcasm. 'You were in Bermuda for what purpose?'

'To talk with Susannah Ranelagh.'

'A woman you had never met before in your life, so you claim.'

'Correct.'

'Yet you travelled halfway around the world to meet her.'

'Yes.'

'And who is now missing.' He paused, like a boxer, watching Harry to see if he flinched. 'Susannah Ranelagh is missing. And Inspector Hope is dead. You're a very dangerous man to be around, Harry.'

Van Buren reached out to grasp Harry's sleeve; such loaded comments weren't worthy of a reply.

'OK, Miss Ranelagh was a lifelong friend of your father, so you've claimed, but you had never met her,' Edwards began again.

'That's right.'

'How strange. You see, she came back to this country frequently after she moved to Bermuda.' He browsed through his paperwork. 'The fact is she used to come back in October every year, regular as rain in the valley, so she did, until ...' His thick forefinger traced through a series of dates. 'Until 2001, it was. After that, not so frequent, not so regular, but there were still the odd visits. And yet you say you never met her, not even the once.'

'If I'd met her or known much about her I'd never have needed to ask for your help in finding her, would I?'

It was meant to be a shot across the bows and van Buren shook himself in both alarm and interest, but the policeman simply stared back at Harry, his pomegranate eyes dripping distrust. 'Yes, that's right. You called me asking me to check into the whereabouts of Miss Ranelagh. Claiming you had no idea what had happened to her. I think that was no more than a sordid attempt to cover your backside and throw around a little confusion. I seem to remember telling you to go to hell.'

'Actually, for the record, you used rather more robust language. Another technical expression. Anyway, Inspector Hope made a formal request only a few days later. I was simply ahead of the game.'

'And my client's been trying to help your investigation ever since,' van Buren added.

'I even offered you a photograph of Miss Ranelagh and my father, which I thought might be of some use, but you weren't interested.'

'It was an informal conversation and I remember it very differently,' Edwards replied evasively.

'I'm still happy to let you have a copy,' Harry declared, wanting to press home his advantage, 'but you've taken my phone.'

'That happens, when you get yourself arrested.'

'No problem,' van Buren said, sensing the DCI wasn't half as confident as he sounded. 'Harry sent me a copy, too. I've got it on my phone. We're always happy to help, Chief Inspector.' He dug into his pocket and, after a couple of taps, the image appeared. He pushed the phone across the table; the DCI and sergeant bent over to peer at it.

'Susannah Ranelagh's in the middle, my father's sitting to her right,' Harry explained. 'Members of the Oxford University Junior Croquet Club. Called the Aunt Emmas.'

'This is useless,' Edwards muttered. 'You told me it was fifty years old.'

'I can't help that,' Harry replied, 'but the fact is that at least two other people in that photo have died before

265

their time. Violently. Croquet's not supposed to be like that.'

'Fifty years,' Edwards repeated doggedly. 'That would make them seventy, or thereabouts. Nothing so surprising in that.'

And Harry knew there was no point. The DCI was interested in Delicious and in Harry and in murder in one of his parks, not in ancient riddles. Yet the sergeant sitting next to Edwards had dragged the phone across the table so it was closer to him. He was staring intently, increasing the size of part of the image, licking his lips. 'It may not be quite as simple as that, sir.'

'What the hell do you mean?' Edwards snapped.

'That one,' the sergeant said, pointing. 'The one on the left. I know he's much younger but I'd swear a week's pay it's him.'

'Who?'

'Findlay Francis. The guy who writes celebrity biographies – you know, about minor royals and that sort of thing. Pretty salacious stuff. Landed himself in court a few years ago, and up against a wall in a dark alleyway once in a while, too.'

'You can't be sure,' Edwards bit back, deeply unimpressed. 'Not even the facial-recognition boys could work on that.'

'No, but ... I've been looking at some of this guy's

books. Like politicians, aren't they? Writers always use much younger photos on their covers. And I'm sure that's him.'

'And what relevance do your reading habits have to our enquiries?'

'That's why I had some of his books, you see. He's missing, too. His daughter reported it last Christmas.'

'I think that's enough for the moment,' Edwards said through gritted teeth, snapping his file shut.

CHAPTER EIGHTEEN

Harry sat out on the sundeck of his houseboat taking the neck off the third beer. It had been a bloody day. He couldn't help but reflect that at one time, and not so long ago, he'd been a soldier, an officer in the British Army and part of the finest support group he could ever hope to find. Even after that, when he'd been a politician, people had queued up to persuade him he was important, special, wouldn't leave him alone. Presidents and prime ministers had competed for his company. Now the world treated him like an open sewer. It would take more than a few bottles of beer to wash away the taste of failure.

The fierce orange sun had sunk lower in the sky and was bouncing off the water, dazzling him even through the sunshades, so he closed his eyes and allowed the warmth of the evening to massage away the weariness he was feeling inside, yet no sooner had he settled back in his chair than his ear began screaming at him, as painful as if it had just been ripped from his skull once more, telling him that he'd screwed up. Again. In the farthest corner of Hell, Johnnie would be laughing.

Harry wanted Jemma, badly, but even more than that he needed to settle with Johnnie. Ever since men had picked up sticks and started using them as tools and weapons, they'd found a need to know their origins, to understand where they came from, what made them different. Harry needed to know his father in order to know himself. Only then could he go back to Jemma, if she was still around. He'd lost too many women in his life to give up on her but because he'd lost so many women he knew he ran a huge risk. She might not still be there. He growled at the sun, sipped his beer, and hurt.

The wail of a police siren from Battersea Bridge away to his left brought back memories of his morning interview with Hughie Edwards. Harry had misjudged him, thought him a friend, but the man had gone sour, and that had made him sloppy. He'd lost control of the interview, told Harry more about Susannah Ranelagh than Harry had been able to tell him, of her constant visits back to Britain. What was that about? And

Findlay Francis. That made five of the seven in the photo either dead or mysteriously missing, so screw coincidence. He beat at the cast on his arm in frustration. With his good arm he reached for another beer.

The bishop was still around, of course, or so he'd been told, yet although Harry had gone about it like a ferret down a rabbit warren he'd still been unable to trace him. *Crockford's Clerical Directory* offered no contact details, only that he'd retired from the episcopate two years previously. Harry had Googled and *Wiki*-ed but had found nothing of use, he'd called the Bishop's House in Burton, where a secretary had patiently explained that it was strictly forbidden to give out Bishop Randall's private details, although she offered to forward any letter that Harry might care to send. He'd even tried Helen in the Steward's Office in Christ Church and got a fulsome expression of regret, but much the same answer. In the end he had no choice. In a mood of deep frustration Harry had written the letters and asked for them to be forwarded.

His mood grew darker as the beer evaporated and a helicopter flew overhead, jarring the air as it made for the heliport upriver. Just a couple of miles on the other side Jemma would be fixing a solitary supper – or would she? There were no agreed rules for their separation, nothing more than the understanding that

Jemma needed space and time 'to make sure that what we're about to do is the right thing'. It had sounded almost reasonable, particularly after she'd finished shagging his brains out on the sofa, but, as the days passed and he became all too familiar with the eccentricities of living on the water, his world began to grow ever more lonely. How much longer? he'd asked on the phone. But she couldn't, wouldn't, say. He'd suggested a drink at their favourite pub but she'd turned him down. It wouldn't help, she'd said. Would they end the evening with a chaste goodbye or making up for lost time behind some park bush? 'This is the biggest step I'll ever take in my life, Harry. Just give me time.'

Time to rip off the top of a fifth bottle, or was it the seventh?

He tried to banish thoughts of Jemma from his mind. Instead, he latched on to the memory of Delicious standing in her shower, but, even as the memory inspired that special sensation of warmth inside, the image changed to the wrinkled face of Susannah Ranelagh. Why had she kept coming back, year after year? Not to celebrate any parent's birthday: they were both probably long gone from this world. And not simply for a holiday, not during the encroaching greyness of October. Harry felt more than a little lost. He sat back, closed his eyes, tried to empty his mind and listen to the music of the old river while its current carried his cares away downstream.

Suddenly and with considerable violence, he launched himself from his chair and clattered backwards down the narrow steps from the sundeck in so much haste that he almost lost his footing. Even before he'd taken breath he was rifling through his bag, pulling out his father's battered file and tipping the contents onto the bed. There it was, the passport. Filled with a chaos of stamps from border-control points around the globe that marked Johnnie's journey through the last dozen or so years of his life. The trading capitals of the world, the powerhouses of global prosperity, set out alongside a clutch of sandy islands that did excellent trade in turtle soup and tax havens. There were no immigration stamps to disclose when he'd come back to Britain – for a British passport holder that wasn't necessary – but Harry remembered the intermittent contact he'd had with his father in those last years, an occasional telephone call to say he was back in the country, a hastily scribbled postcard, a letter on the notepaper of some London hotel, all discarded into the nearest bin. And every one of them, he seemed now to remember, during the dismal months of autumn. Between the stiff covers of the passport he found the evidence – stamps from other jurisdictions that gave date and location for his wandering. His thumbs fumbled in their haste as they picked out visas marking immigration and exit from Belize, Morocco, the United States, Vietnam, Singapore, the Cayman Islands, Norway, Cyprus, Panama, Malaysia, Canada, Russia. Never seeming to settle. And, as he held open the pages and tried to reconcile the markings, he found a hole in every year of the record that could only be explained by one thing. He had come home. In October.

Whatever Susannah Ranelagh had been up to, Johnnie had been there, too.

'What bloody secret are you hiding?' Harry shouted, throwing the passport down in anger. He glared in pain out of the window. The sun was glowering in the evening sky; the waters turned a shade of volcanic red. That was the trouble with rivers like the Thames. No sooner had they shifted all the crap in your life downstream than the tide turned and shoved it straight back at you.

—⁓—

A backstreet in Tottenham, north London. An old Victorian pub with dark tiles and sticky varnish and pies that protested, perhaps too vehemently, that they were a hundred per cent beef. Not a pub that attracted passing trade. Hughie Edwards was sitting in a booth nursing a large whisky, turning the rim of the glass slowly with the tips of his fingers, inspecting it carefully as though hoping to find a part of the glass that held more alcohol than another. He was alone. He stayed staring at his glass until the pub door opened and four men sauntered in; it was darts night. Edwards looked up, nodded. One of the men, a small black guy with nervous eyes and greying curly hair, scowled and muttered to his friends before making his way over.

'Evening, Billy.'

'Hello, Mr Edwards. What a surprise.' The other man's voice with its Trinidadian roots was stripped of any trace of enthusiasm.

'Mine's a whisky. Get yourself whatever you want.'

The scowl came back. 'You can get yourself all sorts of things on a dark night in these parts, Chief Inspector. Like totally fucked. You should be careful.'

'Even on a dark night I would know it was you, Billy-boy, from the smell of all that black bullshit. Make sure mine's a large one.'

Billy swallowed his contempt and trundled across to the bar, returning with a whisky and a pint of lager with the head already taken off. 'As I was saying, it's a great pleasure to see you again, Mr Edwards,' he declared, setting himself down on the opposite bench of the booth. 'What brings you to these parts?'

'Old times.'

Billy sniffed and stared at his glass.

Many years before, when Edwards had been no more than a trainee detective constable at the start of his career, he had nicked Billy under the old sus laws for door handling – being found trying car doors with intent to steal either the contents or the car itself. Billy served only a short period of 'bird', a couple of months, but when, a little later, he'd been discovered to be a minor part of a high-value car-ringing scam and faced a much longer stretch inside, Edwards had given him a break. The policeman's sights had been set on those much higher up the food chain and he'd decided Billy would be more useful to him outside than in. As Billy had discovered on repeated occasions in the years since, ambitious policemen have a need for the sort of support team that never appears on the payroll. He had also discovered that Edwards had a very long memory.

So they sat and they chatted, of times past and times that were to come, both for themselves and for Harry Jones. Totally screwed up Billy's game of darts.

—◆—

It was late, almost touching midnight. The insistent burble of the phone cut through the peace of the hour, echoing through the elegant rooms and tiled corridors of the old house.

'Yes?' an irritated voice responded, although the strains of a Beethoven piano sonata in the background betrayed that he hadn't been asleep.

'It's me.'

There was no need for any further introduction: the caller's voice had always adopted a pronounced sibilance when he was drunk, even when he was young.

The other man didn't respond immediately, wanting to collect his wits, making it clear that the interruption was unwelcome. 'What do you want?' he said eventually.

'Johnnie's son. He's written. Wants to meet.'

'So?'

'But I can't. What do I tell him?' Alarm battled with alcohol for mastery of the caller's voice.

'You tell him nothing. You and Johnnie were university friends and it was all a long time ago. You can manage that, can't you?'

The sound of slurping trickled down the line. College port. He'd never got out of the habit. 'But what if he asks questions?'

'Of *course* he will ask questions. He will ask questions because he doesn't know. Keep it that way.'

'But—'

'You have to meet with him. Otherwise he will become suspicious. Don't do that. Harry Jones is a hunter, he will track you down like a wolf.'

'I don't think I can do it.'

'You must do it. You have no choice. And there is one other thing you have to do.'

'Tell me,' the caller pleaded.

'You will do it sober. We all know that when you drink it brings out the more ... *vulnerable* side of you.' The word came loaded with meaning they both understood but had never discussed, not in all the years. It was the nature of groups such as theirs that they didn't waste their time discussing the finer points of morality. 'Anyway, Harry's doing you a favour, giving you warning. It means he doesn't suspect.'

'I'm just not sure what to say.'

'Praise the Lord and quote some scripture – you can manage that, can't you? For pity's sake, you've had enough practice dodging questions. After all, that's what's kept you one step ahead of your accusers all these years,' he said, not bothering to hide his contempt as he put the phone down.

CHAPTER NINETEEN

Harry stumbled through the night sleepless on a diet of headache and hangover. At around two he had tried to call Jemma but experience had cut through the alcohol and at the last second he had hit the cancel button. He waited until he thought he was sober enough, and she was about to leave for school. His throat felt as if it had been scrubbed with raw chillies.

'Jem.'

'I'm rushing, Harry.'

'They arrested me again yesterday.'

That stopped her in her tracks.

'Are you ...?'

'No, they let me go.'

'What do you need?'

'First thing, to know that you still care. That's very important to me right now.'

'I care. Of course I bloody care, otherwise this wouldn't all be hurting so much. And you sound like crap. Have you been drowning your sorrows?'

'And second—'

'Somehow I knew it wasn't going to be as simple as they arrested you on suspicion of murder. Why should it be simple, just because it's the last week of term?'

'I'm trying to find a woman.'

'Never needed my help for that before.'

'No, a special woman, a specific woman.' Damn, he was making a mess of this. Perhaps he wasn't as sober as he'd thought. 'Don't know her name but she's the daughter of a chap called Findlay Francis. You heard of him?'

'No.'

'I need to find her. Or him.'

'How am I supposed to help?'

'Social media, Facebook, that sort of thing. You're the expert.'

'Any other clues?'

'He's gone missing.'

She sighed, weary. 'No, don't tell me, Harry, I'm going to find him dangling from your wretched family tree.'

'He was a friend of my father. Another one from the photo. Disappeared. That's five out of the seven. This doesn't smell like coincidence, Jem: this stinks like an old abattoir.'

She had to make a decision, and it would be an important one. Harry was asking for help, practically pleading, and that was a first. And she still smelled of Steve, no matter how long she'd stood soaking in the shower.

The ground was shifting; she no longer felt sure of her footing. She had allowed their relationship to restart because it was so superficial that it counted for nothing, nothing more than totally transient sex. Or that was how it had been, but something had changed. Steve had changed. His roving eye now seemed fixed on her, she found it more difficult to brush away the compliments, they sounded sincere, they stuck. Steve – sincere? She'd even stopped finding strange hairs embedded in his brush. He could never be Harry, of course. She loved Harry but – could she live with him? Steve was so predictable, great body, no holes, no scars, no previous, no ambition other than to be a good teacher while Harry ... Steve and she had spent a couple of evenings using the pool and gym, finished off with a game of mixed basketball, nothing serious, only enough to work up a thirst, and the previous evening they'd both gone up for a high ball together and ended up in each other's arms. Sweat, scent, raw sexual tension. 'Love you,' he'd whispered in her ear before chasing off after the game, but the look he threw behind him said he meant it. Damn him! It wasn't supposed to get like this, to confuse her.

Now Harry was on the phone confusing her all the more. One day she'd come to her senses and give up bloody men. One day.

'I'll see what I can do,' she said.

A missing elderly author. A daughter with no name. Not much to go on, as puzzles went, but Jemma had solved much of it in her lunch break between helpings of homemade pasta. In fact, it took less than the time taken to finish a mouthful. She typed the name Findlay Francis into her Facebook account and no sooner had she done so than the screen filled with possibilities. There were more than a hundred hits but only one that was tagged with the word 'MISSING'. A page set up by his family seeking information about a missing father and grandfather. The details were decidedly frugal. A photo of a man in middle age rather than a seventy year old. An acknowledgement that he travelled to many parts of the world for his job but it was believed he had gone missing while back in Britain. 'The police can't help, so can you?' the page pleaded. It was all pretty bald so far as these things went, lacking the passion and emotional incontinence of the genre, which was perhaps why it had been hit by only a relatively small number of 'likes'. And the contact details were restricted to a specially constructed 'findlayfrancismissing' address. Vague to the point of mystery, yet nevertheless Jemma typed in a message about her partner Harry having information that he thought might be helpful and asking for a reply. The bell for afternoon classes was ringing. She punched the button. There was nothing more to be done, except wait.

—⁂—

At last the bishop had replied, sent an e-mail, part-apology for the delay, part-explanation on account of his overcrowded diary, but declaring that he would be delighted to make time for the son of Johnnie Maltravers-Jones. He had a gap, before a lunch appointment, eleven thirty in the restaurant at the top of the Gherkin, where he would be sitting at a table reserved in the name of his host, a leading City financial operation.

The Gherkin, it seemed to Harry, was an unusual hideaway for a man of religion. Built on the ruins of the old Baltic Exchange after it had been blown to oblivion by an IRA bomb, along with a fifteen-year-old girl and two others, the forty-one-storey structure clad in glass had rapidly established itself as one of the delights of the City's skyline. It was an unabashed exercise in phallicism or picklery, depending on one's viewpoint – and, of course, in money, vast amounts of it, which accounted for the heavy security and exceptionally clean windows. Harry had to change lifts in order to get to the top of the building and found the bishop sitting at a window table where a bottle of exotic glacier water cast a shadow on the crisp white table-cloth. The cleric was twisting a large amethyst ring on his right hand, seeming lost in thought as he gazed out at the view that, from nearly six hundred feet, was breathtaking. To one side he found the royal medieval walls of the Tower of London and the cupola of St Paul's Cathedral; to the other Harry could see down to the honey-cake crenellations of the Houses of Parliament. The Gherkin looked down on them all.

The bishop looked up. 'Welcome,' he said, extending a hand. The fingers were thin, almost clawlike, the sensation of awkwardness exaggerated by the missing top of his little finger, and a body that once had been a power on the rugby pitch was now wizened and slightly bent. A man past his prime. There was an air of sadness about his pale eyes; the lips were pink and moist, constantly moving as though searching for some elusive word. A band of white hair curled around the margins of his otherwise bald head in an echo of the clerical collar he wore above his black clerical shirt, and around his neck he wore an elaborate pectoral cross in the Anglo-Catholic tradition. 'It's a pleasure to meet with you, Mr Jones – may I call you Harry?'

Even as Harry took his place, looking down the meander of the Thames to the haze-covered country-side of Kent beyond, a waitress appeared at his elbow.

'Tea? Coffee? Something stronger?' the bishop enquired.

'Tea, thank you. Indian.'

The waitress moved serenely away.

'Quite a place you have here, Bishop Randall,' Harry said.

'Not my perch, of course. This is the world of Mammon and I'm no more than an occasional visitor. I try to catch a few crumbs from the tables. The Church so desperately needs them.'

'I suspect there are some pretty impressive crumbs.'

'Yes, but from this height they tend to fall a long way. My task is to persuade those men of very profound wealth that they can afford not only their yachts, several ex-wives and assorted young companions but also a conscience.'

'You had a career in the City before you joined the Church, didn't you?'

'Ah, you've done your homework,' the bishop chuckled, his lips moving like the ripples on a pond – although in truth there had been remarkably little information about the bishop to be found: a sparse *Wiki* entry, few interviews or profiles, no evangelical out-pourings. 'I found the City ... unfulfilling.'

Harry's tea arrived; he let it stand for a while.

'But we have so much to talk about and so little time,' the bishop said, moving them on. 'How can I help?'

'I was hoping you could tell me a little about my father.'

'Ah, the Blessed Johnnie. Did you know he was a very fine scrum half?'

'I had no idea.'

'Could have got a blue if he'd applied himself.'

'You did, didn't you?'

The bishop nodded. 'But for Johnnie there were always ...' – he sighed – 'too many distractions.'

'What sort of thing?'

The bishop began, picking his words with care. 'He was always very ... enterprising. Had no money and not much background. In places like Christ Church at that time such things mattered. Every staircase had its earl or an honourable, there was even a maharajah floating about the place. It was still very *Brideshead* but Johnnie never let such things stop him. He made himself useful.'

'How?'

'He would organize extravagant trips during the vacations. Skiing at Klosters, summers in Venice, that sort of thing. Always led from the front, did Johnnie. First down a black slope, first into the bar and' – the damp lips wobbled in amusement – 'it has to be said, he was always first up to the prettiest woman in the room. Your father always made his mark.'

'Took risks, you mean?'

As Wickham reminisced he ran a finger down his crucifix. Harry noticed that his fingers were beautifully and almost certainly professionally manicured. Perhaps he was making up for the fact that he was down on the digit count. 'You have to remember it was the sixties. The Vietnam War, the Beatles, Profumo, the Pill. The world trembled, everything seemed to be up for grabs, every rule was questioned. It was a time when, for a while, I lost my own faith. But your father never had much time for rules. What he had instead was a large number of friends. Extraordinary. I think Johnnie invented the game of networking – everyone from aristocrats to an engineering student from Worksop. Named

Richards, I think he was, quite brilliant academically but without a single social skill that anyone could discover. Latchkey kid with a working-class grudge, hated Oxford. But Johnnie made friends with him and discovered he had a peculiar skill with telephones. Could beat the system. In those days when you wanted to make a call you had to drop four large old pennies into the slot before the operator would connect you. Richards discovered that simply by tapping the receiver in the right way he could mimic the sound of the coins dropping and get his call home for free. Then he expanded. Built himself a little gadget tied together with tape and with wires sticking out of it that enabled him to make calls to any part of the world. In those days you had to book international calls and they cost several fortunes. Johnnie had a lot of pals with girlfriends in the States or Switzerland or Australia, rich pals who were more than happy to pay for the pleasure of chatting up their young ladies, particularly if at the same time they could add to it the exquisite titillation of cheating the General Post Office. Johnnie and Richards went into business together and made some very serious money.'

Harry was astounded, almost breathless in anticipation. It was as though a page of history – his own history – was being turned for the first time. 'What happened?'

'Richards got caught, of course. Got himself arrested and charged with some ludicrous offence like misappropriation of Her Majesty's electricity. The authorities were making it up as they went along. They'd never come across anything like that before. Ridiculous, couldn't make it stick. Richards was found not guilty and as he walked down the steps of the court the men from the GPO came to their senses and offered him a job.'

'And my father?'

'Always one step ahead. Nobody could lay a finger on Johnnie, got away with it, always did.'

'I suppose he did,' Harry muttered, an edge of bitterness souring his tone. 'You and he were good friends?'

'For a while, yes. It was a time of sharing. Pimm's, poetry, long afternoons in punts, and exceptionally pretty people. Everyone was pretty in the sixties.'

'And the Aunt Emma club.'

'Ah, yes, the Aunt Emmas. Just an informal gathering, very gentle. At that time we undergraduates weren't allowed in the full university club, so we called ourselves the Junior Croquet Club and hacked away on college lawns. And your father, Harry, was the meanest man with a mallet I ever knew.' The bishop laughed. 'A total tiger in front of the hoops, while I was always a bit of a headless chicken, I fear.'

'And after university? You kept in touch?'

'Summer's colour fades. Young people drift apart. I went into the City while he ... well, Johnnie continued making friends, finding opportunities wherever he could.'

Harry reached for the photograph in his pocket, realizing that the bishop's stories had already swallowed up so much of his time. 'These people ...' He put the photo down on the crisp linen tablecloth and pointed. 'There's you. My father.'

'Well, well,' Wickham said, fumbling for his pince-nez glasses, which emerged from his suit breast pocket attached to a thin gold chain. He was almost foppish but a bishop could get away with it.

'You were both friends of Susannah Ranelagh.' Harry pointed once more.

'Yes, her name strikes a chord. Not close friends, not in my case, at least, no more than an occasional leap around the croquet lawn. I wonder what became of her.'

'This is Christine Leclerc. And the one she's got her arm around is Ali Abu al-Masri.'

'Yes, I remember them. Followed their careers from afar. So sad.'

'And this one's Findlay Francis, isn't it?'

The bishop squinted. 'Is it? Was that his name? I

don't remember, it was such a long time ago. Mind you, at my age most things were a long time ago.'

'It just struck me as strange that so many members of your croquet club seem to have come to a sad end.'

'Three score and ten.'

'I think it was more than that.'

The bishop's lips lost their rhythmic beat and pursed in curiosity. 'What do you mean, Harry?'

Harry searched the cleric's eyes. 'A plane crash. An assassination. A sudden heart attack. Now both Susannah Ranelagh and Findlay Francis have disappeared.'

'Have they? I didn't know.'

'I think my father and Miss Ranelagh kept in touch. I think they met up every year, in October.'

'Really? How good of them.'

'I was wondering, do you know anything about that? Their friendship? Their meetings? Was it an annual get-together of the Croquet Club, something like that? And who was this third woman? She's a total mystery. Do you have any idea?'

The bishop dragged his eyes away from the photograph and took off his glasses. 'Harry, you know more than I do. I'm afraid I can't help you.'

'You didn't keep in touch with other members of the club?'

'The other Aunt Emmas? No, not really, not even your father. He travelled so much.'

'Can I ask when you last met him?'

'You know, I'm not entirely sure. Perhaps during a gaudy at Christ Church, a reunion dinner. But there would have been so many others there and old minds grow weary—'

'I'd like you to think about that really hard if you would, Bishop Randall. Any little connection, any detail you might be able to remember, no matter how small.'

'Of course, I shall. And if it doesn't offend you I'd like to remember him in my prayers. But I fear there is little else I can do for you, especially today.' He glanced at his wristwatch. 'I hope you'll understand and forgive me. My luncheon companion will be here any minute. I'd love to introduce the two of you but he and I are about to have a . . . a very delicate discussion.'

'Falling crumbs.'

'Even the Good Samaritan required a few crumbs to undertake God's work. So if you'll excuse me, Harry . . .' He pushed back his chair and rose, extending both hands, which wrapped around Harry's own.

'Might I have an address for you, a telephone number, Bishop Randall?'

'Of course, but I . . . I travel rather a lot. You can

always track me down through the Church Commissioners' office, that's easiest. They always know where I am. Or e-mail.'

It didn't sound like too much of an excuse, not from a man of his age.

'God guard your every step, Harry.'

The bishop released his grip. As Harry turned and walked towards the lift, he realized he hadn't even touched his tea. And the bishop, who could remember every detail about an engineering student named Richards, could barely recall even the names of his own friends.

—∞—

Long after dark and still hours before dawn, Billy stood in the cover provided by a bookie's shop doorway. It hadn't taken much to find Harry's old Volvo parked in a side street. Edwards had provided the registered address and, with parking restrictions in London as tight as a Chancellor's purse, the car was never going to be far away. Billy eyed the street one more time. Nothing. He stared contemptuously at the car. It would have taken him less time to break into it than it would to hit a dartboard from three feet, but there was no need. He knelt down beside the rear number plate, peered underneath to make sure there was no obstruction, then

293

wriggled his way beneath until he was alongside the line of the exhaust pipe. With a pencil light clamped between his teeth he inspected the underside of the car above the rear axle and, with a wire brush he pulled from the pocket of his camouflage trousers, scraped the thin layer of road dirt away until he had a sound surface. From his other pocket he produced a gadget barely larger than a box of cooking matches. Mail-order. A vehicle tracking device. GPS straight to your mobile phone. Battery life of three weeks, twelve months on standby. Real-time locations, password-protected and lots of other crap Billy didn't need to understand. 'An ideal solution to the challenge of tracking company employees who are not working diligently. Also for use in domestic circumstances for resolving relationship issues.' The tracker had three large magnets that he used to attach it to the scrubbed area, where it located with a satisfying clunk. He allowed himself a smile. This was so much easier than the usual shit Edwards insisted that he jump into. Perhaps the dick-head policeman was going soft in his declining years. Maybe it was time to stand up to the slime-ball. For sure, next time, maybe, probably, that's what he'd do. What goes up can be shoved further up. But no sooner had he vowed on the virtue of a hundred virgins that he'd quit being a loser than Billy froze. Two piercing bright eyes were staring at him. He jerked his head in panic and banged into the underside of the axle. As if someone had hit him with a hammer. As Billy let out a stream of curses, the old dog fox sauntered away.

It was only as Billy was kneeling in the gutter brushing the dirt from his shirt that he noticed the fox had left something behind, something that he was now kneeling in. Edwards's fault. One day he would make sure that bastard got what was coming to him. Meanwhile, and accompanied by another bout of cursing, Billy followed the fox into the night.

CHAPTER TWENTY

It was the weekend, a lazy start to the day, and necessary after the previous evening, which had involved not only an hour of mixed basketball but also an intense time at the bar afterwards when Jemma had been interrogated by another couple, friends of Steve. They had probed and pushed, particularly the woman, testing her about the relationship with Steve when he disappeared to the toilet. It had made her feel uncomfortable. 'Just good friends' didn't hack it: they'd clearly got a very different impression from Steve. She hadn't been much of an active participant in the sex when they'd got back to his place. She hadn't slept well and was up early, making coffee, when she heard her laptop warbling from within the depths of her overnight bag. She flipped it open on the kitchen table and saw it was a Skype call. From 'findlayfrancismissing'. She ran a vague hand through the mess of her hair and hit the video button. Her face popped up at the bottom of the screen and she immediately regretted opening the video link: her hair screamed of Friday night fornication. But the rest of the screen remained blank. The caller was being cautious.

'Hello, this is Jemma Laing.'

A woman's voice, hesitant. 'This is Findlay Francis's daughter. You wanted to talk.'

'That's right.'

'Hope you don't mind me not showing my face but when you post a missing-persons page it seems that almost every sicko in the business climbs on board.'

'Fair enough.'

'That's why I called early, before the sickos get out of bed.'

'Nearly caught me out, too.'

'Sorry,' the woman apologized but the voice was still uncertain, unconvinced.

'No problem. I'm a teacher, my body clock kicks me out of bed early every morning.' She ran another desperate comb of fingers through the mop of auburn hair. It appeared on the screen like a gushing spring. 'Can I have a name?' she asked.

'I'm Abigail. You can call me Abby.'

'Morning, Abby,' Jemma responded, trying to reassure, sipping her mug of coffee.

'You said your partner, Harry ... that he wanted to talk about my father. I have to tell you right from the start there's no reward, nothing like that.'

'That's not why he wants to talk.'

'So what exactly does he want?'

'I'd rather he explained the details himself. Your father and his father were friends at Oxford, apparently. And it seems that several of the friends they shared have gone missing.'

'He thinks there's a connection?' Abby said, her voice rising in alarm.

'I think he wants to swap stories, show you some photos. Shake a few memories.'

'Oh dear. What happened to his father?'

'He died of a heart attack some years ago. Before Harry and I got together.'

'Sorry but ... I'm just not sure. The last person who promised to help me turned out to be a spiritualist; the one before that wanted me to join their prayer group. I really don't know.'

'You might think Harry was even worse. He was once a politician.'

A squawk of surprise that might have been misery came from the laptop.

'Look, Abby, his father was Johnnie Jones – I think he called himself Maltravers-Jones. Both he and your father were at Oxford in 1962. Ring any bells?'

Suddenly the full screen came to life and Jemma saw the round face of a middle-aged woman with spiky purple hair and dark eyes hidden behind oversized spectacles the colour of daffodils. She was wearing a T-shirt decorated with the image of an elephant and she was sitting in a makeshift domestic office in front of an overcrowded noticeboard made up of cork tiles. The overriding theme of the room appeared to be chaos and cats. A long-haired tabby was sitting on the bookcase while Abby was sucking her lip nervously.

'Hi, Abby!' Jemma waved a hand in greeting. 'Nice to meet you properly.'

'Hello, Jemma. Me, too. If – *if* – I agreed to meet him, would you be there, too?'

'Er, would that be entirely necessary?'

'Yes, I think it would. I'm not meeting any more men on their own.'

'Abby, if you're to make any progress finding out what happened to your father I think you're going to have to take the risk.'

'Maybe.' Suddenly Abby's eyes widened in surprise and she leaned forward intently into the screen. In the box at the bottom of Jemma's screen, showing what her camera was revealing to Abby, a body was moving in the background. A naked body. Steve. Ears plugged into music. Scratching himself. Utterly heedless. Heading for his coffee.

'Is that Harry?' Abby whispered.

'Um, no. It's complicated.'

'I bet.'

'Sorry, I didn't mean to offend—'

'You haven't, Jemma, believe me. Made my day. I was young. Once.' She giggled, stifling it with her hand. 'Look, if you're willing to take risks, I suppose I am, too.'

—∞—

'You ever think about coming back to this place, Harry?'

'No, but occasionally I think of doing a little root-canal surgery on myself.'

'In which case, you'll be needing a touch more anaesthetic.' Cyrus Harefield leaned forward and poured more Sauvignon. Harefield was a senior Member of Parliament – 'the crust on the vintage port', as he described it – and also sat as a Church Commissioner, a member of the group responsible for safeguarding the property and other assets of the Church of England. The Terrace of the House of Commons was a favourite hiding place, away from the turmoil of the chamber and the interminable plotting of the younger brethren. On the other side of the river the multicoloured lights on the wheel of the London Eye turned slowly through the night while the sound of bagpipes drifted from the direction of Westminster Bridge. The neon-blue lights of an ambulance sped towards St Thomas' on the other bank. Nothing had changed, it seemed, since Harry had sat here in his own right and poured his own wine.

'But you should, you know,' Harefield continued as he dunked the empty bottle back into the ice. 'You were the best and the brightest, Harry, yet you got shafted. You could right that terrible wrong. Damn, but we need you.'

'You seem to have survived without me.'

'Perhaps too well,' Harefield said, tucking a thumb into his belt, which seemed to have gained a notch with every election campaign. 'At times I feel my job is to eat for England – or, at least, the *Church* of England.' He chuckled. 'You look as if you could do with a few extra pounds. Come back, find your feet once more.'

'I don't feel at home here any longer.'

'We could put you in the Lords.'

'It's come to that, then, has it?'

Harefield roared with laughter at his old friend, sending an inquisitive seagull scurrying away along the parapet. 'Yes, I suppose ambition should be carried

302

on rather more supple thighs.' In the middle of the channel a pleasure cruiser was turning, its screw beating the river and sending a bow wave slapping against the embankment. They watched its battle with the tide before returning to their conversation. 'So, you wanted to know about Bishop Randall. What, *precisely*, did you have in mind?'

'He is, of course, a good man of the cloth.'

'Diligent, godly and sober. Or most of the time, anyway. OK, we've got that out of the way, Harry, so what more do you need to know?'

'I think he's false and entirely two-faced, Cy. You tell me.'

Harefield mined a bowl of nuts and began throwing them one by one into his mouth as he considered the request. 'It's no great secret that Bishop Randy is a man of more than a little controversy. But why do you think he's a shit? I thought you said he was a friend of your father's.'

'Being a friend of my father's doesn't help.'

'Ah.'

'There's too much about the bishop that doesn't add up – or perhaps adds up to too much. His nails are manicured, his teeth too expensively capped. He wears a tailored suit you couldn't afford and a watch that is simple and elegant, and also very Swiss.'

'Yes, for a humble man of the cloth he has it cut from a rather splendid fibre.' More nuts disappeared, fuel for his thoughts. 'But Randy is controversial in part because he's so bloody successful. Climbed his way up the greasy pole of clerical preferment, ended up in a bishop's palace. You don't do that without stepping on a few bunioned toes. Yet I do so hate this evangelical need to decry success. God knows, the Church could do with a little more of it rather than spitting in its face. And, yet . . .' Harefield sighed. 'Envy isn't very ecclesiastical, Harry, but it's hellish common. And the man simply refuses to stop.' He reached for his glass.

'So what's the other part? You said his success is only one reason for his notoriety.'

Harefield savoured his wine as if it held many secrets before he returned to his tale. 'He was a City slicker in his early days. Got himself involved in a lot of controversial takeovers in the eighties. It was a little like the Wild West, plenty of shootouts and shady deals, bodies being dragged away. There were some who thought that Randy should have been one. The Serious Fraud Office had their eye on him for some time; he was arrested more than once but never charged. There are some who believe that it was the heat they put on him that forced him out of the City.'

'Into the hands of God?'

'Where he has used his talents to considerable effect. I only wish I had his wisdom, or his luck. There are those who accept that his talents are God-given and, anyway, don't give a damn who's driving the fire engine when the bloody house is on fire. And there are those ... yes, there are those who think that the support he gives God has a good deal of help.'

'Inside help?'

'Who's to know? He delivers. Harry, last year more than a hundred churches closed their doors for good. Our pension fund's hollowed out, there are retired vicars living below the poverty line and you can buy an old church and turn it into a carpet warehouse, theme bar – even a mosque. So for everyone who has their doubts about Randy there are a hundred who fall onto their knees in thanks. And he's devoted to his duties, there's no doubt about that. Well, I suppose you can when you're unmarried.' Harefield left the words dangling in the night air.

'I see.'

'Do you? Do you, Harry? Because I'm damned if I do. I just refuse to believe those twisted little rumours that float around in dark corners, they sicken me. But ...' He blew out his cheeks as if about to climb a very high wall. 'There were accusations of molestation made against him at one of his early parishes.'

305

'Molestation?'

'Young boys. In Penrith.'

'What happened?'

'What all too often happened in those days. They weighed a frightened child's word against that of a man of God and transferred Randy to a living in the West Country.' His hand scrabbled in the bowl of nuts but they were gone.

'Sermons and secrets.'

'Not an exclusive preserve of Catholics.' Harefield reached for the bottle. 'Ah, the Sauvignon's finished. Dare we try another? I have this terrible taste in my mouth that I'm desperate to wash away.'

'No, thanks, Cy.'

'You're probably right. Been too indiscreet as it is. And I don't have a shred of evidence against him, perhaps nothing but prejudice. Still, as an old friend, my advice is to steer well clear of him.'

'Can't do that,' Harry replied. 'Seems I need him more than ever.' And already he was tapping his iPhone asking for another meeting.

CHAPTER TWENTY-ONE

Harry didn't hear back from the bishop. Wickham was another one who seemed to have vanished. In spite of repeated requests directed both to his e-mail and through the Church Commissioners, Harry heard nothing, but after his chat with Cy Harefield it came as no great surprise. So once again he followed his father's footsteps back to Christ Church, where it had all started.

He didn't make an appointment, preferred the element of surprise, but he took the precaution of arriving with a box of chocolates wrapped in a bow. The green stretches of Tom Quad had a different air from the last time Harry had been here: the academic year had come to its glorious end and the undergraduates were gone, leaving the hallowed cloisters in the possession of fee-paying tourists who arrived by the busload, yet Helen was still in her place of command in the Steward's Office. He knocked on the door and walked in.

She looked up from her computer. 'Oh, hello, Mr Jones,' she said. 'What brings you here again?'

'I was passing, brought you these. A token.'

'Why, thank you, that's so kind. And I'm sorry about the bishop's details but—'

'Actually, I wasn't just passing. I need to ask you another favour.'

'And these chocolates are . . .'

'A bribe.'

She smiled at his audacity. 'I'm an old-fashioned girl, Mr Jones. A walnut whip could never be considered a bribe, more an offering.'

'Then may I offer you these?' Harry said, handing the box across. He felt he could do business with this young woman.

She was in her late twenties and wise for her years, used to dealing with all sorts from pompous Privy Councillors to confused Japanese tourists. She appreciated Harry asking for a favour rather than simply making demands, although the gentle bribe suggested the possibility of choppy waters. From outside the thick walls of her office came the sound of Old Tom striking the half-hour. 'Look, I'm just about to have my morning coffee break and it's far too nice a day to spend it inside a stuffy office. Would you like to join me for a walk around the Master's Garden?' she asked, rising from her chair.

They walked through the ancient cloisters with their worn stones and soon were in a walled garden. The day was gentle, the birdsong brisk, the breeze dancing through the army of lilies, sunflowers and roses that crowded the borders. A gardener was mowing the wide expanse of lawn that backed onto the cathedral, pulling out the croquet rings that barred his way. The sweetness of freshly crushed grass filled Harry's nostrils.

'My father,' he began as the gravel scrunched beneath their feet, 'was a rather untidy man in many ways. He left behind him quite a lot of loose ends, unfinished business, some of which involves his old university friends.'

'Like Bishop Randall. I did forward your letter. Have you not heard?'

'Yes, I did, thanks.' She seemed relieved. 'There were others, too. A man called Findlay Francis. I know he was up here at Christ Church, it was mentioned in his *Wiki* entry.'

'I'm sure I remember the name.'

They were at the halfway point on their stretch around the garden and sat on an old teak bench in the shade of a towering sycamore. 'Can I ask you how long you've been working here, Helen?'

'It's around five years now.'

'You see, until the time my father died in 2001, no matter where he was in the world, whatever he was up to, he came back to this country for a week or so. Always in the middle weeks of October. Religiously. Almost like a pilgrimage. And I think while he was here he met up with other Oxford friends, so I was wondering . . .'

'If they met up here?'

She was sharp as well as attractive.

'That's right. Look, October's the start of the academic year, Michaelmas term, and it would be a natural place to hold any reunion.'

'We encourage our alumni to visit. Bring their goodwill with them. And hopefully their money, too.'

'Old habits.'

The gardener had finished trimming the lawn and was knocking the croquet hoops into place with a wooden mallet. The sound of wood on iron echoed from the warm sandstone walls.

'So if they came back to Christ Church,' Harry continued, 'they'd probably have dinner at High Table. Maybe run up a bar bill in the SCR, stay overnight in the guest room, just as I did.'

Helen nodded.

'So I wondered if there might be any records.'

'Ah,' she sighed. She wrinkled her nose.

'Helen, I can't emphasize enough how important this is. All I need to know is if my father came back and, if he did, who he was with. That can't be covered by any privacy code, can it?'

'Frankly, I'm not sure. It's an odd one.'

'We're talking twenty, thirty, maybe forty years ago. Not even Cabinet papers are kept secret that long.'

She shook her head.

'There's a problem?'

'Even if it were OK to release that information – and I'm not saying that it is, you understand – I've no idea what sort of records there would be. It's pre-digital, nothing but scraps of old paper.'

'We could say I was undertaking research for my thesis.'

'Are you writing one?'

It was his turn to frown. 'Let me take a look. Please.'

'You want all of that for a walnut whip?'

'I swear I saw some champagne truffles in the box, too.'

She shook her head once more. 'Oh, Mr Jones, you're really rather wicked.'

'You see right through me.'

She sat staring at him while the breeze rattled the ancient branches above their heads. 'Mr Jones—'

'Harry, please, since we're almost partners in crime.'

'I've no idea whether this information should be regarded as confidential, and I doubt if anyone else does, either. They'd have to convene a committee, dust off the precedents, submit proposals to the proctors. And the proctors would only suck their thumbs for a while, then cover their backs by seeking the view of the Vice-Chancellor. Harry, this could get very messy, take months.' She paused for a final moment of reflection. 'So I'd better not ask.'

'Helen, I don't want to get you into any difficulties.'

'You won't. What you will do, Harry, is come to my office at three thirty. That's the time for my afternoon tea break. But you may find that I'll be out taking a walk along the river. Eating chocolates.'

—⁂—

Old Tom was ringing the half-hour as Harry rapped on Helen's door. There was no answer. He stepped inside and closed the door carefully behind him. The office was much as he had remembered it that morning, except the box of chocolates on her desk had been opened and both the walnut whip and the champagne truffle were gone. And, in the corner, an old filing cabinet stood with one of its drawers gaping open. In the rack of files there was one set apart from its neighbours. It was marked 'High Table: Guests'. The papers inside were old, chaotic, far from complete. Many of them consisted of no more than flimsy carbon copies.

But they were enough.

—ᴍ—

Waterloo train station. The place on the concourse level that had never quite decided whether it was a wine bar or a coffee shop. Overstuffed armchairs and tiny tables. It was the first occasion Jemma and Harry had come face to face since their time-out. She hadn't wanted to be there, to be any part of this, but Abby had insisted and Jemma had found it impossible to deny her.

'I'm not comfortable,' she'd explained to Harry. 'I'm not ready yet.'

'Have you stopped loving me, Jem?'

'No, but we both know that simply loving you was never going to be enough. It's working out how I might ever be able to live with you that I can't get my head around.'

She wasn't the first to have said something like that. Harry knew that if he tried to push things he would reopen wounds, perhaps do lasting damage. He'd have to make do with a double espresso.

Abby had suggested the meeting place and Jemma pointed her out to Harry as she stepped onto the escalator. Abby hid a good figure beneath shapeless clothes, wore a battered straw hat with an oversized brim and had a canvas bag slung over her shoulder that was large enough to carry essential supplies that would outlast the Apocalypse. As she drew nearer they saw she had an intricate henna tattoo covering her wrist and the back of her hand. Jemma waved, got a kiss for her troubles, while Harry got a guarded greeting and a handshake that made the army of bangles on her wrist jangle. She held his hand for several moments, as though trying to read his chakras, then seemed to find something of which she approved. 'Peace and love, Mr Jones.'

'Wouldn't *that* be nice?' he replied before disappearing to arrange an order of herbal tea and espressos.

Abby watched him go, studying the muscular body beneath the loose summer shirt and tightness of the trousers around his butt. 'Him – *and* the other?' she said to Jemma, in awe. 'As I said, I used to be young once, but never that young.'

'OK, Abby, these are the rules of engagement. You and Harry tell each other your secrets, you keep mine.'

'Do either of them have brothers?'

But already Harry was returning from negotiating with the waitress behind the bar and soon they were sipping their hot drinks. Harry produced his photo. 'Your father. My father,' he declared, pointing.

She whispered something inaudible and then sat silently, running her fingertip with its violently painted varnish across her father's face. It was clearly a moment of emotion and there was mistiness in her voice when she spoke again. 'I've never seen anything like that before. Old photos. When he was young.' When she looked up from the photo her eyes were filled with gratitude, and also with trust. 'I didn't really know my dad terribly well, you see. He split up with my mum when I was young, about ten, and after that he was little more than a visitor in my life. He wrote – you know that, of course – and that kept him travelling around the world. I can't say we ever had a proper relationship.' It was clearly a source of pain. 'But he did keep in contact. You know, it doesn't sound much, a postcard, but he sent me one every month from wherever he was. And he always sent me a dedicated copy of his books, nearly twenty of them, all told, about oil sheiks, film stars, disgraced politicians, royalty. Not my sort of stuff, really, but in every one he wrote a special message for me. He tried, I know that. He just wasn't very good at it.'

'Do you recognize the other faces?' Harry asked, indicating the photo.

Abby shook her head. 'I don't think I ever met any of his friends.'

'Where did he live when he was in this country?'

315

'He had a flat in Brighton for many years, overlooking the sea. Always loved the sea, said it helped him concentrate. But he had a problem – oh, it must have been about ten years ago, maybe a bit more. He was walking back home late one evening from his favourite drinking place, cutting through The Lanes, one of the alleyways a little back from the seafront, when he was attacked.'

'Mugged, you mean?' Harry asked as Abby took a sip of her tea.

'No, very badly beaten. Spent a couple of weeks in hospital. Could have been far worse but a couple of policemen heard the shouts and when they appeared the attackers ran off.'

'Who were they?'

'Never found out. The police decided it was probably a bit of gay bashing that got out of hand – but Dad wasn't like that; my mum used to say he wasn't very much inclined either way. The beating affected him, very much so. He told me it was to do with the book he was writing, someone trying to put him off. And it worked. He never finished it, started on something else.'

'Do you know who the book was about?'

'No. He wouldn't even discuss it. He didn't mind suffering for his art but no way was he going to die for it; he said no book was that important. Became very secretive, sold up in Brighton, moved.'

'Where?'

'I don't know. He became paranoid, hid himself away. Stopped using credit cards, it was always cash, didn't have a regular phone number. He spent much more time out of the country, said he was afraid they were still after him. But I never found out who "they" were. And I'm not even sure where he stayed when he was in Britain – somewhere in the West Country, that's all I know. He would come to see me in London and this is where we'd meet, Waterloo station. He got very cloak-and-dagger.'

'You said he travelled a lot for his work.'

'Seemed to spend half his life on planes and in hotels.'

'Did he come back to Britain regularly?'

She nodded. 'Yes. Every year. He'd research his subject, then come back here to write it all up. But only for a couple of months or so. He said he could write three thousand words a day so long as he was left alone.'

'Tell me, Abby, was there any particular time of year he came back home?' Harry asked, an edge to his voice.

'Yes, always in the autumn.'

'October?'

'That's right. September–October. Then sod off

317

before the snow, that's what he used to say. Before they caught up with him again.'

'So your father changed his life after the attack?'

'Completely.'

'Can you remember exactly when that was?'

'As I said, around ten years ago. No, perhaps a little more. I was still in my twenties.'

'Might it have been 2001?'

'No, no, not then. It was the autumn of the following year, 2002. I'm pretty sure of that,' she said, nibbling at her thumb as she concentrated. 'But we were all getting paranoid then, weren't we? After 9/11, just before the Iraq war.'

'And after that you saw him ...?'

'Once a year. He'd send me another postcard, arrange a meeting place, here, or sometimes at a Cuban restaurant around the corner. Only a couple of hours, it was never more than that. But, you know, he was always excited to see me, always apologizing for screwing up.'

The memories were getting to her; her lip trembled as Jemma squeezed her hand.

'And the last time, Abby?' Harry pressed. 'I'm sorry, but we have to know.'

She hesitated, reached inside her bag and produced a roll of kitchen towel. She tore off a sheet and began dabbing at her nose. 'At that table in the corner right there. Said he was working on a new book that was going to be the most important he'd ever written.'

'About who, what?'

'That's the scary thing: he said it was about himself. That it was time for the full story to come out.'

'And when was that?'

'The third of October last year. Then he went missing. I knew something had happened, you see, because the postcards stopped. I waited a few weeks before I went to the police but they didn't seem very interested, said there was no evidence he was still in the country, that he could have left on a ferry or something. He often did that.'

'And?'

'I pressed, of course, insisted they look, but he had no registered address, no car, no bank account, hadn't paid tax in Britain for years. I tried to explain but the policeman just kept sucking his pencil and shuffling papers around in his file. He said Dad had no real link with this country any more, so I said, "What about me?" He said a daughter he saw only once a year wasn't much of a link. I felt so . . . humiliated.'

A flush of emotion had risen from her chest and spread around her neck. Jemma squeezed her hand some more. Harry fiddled with an unused stick of sugar.

'So do you think you can help me, Mr Jones?' Abby said, giving her nose a defiant final wipe.

'I don't know.'

She shook her head bitterly.

'But I'll try.'

Her eyes came up, in despair, in hope.

'Somehow it's all linked to this photo,' he said. 'I think they met up every year. In October. Old friends who had a secret that kept drawing them together. Very successful friends, too – an international businessman, a wealthy single woman in Bermuda, a powerful official in Brussels, your father the biographer of the famous, my father the buccaneer, and even a bishop. Then something went wrong. This woman' – he began tapping the photo – 'Christine Leclerc, dies in a plane crash. That was in 2000. Then the following year this man, al-Masri, was murdered. My father died of a heart attack. Soon after that your father was beaten up, perhaps in an attempt to murder him, too. All around the same time. Then a few months ago your father went missing and this woman, Susannah Ranelagh, she's gone missing, too.' He looked directly at Abby, willing her to be strong. 'The police believe she may have been murdered.'

Abby let forth a soft moan but she didn't break down. 'My father isn't missing. He's dead. I know that. I think you know it, too.'

'What makes you so sure, Abby?'

'Thirty years of postcards. Every month from every corner of the world, even one time when he was in the hospital he got a nurse to write it. He would have sent me a postcard even if he'd been nailed to a cross. I think he was carrying too much guilt not to.'

'Too much love, Abby,' Jemma prompted.

Abby nodded, grateful. 'And now, nothing. I'm not going to find my father, I know that. But I would like to find the truth.' A change had come over Abby. Any sign of vulnerability had gone and in its place was heat and determination. 'That stupid policeman asked me why it mattered so much. "Your father spent less than a day with you in a decade," he said. Idiot. He was my father!'

'I understand, Abby,' Harry said, very softly.

They shared something unspoken between them and for a heartbeat Jemma felt a scratch of jealousy, cut out of the circle. 'We somehow need to find out where he was living,' she said.

'The police reckon he must have been renting a place, informally. Well, he did everything cash-in-hand. Paid no council tax, didn't appear on any electoral register. Probably rented a car the same way when he needed one.'

'The postcards.'

'Yes?'

'Did you keep any?'

'But I kept them all,' she replied, leaning down to her bag and hoisting it onto her lap. 'All three hundred and fifty-seven of them.' She reached inside and produced a shoebox, its lid secured with a leather strap. 'My father's life – in a stupid shoebox.' She undid the strap and lifted off the lid to reveal cards, bound with a strand of red wool for every year, in a neat row. Harry looked on wistfully – it was his turn to feel a scratch. All those postcards and letters from his own father that he'd thrown away with the rubbish, some of them unread. Thoughts offered, only to be discarded, memories lost. Perhaps if he'd kept them he would have understood them better now.

'May we look?'

'Yes, please,' she said. 'I want to share them with someone who believes.'

Carefully, respectfully, both he and Jemma unwrapped the woollen ties, a year at a time. Harry concentrated on the years since 2002, the year of the beating, and in particular the months Findlay had been in the country. And, like his father's passport, the postcards gave up their story. Most were scenes of coastlines and seaside towns. Chesil Beach. The Fossil Cliffs of West Bay. Two from Abbotsbury with the swans. One of the Cerne Abbas giant with the huge phallus cut from the chalk. Another three from Dorchester, Weymouth, and Burton Bradstock. From other places, too, but a pattern was emerging. He pushed aside their mugs to clear space, then laid a selection of the cards on the undersized table. The two women crowded round; he could feel Jemma's shoulder digging into his, the closest they'd been since – since too long. He flipped open his iPad and pulled up a map of a stretch of coastline, with an endless beach of shingle and pebbles rounded by the rocking of waves that created a lagoon stretching from Portland Spit almost to West Bay. Francis Drake had known this place, sheltered his ships here. Now Harry began pointing silently to the names of the towns and villages. They were all there, from the postcards. Every one of them.

'West Dorset.' The words came almost at a whisper. And even as he spoke them the station loudspeakers burst into life to announce that the direct service from Waterloo to Weymouth would be departing from Platform Four in fifteen minutes.

'It's still a pretty big area,' Abby said, not daring to raise her hopes too high.

'Thirty miles, thereabouts.'

'But sea. I'm sure he'd be by the sea, somewhere he could see it. Not inland.'

'Which means ...' – Harry wiped his fingers across the screen to enlarge the map – 'somewhere between here and the shoreline.' His finger ran along a coastal road, the B3157, that stretched west from Weymouth and passed through Abbotsbury and Burton Bradstock, hugging the coastline in places, veering away from it at others.

'Any family connection?' Harry asked.

'Not that I know of.'

'Then we'd better go look.'

'I'll take some time off from my job,' Abby pronounced.

'No, Abby.'

Harry contradicted her, perhaps a touch too firmly, and suddenly Abby went cold. She knew this wasn't to be the stuff of happy endings, yet she couldn't avoid whatever was waiting for them out there. 'He's my father, Harry.'

Harry hesitated, then nodded slowly in acceptance. 'Of course.' He turned to Jemma. 'You, too? I can't drive all the way there, not with this.' He waved his cast.

'It's coming off in a few days, so you said,' Jemma objected.

'They also said it would need weeks of physio.'

Jemma found their eyes on her. What choice did she have? Damn you, Harry!

'Thanks, Jemma,' Abby said, giving her a feminine look of understanding and encouragement. 'But, tell me, who are the other two in the photo?' She laid it on top of the postcards and leaned forward to interrogate it.

'Good question,' Harry replied before Jemma had time to change her mind. 'I don't know the woman, she's a complete mystery. Can't find anyone who says they remember her. But the man you're crushing beneath your forefinger is the former Bishop of Burton. His name's Randall Wickham.'

'And is he . . .?'

'Dead? No. But he's gone missing, too, in a manner of speaking. Gone into hiding, really. All of a sudden he's not returning my messages.'

'Is that important? Is he involved in all this?'

'Oh, yes, I think he is. Right up to his spotless clerical collar,' Harry said, tugging at the stick of sugar so hard that it suddenly burst and sent white granules scattering across the table.

—⁂—

At first the murder of Inspector Hope had seemed like a good break for Hughie Edwards. A pity, of course. Wouldn't wish that on anyone, least of all a professional colleague, but Edwards's career had spanned many years and even more murders. Business was business. And getting a result would be just what he needed to snatch that late promotion to superintendent he was after. The 'dash for cash', they called it. He wouldn't get another go, was fast running out of years, and had failed the process twice already. His last chance. So a body in the park within sight of Downing Street was a lucky break.

It had been something of a soft landing, so far as murders went, because it had been some time before they'd been able to confirm it was foul play; up to that point it had simply been a stray body, and a foreign one at that. Media interest had drained into the dry summer soil. There were no hassling reporters, no excitable press conferences. Hughie Edwards was in control of this one. Yet with every day that passed without progress his authority was slipping away. The stiff dicks that waved above his head were beginning to ask questions. It was, after all, a murder, and of a fellow police officer. Where are we on this one, Hughie? What forms have been filled, what boxes ticked?

The answer was that he was getting nowhere. What had started out as an opportunity was now beginning to undermine him, to bugger up his prospects of promotion. So he went for one of his long walks.

Hughie Edwards walked because he was Welsh,

because it helped him wear off two pints too many, and because he was an essentially lonesome type, most comfortable in the company of his grudges. He burned a little leather and found himself on the Jubilee footbridge spanning the Thames between Charing Cross and the South Bank. There was still plenty of foot traffic even at this late hour as people drifted away from the Festival Hall arts complex. A performance of *Look Back in Anger* had been playing at the National. Fitted Hughie's mood. A couple of young tarts had smiled at him as he'd passed, East European, novices, unsure of the rules of engagement in this foreign city. He ignored them; instead, he stood in the middle of the bridge, thinking of Delicious, smoking a cigarette, his dark thoughts swirling with the tide.

He knew it was Harry. Had to be. Four weeks on and still not a whisper of another suspect. The murder had had to be planned, which meant a link to Bermuda, and, despite an avalanche of e-mails and faxes trying to pin down any Bermudan with a British connection who might have a reason for wanting Delicious dead, not a single name had stood up to even the gentlest of testing. Which left Harry. A former soldier trained for violence whose life had suddenly been tipped over the edge and into the slurry pit that waited for failed politicians. That must have hurt, left him in all kinds of emotional turmoil – the profilers would have a field day with that – yet Harry had proved to be a canny bastard and now his superiors were growing impatient. You didn't win your super's spurs on unsolved cases. Edwards needed a name. He needed Harry.

He took a long draw on his cigarette and let the sultry air carry the smoke away. He took pride in being a decent cop, wouldn't fit Harry up, not on a charge of murder; but, precisely because it was so serious, it made it all the more important to get a result and, in Edwards's experience, reading the rule book never got you out of the sodding library. They'd get a break in the case eventually – they almost always did – but eventually was no bloody good to Edwards. Eventually sucked; eventually he would be out of the force and on his uppers. The case – Harry – needed a bit of a shaking, given a nudge in the right direction.

He took a last pull on his cigarette and watched the glowing butt spiral down into the flowing darkness below. He glanced round, almost nervously as if someone might be reading his thoughts, but there was no one. Even the hookers had gone. No, he was going to be all right, get Harry Jones sorted, banded and de-bollocked like a day-old lamb with a sprig of rosemary and the roasting tray already waiting. Harry was going to go down. He'd bet his super's pension on it.

CHAPTER TWENTY-TWO

Albany was one of the most prestigious yet peculiar addresses in central London. Built in the late eighteenth century for the first Viscount Melbourne, it was later converted into a series of 'sets' or apartments for eminent bachelors. One of them was Lord Byron, the poet-politician who proceeded to behave outrageously with Melbourne's daughter-in-law, Lady Caroline Lamb. What made the liaison all the more disreputable was the fact that she was married to the second Viscount Melbourne, one of Queen Victoria's favourite prime ministers. Discretion required disguise, and Lady Caroline was smuggled into the strictly all-male preserve of Albany dressed as a page boy.

In the two centuries since, the residents' behaviour may have been toned down and the rules relaxed a

little, but Albany is still a socially exclusive enclave
tucked away behind the urban bustle of Piccadilly from
which children, pets and unwanted visitors are banned.
Which presented Harry with a problem. He knew this
was where Randall Wickham lived – thirty seconds
interrogating Helen's computer had told him as
much – and he also knew the bishop had just arrived
home because he'd seen him climbing out from his taxi.
But, by the time Harry had tumbled from his seat in the
window of the coffee house from where he was keeping watch, the bishop had disappeared inside. The
pillared entrance was guarded by two porters in uniform whose jobs depended on maintaining the sanctity
of the place. Harry strode hastily up the steps. A porter
stood at the top, barring his way.

'Afternoon, sir,' he said. 'Can I help you?'

Harry produced his wallet from his inside pocket
and brandished it at the porter. 'I've just been having
lunch with Bishop Randall,' he explained, 'been trying
to catch up with him. He left his wallet behind.'

'Thank you, sir, I'll make sure he gets it,' the porter
replied, stretching out his hand.

'If you don't mind, I think I ought to hand it over in
person. I know he's only just beaten me here. Would
you mind calling up and telling him I'm on my way?'

Without waiting for an answer and with an air of

social authority, Harry passed by, grateful that despite the heat he'd chosen to put on a well-tailored jacket that morning. He could sense the porter's indecision but Harry was already heading up the stairs. As he reached the top he could hear the porter muttering into his internal phone.

The bishop lived in the main block of Albany, its oldest part, and Harry was surprised how simple and almost institutional the common parts were, with a few doors coming off the landings around a large and rather dark central stairwell. He knew which one was the bishop's because, even as Harry approached, it was already open. The bishop was standing in the doorway, clad in a smoking jacket. From several yards away Harry could see the storm of surprise and apprehension that was sweeping across his face. The thin fingers were white upon the door, moist pink lips moved, then froze, as Wickham debated whether to open the door wider or slam it in Harry's face.

'Harry, my dear friend, what a surprise. What brings you here?' The lips split in a tight smile while the eyes danced with caution. 'The porter was suggesting something about a lost wallet?'

And slowly, as if on rusted hinges, the door was opened a few further inches.

'Wallet? I've no idea what he was talking about. I just

saw you in the street and chased after you. I hope you don't mind, just wanted to say hello. I've got some more news about your friends from Oxford. I wonder, do you have time for a cup of tea?'

The cleric's certainties in life tended to be of an eternal nature; he didn't have much practice at inventing excuses on the spot. 'Do come in,' he found himself saying.

Harry found himself in a high-ceilinged hall. The contrast with the bland hallway outside couldn't have been more stark. The walls were dressed in rich silk wallpaper and an ornate bureau stood against one wall. Across from it, in a gilded frame, a Pre-Raphaelite scene of the Crucifixion stared down at him. A staircase led up to a further floor; other paintings lined its walls. Harry didn't have time to take in more as he was ushered into an inner room that seemed womblike. It had no windows and was lined with bookcases while every spare section of wall was covered in oils and watercolours. A desk faced the door; behind it was a white marble fireplace with its mantelpiece so crowded with elegant objects and invitations they threatened to push each other off the top.

'Er, tea, you said. Wait here. I'll fetch some.'

Harry guessed that Wickham had no desire to leave him alone but equally the man needed time to collect his thoughts. The bishop disappeared through a doorway that was hidden behind a crimson crushed-velvet curtain and soon Harry could hear clattering from a nearby kitchen. He didn't have long. He made a rapid inspection.

His eyes wandered to the bookshelves with the keenness of a man who had once collected first editions before he had been dragged to the brink of financial despair. He pulled one out at random, attracted by its intricately tooled spine, ran his finger slowly down the ancient leather. The Book of Common Prayer, a 1650s edition. On the shelf above were beautifully bound biographies of Pugin, several popes, Martin Luther, Cranmer, Ridley, and at the end, to his astonishment, an edition of *Mein Kampf*. Judging by the grubby state of its binding, it was prewar. An original.

Now his eyes raced around the room. On one wall was an oil showing several youths on a rock above a swimming hole, superbly executed, probably American, and above the fireplace in a simple gilded frame was a large charcoal sketch of another youth, limbs stretched, chin high, seated on a beach, soaking up sun. This youth, like all the others, was beautifully conceived. They were also all completely naked.

On the wall opposite the entrance to the kitchen hung another velvet curtain. Listening to make sure

Wickham was still clattering around the kitchen, he pulled the curtain back to reveal a door, and on its other side he found a dining room so filled with *objets d'avarice* it took his breath away. Nothing was less than Victorian: the lustrous dining table was Georgian and the two classical busts on columns in the corners of the large window were battered enough to be at least two thousand years old. An entire corner was devoted to a display of Orthodox icons and a painted wooden altar triptych whose age was so great it was preserved behind glass. Yet even as he tried to understand what he was seeing, Harry stiffened. The kitchen noises had stopped. He rushed back to his chair, just in time to see the bishop brushing aside the curtain and bearing a tray with two mugs and a bowl of sugar. Mugs seemed entirely out of place in these surroundings; the bishop wasn't extending himself for Harry's benefit.

'All this,' Harry said, waving his unbroken arm around the room, 'is stunning.'

Wickham was clearing a space for the tray among the paperwork that was spread across his desk, moving an old green glass gourd that still had soil from its excavation inside it and that Harry suspected was Roman.

'A lifetime of careful collecting,' Wickham acknowledged, 'and with no children to support.'

'I thought a bishop's salary was disgracefully modest.'

'Indeed it is, as it should be, which is why almost everything here is a copy. Well crafted, handsome, but not the real thing.'

'Fake, you mean.'

'If you will.'

Harry cast his eye across the bookcase. Bugger-all fake about that lot, but already the bishop was hastening on.

'I'm so sorry not to have been in touch, Harry, but I've been having a little eye trouble. Age, you know. And my entire computer system crashed. I've only just picked up your messages.'

Two excuses. One too many, Harry thought.

'Please forgive me,' the bishop said, settling behind his desk and throwing Harry a timid smile.

'I'm not sure I can.'

'I beg your pardon?' the bishop snapped, alarmed, spilling his tea across his paperwork.

'You weren't truthful with me.'

Wickham said nothing, stared in anger, then in a fluster began to rescue his damp papers.

'You said you didn't know Susannah Ranelagh,' Harry continued, 'yet you arranged dinners at Christ Church which she attended.'

'I . . . I . . .' Wickham stopped fussing over his paperwork and confronted his guest. 'It's possible. I was

335

asked to make arrangements with the college for a few old friends. I didn't attend them all. Perhaps she was there when I was not.' The words were defiant but suddenly he broke into an avuncular chuckle. 'Harry, please, I know you're upset about your father but don't badger me. You have to understand that I'm old, the grey cells sometimes slide by each other nowadays, don't connect like they used to.'

'But it wasn't just Susannah, was it? The others were there, too. My father. Findlay Francis. Leclerc. Al-Masri.'

'That may be so, but the dinners took place at the request of others. You can imagine what my life is like, my duties are heavy, my diary all but overwhelmed. Just because I did a favour and helped with the organization doesn't mean I attended them all. Anyone could have been there without my knowing—'

Harry cut him off. He knew it was a lie, a whole series of lies. He wanted to keep the other man under pressure. 'Strange, isn't it? You remember so much about a student named Richards, even down to the tape on his little box of tricks, and yet you can't even remember your close friends.'

'Scarcely friends—'

'Members of the Croquet Club. What were you all up to?'

'I'm sorry, Harry, I simply don't know what you're

talking about. You must understand, show a little pity. When you get to my age you, you …' He trailed off, his eyes flooded with distress and anger.

'Your memory becomes partial, convenient. Like your explanations, Bishop Randall. '

'Enough!' Wickham growled. 'I will not be insulted in my own home.'

'What happened to Findlay Francis?'

'I have no idea.'

'So you admit you knew him.'

'I admit nothing.' The bishop spat out every word. A crimson tide of outrage was spreading up from his collar of hair across his shining scalp.

'That's strange, since he was at all your reunion dinners. Even if you didn't attend them all you would have met him frequently.' This was no more than an assumption – the Christ Church files had given Harry no more than the name of the old member who had been responsible for making the arrangements – but the increasingly florid sheen that had taken hold on the bishop's face told Harry it was true.

'Why are you persecuting an old man?'

'I'm not persecuting you, Bishop Randall, I'm just doing a little prodding.' Harry's eye rose to the sketch of the naked youth behind the bishop's head. 'That's an Augustus John, isn't it?'

'I told you, a copy. By one of his followers.'

'A very good copy. I see they've even copied his signature.'

'Out!' The bishop sprang to his feet with remarkable agility for an elderly man professing all types of infirmity. 'Out now!' His finger shook wildly as it pointed towards the door.

'But I haven't finished my tea.'

'I only have to press a button on this phone and within seconds three men will be here to throw you out!'

'A panic button? You should press it. You need to panic. I will find out, you know.'

'Go!' Spittle cascaded from the damp lips.

'I thought you were a friend of my father.'

The bishop's eyes flared. 'Oh, and in every detestable detail I see you are his son.' His hand was still shaking as it reached for the phone.

'Don't bother. I'm going.' At last Harry rose to his feet, slowly, in contempt. 'Five of them gone, Bishop Randall, and you're the only one still left so far as I can see. You know what that means?'

'What?' the bishop all but screamed.

'I'm coming back.'

Harry took one last look around the room, brimming with so much elegance and opulence, and left. As he closed the door he thought he could hear the sounds of sobbing.

—⚬—

When Jemma had woken that morning she had realized that the thrill of playing out of bounds with Steve had begun to fade. She had slept listlessly, lying awake, feeling the rise and fall of his body, and worrying what the hell she should do. She'd confided in a girlfriend whose advice had been simple: 'Make your mind up, silly.' But, lying next to Steve, she knew it wasn't a matter of mind, you couldn't do this with a list of pros and cons scribbled down on the back of an envelope, although to her shame she'd tried that several times. In the end she'd realized it wasn't about Harry or Steve, it was about herself.

Steve had begun making his feelings more obvious, and in public. The previous evening he'd tried to drag her into the showers of the gym once again but this time their friends had been outside, whispering, giggling. It was a display of ownership; it wasn't helping. It was all very well Steve pounding her brains out but, when he'd finished and rolled over and fallen asleep, when the bells had stopped ringing and she could hear nothing but his gentle snoring, it was time for her to gather up her scrambled senses. She was young, full of passion and loved giving up her body, but she was also Scottish, a little stubborn, insisted it was on loan, and on getting possession back. For Steve that was no longer enough. He insisted she decide. Her time was running out.

She had left Steve's apartment early, made some excuse, hadn't stayed for breakfast, needed space. She hadn't bothered with the bus but had walked, making her way past the shopkeepers who were setting out their pavement stalls, avoiding the piles of accumulated night-time rubbish, dodging cyclists, her head down as she tried to drain it of confusion. Her head was still down some time later as she turned the corner into her own street. As a result she almost walked into the huddle of men and a few women that had gathered outside the communal door leading to her top-floor flat. They had cameras, microphones, notebooks. Jemma jumped in alarm. Journalists, packed so tight on the pavement that a young mother with a pushchair was forced into the busy road to pass them by. The media had arrived. She hadn't a moment's doubt what they were after. Harry.

Her first instinct was to turn and run, back to Steve, but suddenly a bolt of awareness shot through her. No, not Steve. That wasn't what she wanted. And, even as that realization dawned, she remembered that her

forefathers had fought at Culloden and had never had
enough bloody sense to turn back. Almost before she
realized what she was doing she was using her shoulder to push her way through to her front door. They
turned, as one, as packs do, a TV light was shining in
her eyes and questions were being thrown at her from
all sides. They didn't appear to know who she was; it
was enough she lived in the same building as Harry
Jones. Do you know him? How long has he lived here?
Have you seen him recently? Did you know he's been
arrested in connection with a murder?

Jemma held her key out in front of her, forced her
way to her front step, put her key in the lock, opened
the door a couple of inches, had said not a word. Then
she found a young woman at her side, tugging at her
sleeve. 'Are you having sex with him?' The young
woman was a 'shouter', a junior at some television
company who was paid to hurl insinuations and accusations at those, mostly politicians, from whom her
bosses wanted to capture some sort of reaction. 'Are
you going to resign, Minister?' 'How can you face your
wife after those headlines?' 'Did you really employ
your secretary for her filing skills?' But it was summer,
the politicians had all disappeared.

Jemma turned slowly to face her. The others crowded
round.

'Are you having sex with Harry Jones?' the young woman demanded once again, though less forcefully now she was looking into Jemma's eyes.

Jemma's eyes dropped, inspected the young woman. The reporters grew silent, waiting.

'Sex? You want to know about sex?' Jemma said as the young woman pressed forward in expectation. 'First thing is, I'd change that bra. It's not doing a thing for you.'

As Jemma closed the door behind her she could hear the pack of journalists still mocking their colleague, but suddenly she was trembling so much she could scarcely move. The keys clattered from her hand; she leaned against the wall for support, slid by inches to the floor. Only when she heard the reporters drawing back from her doorstep did she allow herself tears.

—⚮—

Harry stepped out of the shower, still sweating. The heat was persistent, intrusive, even on the river with all the windows thrown open. As he towelled himself he heard his phone vibrating on the dining table. He didn't catch it in time, even though he'd left a trail of dripping footprints across the wooden floor, and was surprised to see he had seventeen missed calls and almost as many messages. Not bad for a short soak in the shower.

Journalists. Hunting as a pack. Tasting blood. Someone had told them he'd been arrested in connection with a murder and Harry had no doubts who that had been. The police – or one policeman in particular. Edwards. As he flicked through the messages they became depressingly consistent. What was his relationship with the deceased? Would her murder affect any political comeback? Surely he would like to give his version of events? Even sell his story? Or comment on rumours that he first had sex with Delicious in a hospital bed?

One was a friend. 'Sorry, Harry, old chum, I hate to do this but my editor's insisted and, well, you know what a bottomless pit of venom she can be. Look, I'm so sorry you're in the shit again, truly. You know my colleagues in the press will turn you slowly on a spit but – Harry, face it, you know they can't ignore a murder rap. Look, any chance of meeting up? I'll do the story as gently as I can. Over a drink, perhaps? Just name the place and I'll be there for you, Harry.' That was followed by a short pause. 'And, er, any chance of a photo?'

Thank the Almighty they didn't know where he was, that Edwards still thought he was with Jemma. Oh, screw you, Hughie, I'll rip your tongue out through your butt, for what you must be putting her through. He tried to call, warn her, hoping it wasn't too late, but it went straight to her voicemail.

He sat, naked, bent, sweating, dripping onto the polished floor, ashamed for what he had inflicted on her. This was his fault.

Yet he might have known that Jemma was not simply a child of Culloden but also of Bannockburn, a proud woman who could meet both disaster and triumph with a straight eye. She hadn't switched her phone off as Harry had surmised but was talking on it. To Steve. Trying to let him down gently, even as the door buzzer was hissing at her relentlessly.

CHAPTER TWENTY-THREE

Findlay Francis had taken the train to Weymouth, by his beloved sea. His postcards had been purchased at places along the stretch of coast road that ran like a lazy ribbon from the town to West Bay. So that was where they went, early the following morning, Friday, in Harry's trusty Volvo, with Jemma sneaking out of a back door, trying to leave the baying of the pack behind them. It was precisely what Edwards had wanted, of course. Action. When the rabbit decides to make a run for it.

Harry, Jemma and Abby started early, sharing the driving, taking the road southwest until they ran out of motorway and were left with cluttered A-roads. It took them more than three hours and in some discomfort: the air-con wasn't up to it.

345

'What, precisely, is the plan?' Jemma asked from the passenger seat, throwing aside the last of the newspapers. Harry had made them all, and, although they had been careful not to suggest he was guilty and get their libel lawyers in a froth, terms like 'disgrace', 'humiliation' and 'shamed' wound through the copy like a noose around his neck.

'Nothing precise,' Harry said in reply to Jemma's question. 'Nothing you'd call a plan, really. Just a day by the sea.'

'I forgot to bring my bucket.'

They were all sleepless and more than a little apprehensive.

'Abby, do you think your father might have stayed in Weymouth itself?' Harry asked, throwing the question over his shoulder to Abby, who was sitting clad in a floppy straw hat in the back seat.

'No, I don't think so,' she said eventually. 'I'm pretty sure of that. He always wanted total peace for his writing, isolation, not crowds.'

So that was where they decided to start, on the coast road west out of Weymouth that wasn't even up to being an A road. They passed through the small town of Chickerell without pausing until they hit the open countryside beyond, and it didn't take them long to become aware of the flaw in their nonexistent plan. It was all very well for Abby to suggest her father would have sought somewhere isolated, but so much of this part of the Jurassic coast stood up to that description. If Findlay had been looking for a place to hide away from prying eyes he would have been spoiled for choice. Between the gentle green folds of the hills and back from the stark cliffs that faced the sea there were kinks and crevasses in the countryside that could have hidden several armies. For centuries this coast had been the place of fishermen, pirates, smugglers, shepherds, those who valued their invisibility. Away from the coast road ran any number of lanes, farm tracks, bridleways, footpaths, walkways and meandering badger runs that had never been marked on any map, many of them too small for a vehicle and now overgrown with summer's abundance. They tried each in turn yet found nothing. For a few minutes their hopes rose along one lane where the grass showed signs of ancient vehicle tracks, but at its end they found only a tumbledown cottage whose roof had disappeared decades earlier and whose empty windows stared blindly back at them. They pressed on. They had no choice.

It was well into the afternoon and Jemma was driving down a lane between steep banks, topped by thick hedgerow and overflowing with fronds of bracken and bramble, which began to narrow with every new yard.

Soon the thorn bushes were attacking both sides of the car and the pavement had completely disappeared. Nothing had passed this way in many moons. Another dead end. There was no turning place and Jemma had no choice but to push the gearstick into reverse and thread her way backwards. She gained speed as the brambles retreated and the road widened. She was a good driver, confident. She twisted in her seat, and the engine whined while Abby ducked her head to give Jemma a clear view. Harry had his eyes closed, his shoulder weary from the day's drive. Suddenly there was a chilling crack from the back of the Volvo and Jemma cried out as she slammed on the brakes. They'd hit something, hard.

As they spilled out of the car they could see what that something was. It was lying in the road. A young buck fallow deer, its antlers not fully grown, its chestnut flanks mottled and its foreleg broken through the skin.

'I didn't see it,' Jemma gasped. 'It just jumped out . . .'

They could see the gaps in the hedge that the deer used as their crossing point. No deer born in the last five years would have expected a car to be passing here.

Abby began to moan in distress and Jemma put an arm around her to console her, and to comfort herself. The animal was twitching in pain and terror. Harry moved forward and bent to inspect it. The dark eyes

stared wide and swollen, filled with shock, its eye-
lashes almost human while its dark-rimmed nostrils
flared as it tried to suck fresh oxygen into its lungs. A
dry, hoarse cough came from its throat, past the tongue
that hung listlessly from its gaping mouth. It was in its
death throes, but for how long would it linger?

Harry left the deer and walked back to the women.
'Take Abby down the way a little, will you?' he asked
Jemma.

'What are you going to do?'

'Nothing you'll want to see. Please.'

The two women retreated down the track until they
found the shade of an old tree where Abby stood, crying
softly. Jemma put her arms around her once more,
shielding her from any sight or sound but all the
while staring back down the way to Harry. He was
looking at the whimpering deer. It was far too large to
throttle and he had no faith that with his left arm he
could hit the deer hard enough or accurately enough,
with the car jack perhaps, to dispatch it swiftly. He
reached inside the car and retrieved his jacket, walking
back to the deer and laying it gently across its head.
Whatever he was about to do, the deer should know
nothing of it. Then he climbed back into the driver's
seat and put the car in reverse once again, and on a
summer's day with the light dappling through the

swaying trees, their branches laden with fruit, their roots surrounded by sweet-smelling wild garlic and the eyes of red campion, with as little sound and as much care as he could muster, he backed the car over the neck of the deer, then quickly repeated it, again and again, until he was sure. When he went back to lift his mangled coat, the soft eye stared back at him sightless.

—⁓—

The death of the deer stripped them of any sense of adventure they might have had. They kept to the task for several more hours until even the most optimistic of souls would have had to declare their mission fruitless. There were simply too many grassy tracks, too many overgrown lanes to have any chance of making a thorough search of the near twenty miles of road that led to West Bay and its neighbouring town of Bridport. They fell silent as the sun hid behind a bank of clouds, taking their hopes with it. Harry was driving, tapping his fingers on the old leather steering wheel, when he turned to Abby. 'Did your father drink?'

'You suggesting he was an alcoholic?'

'No, not at all, but I was wondering whether he liked a pint occasionally.'

'No, not occasionally. Dad was more of a four-pints-a-night man.'

'So he would have known the pubs near where he was staying. And they would have known him.'

'What are you suggesting?'

'We stop driving blindly around the countryside and go to the pub.'

So they stopped off at every pub they came to, showing photos, asking their questions. But the men and women of Dorset are not like the Greeks, they don't throw open their souls at the first sight of a stranger, and all they gave up was a distracted shake of the head. The day grew more depressing and soon it was gone eight.

'OK, decision time. Do we carry on with this and stay over or head back to London? Try another day?' Harry asked.

'One more pub, see if they do B&B,' Abby proposed. 'If not . . .'

The Gathering Storm was a little off the main route, down a side road and traceable only by an old sign that leaned precariously at the roadside. A locals' pub, not one for the tourists. Everything seemed to lean. The horse chestnut beneath which they parked sagged and creaked, the old walls were buckled, the front door was barely a match for its tilting jambs, but it had the sense of having been much like this for at least four hundred years. The half-dozen drinkers inside all stopped talking and stared as Harry, Jemma and Abby walked in; it was almost as if they'd interrupted a gravediggers' convention.

'Do you do bed and breakfast?' Harry asked the stout woman behind the bar.

She continued polishing glasses as she inspected them. Her eyes snagged on the henna tattoo on Abby's wrist. 'How many rooms?' she asked in a tone that suggested she suspected them of several kinds of debauchery.

'Two.'

'I got a twin 'n' a single. Nice rooms. Clean.'

'*En suite*?'

She went back to polishing as if the question offended her.

'And perhaps something to eat?'

She nodded and at last let go of her polishing cloth.

'That's very kind of you,' Harry said, trying to establish some form of human contact.

The landlady led them up the leaning stairs, along a passageway of uneven floor and threw open the door to a room with a sloping ceiling supported by buckled beams. 'The twin,' she announced as if revealing the secrets of the Shroud.

At the end of the passageway was another door. She made no announcement as she opened it, and none was necessary. It was clearly a bedroom only inasmuch as it had a bed squeezed inside so tight that the door was unable to open fully. The window was small enough that it might once have been used as a dovecote. Abby knocked her hat off as she tried to get through the narrow door and sat on the bed. It had more lumps than a pile of broken bricks. Jemma's silence screamed rebuke.

'It's fine,' Harry declared, his heart sinking as he knew what he had to do. 'I'll have this one, you girls can make yourselves comfortable in the twin.' Abby cast a net of pity that all but smothered him.

'The bathroom's down other end, hot water seven to nine, morning 'n' night,' the landlady declared.

'And food?'

'I'll see what I've got,' the stout woman sniffed, disappearing downstairs.

An hour later, as they sat at their table in the small dining area, the welcome had warmed. The offering of meat pie or fresh fish had been excellent, the crumble was homemade, and while it wouldn't win awards their meal had restored their spirits. What did it matter if the table legs were so far out of true that Harry had to stick his foot under one to keep the plates from sliding off? When Abby complimented the landlady, she got a brief nod and smile in return.

Harry seized the moment. 'Do you mind if I ask you something, Mrs Butt,' for that proved to be her name. 'We're down here looking for a friend.'

'Friend?'

'Actually, Abby's father. You see, he used to come to these parts very regularly.'

'He's gone missing. I'm worried about him,' Abby added. 'I do hope you can help.'

Mrs Butt stood her ground. Harry showed her the photo on his phone and it was clear from her expression that she recognized the face. She looked closely at them once more, her suspicion returned, then went to the door that led to the bar area. 'Bert!' she cried.

Albert Butt appeared through the door. He was as stout as his wife but his face was weaker, his drooping eyes and shambling gait those of a drinker, his thin hair plastered to the sides of his head.

'These got questions,' his wife barked.

'I'd be grateful,' Harry said, 'but maybe we can do this over a drink. Can't enjoy a good meat pie without something to wash it down. A pint, perhaps? And whatever you're drinking.'

'I'll get 'em,' the wife said, and disappeared back through the door.

Bert drew up a chair. The girls made a fuss of him,

thanking him for his kindness. Unaccustomed to such praise, he gave his mouth a cautious wipe with the back of his hand.

'This man, Abby's father,' Harry began, pushing the iPhone at him. 'His name was Findlay, probably called himself Finn. Used to come here regularly, I believe. But only in the autumn.'

'Tha's right.' They appeared to know as much as he did; there seemed little point in denying it.

'And last autumn?' Abby asked eagerly.

The man considered. 'No, not for a while.'

His wife returned with Harry's pint and a remarkably generous whisky and ice for her husband.

'Do you know where he stayed when he was down here?'

The landlord shook his head. 'But couldn't be far, not the way he used to drink. Didn't say much but he knew 'ow to swallow.'

'He rented somewhere, didn't he? Must have done. We'd know if he'd bought,' his wife chipped in.

'I reckon he rented a place on the old Farleigh estate – sure he did, come to think of it. Most times used to walk here and stumble back, so it's gotta be local, and the Farleighs own most of what there is round these parts. Old man Farleigh'd know.'

'Can you tell us how we can find Mr Farleigh? We'll

go and have a talk with him first thing in the morning,' Harry said.

The landlord began laughing. 'Go find him? No need for that,' he said between chuckles. 'Why, he's sitting in the next-door bar.' He took a swig of his whisky. 'But you be careful now, you hear. He don't take kindly to most, specially women. Can be a prickly old blighter.'

Still chuckling, Albert Butt picked up his drink and disappeared.

—◊◊—

More than a hundred and twenty miles away and earlier that day Edwards's phone had sparkled into life. He'd fished it from the depths of his jacket pocket and his wrinkled face had brightened as the tracker app flashed insistently at him. He had pushed aside his bacon butty and stained coffee mug to clear a little free space on his crowded desk and bent over the flashing dot as it had moved down the M3 motorway heading southwest.

'Oh, my little beauty!' he had cried and had begun pounding his desk in delight so that the others around him had turned in curiosity. 'On! On! Straight into your Uncle Hughie's hands!'

—◊◊—

Friday evening, gone nine. They hadn't met face to face for several years. Distance takes root, grows, particularly when a close group is torn apart. Those who are left often feel a sense of shame, of guilt for being survivors, and there were so few of them who had survived. That was why the two men had chosen a spot where their emotions couldn't be put on display, a spot that was public yet expected of them some measure of reserve. The Royal Academy.

The Academy was one of the most respected art galleries and institutions in Europe and only a few minutes' walk up Piccadilly from the bishop's set in Albany, but by the time the other man arrived and had gained entrance he found Wickham already there, sitting quietly on a bench, studying an extravagant bronze of St Sebastian, a modernist piece with many twists and turns of its dark metal construction that seemed to mimic the agonies of the martyr. The bench on which he sat dwarfed Wickham. He appeared to have shrunk since the last time they had met. Now he was bent, leaning over his catalogue. They were all getting old, so old that they surely didn't deserve this, the past coming back to haunt them. The man settled down on the bench, his eyes cast at the bronze.

'He knows everything,' Wickham whispered hoarsely

from the corner of his damp mouth, not looking at the other man, like a guilty schoolboy.

'He knows nothing!'

'The croquet club, the reunions. Knows almost every one of us. Not you, of course, but Christine and Ali. Asked what had happened to Finn.'

'Faces from an old photograph.'

The bishop shook his head defiantly. 'He promised he would come back. He's out to get me. I'm not sure I can take any more.'

'What does he know about you?'

'Not a thing! Except ... He saw too much in my home.'

'You let him in?' the other man snapped contemptuously. 'You were stupid enough to let him in?'

'I had no choice!'

'What did you tell him?'

'Nothing! But ...' A gasp. 'I think he suspects.'

'Suspects what?'

'My collection.'

'And ...?'

The bishop made a choking noise. The lips moved but didn't work. His head sagged.

'Damn you, you always were so weak, Randy. Made yourself so vulnerable.'

'I've done none of that for years,' Wickham sobbed in protest.

'Of course not. You're too old. But your age is unlikely to generate a lot of sympathy for a man who spent so many years getting sucked off in a surplice.'

The bishop clenched his fists, the knuckles white with tension. Tears began to fall, one by one, onto his hands, like drops of acid.

'We've got to deal with it, Randy.'

The bishop's head slowly came up, his eyes beginning to glow with hope that there might be a way out.

'*You* must deal with it, Randy.'

'Me?'

'Your problem. Your fault. You lied to him. Caught you out.' The voice was hard, an edge that cut through the bishop's hopes and left them once more flapping like old sails. 'If Harry talks, you're ruined. You'll end up just like that bloody bronze.'

In front of them St Sebastian's limbs and entrails seemed coiled in eternal agonies.

'You'll burn in whatever very special Hell is waiting for you, Randy, and the only relief you'll get is when all those righteous men you once thought were your friends gather to piss on you.'

'No!' Wickham burst out, shifting on his seat. Only the public surroundings enabled him to keep any sort of hold on the torment that was ripping him apart.

'Then you're going to have to stop him, Randy.'

'But how?'

They sat in their huddle, yet at a great distance from each other, talking until the attendant announced that the gallery was about to close.

CHAPTER TWENTY-FOUR

Jason Farleigh sat on a bench in the bar with a younger man who was clearly his son, their backs against the wall. The sleeves of the older Farleigh's faded cotton shirt were rolled up tight, exposing weather-burned forearms that might also have hidden a deal of grime. Everything about him appeared frayed, from his stiff hair to his greying stubble, his limp collar to the pockets of the smock he wore, even in this heat. His eyes suggested a temper to match; they were old even for his fifty-odd years and stared straight ahead, pugnacious, discouraging any form of interruption. Beside him the son sat with eyes downcast as though afraid of what he might find if ever he looked up.

Despite the warning in Farleigh's manner, Harry had

361

to risk it. 'Mr Farleigh? My name's Jones, Harry Jones. I'm hoping you might be able to help me.'

The old eyes, filled with caution that ebbed into suspicion, locked onto their target slowly as if taking aim. He said nothing.

'My apologies for interrupting, rude of me when you're relaxing. Look, can I get you gentlemen a drink? Least I can do.' Harry produced a crisp red £50 note from his emergency supply in his wallet and hovered expectantly, dangling the bait.

The farmer eyed it, ran a tongue around his lips. 'Since you're offering. I'll have a large whisky,' he muttered in a broad Dorset accent, downing the remnants of his half-pint of bitter and staring at the cast on Harry's arm. 'Peter here will get 'em in, don't want no spillage, do we?'

Harry handed over the note and pulled up a stool so that only a low table separated them. Peter gathered up the empty glasses and disappeared.

'I'm looking for a man named Findlay Francis,' Harry began, pushing his phone with its image across the sticky varnish.

Farleigh looked at the image, sucked a tooth as though looking for scraps but offered no other reaction.

'I'm told you might have given him some help. Some *informal* help. He was a very private man.'

'Private is as private does.'

'Yes, of course. He came down here to get on with his work, to do his writing.'

'What's this man to you?'

'He was a friend of my father. And I'm down here with his daughter. No one's seen him for many months.'

'Like you said, if your man was private. No crime in that.'

Harry sighed inside. This old bugger was going to take some breaking down. The son returned with the drinks, old man Farleigh's whisky and half-pints for himself and Harry. He glanced at the photo of Fat Finn and lingered on it, but a glance from his father warned him off. He placed the substantial amount of change in a pile near to Harry. Harry pushed it into no-man's-land between them, as if it were waiting for further business to be transacted.

Old man Farleigh picked up his glass, inspected the contents as though he might have been given a short measure. He looked across the rim of the glass at Harry, provocative, mean, then he downed the whisky in a single gulp.

'It's very important,' Harry pressed.

'So's my peace and quiet.'

'Mr Farleigh, I've already apologized for disturbing you once. Where I come from, once is enough,' Harry said, meeting the challenge but not raising his voice.

'But since you've already finished your drink I think the least I can do is get you another.' Without taking his eyes from the other man he produced another £50 note from his wallet and laid it on the pile of change. 'Peter, would you mind getting your father another?'

The son didn't move, waiting for the sign, like a collie. Then his father gave the slightest hint of a nod and the younger man disappeared once again.

'We don't much care for strangers sticking their noses into private business in these parts,' the farmer muttered.

'I understand. And, whatever your business with Mr Findlay, it will stay private so far as I'm concerned.'

'I didn't say I had any.'

'You must have met him. He drinks here. Not the busiest of pubs in the world.'

The farmer stared. 'Don't take much notice of others.'

'You own much of the land around these parts, so of course you do. I'll bet you a half-pint to another fifty-pound note' – he produced yet another and placed it on the pile – 'that you see everything that burrows or bleats or barks. This is your world, Mr Farleigh. So I'm not surprised you're so protective of it. I don't want to disturb it.'

'How do I know that? You could be anyone. A snooper, a . . .'

'The police? Or Revenue and Customs come to dig away in your backyard? Someone from the council come to see if you've got the right planning approval for every little shed or stable, a taxman come to see if your accounts have got more holes in them than your stock fence?'

The farmer's stare was bitter. Harry looked around the bar and saw a copy of the *Daily Express* abandoned on a nearby table. He retrieved it and opened it at page five. His own photo stared back at him above a lurid report. He pushed the newspaper into Farleigh's hand.

'You this bugger?' the farmer said as he finished reading.

'Arrested. Not charged. And, before you ask, I didn't do it. But either way I'm not likely to be running off telling tales out of school, am I? All I want is to find out where Mr Francis is.'

The son was back with more whisky. And more change. The pile of money was growing. Harry took yet another note from his wallet, making sure Farleigh could see that it was his last, and placed that along with the rest. 'For the next round, too.'

Still there was silence.

'Look, Findlay Francis comes along, asks you for a very quiet place where he can hole up for a couple of months every year, do his work, visit his daughter in London, no questions asked and, most importantly for him, no questions answered. I'm guessing you did a deal with him, in cash, like you've always done in these parts, and I'm pretty sure he would have been generous. Paid for your silence. I understand your reluctance – it's the decent thing to do – but let me assure you there's nothing Mr Francis would like more than to speak with me right now.'

'And why's that?'

'Because I think something's happened to him.'

'Why's that?'

'Why do you think he was hiding? Somebody didn't like him very much.'

The son began to shift uncomfortably on his bench. 'We don't want no trouble,' he bleated.

'Trouble doesn't wait for an invitation.'

'But he said we wouldn't—'

'Shut your face, you little prick!' the father spat.

The son's face churned in pain as if he'd been physically slapped and retreated inside his skin.

The father leaned across the table towards Harry so that his words would be incapable of misinterpretation. Flecks of contempt swam in his eye. 'You're trouble, Mr Harry Jones, and I don't remember no one inviting you, either. So why don't you crawl off back under whatever rock you calls home and leave us folk in peace.'

Harry had wasted his time. He sighed and reached out to scoop up the money on the table but Old Man Farleigh was ahead of him, his large farmer's hand with its walnut knuckles and broken, dirty nails smacking down possessively on the pile of change. 'Let's call it my consultancy fee, shall we?'

'Let's not. You haven't given me anything.'

'But I don't suppose a chap in your position's in much mind to go calling the police. I did warn you not to go sticking your nose into other folk's business.' He smiled, coldly, then turned to his son. 'You go get the pickup while I take a slash. I think our evening here's done.' He disappeared into the rear of the pub while his son, not wanting to be left alone with Harry, scuttled out the other way.

Harry gave it thirty seconds, then followed the father. In many parts of the world they call such facilities rest rooms or comfort stations; this was neither. It was a bare, bleak room with scratched paintwork and an old porcelain urinal that dominated one entire wall. A single stall with a crooked door was at one end next to a basin that appeared to have been recycled from a tip. The place stank of stale urine, and the farmer stood at the urinal adding to the stench while scratching a new graffito with his thumbnail on the wall alongside a host of others. He stared in total indifference at Harry.

'I think we have unfinished business,' Harry said quietly.

'I have.' The farmer went back to it.

'Don't let's fall out, there's no need.'

'What's that you say?' Farleigh said, turning to Harry. He was still pissing. It streamed close to Harry's shoes.

'I wish you hadn't done that.'

'Who d'you think you are, the one-armed bandit?' the farmer sneered. His words were slow, with a slight slur; the last whisky had done for him.

When he was finished he shook himself and zipped up his trousers. 'You reckon you're man enough for me, then?'

'Oh, I think so,' Harry said, taking a small step forward.

That was when the farmer took a swing at him, putting all his bulk behind the blow, but it was too well telegraphed. Harry swayed back just far enough for the clenched fist to miss. The farmer swore and swung again with his other hand, a long looping hook that, when it missed, spun him round. Harry was now behind him. He shoved Farleigh face first against the wall, hooked his cast around his neck and grabbed the middle finger of his left hand, wrenching it up over his shoulder and bending it back fiercely. The farmer screamed in shock and pain.

At that moment the door swung open and Peter stood, staring, hesitating.

'Get him, you useless bastard!' the father cried.

Yet still the son hesitated, looking at his father, then back over his shoulder to see if there were someone else he might summon to help. And Harry twisted the father's finger once more. It wouldn't take much more to break it. In agony the father sank to his knees.

'You sure we can't do a deal here?' Harry said. 'You keep kneeling in your own piss much longer and those trousers of yours will be ruined. Not to mention your finger.' He gave it another savage jerk.

'There – there *was* a man who looked a lot like the one you're after,' Old Man Farleigh gasped, his teeth gritted against the pain. 'Wanted a place to think, so he said.'

'That's right.'

'Said he'd do the place up a bit. It needed work.'

'What place?'

But Farleigh struggled, tried to release himself. Harry's voice went cold as he leaned his weight on the finger and brought it to breaking point. 'My trouble is, Mr Farleigh, I get very impatient. It's a fault, I know.'

It was Farleigh's resistance rather than his finger that

was broken. He gave a huge sob of despair and his body sagged in submission. Harry let him go. He fell sobbing to the floor, almost into the filthy water.

'The old keeper's cottage,' Peter whispered, aghast at the sight of his father. 'We don't have no keepers no more; no one ever goes up there, not in years.'

'So when did you last see him?'

'Last September. When he usually arrived. Sometimes he'd borrow our old Land Rover. Carry his supplies, fresh gas canisters, that sort of thing. Then he'd pay for its annual service. That's always in September, once the harvest were done.'

'And where is this keeper's cottage?'

''Bout half a mile down the Burton Bradstock road, up in the old wood. Just past what's left of the oak that got done by lightning a couple of years back.'

'Then I shall go and visit him.'

'He won't be there.'

'I just hope you're right.'

The father straightened, clutching his hand in pain. 'I think you bloody broke it.'

'No, I didn't. It'll only feel like that for a couple of days. Believe me, if I'd wanted to break it you'd have known all about it.'

'Dad, shall I call the police?'

'Why not, after all?' Harry interrupted. 'We can meet

them at the back of your farm. The way you like other people's money I'm guessing – what? Holiday lets without planning permission? A little illicit asbestos dumping or a bloody great hole filled with old tyres? Something like that. I'm up for it if you are.'

The father snarled and swore at him but kept his eyes lowered.

'Keep the change. You'll need it to clean yourself up,' Harry said as he pushed past the son and disappeared out of the door.

—⁓—

They said goodnight at the top of the leaning stairs. The girls' room was to the right, Harry's to the far left. Abby threw her arms around Harry. 'Thank you,' she breathed in his ear, kissing both cheeks.

'For what?'

'For being a very special sort of man. For taking care of that darling deer.' A brave smile. 'For whatever happens tomorrow.'

He had told them only some of what had taken place with the Farleighs, that they'd given him a few good clues they could follow up in the morning. He didn't want to raise their hopes, he had too many fears of what they might find.

'And for taking care of us,' Abby whispered, giving

him a hug that squeezed the breath from him before heading for her bedroom.

It was Jemma's turn, reaching up to kiss him, on the lips, the old elm floor creaking beneath her feet as she stretched. No words. Just a strange look. Then she, too, was gone.

—◊◊◊—

Harry was woken from his bed of lumps by a noise. It was as dark as a coal seam in the room with only starlight for company, but he wasn't alone; he heard the noise again. A creaking joist from outside. Slowly the door opened, an inch, then more, casting a pale light onto the bedroom floor. He saw Jemma's unmistakable profile. She crept in, on tiptoe, closed the door behind her, shutting out the light once more and finding the edge of the bed by touch. She reached for his hand.

'I saw a new side of you today, Harry,' she said, her voice so low he daren't breathe for fear of missing it. 'I'm so used to chasing after you, trying to keep pace, feeling so bloody miserable when I fail. But this afternoon, in that lane, you stopped for a while. To deal with the deer.'

'Someone had to.'

'It's easier to love you when I don't have to run.'

He nodded in the darkness. How often had he heard that before?

'At times you seem to drag all the cares of the world behind you. It gets messy. That's not easy for a girl to deal with.'

'I'm sorry.'

'But this afternoon, with that poor creature, I was so glad it was you. Not anyone else.'

He wasn't sure where this was headed, stayed silent.

'Harry, I wanted you to give me space because there were some things I needed to find out. About myself.'

'And did you, Jemma?'

'I think so. But, Harry, I couldn't find the answers to those questions on my own.' The tremble in her voice told him all that the words did not.

'I didn't assume you'd stay at home every night knitting, Jem.'

'I don't knit.'

'I know.'

'You ... didn't mind?'

'Of course I minded, particularly when I saw you dancing out of the cinema hand in hand with Steve.'

'You followed me?'

'No, I was just passing. Coincidence.'

'But I didn't think we believed in—'

'You know, every time I use that word I feel like I've swallowed old fish guts. Yes, but that's all it was, coincidence. Seeing you with your old flame. Do you remember you once told me you only ever went out with him for one thing?'

It was her turn to stay silent.

'Mad as bloody hell I was when I saw you. But then I got drunk, and while I got drunk I got to thinking. I'd asked you to share our bed with another man. My father. I guess I can understand you wanting to get your own back.'

'It wasn't like that.'

'Whatever it was like, so long as it's over I can deal with it.'

'The gentle Jones.'

'No, the very practical Jones. I want you, Jem, and there's a price we all have to pay for what we want.'

'What price do you want me to pay, Harry?'

'Help me finish what I'm doing.'

'Kicking open coffins?'

'That sounds a bit graphic.'

'It's what it feels like.'

'It's too important for me not to do it and too important for us not to do it together. I think we're getting close, near the end. Then we can get back to the real world of you and me.'

'We don't have to wait, Harry.' She leaned forward, searching for his lips.

'What will Abby think?'

She smiled even as she was kissing him. 'Oh, I know what Abby thinks. She told me she'd kill me if I came back before breakfast.'

CHAPTER TWENTY-FIVE

They had found it the next morning, less than half a mile beyond the turning that led to the pub. A small lay-by on the side of the B-road that in its summer grab seemed little more than a slice of wayward grass verge. From the direction in which they came they could see nothing that gave any clue, but once they'd parked up and walked back they found the suggestion of a track leading away through the overgrowth. From the road where they stood the track seemed to come to a rapid dead end but, as they forced their way through the tentacles of ferns and summer grasses that reached out to grab at them, they saw that it turned and headed up the hillside in the direction of the thick woodland that dominated the brow. The day was young, fresh, the air still, the path ahead of them untouched and filled with daisies and hogweed and the sound of foraging bees. As they climbed they could see behind them the extending vastness of the sea, while up ahead they found nothing but trees. Then the earth dipped to form a fold, a crease in the hillside. That was when they saw it, nestling in the margin of the woodland. A small cottage hidden from the road by the lie of the land, backed into the trees yet open to the sea views, the hillside that led to its door sheep-mown, its small windows squinting out to the endless stretches of Chesil beach and the Channel beyond. Fat Finn's place. As Harry led, the two women began to drop behind, cautious, a little afraid, reaching for each other and holding hands.

The brick-built keeper's cottage was Victorian, one floor, built around a central chimney with a small room at either flank. It was of the greatest simplicity in design but showed signs of recent attention: the roof had been patched with tiles that hadn't weathered, one of the windows had been replaced, the solid door repainted. Harry felt foolish as he knocked. There was no answer. He tried the handle but it was locked, top and bottom, bolted, and the windows had enough dirt to offer almost no view of the interior. He circled around the back. The trees crowded around the rear of the cottage, protecting but also darkening, casting deep shadows in the morning light. A small extension had been built at some point in a different brick that jarred; it had a door with old, blistering paint that Harry once again tested, but it, too, was locked. A large red propane gas cylinder stood to one side, which Harry instinctively rapped; it rang hollow and empty. Beyond a crumbled stone wall whose purpose had long since been lost there was a small outhouse overgrown with ivy that at various points might have been privy or dog kennel or lock-up; now the door swung open on a broken hinge to reveal a stack of firewood. Despite its signs of recent repair the cottage screamed desertion.

He peered through the only window in the rear extension, wiping the grime away with his hand. He found bottles lined up on the inside, impeding his view, although he could see signs of a kitchen area. A two-ring gas hob set in a wooden counter. Wall cupboards on the far side. He thought he could hear a tantalizing buzzing sound; he stood still, his ear to the window, straining to identify the noise. It came from inside. Perhaps a fridge. He walked back to the rear door, tried the lock once more, put his shoulder to it to test it. It rattled in its frame, less secure than the door at the front. The women watched from a distance, Abby seated on an old tree stump, Jemma hovering protectively at her shoulder. Here, in the deep shade away from the morning sun, it felt dank, a place of shadows and dark thoughts.

He had to do it. Harry nudged the door once again, more firmly this time, then took a step back and with his sound side flew at its painted wooden panels. It retreated but wasn't yet ready to surrender. Three good kicks with the heel of his boot around the lock produced sounds of splintering wood and tumbling screws, and with one further kick it was done. The door lurched open, still reluctant, scraping the floor in complaint as he gave a final push, and at last Harry stepped inside. What he saw, and sensed, and smelled, made him reel in horror.

He bent over in the fresh air and leaned on his knees, panting, trying to scrub his lungs clean. Jemma began to move towards him in concern but he waved her back. 'Just winded myself,' he lied, coughing, spitting. 'Stay there. Don't come any closer.'

She knew he was lying. Not anything as simple as a simple fib but a dark, hideous falsehood that he'd concocted to protect her. So she stayed where she was, holding Abby's hand.

—∿—

It had taken a hell of an effort to kill Fat Finn. Overweight, often underscrubbed, didn't take care of himself. And suddenly, during one of their reunions, it seemed as if a switch inside him had been thrown. He looked older, still more bedraggled, complained about having been beaten up, almost killed. He couldn't control his drink or his tongue any longer, kept repeating himself, blurting out confidences in the presence of waiters, said he was writing a book about it all. The situation couldn't go on. Fat Finn couldn't go on.

Getting Finn drunk almost to the point of unconsciousness a few weeks later hadn't been difficult and a bottle placed in the front of the car kept it that way as he'd been driven home. Scrambling up the wretched track had been the most difficult part, at their age and with Finn's weight. He'd stirred as they'd made it to the rear door but he'd been given another drenching of whisky, most of which went down his shirt, quietening him once again. He'd known nothing. When eventually his legs had given way he'd been dragged across the threshold into the tiny kitchen, recently renovated, with none of the draughts of most nineteenth-century rural hovels, and so proved brilliant for the purpose. Windows shut tight, two gas rings lit, the door locked just in case Finn came round, the empty bottle of whisky lying at his side to tell wicked tales. Gloves, no prints. And Finn's tiny study ransacked, his laptop and papers squashed into a bag, just in case.

Propane isn't itself poisonous but when it burns it produces carbon monoxide, which most certainly is.

Gentle, painless, deadly. By the time it had killed Fat Finn his murderer was already miles away.

—⚬—

It took some while before Harry felt up to returning to what lay inside. He gazed up to the sky as though trying to drag its light back into his life, then took one step inside. He needed no more.

On the floor of the cramped kitchen was a body, although it was difficult to recognise it as such. The soles of the shoes that pointed towards him gave the first clue. The stench was hideous. The buzzing sound Harry had heard from outside was caused by a swarm of engorged flies that circled like a storm system above the body, and on it. They had called him Fat Finn but the body now seemed shrivelled within his clothes, had leaked away in hideous stains, and even though Harry knew his facial features there was no way to tell that this was Findlay Francis. The rats had seen to that.

—⚬—

Once more Harry returned outside, grabbing for the clean air. He crossed to the two women and found Abby silently weeping, her cheeks smeared with tears. She knew.

'Abby, I'm so sorry.'

'Can I . . .?'

'No.' He said it firmly, perhaps too much so.

She looked up at him, her damp eyes pleading. 'How?'

'I don't know. A heart attack, perhaps.'

'Like your father?'

Her question had an edge that struck him like a bull-whip, unleashing thoughts he had been trying to suppress. Of all the members of the clique of old friends who had died, Johnnie had been the only one who'd had the dignity of dying from natural causes. Or had he? Harry stood blinking, as though fighting a storm.

'Abby, forgive me, I hate to ask you this, but I have to. Was there any chance your father was somehow . . . depressed?' He searched for the word, trying to soften the blow. There was no need: she was entirely up to pace.

'Killed himself?' She shook her head doggedly. 'He was scared, not suicidal. Anyway, do suicides bother to lock the door?'

'That's a very good point.' She had kicked something in his mind, got his ear burning. 'Give me a moment.' With considerable reluctance he returned to the kitchen door. The stench was less virulent, diluted with fresh air, but the vampire flies still swarmed and circled. He inspected the inside of the battered door. The key wasn't in its lock, nor had it spilled to the floor. And every instinct told him he wouldn't find it in Findlay's pockets, not that he had any desire to check. Which meant the door had been locked from the outside. He remembered the empty gas tank. There was no room to move around the body so with great care he stepped over it in order to get to the gas rings. He tried the taps. Both were open. No, not a heart attack, then. And not suicide, not if the door had been locked from the outside.

He stepped back out into the summer light and fresh air, wondering if the sweet sickly smell of Death would ever leave him. All his adult life Death had had a habit of tracking him down, even when he wasn't looking for it, even to the depths of the West Dorset countryside on a day that was glorious with life. He led Abby and Jemma round to the front of the cottage, where they found a grassy knoll surrounded by daisies and overlooking the hillside and distant sea. He put his arm around Abby's shoulder. 'You OK?'

The tears were gone, her cheeks brushed dry by the breeze. 'I told you that I knew we'd never find him, not alive. But I do need to know the truth. You haven't told me.'

'Somebody tried to make it look like suicide but I think you were right. He didn't kill himself. He was murdered.'

'Why?'

'Same reason as the others. He knew too much.'

'They were all murdered?'

'It wasn't just Delicious. Al-Masri certainly. Susannah Ranelagh probably. Who knows about Christine Leclerc? Her death was certainly violent enough. Your father. And right now I'm even beginning to wonder about my own.'

'It was a heart attack,' Jemma prompted.

'I'm wondering about that,' he replied.

'All members of the croquet club,' Jemma said.

'And then there were two,' Abby added.

'Not for much longer. Not at this rate,' Harry suggested.

'The bishop and that strange woman. Who on earth is she?' Jemma asked.

'I haven't even a glimmer of an idea.'

They sat lost in the maze of sorrows and surmise. Overhead a pair of buzzards circled languidly on a light sea wind and in a distant meadow a roe deer grazed the lush grass.

'We should call the police,' Jemma said eventually.

Harry reached into his pocket to retrieve his phone. 'Well I'll be . . .' he breathed as the screen came to life.

'Harry?'

'Our bloody bishop. He's just resurfaced, sent me a message. Wants to see me.'

'And we don't believe in coincidence, do we?' Jemma said.

'He's got to be involved. In one way, or the other,' Abby suggested. 'Be careful, Harry.'

'Or be a bloody fool,' he muttered.

'Sorry, Abby, Harry here doesn't do careful,' Jemma added ruefully.

He reached for Abby's hand. 'Abby, I want to ask you a very great favour. I don't know how I dare but ...'

'You don't want to call the police, do you?'

'No, not just yet. I'm out on bail on suspicion of one murder and if I'm found at the scene of another, Chief Inspector Edwards will take a distinct personal pleasure in burying me so deep it'll take an Act of Parliament to get me released. Returning to the scene of the crime, he'll say. And, unreconstructed idiot that I am, I've even left my prints on the gas taps for him. Our bishop friend wants to see me. Let me at least find out what he's up to before we do anything.'

'You think it's him?'

'The odds are getting shorter.'

'But if it's him ...' Abby didn't want to finish the thought.

'I'm on my guard. I'll draw him out. Take the risk. I owe it to you and your father.'

'Your own father, too, remember.'

'Old Bishop Randy wants to see me tonight. Shall we head back to London?'

Abby didn't respond immediately. From somewhere nearby a newly fledged seabird was calling, a lonely, plaintive cry that mingled with the sound of the waves falling on the distant shingle. The mackerel sea melted into a sky of finest blue silk woven through with clouds of English lace. Somewhere out there, in the infinity that lay beyond the horizon, were the fading echoes of her father. She wanted to capture them while she still might. 'I think this was where he sat, right here. Where he was happy,' she whispered. 'Let me have a few minutes here with him, will you?'

Jemma kissed her, then walked hand in hand with Harry to the car waiting for them on the road below.

—⚬—

It didn't matter a mouldy fig that they hadn't called the police. With the app on his mobile phone in front of him Edwards had been spying on their every move, every twist and turn of the wheel through West Dorset, where they slowed, where they stayed. He knew Harry: the bugger was mental, didn't know when to stop, couldn't help himself. Edwards was certain that whatever he was up to would be connected with the case; Harry Jones didn't take holidays. Yet there was a puzzle. For more than an hour Harry had stopped at the side of some rural road by the sea and none of the maps that the chief inspector had to hand or could summon up from the Internet suggested there was anything at that spot. But something had to be there, something that had drawn his man to a very specific spot on the map and kept him there for some while.

Edwards waited until the Volvo had reached the motorway and was on its way back to London, then he called a colleague in the local Dorset constabulary, a fellow officer he'd met on a homicide investigators' course at the National Crime Faculty in Bramshill. Not an official request but one that was off the radar, not logged, no paperwork. 'Just my old copper's nose twitching, Derek,' he explained. 'Can you kick a couple of your layabouts and get them to give their eyes some exercise?'

'What are you looking for, exactly, Hughie?'

'No idea. But this is a murder investigation.'

'Casting a few flies?'

'Something tells me this is good fishing weather, Derek.'

Hughie Edwards liked fishing. It taught him patience, not a natural side of his makeup, and he needed to be patient just a little longer. Harry was still the only suspect, the only one he was after. He'd soon have the bastard in his net.

CHAPTER TWENTY-SIX

Shades of confusion, and enough of them on the trip back to London to raise a sweat and a muttered curse inside the Volvo. Abby hadn't returned with them, saying she wanted to spend a little more time along the soaring coastline her father had loved – not near the cottage, of course, although for one so free with tears she displayed an emotional core of oak. She'd known her father was gone, she'd said, so it was time to celebrate what he had rather than to mourn what she had lost. Yet there were fresh tears when she kissed them goodbye.

Harry insisted on driving even though his shoulder ached, an inevitable after-effect of knocking down locked doors and half-strangling local farmers. The muscles were out of condition. Yet no sooner had they passed the Fleet service area than the brake-lights of the Friday-night traffic in front of them lit up like a Californian rock concert. They sat and tried to be patient, seeking distraction. Jemma was wearing shorts that exposed almost all of her thighs, which stretched out provocatively. Harry had been studying them.

'You're staring,' she said.

'Any chance?'

'Not with that lorry driver hanging out of his window to get a better look.'

'Then I'll cut the swine up first chance I get.'

But the opportunity never came. The delay dragged on, their whimsical humour evaporated and Harry kept glancing at the car clock, checking it against his father's wristwatch, which lied and said he had a few minutes more. Was it fate? He was on his way to what he sensed would be one of the most profound confrontations of his life, yet he was stuck in the most impenetrable traffic jam. Fuck coincidence.

—᙮—

The patrol car was sent out from the station at Dorchester. The two young police officers, one a newly qualified constable and the other a female probationer, went first to the Gathering Storm. Yes, Mr Jones had been there, even signed his name in the register, although Mrs Butt admitted to being surprised when she'd been told that was his real name. She was a professional sceptic when it came to any man who booked in with two women and kept the floorboards creaking half the night. And, as if that hadn't been enough to arouse her suspicions, there'd been some sort of trouble in the toilets with a couple of the locals. Nasty sort, that Mr Jones.

With the directions supplied by Chief Inspector Edwards the two constables then found the lay-by just beyond the blasted tree, where the lush summer grass bore the signs of having been crushed by a parked car. The overgrown track up the hillside also showed the marks of where someone had recently passed back and forth. The officers followed the trail that led to the thick woodland on the skyline above.

—⁓—

Their progress on the motorway was so poor they turned off at Farnborough. 'I'll jump on a train,' Harry had said. 'Might just make it in time.' He'd left Jemma in the Volvo to continue the struggle into London.

And he made it in time, with minutes to spare and sweat on his brow from the stewing pot of the Underground. Wickham's message had said they should meet at St Stephen's in Walbrook. Harry scrambled up the stairs of Bank station and into an evening already grown dark. During the day these pavements were packed with workers from every corner of the financial world but now most of them had disappeared off to their homes or into the wine bars and pubs. It was a reasonable bet that Harry and the bishop wouldn't be disturbed, not in a church.

Amid the medieval clutter of streets and alleyways that still left its mark on the City of London, St Stephen's was like blossom on a bare branch. The Walbrook, on which it stood, was one of the old streams that had flowed through and now under the streets of London. Hemmed in and squeezed on all sides, the church had been burned, ransacked and bombed, its exterior still bearing the scars of endless repairs, yet from its ruins grew a rose of extraordinary beauty. Christopher Wren had rebuilt it after the Great Fire, conjuring up a domed structure that he used as a template for his later construction of the cathedral of St Paul's a few hundred yards to the west. Three hundred years later another genius, the sculptor Henry Moore, had been summoned to add yet another transcending touch. He had taken a slab of raw travertine marble from the quarry where Michelangelo had taken his own material and from it had created a great circular altar, which now sat beneath Wren's soaring dome and had become the reborn heart of this old church. It was there, at the altar and in a pool of light that reflected off the white marble, that Harry found the bishop. Wickham was kneeling, his old back bent, his forehead resting against the smooth cream-grey marble, deep in prayer.

—⁓—

Edwards was still tracking the icon on his tracker screen with the remorselessness of a cat pursuing its dinner when his colleague from West Dorset called.

'Hughie, you might have given me a little more warning,' he complained.

'What the hell d'you mean?'

'I've got a probationer who wants to quit and a constable who's still wiping the sick from his sleeve.'

'What did they find?'

'A stiff. Elderly. Male. Not in very tasty condition.'

'Another? Damn his hide, he's making a collection.'

'Who?'

'My suspect.'

'I can't yet confirm that it's suspicious.'

'Of course it's bloody suspicious or why didn't he report it?'

'Certainly messy. Could take a while to confirm the cause of death.'

'No matter. It's enough. The slippery sod's mine.'

—⚉—

The bishop, on his knees, was wearing a rich purple cassock with a silver rosary around his neck. The pool of light that adorned the central altar emphasized the bareness of his scalp and gave the scene a medieval, monastic quality. His hands were clasped in front of him, high, and so hard the fingers were like ivory. He seemed startled, hadn't heard Harry's footsteps, turned suddenly, eyes swimming in agitation.

'I'm sorry.' Harry found himself apologizing – for what? He'd been invited, summoned.

'No, Harry, I'm the one who owes the apology,' Wickham said, rising from his knees. His ornate crucifix swung from the rosary around his neck; he held it, put it to his lips. 'I haven't been entirely forthright with you.'

'I know.'

'Time to settle things.' He turned once more to place his fingers on the polished surface of the altar, running them across its smooth planes, almost sensuous, like a keyboard. 'Do you like this, Harry? Some loathe it, mock it as nothing better than a chunk of old Camembert. Philistines!' He shook his head in incredulity. 'Yet there are those of us who see it as a reminder of our origins, like the rock where Abraham came to sacrifice his son, Isaac. Do you fear God, Harry?'

'He's never been around much when I needed him.'

'This altar caused the most enormous fuss when it was first placed here. So many narrow minds. You know, Moore spent five years coming to this church, sitting quietly, soaking in the atmosphere, catching the changing light, the echoes of the place. And the result is . . .' His moist lips hovered, searching for the words. 'A gift fit for God himself.'

'A sacrificial stone?'

The bishop turned sharply in annoyance. Harry seemed intent on provoking him once again.

'I found Findlay Francis a few hours ago. Or what was left of him.'

The bishop's face twitched, the flash of ill temper that had filled it as quickly transformed to anguish. 'I did not know. Poor, poor Finn,' he whispered, the words struggling to find their way past lips that had suddenly grown parched in pain.

'You must at least have suspected.'

Wickham shook his head again. 'You think me capable of such things?'

'You steal from the Church, that's pretty obvious.

There are other parts of your private life that might pose a few problems, too, if they were thrown open to the daylight.'

'Enough!' The bishop's anger echoed around the empty corners of St Stephen's. 'Do you know how many churches I have saved from closure? How many letters of gratitude fill my desk from charities that would otherwise have folded? How many vicars who have given their lives selflessly to God whom I have saved from an old age of grinding misery? I ... I ...' He was pounding his chest histrionically, boastfully, his amethyst ring sparkling in the light like an angry eye. 'I, Randall Wickham, have raised more money for the Church than perhaps any man alive.'

'And poured quite a chunk of it into your own vices. You know, Bishop, when you go and join the Almighty, the curators of every museum in the country will be tearing each other's arms off to be the first through your door.'

'You know nothing!'

'Then try me.'

Wickham stared as if explanation were beneath his dignity, then relented. 'It was my first visit to Russia, when it was still run by Communists and God-deniers, long before the Wall came down. I met an old Orthodox priest in a suburb of St Petersburg. He was dressed in rags and thin as a winter tree. He found me praying in his church and handed me an icon, begged me to keep it, preserve it. He told me that if it stayed with him it would soon be lost for ever. They were such desperate days. So I brought it back home. The piece turned out to be of very considerable value.'

'On your wall.'

'Yes, and of greater value with every passing year. Ever since that day I've been rescuing special works, putting them to one side for safekeeping. I'm no more than their custodian. When I die every one of them will go to the Church.'

'May your God forgive you.'

'He will! He understands.'

'He understands about the boys, does he? Lead us not into temptation but deliver us from evil. He sure screwed up on that one, didn't he?'

'Stop!' Wickham struck the altar with his palm, gasping for breath and excuse. His head sagged, but when it came up again crimson spots of defiance were burning on his cheeks. 'There may have been moments in my private life, times when I've been totally exhausted by my work, made vulnerable, that I've fallen prey to ... distraction.'

'You call young boys distraction?'

'I have done nothing – nothing! – that is unlawful.

Not a single one was below the age of consent.' The lips were once again moist as they lied. 'Many were just friends ...'

'I'm sure the archbishop would understand. Not so sure about the *Daily Mail*.'

'If I hadn't devoted my life to the Church I would be wealthy, I would be honoured and no one would give a damn about the boys.'

Boys. Harry noted the word the bishop had used and the admission it contained. 'Is that why you asked to see me, Bishop? To hear your confession?'

'In a manner of speaking.' He was calmer now. 'I want to talk about your father.'

—⁓—

Jemma scolded herself. She'd been determined that she would have nothing to do with Harry's bloody father, had washed her hands of the matter, almost of Harry, too, yet, despite herself, she found that questions about Johnnie and the Aunt Emmas kept wriggling their way into her mind. A matter had begun with a meaningless black-and-white photograph but now all those faces had transformed into people who were very real, and very dead, except for the bishop. And perhaps the mysterious woman with the thin face and those nervous, aching eyes, like a sparrow. It was inconceivable to Jemma that such a fragile bird could be responsible for such malevolence as was unfolding, yet there could be no doubt she was part of the secret.

Parliament Square. Once more stuck in traffic as it snaked past the honey-coloured palace with its soaring clock tower. As she waited for the lights to change she was distracted, temporarily blinded as a group of tourists snatched their moment in front of Big Ben and their cameras flashed, each taking it in turn behind the lens to capture the moment. Mrs Butt's face had been a picture, too, as she and Harry had come downstairs to join Abby at the breakfast table. She had deliberately overcooked the eggs and left the toast like a doormat, banging their plates down in disapproval. As her thoughts wandered, Jemma was brought back to the moment by the black cab that had been following her around the square and was now blowing its horn in impatience. She slipped the gear and was soon driving along the bank of the river once again, yet still she couldn't rid herself of the question: the woman in the photo, who the hell was she?

Suddenly she wrenched at the wheel and pulled over, violently, resulting in another chorus of objection from the black cab. The driver waved a finger of reproach and mouthed something rude; in return she blew him a kiss of excitement. They'd been stupidly blind, missed the point. The woman didn't matter after all, or not that much. Both she and Harry had been staring at the bloody obvious yet managed to overlook it all this time. As the taxi drew away she glanced at the clock. Harry would still surely be with the bishop. She couldn't call, disturb him, but he would need to know. Her thumbs were shaking with excitement as she texted him.

CHAPTER TWENTY-SEVEN

'I want to show you something, Harry,' Wickham said. 'Come with me.' The priest led the way from the light of the stage on which the altar sat to a doorway in a darkened corner, then through a door of studded oak that Harry guessed was perhaps salvaged from an era even earlier than Wren. It led to a circular stone staircase, narrow, dark, tight, whose treads were marked by several centuries of wear. Both men took care as they made their way upwards. The stairs became dustier, marked by pigeons and crumbs of ancient masonry; the bishop paused for breath as they reached the level of the bell hanging in its cradle of wooden beams, then pushed on. Harry had lost count of the number of steps by the time they came to a door; the bishop tugged, struggling to open it until it came free with a sharp scraping noise and he stepped out onto the narrow roof of the bell tower. The atmosphere inside the old church had been cool; now the humidity of the summer's night washed around them. For a moment Harry was mesmerized by the light pouring from the buildings that crowded in on all sides. Most were mercantile, many of them banks, but in the distance he could see the cupola of St Paul's and, in the darkness between, the outline of the bronzed figure of Lady Justice that hovered above the Old Bailey. In front of him at the edge of the roof was an old stone parapet. It was low. Like the staircase behind, it had been built for an age of smaller souls.

The bishop waved an arm. 'From here you can see everything, the entire machinery of civilization,' he began. 'The towers of commerce and the temples of the soul.'

'God and greed. Greed seems to be winning.'

'You're so very like your father,' Wickham said, un-amused. 'Always a word wiser than anyone else. He'd argue the wings off an angel – if ever he stumbled over one.'

'I wish you luck, too.'

'The point I'm trying to make,' the bishop said testily, 'is that these things are what life is about. Body and spirit. Sometimes in harmony when we get it right, other times at each other's throat, but we've always needed them both. Two thousand years ago there were slaughterhouses on the banks of the Walbrook. Next to them, Roman soldiers built a temple dedicated to Mithras. Why? So they could bathe in warm bull's blood while they paid homage. It's all gone now, of course, the slaughterhouses, the temple, but in a sense so little has changed. In their place we have the towers of the Lord and of Mammon. Still side by side, and sometimes hand in hand.'

'What happened to the meek inheriting the earth?'

'A little naïve, Harry, I'm surprised at you. Your father would never have felt that way. No, not Johnnie.' He steepled his fingers at his lips, as though in prayer. 'He used to talk about you, you know.'

'Me?' Harry couldn't hide his surprise; suddenly he was on the back foot.

'But of course. He was very proud of you.'

Harry wasn't sure what to say, so he said nothing, waiting.

'Your father and I were friends for many years, Harry.'

'The Aunt Emmas.'

'Yes, and as you rightly suspected we continued to gather together, every year at the start of the Michaelmas term.'

'To collaborate.'

'An ugly word. It began as youthful arrogance. We were better than the rest, we thought, each of us bringing our individual perspectives and skills, which we could exploit better together than alone. It started as fun, nothing more, yet over the years it became serious. Almost too serious.'

'Insider trading.'

'We never deliberately conspired. We exchanged views, experiences, as friends, and as we made progress along our chosen career paths those experiences became more valuable.'

'Even Findlay Francis? He was a writer.'

'Poor Finn never made much money out of the rest of us, that wasn't his interest, but he was always so keen to tell the story of what he'd discovered from those rich and powerful figures he was writing about. He preferred the telling to the taking, God rest his soul.'

'And my father?'

Wickham recognized the anxiety in Harry's voice and rejoiced. He'd got Harry to where he wanted. He had the advantage; now he needed to make sure. 'Yes, Johnnie turned up every year, without fail. And every year he'd bring with him tales of what you'd been up to.'

'But we scarcely talked. Almost never met.'

'He followed your career in the Army as best he could. You kept getting mentions in despatches, promotions, medals, accolades. Then you became a politician.'

'The year before he died ...'

'By then you were scarcely ever out of the news. And Johnnie brought every scrap of it to us.'

'But he never had any time for me.'

'He wrote to you, that's what he said. It was you who turned your back on him.'

'No, no, he ...' But the half-formed excuse disappeared within a fog of confusion. Suddenly Harry began to understand how skilful the bishop was in spotting and exploiting vulnerabilities, in creating distractions in a way that had kept him out of reach all these years. Harry had hoped that unravelling the truth about his father would settle things, flush out the pain that had been lurking deep inside ever since he was a boy. He'd thought it would enable him to purge the memory of his father's ghost, to move on. Instead, Johnnie was coming back to haunt him.

—ɯ—

Friday night. No parking restrictions. Jemma stopped a little way down Walbrook, keeping the front of St Stephen's in view, and waited, windows open, the heat of the city trickling down the nape of her neck. As she sat behind the wheel of the old Volvo she wondered at the ridiculous way in which women made up their minds. A few nights earlier she'd been driving around in Steve's car. It was almost new, bright red, air-conditioned, fun – and, yes, even a little flash, and smelled of an air freshener that claimed it was natural pine and dangled from the driver's mirror. Harry's old Volvo, on the other hand, was an entirely different world. Old leather, the slightest tang of oil and a heavy, complex sweetness that reminded her of freshly cracked walnuts. There were other contrasts, of course. He was more than a dozen years older and her mother definitely didn't approve of that, or him, or the fact that he was sharing a bed with her daughter. Perfect.

—⁂—

'Who killed Findlay Francis?' Harry asked.

'I don't know,' Wickham replied.

'And Susannah Ranelagh?'

'Is she dead? I suppose she is. Sweet, lonely Susannah.'

'And the others? Why did they all die?'

The shadows hid the bishop's eyes, made his face appear shrunken, skull-like. His voice had an air of resignation. 'I can't say. Sometimes God appears to sleep. I hope he does, for my sake.'

The last words came out as a sigh, so soft that Harry scarcely caught them. It sounded like an admission of guilt. In his pocket he was vaguely aware of a tingling sensation from his phone that told him he had a new message. He ignored it.

'Downstairs, Harry, at the altar, I was praying for us both.'

'I don't need your prayers, Bishop, just the truth. Tell me. What happened to my father? Did he really die of a heart attack?'

'Why do you doubt it?'

'Because I'm beginning to doubt everything I've ever been told about him.'

—ᴀ—

Chief Inspector Edwards stared at the tracker icon, making certain. There was no doubt. It had come to a halt, marking a spot in the heart of the City. He felt a flush of excitement. The bait had been taken; the float at the end of the line tugged beneath the surface. Time to strike.

'Staunton?'

'Yes, Guv?' the sergeant responded from his desk a few feet away.

'Drop whatever it is you're wasting your time on and bring round the car. You and me, we're going to take ourselves for a little drive.'

—⁂—

Wickham had stepped out from the shadows of the church tower and was leaning on the low parapet, looking out across the spectacular skyscape. Harry came to join him, to make sure he heard every word.

'I know nothing of your father's death, Harry,' the bishop said. 'I can only tell you how he lived. Most men have a time in their lives when they struggle with their conscience, but Johnnie ...' Wickham waved his hand towards the forest of towers that surrounded them. 'You talk about that gap between God and greed, but Johnnie never had any doubts about which side he pitched his tent. He wasn't like the rest of the Aunt Emmas. While we got together to share, not just what we knew but what was important to each of us, as friends, as we'd always done, Johnnie somehow changed. He seemed only to want to use us, to grab every plate that was put upon the table. Finn put it bluntly, in that way he had with words. Johnnie was raping our minds. We were supposed to be his friends.'

Harry flinched, his hands scraping in shame along the rough stonework.

'In our different ways the rest of us gave, to each other and often to those beyond. I'm proud of what I've done for the Church and for many other causes, but Johnnie – he only took. Left nothing of value behind. And yet you come here with your cheap morality, a man whose life has been built on what his father took from others. How dare you?' The words were spoken softly and in accusation.

The bishop took a step or two backwards, as though he found Harry's company repellent. Harry was left leaning on the balustrade, breathing heavily as confusion and guilt tumbled through his mind. God, it hurt. He knew now that he'd always wanted to find something in his father he could admire, some spark of love he could revive, but that was all gone. He'd been such a fool. He'd kicked the lid off the coffin, shaken the dead, and now his father's ghost had come back to torment him.

Far down below in the street, out of reach, was a world of ordinary people. The wail of a Friday-evening siren floated up; to Harry it was the sound of his father's mockery. Damn you, Johnnie, in whatever corner of hell you're hiding.

It was at that moment, lost in misery, that he heard a scuffling noise behind him. Harry turned, but by then it was too late.

CHAPTER TWENTY-EIGHT

Harry had only half-turned when the bishop hit him. Wickham had thrown himself at Harry using the full weight of his elderly body. Taken unawares, off-balance, Harry could feel himself toppling over the balustrade. There was no time for fear, only instinct. As on other occasions in his turbulent life when he'd been about to die, time slowed, every fraction stretched out so that he knew he was falling, his senses tumbling, screaming at him to save himself, but he couldn't. As he looked down he could see only pavement, a hundred feet below, where he was going to die.

His good hand clawed at the darkness, desperate for something to hold, but found only the bishop's cassock. His fingers closed around it, for dear life but too late. He succeeded in doing no more than dragging Wickham after him.

The bishop's momentum spun Harry around and together they toppled over the weathered stone rail. That was when the cast on Harry's broken arm snagged on the top of the balustrade, like a grappling iron. Suddenly both his own weight and that of the falling bishop were ripping at Harry's shoulder. He could feel something tearing inside it; a fire exploded that instantly caught hold in the elbow joint, too. Harry cried out in pain. Without the rigid, unyielding cast he would have been forced to let go but instead he was left dangling, in darkness, in agony. Beneath him he could feel the bishop scrabbling for purchase on his other arm yet his fingers were old and frail; it was only Harry's reflex grip that prevented him from falling.

The shoulder joint was being torn from its socket as though he were being racked by some medieval inquisition. He bent his neck, found Wickham, face twisted in horror.

'Help me! For God's sake, help me!' the bishop cried. His fingers were slipping on Harry's arm, his feet kicking frenziedly at thin air. One of his shoes went spiralling down to the street below. It seemed a long time in falling.

'I beg you, Harry,' the bishop whimpered.

Every tendon and muscle, every corner in every joint of Harry's arm was screaming. The cast was slipping, losing its purchase on the stonework as the bishop fought. Wickham reached up, in despair, clawing, his nails leaving dreadful gouge marks in Harry's skin as they slipped further down his arm. At the last they closed around the watchstrap. Harry's own grip was failing, the cloth of the bishop's cassock too fine, too smooth. A button burst, then another; the bishop gave a jerk, dropped a few further terrifying inches.

Dread had frozen every sense in Randall Wickham. He stopped thrashing, hung helplessly in the air. Every ounce of willpower was directed towards Harry. Their eyes locked, reading each other's thoughts, their fears.

'In the name of God,' the bishop begged.

'I think,' Harry whispered slowly, 'we'll let your God sort this one out, shall we?'

Then he opened his hand.

Randall Wickham screamed as he fell, his fear echoing back from every wall, until the moment he hit the pavement.

—⁓—

Edwards never made it as far as the Volvo. As Sergeant Staunton turned their car from the ancient thoroughfare of Poultry into Walbrook they discovered a disturbance.

A group of passers-by was gathered in a huddle at the base of the church tower. As they drew closer they could see one woman turn away and begin to scream, while a man was bent double while throwing up in the gutter. Others were taking photos, the flashes of their camera phones giving a garish, disconcerting light to the scene. A vivid purple stain was stretched out on the pavement.

'Stop here, Staunton, I need a closer look.'

The huddle of onlookers was already becoming a crowd and as he pushed through them he saw what had drawn them. At that same moment he saw Harry stumbling from the church.

'Christmas in July,' he whispered to himself before calling for assistance.

—⁓—

Jemma heard the scream, saw the body falling from the tower, just a flash, almost a shadow, so quickly she couldn't make out its shape. She heard the noise it made as it hit the pavement. At first she thought it was Harry and screamed, silently, through frozen vocal cords, until she saw that it was clad in purple clerical garb. Then, as a crowd began to gather around it, a different fear took hold. Another body, and as Harry had said, in rather more colourful language, coincidence was only for the feeble-minded. He was never going to dig his way out from under this one.

She didn't ask herself whether Harry was responsible. Part of her wouldn't accept the notion, even as another part of her acknowledged it was entirely possible. Harry had form when it came to corpses. But whatever had taken place inside the church, Harry was going to need help – and right now she was the only one who could supply it. She had to find him. Yet even as she stepped out of the car she saw him, stumbling from the shadows, his body strangely twisted, in pain, clutching his shoulder as he walked straight into the arms of a waiting policeman.

—⁂—

'Central Command, this is DCI Edwards from Charing Cross. Require assistance in Walbrook in the City. We have a suspicious death in the street,' Edwards barked into his radio.

'What assistance do you need, Chief Inspector?'

'The whole bloody army, love,' he said. 'You can get those layabouts from Snow Hill to put down their snooker cues and sarnies for a minute and get over here like it's open day at the brewery. We've got quite a little crowd gathering. Oh, and did I tell you? I've already got the blighter who did it.'

Don't panic, don't you dare panic, Jemma whispered to herself. Think!

She sat in the shadows of the street, away from the mêlée that was growing around where the body lay. More police had arrived in a collection of cars and vans, their flashing cobalt-blue lights and the gathering press of onlookers turning the scene into an evening at a fairground, and turning her mind to mush. Think, Jemma! Think!

Everything she knew, or thought she knew, had been thrown into confusion, like a kaleidoscope that had been kicked down the street and landed in the gutter with all the pieces in a new, confusing order. The photograph was crucial but it hadn't been telling the whole story, and she'd only begun to realize that as she had driven past the cavorting tourists. A piece was missing: the identity of whoever took the bloody snap.

She watched in misery as Harry was being led away. The police reinforcements were pushing back the crowd. An ambulance joined the fray, edging forward to stand beside that terrible spot where two forensics officers in white suits and hoods were bent over their work. Think, woman! But she couldn't, her mind and emotions in too much turmoil. Yet as tears of frustration gathered and demanded that she give in to them she became aware of a man who could, someone who might be able to understand the images in this darkened mirror and make sense of the way in which the pieces had fallen.

Once more she reached for her phone, pressed buttons, waited for an answer. When she got it, and had spoken briefly, she restarted the engine of the trusty Volvo, slipped it gratefully into gear and left the pandemonium of Walbrook behind.

CHAPTER TWENTY-NINE

No one could have been more surprised, or equally more delighted to the point of ecstasy, than Hughie Edwards when he saw Harry stumbling directly into his arms only feet away from where the body on the pavement was still leaking. More blood was trickling from gashes on Harry's forearm and the manner in which he was buckled like Quasimodo said he'd clearly been in a fight. Edwards was chapel, didn't go in much for miracles, but right now he was changing his mind.

'Hello, Harry.'

Weary, pain-stricken eyes were lifted, then spent some time hovering over the body before Harry once more returned his attention to the chief inspector. 'Randall Wickham,' Harry muttered. 'Used to be Bishop of Burton. Before you ask, I didn't kill him.'

'And, before you say another word, I'm arresting you on suspicion of murder,' the Welshman began, his lilting voice almost singing in enthusiasm. 'You do not have to say anything but it may harm your defence ...'

Once again Harry was forced to listen to words that had become all too deeply embedded in his life and that were sucking hope from him. A police photographer was dancing around the body, bending, searching for a better image. Wickham's ornate crucifix lay by his side, the strands of the silver rosary snaking their way from his lifeless fingers. Poking out from beneath the purple cassock was the wristwatch. Smashed to fragments. Covered in the bishop's blood. Another nail in Harry's coffin.

'Put the cuffs on him, Staunton,' Edwards instructed the sergeant. 'I don't want this bugger slipping away, again.'

The sergeant reached for Harry's arm; Harry cried out in pain, dropping to his knees. 'I think I may have busted something else.'

'No matter. Cuff him all the same,' Edwards insisted.

Yet regardless of the pain it proved impossible to secure Harry's wrists behind him because of the cast, so they had to compromise, bind his wrists in front. They couldn't doubt that Harry had taken a beating: his face was like ash from a cold fire. The sergeant guided Harry's head beneath the roof of the car as he put him in the rear seat, climbing into the driver's seat to keep an eye on him even though the locks were on the rear doors, while Edwards finished giving instructions over the body.

Slumped in the back seat of the car, Harry tried to focus his thoughts but found it impossible. His shoulder was still screaming in outrage but at least he could move it – perhaps nothing was broken after all. Through the windscreen he could see Edwards holding up a plastic evidence bag. It contained his wristwatch. Edwards was smiling. As Harry closed his eyes in resignation he became aware of the phone vibrating in his pocket once more, and suddenly he remembered Jemma. He needed her, more than ever. Slowly, gritting his teeth against the hurt, he twisted to allow the fingers of his left hand to close around the phone.

'No you bloody don't,' the sergeant growled, snatching the phone from Harry's grasp. 'Not having you messing with any evidence.' Yet even as he claimed his prize the screen lit up, trying to deliver its text message once again, and his nose twitched in curiosity. 'Nothing for you to worry about, anyway.'

Harry could see the message was from Jemma. 'What does it say?'

'*Who took the bloody photo?* What does that mean?'

'I've no idea. Any chance I can give her a call?'

'You can't be serious.'

'You're all heart.'

'And you, Mr Jones, are in very, very deep trouble. About as deep as it gets.'

Harry sighed, exhausted, trying to clear his mind, to concentrate what energy remained on doing battle with his pain, but his thoughts kept snagging on things, wouldn't let him rest, tripping over the bishop, and Jemma, and Johnnie, and over what Hughie Edwards was about to do to him. And the photograph. Now they were all dead, every one of those faces, and that included the unknown woman with the nervous eyes, had to. Once again, he went round the faces, one by one. Then he sat up so sharply he couldn't hold back the cry of pain. 'Get Edwards,' he gasped. 'We need to talk!'

'Oh, he'll be wanting to talk to you, all right, and all night, too, I've no doubt, as soon as we get back to the station.'

'No, now!' Harry raised his voice, grabbed the handle of the rear door, tried to open it but the child lock refused to budge. 'Now!' He began kicking the front seat in frustration.

'And what the bloody hell's going on here?' Edwards demanded as suddenly he appeared, climbing into the front passenger seat, ripping off his latex gloves and dropping them into the footwell.

'Hughie, listen to me!'

'It's Chief Inspector Edwards so far as you're concerned.'

'I know you reckon I'm the greatest mass murderer since Caligula . . .'

'Who?'

'But you've got it all wrong. That photo I showed you, it holds all the clues to what really happened.'

'I think you may have a point there. Know what I'm thinking? That your old man was involved in some dodgy dealings, you see, and when he fell off his perch with that heart attack of his, I think he was cheated by his old chums, and you've been getting even with them ever since. Something like that. Shall we run that one up the flagpole and see how many jurors salute?'

'Hughie, you've got bollocks for brains.'

'Nice start to the game, Harry. Fifteen–love to me.'

Harry bit his tongue in pain, in remorse. He'd have to handle things better than this. 'Look, my fiancée, Jemma.'

'Attractive girl, that. Seen the photos. I wonder if she'll wait for you, Harry. By the time you get out she'll be – what? Fifty? Sixty, maybe?'

'She's waiting down the road in my car. You need to speak to her.'

'My next stop. We need that car as evidence and it's parked just along the way, I'm thinking.' But, as he consulted the screen of his mobile phone once again, he swore softly. 'What the hell's going on here, Harry?'

'What do you mean?'

'Forty minutes ago your car was parked at the bottom of Walbrook. Now it's halfway to the bloody seaside.'

'Where?'

Edwards tossed the question around for a second. What did it matter if he let Harry know? He might even learn something. 'The A12 heading out into Essex. And going at a rate of knots by the look of things.'

'But . . .' For a moment the pain was buried beneath a surge of anxiety. 'She doesn't know anyone in Essex, not anyone she'd go to right now.'

'Maybe she's decided not to wait for you after all.'

'Stop her.'

'Whatever she's up to you can tell us all about it when you get back to where you belong, boyo, in my nick.'

'Hughie, no . . . No, no, no, no!' His eyes were dancing, seeing too many things. 'Oh, you idiot, Jones! You, too, Hughie. Why didn't we see it?'

'See what?'

'The bloody photograph! Seven. There were seven people.'

'That's right,' the chief inspector groaned in boredom.

'But who the hell has seven for dinner? There was an eighth person, of course there was. A gap at the table. A missing face.'

'Who?'

'Whoever was taking the photo. Jemma worked that out. Sent me the text.'

'What flaming text?' Edwards demanded, no longer bored.

The sergeant fished out the phone, showed it to his boss. Another curse, less soft.

'Hughie, you've got to stop her,' Harry pleaded.

'You think I'm going to close down the entire A12 just for your girlfriend?'

'I don't know where she's going but it's got to be connected with all this. That puts her life on the line.'

'Not a flaming chance. Closing down half of Essex is chief constable territory and there's no way I'm going to—'

Suddenly his words were cut off. Harry had stretched his arms around the front seat so that his handcuffs were under the chief inspector's chin and he was pulling back on them, hard. Edwards couldn't speak, couldn't breathe, he was choking. All three men knew that one severe jerk on the manacles could kill him. Harry was gasping with pain but he kept the pressure up on the policeman's neck. The sergeant, in the driver's seat, was frozen, unsure what he should or even could do.

'Hughie, you'd better hope I'm not that murdering psychopath you're after. You understand?'

Edwards was making desperate gurgling sounds. He managed to nod his head.

'So I'm going to let up. Just a bit. Your sergeant's going to sit there as quiet as if he's got scorpions crawling up his leg. And you're going to listen to me. Are we clear on that?'

More choking. Another stiff nod. And slowly Harry released the pressure, just a little. Edwards started coughing, breathing once more, and almost immediately cursing profoundly. Harry ignored it.

'Someone else at the table, Hughie. Does that make sense?'

'Could do.' The policeman's voice was hoarse.

'If you don't stop her, if something happens to her just because you're too busy gloating over me, they won't give you time to pack a cardboard box before they kick your sorry Welsh arse out the force.'

Edwards took his first full breath. Damn, but this had been going so well, his superintendent's badge already warming a spot deep in his trouser pocket, but what Harry had to say had begun to sow doubts. He couldn't afford to ignore them. He wasn't a bad copper, certainly not a bent one, but he'd always been in a hurry, which meant he cut a few corners. Results, old boy, results. And maybe he'd hit the kerb a little too hard on this one.

'I'm not going to stop her, Harry. If she's involved she might be leading us to the proof we need to sort this. I can't ignore that possibility. What I can do is follow her, see where she's going. Keep her company.' His words still came as though sifted through gravel.

'A helicopter?' Harry moved the handcuffs back against his throat but the policeman refused to be bowed.

'Not a chance. If this *is* all down to you, Harry, as I still think it probably is, then I'm not going to make a complete bloody fool of myself by calling out the cavalry. This is down to just you and me.'

'But she's got almost an hour's head start.'

'Then we'd better pull our bloody fingers out, hadn't we?'

CHAPTER THIRTY

The journey out of London had been smooth this late in the evening. Jemma didn't push the old estate car to its limit: it had enough miles under its cambelt to feel the potholes. In any case, she wanted time to think. She had never wanted to be involved, yet now she was being dragged in deeper than she could ever have feared. She couldn't avoid it: she owed Harry, for Steve, for doubting him. So she had called the only man she knew who might help cast a little light into the dark corners of the croquet club.

She was off the main carriageway now, into the depths of the flat Essex countryside, following the instructions he had given her. The beams of her head-lights picked out deserted roads, nothing but trees and hedgerows to see her on her way. A final village, which seemed to consist of no more than a dozen homes, doors firmly closed against the outside world, then she saw the driveway opening up to her left, guarded by red-brick pillars and towering ash trees, and places where elms would have stood before the blight got them. Up ahead, silhouetted against a pale half-formed moon in a cirrus sky, she saw the outline of chimney-stacks with their Tudor crenellations that grew from the roof of the gabled house. A light shone from a down-stairs window, another from above the weather-stained timbers of the oak door. As her tyres came scrunching to a halt in the gravel, the door opened. He stood on his step, waiting for her.

'Jemma, welcome. I'm so glad you called me.'

—⁓—

'Give it some welly, man,' Edwards growled at his sergeant. They were already well above the speed limit, the lights flashing through the night, the siren blaring in warning. With every moment the chief inspector had grown more impatient, glancing at the icon on his tracker screen. Jemma was still many miles ahead but now she appeared to have stopped.

In the back seat Harry made little sound apart from an occasional groan as he drifted through intermittent bouts of pain and dark dreams.

Edwards picked up his radio. 'Central Command, Chief Inspector Edwards.'

'Go ahead, Chief Inspector.'

'I've got a location I want you to check. I want to know what it is, who lives there, anything you can tell me about it. And I need it all about five minutes ago.'

They had left the A12, their pursuit slowed by roadworks and roundabouts. Staunton skimmed one a little too closely, throwing the car around, rousing Harry. He moaned, struggled to sit upright, to focus his thoughts.

'It's the snake shit, don't you see, Hughie?'

'Don't I see what?'

'The synthetic cobra stuff. He's a biochemist.'

'What are you prattling on about, Harry?'

'The man behind the camera. The missing diner. The man who murdered Delicious and who probably killed Finn Francis and, I guess, Susannah Ranelagh. The others, too.' He caught his breath as the car hit another pothole at speed and played havoc with his senses. 'He told me. Done all sorts of cutting-edge research. In bio-chemistry. He was a young research fellow, a lecturer. At Brasenose.'

'And where's that when it's at home?' Edwards asked, perplexed.

'Piss out of the front door of Christ Church and

you hit it.' He gasped once more. 'It's Alexander McQuarrel.'

'And he is?'

'One of my father's best friends.'

Harry cried out yet again, more sharply, in a deeper state of torment. 'He killed them all. He'll kill Jemma, too, Hughie. Please. Please hurry.'

—⁓—

Jemma couldn't contain her surprise as she walked across the threshold and into the house. The darkness had hidden the size of this manor house, and much more. The old red-brick porch that protected the main door gave way to a hallway of extraordinary, almost palatial proportions. The flagstones were softly worn, the dark oaken central staircase with its elaborately carved newels was wide enough for a man to lie across at full length, while every wall was covered with portraits, escutcheons and other evidence of McQuarrel's Scottish roots. Against the wall on one side of the hallway was a broad stone fireplace; against the wall on the other was an elegant coffer covered in framed photographs.

'I never expected anything like this,' she said, breathless with wonder.

'My family came down from Scotland with King

James four hundred years ago,' he explained, an unmistakable tinge of pride in his voice.

'It is beautiful.'

'Thank you, Jemma.'

She continued to gaze around in awe. A piano, a baby grand of considerable age, stood in a place of honour near a mullioned window. 'You play?' she asked.

'No, that was my wife. And that,' he said, indicating the piano, 'is a Broadwood. When she played it her music floated to every corner of the house. But come, you said you have news of Harry. Let's go through to the library.'

He led the way but Jemma hovered by the mirror above the coffer, seemingly distracted by the need to tug at her hair. McQuarrel thought it an unnecessary expression of vanity. 'You said the news was urgent.'

'I'm sorry,' she said, and followed meekly. Flagstones gave way to polished wood and soon she was sitting in a cracked leather armchair set by another hearth, surrounded by soaring overstuffed bookcases and the warm paraphernalia of an academic's study.

'You look as if you could do with a drink,' McQuarrel said, his hand already on the decanter. 'A little of our Scottish water?' He raised an enquiring eyebrow, Jemma nodded, and he busied himself pouring measures into two crystal tumblers. Jemma couldn't take her eyes off him. He handed one of the glasses to her and settled in a winged chair opposite, separated from her by a low table. Beyond his shoulder and through the garden windows she caught the reflection of the moon shimmering on the dark waters of a lake.

He studied Jemma; she seemed disorientated, her eyes and thoughts unable to settle. *'Slainte,'* he murmured, raising his glass. She followed his lead, and drank; he noticed her hand was trembling.

'Jemma, whatever it is, please let me help you.' His voice was warm, smoothed by the wisdom of many years. 'When you called you mentioned that something had happened to Harry.'

'He met with the bishop this evening.'

'Bishop Randall?'

She nodded. 'He's dead.'

'Harry? May God have mercy,' he blustered in alarm.

'No, not Harry. The bishop.'

He didn't press for details. Instead, he sat cradling his whisky, and his thoughts. His mood grew sombre and Jemma had the impression that the walls and bookcases were drawing in on them, the atmosphere suddenly claustrophobic, heavy with misgiving. 'What would you like me to do?' he said eventually, his voice soft and painfully solemn.

'Help me. Help Harry.'

'Shouldn't we leave all that to the police?'

'They think he's guilty.'

'What is it, precisely, you would like me to do?'

'I don't know. Ask questions. Make a fuss.'

'With what?'

'The photo of the Croquet Club. We're sure the answer is in there somewhere.'

'Ah, Oxford.'

'You were there with them, weren't you? Do you have a copy?'

'Of the photo? I've seen it, of course. Harry showed it to me.'

'But you have your own copy.'

'What makes you think so?'

'Because I think you took the photo. And because your wife was in it.'

—⚉—

Harry no longer had any ability to fight. His physical pain had become so twisted up with his fears for Jemma that they had become one, leaving him exhausted, numbed, beyond the point where he could even groan to express his torment.

He'd lost other women, other immense loves in his life. Lost? The wrong word, made it sound no more than clumsy but Julia, his first wife, had been killed in a

435

skiing accident. His fault. And Martha the irrepressible, impossible American, on yet another mountainside, and again down to him. Now Jemma, too?

And, of course, his mother. Like all children he had blamed himself for what had happened, carried the guilt for his parents, no matter how unreasoning such guilt was. That burden was in part why he'd wanted to find out more about his father, to settle old scores; instead he'd discovered altogether too much.

'Please hurry,' he pleaded once more.

—◊◊◊—

'How did you know it was my wife?' McQuarrel asked, almost casually as he rose to refresh their drinks.

'The photographs in the hallway. The biggest one, of your wedding. I got a good look at it. Unmistakable. The same sensitive eyes. Fragile face.'

'Yes, she was fragile, that's an excellent description. My poor Agnetta. Leukaemia. That was almost ten years ago, with many more years of suffering before that. For us both.' The voice was dry, like the rustle of dead leaves in an autumn wind. With his back to her he poured two substantial whiskies, bigger than the first, and set them down on the table, but then retreated to his desk and began sifting through the contents of a drawer. He returned, clutching his own copy of the photograph and set it on the table before her.

'The Aunt Emmas,' she declared.

'My dear, dear friends.'

'And every one of them dead.'

He gazed at the photo, inspecting every face, naming every one. 'We should salute their memory.'

He raised his glass, Jemma too, and they drank. Was it her imagination or did the whisky burn on her lips and throat?

'I wasn't surprised to get your call, Jemma,' he began again, wiping his own lip with a forefinger. 'I knew Harry and Randall were meeting but I have to admit I was expecting a rather different outcome. How much of all this do you know?'

'Harry told me everything. So as much as him. And perhaps a little more.'

'It wasn't meant to be like this,' McQuarrel whispered. 'I'd like you to believe that. We all had our dreams. Ali would bring peace to his world, Finn wanted to win a Pulitzer, Randy would sit at the right hand of God, while Christine glittered throughout every chancellery in Europe.'

'And Johnnie?'

'Ah, Johnnie. I must admit he was a bit of a mystery. Skated deeply across the surface of things, that's what

437

he used to say about himself. At times he could seem extraordinarily superficial. He never quite convinced me of that. It was all diversion.'

'And you, Alex. What about you?'

'Me?' The question took him aback. 'I never wanted anything more than Agnetta. And this house.'

'But it was already yours.'

Yet even as she spoke he was already shaking his head. 'It was our family seat for three hundred years. A place of safety throughout all the turmoil. How many Scottish families can say that? Until the time of my great-great-grandfather, Lachlann. A mighty useless specimen. A drunkard, a weakling, a numpty, all of that and more. But he was also a gambling man. It might even have been in this very room, at the cards, and he was losing badly, couldn't find his way out. So the fool bet everything he had on the turn of a single card. And lost. Left with nothing but his name and he'd made that worthless. The story has it that when he realized he was ruined, the man he had lost everything to took him to the front door and cast the offending card into the wind. "Wherever it flies, McQuarrel, will be your home from now." The card landed where the village grew. It was where my father was born, and I after him, living in the shadow of our family's shame.' He reached once more for his drink, trying to wash away the bitterness. 'My

438

father's dying wish was that I would find some way to take this place back, restore it, along with our family name. That's what I've spent my life doing. With Agnetta. Did that seem so wicked?'

'That depends.'

'We chased our dreams and we went too far. All of us. We shared everything, made merry, made love, made money, lots of it, and by the time we understood what we had done it was too late to go back. The Rubicon had been crossed, our feet were wet, our hands filthy.' He shook his head in a manner that seemed to carry all the sorrows of the world. 'None of us wanted that or ever intended it. When Christine was killed it seemed like some sort of divine retribution, but then the following year Ali arrived with the most extraordinary news, information that could make every one of us wealthy beyond any further need. One last throw of the dice, he said, and we could walk away from the casino for ever. But it seems others got to find out what he knew and killed him for it.'

'Along with his entire family. Even the children.'

'It was the end for us, the Aunt Emmas. It was no longer a game. From that day we began to fall apart.'

'Do you have any children?'

'No. Agnetta was, as you say, fragile.' For a moment he stared into the bottom of his glass, swirling what was left of the whisky as if it held more secrets that needed to be set free. 'There was a time when I thought Harry might be my son.'

Jemma choked in astonishment.

'We shared everything, and too much. Harry's mother Jessie, too, was fragile, in her especially beautiful way.'

'So how do you know you're not?'

'Not Harry's father?' McQuarrel laughed drily in dismissal. 'You only had to watch the boy grow. Just like Johnnie.'

'Johnnie knew about it?'

'Perhaps. I wasn't Jessie's only distraction. She wandered far and wide but Johnnie loved her, always brought her back, rescued her from every rock on which she'd foundered. He was devastated when she died. Hid it, of course, tried to find comfort elsewhere, but in the end I think he died of a broken heart.'

'Is that what killed Susannah Ranelagh?'

'No, of course not. She was like Finn, got spooked, couldn't be trusted.'

'So?'

'So there was no choice. It was either Susannah or us.'

'You mean Susannah or you. The rest of the Aunt Emmas were pretty much all gone by then.'

440

'Except for Randy.'

'And now ...'

They had come to the moment where there was no more point in pretence.

'I watched Susannah, watched her as she died. In that chair where you're sitting, Jemma. She was looking out over the lake.'

'It's dark, the moon's gone. I can't see the lake.'

'You see the truth.'

She stared into his cold, soulless eyes and knew what he had done.

'It's all Harry's fault,' McQuarrel said bitterly. 'If he hadn't chased around the world stirring things up, Susannah would still be alive. Randy, too, and the black Bermudan policewoman.'

'And me?' she whispered.

'There will be no pain, Jemma, I promise you, just a gentle numbness, a shortness of breath. It's what Agnetta chose.'

'What have you done?'

'It's a neuro-muscular drug. A company I was involved with spent years trying to develop it. Agnetta worked there, too, before she became ill. The sort of potion neurological surgeons need for the removal of a brain tumour, that sort of thing. It keeps the patient totally immobile yet still conscious, so the surgeon can test their reflexes. Based on the same chemical composition as snake venom. The early trials seem to suggest it was highly effective but, alas, it proved inflexible. No reliable reversal agent, and none at all in large doses.'

'How ...?'

'When I topped up your drink. Oh, my, but we have been talking a very long time. I expect any moment now ...'

CHAPTER THIRTY-ONE

The police car sent the gravel flying as it skidded to a halt beside the Volvo. There was no sign of life around the house. Edwards and Staunton jumped out of the car, pursued by Harry's cry.

'Hughie!'

The chief inspector turned.

'You daren't leave me on my own,' Harry shouted.

Edwards stamped his foot in indecision, knowing Harry had a point, but knowing he daren't take Harry with him, either.

'Oh, you'd better be on your best bloody behaviour, boyo,' he growled, heaving open the rear door of the car, 'otherwise you'll find me breaking something else of yours.'

The sergeant was already pounding on the old oak door. Nothing stirred inside.

'You come with me round the back,' Edwards snapped at Harry.

Edwards ran, trying windows, testing doors, while Harry, still handcuffed, stumbled on in the policeman's wake. At the rear of the house they found a lake, with a ruined boathouse and a willow tree. They also found an unlocked door. Edwards rushed through it, Harry close behind, their voices raised, calling for Jemma.

Then Harry found her. He saw a light beneath a door and burst into the library. He could see the back of her head above the cracked leather of an old armchair. Rich auburn hair, always tussled, as if it had come fresh from his pillow. And in the chair opposite was McQuarrel, staring at her.

'No!' Harry screamed.

And as he cried out, Jemma turned her head and rose from her chair. 'What are you complaining about this time, Jones?' she said, sobbing, the tears cascading down her cheeks.

Suddenly Edwards and Staunton were in the room with them, the chief inspector barking instructions that they were to touch nothing, the sergeant checking for a pulse on McQuarrel.

'Well?' Edwards roared at Staunton.

'I'm not sure, Guv. Might be one, very faint.'

'There's no point, no way back,' Jemma interjected. 'He told me so himself.'

'What the hell, Jem?' Harry whispered in rebuke, even as he tried to staunch the flow of tears with his thumb.

'There's a photo in the hall of his wife,' she began. 'She's the other woman in the croquet photo. So it had to be him, didn't it? He was the only one left. He'd poisoned Delicious, I knew he'd try the same with me, so when he gave me a whisky and turned away to fetch the photo of the Aunt Emmas . . .' She paused as she relived the moments, 'I switched the glasses around.'

'For pity's sake, that was taking one mother of a chance, miss,' Edwards scolded. 'I mean, what if he'd known the game was up, poisoned his own drink? You know, some sort of grand farewell.'

'He'd already killed so many I thought he'd rather kill me than kill himself. You know how selfish men can be, Chief Inspector.'

But her simulation of defiance was done. She rested her head on Harry's good shoulder and he felt the warmth of tears soaking through his shirt.

'You took that risk, for me,' he whispered.

'No, not for you, Harry. For us.'

'But why, Jem?'

'Because you'd have done the same thing yourself stupid.'

—∿—

They left it until the calmer weeks and cooler winds of September when the earth had stopped baking before they sailed into the port of Patras. Johnnie's grave was there. The last of the Aunt Emmas. It seemed the thing to do.

Harry and Jemma had arrived by gently rusting ferry from Venice, their arrival delayed by several hours because of an unscheduled strike. They had tried to make rudimentary arrangements by phone, had promised to be at the cemetery by noon, but by the time they struggled up the hill from the port in an over-worked taxi the shadows of the pine trees were already stretching out to greet them. The iron gate that led to the graveyard creaked with age as it swung back to let them enter, its hinge held together with wire. They gazed around. The place seemed deserted except for the flapping of crows in the trees. Then they saw the approaching figure of an old man, summoned by the complaining gate. He was grizzled, unshaven, his face like new-ploughed earth, his legs bowed from carrying so many years. A battered straw hat rested on top of two corrugated ears.

'*Kali Mera*,' Jemma greeted him, resurrecting a phrase she had picked up during the low months of a gap year.

'*Kali Mera. Otheos Mazisou.* May God be with you,' the old man replied, gazing at them with a quizzical frown that added more furrows to the face. His teeth were remarkably white and natural. 'Mr Joh-nas?'

'*Nai*, Jones,' she repeated. 'Sorry we're late.'

'*Dhen Peirazi.* No matter.'

The ancient caretaker wiped his brow with a large handkerchief before turning and shuffling off, waving for them to follow. He led them further up the hill to a distant corner of the cemetery, past orderly lines of tombstones, some marble, others painted in whitewash and azure, adorned with lanterns, images of the dead, summer-blighted flowers and passages from biblical scripts. Not all the graves were Greek, or Orthodox. Up ahead, almost hidden among the trees, they could see a small collection of graves in a patch that was relatively neglected and unkempt, with Stars of David on the stones. In Patras, death didn't discriminate. One tomb they passed was dedicated to an Englishman. 'Fondly Remembered', so its inscription claimed. 'Not Johnnie, then,' Harry muttered, walking on. He was sombre, hadn't talked much all day.

He and Jemma walked slowly, hand in hand as

447

they climbed. Then the old man stopped, pointed to a stone in the lee of an ancient cedar whose spreading limbs were like arms reaching out to protect something. Johnnie's grave.

It was of dark-grey marble, not the colour of fresh cream like the others around. Harry's pace became slower, heavier, as he drew close.

It bore a simple inscription.

J E MALTRAVERS-JONES. 1941–2002.

Underneath was another short line.

NO EXCUSES. NO REGRETS.

'Typical. He always had to have the last word,' Harry breathed. Jemma noticed he was biting his bottom lip as though something hurt. The wizened caretaker had drifted away, leaving them alone with their thoughts. As he disappeared an early-evening breeze began to shake the branches of the tree, casting dappled shadows across the grave. The scent of pine resin and cedar, as sweet as it was heavy, carried on the air. Harry squeezed Jemma's hand, a fraction too tightly.

The grave was in its own plot, covered in bleached pebbles and marked out by a narrow marble surround. Fresh flowers stood in a pot of water at the end of the grave but the elegance of the scene was spoiled by a cheap plastic toy that someone had left. It was of a dragon and dressed in a bright red rugby shirt that marked the famous Welsh victory in the Grand Slam of the previous year. The toy was propped up awkwardly, at an angle, embedded in the pebbles at the base of the headstone. It was no more than a trinket, a silly gesture for such a place, as though Johnnie were still laughing at the world from the other side.

Harry said nothing for several minutes; Jemma could see his lips moving but it was a conversation he was having on the inside, alone with his father. She could see great sorrow in his eyes and also resentment. Eventually he turned, whispered one word: 'Enough.' Then he left.

His stride was now purposeful, he wanted to leave, get out of this place, and Jemma was forced to hurry in order to catch up with him. He took her hand, held his head high to the setting sun, trying to hide the tears, his thumb stroking the new ring on her finger as though in search of reassurance and some meaning to it all.

They had arrived back at the iron gate. Once again it complained as Harry stepped through it, but Jemma tarried, reluctant to leave. The tip of her nose was bobbing in the way that it did when she was puzzled, or thoughtful, or both.

'What's the matter, Jem?' he asked, impatient to get on.

'I'm not sure. It's nothing, but . . . Who put the flowers there, Harry? And that silly plastic toy?'

—๛—

They found the caretaker in his hideaway at the back of the cemetery, beneath a rush awning that stuck out from the front of a ramshackle work shed. He was sitting on a battered chair beside an equally forlorn table, cracking pistachios between his teeth and staring out towards the distant sea.

'*Sighnomi* – excuse me,' Jemma began, leaning on more of her youthful Greek.

The old man smiled in encouragement and pulled himself, willing but wearily, from his chair.

'The flowers – *Louloudia*. Who put them on the grave?'

The old man tapped his chest. 'Me,' he replied, revealing broken English.

'But why?'

He rubbed his thumb and forefinger together in the universal language of money.

'You want paying?' Jemma asked, taken aback but nevertheless reaching into her bag.

'No! No!' the caretaker insisted, his cracked face suddenly flushed with insult. 'Money, it come by post. Every year.'

'But who? Who sends it?'

The old man shrugged his shoulders. 'Three hundred fifty euro. Every year. In letter.'

'From where?'

The old Greek struggled and spread his hands in a gesture of impotence.

Harry jumped in. 'These letters. Do you still have them?'

The caretaker shook his head once more.

'Then the toy, in the red shirt,' Harry said, trying to draw its design on his own chest, 'where did that come from?'

But the old man seemed bemused.

'The red shirt!' Harry said, more forcefully, as if raising his voice would help scatter the old man's confusion.

The Greek gazed from Harry to Jemma, then back again. Their misery was unmistakable. Yet suddenly his face burst into a broad smile. He reached into his pocket and brought out his phone. He called someone, gabbled a few words, placed a gnarled finger on the button to activate the speakerphone, and with an expression of pride held it out towards Harry. A woman's voice came from the phone, in accented but excellent English.

'Mr Jones, my name is Iro. I am Mr Kottikas's granddaughter. How can we help?'

451

'Thank you. Thank you, Iro,' Harry said, nodding his thanks to the old man. 'Your grandfather has been very kind but ...'

'I'm afraid his English is like a banker's virtue, Mr Jones. Sadly unreliable.'

'I've been visiting my father's grave. There are fresh flowers on it. Your grandfather says someone sends him money every year for them. I'd very much like to know who.'

'I'm sorry but we don't know. It's been going on ever since your father was buried. A note came asking for the grave to be tended and saying money would be sent every year. And so it has. Cash. But never any name. It surprised us, too.'

'Then what about the plastic doll? Where did that come from?'

'Excuse me, Mr Jones, while I speak with my grandfather.'

A cascade of Greek followed before Iro returned her attention to Harry. 'It seems the doll of which you speak was sent with last year's money. In a small parcel.'

'You must have some idea who sent it,' Harry insisted, struggling to hide his exasperation.

'I'm so very sorry but—'

Suddenly the old man gave a cry and began wagging

a finger. 'Stop, stop! One ... minute!' he exclaimed before disappearing inside his patched-up shed. Moments later he returned, clutching a small cardboard box. He tipped its contents over the table. Screws, bolts and other fixings tumbled out, clattering onto the battered top. Then he handed the box to Harry. It was robustly constructed, ideal for storing old screws, and just big enough to hold a small plastic doll.

There was nothing inside, no letter, no markings, but on the outside of the box, in carefully formed capital letters, was Mr Kottikas's name and address. Two stamps were fixed to the parcel to cover postage. British stamps, franked and cancelled by the seal of a local postmaster. A seal that was smudged but still legible.

As he read it Harry's hand was shaking. 'No, impossible. It can't be,' he whispered.

CHAPTER THIRTY-TWO

The Isle of Man. Part of Britain, but part not. An isolated and often storm-swept rock in the middle of the Irish Sea. There is a saying that on a clear day and from its highest point a man can see five kingdoms: the kingdoms of England, Ireland, Scotland, Wales – and God. A place of raw beauty, of moorland, of mountain, of uninhabited beaches where oyster catchers and seals keep a wary eye for intruders. Yet, despite its physical attractions, at least half of the inhabitants come to the island not for its views but because of its status as a tax hideaway, for the island is also a place of investment funds, offshore advisers and audacious accounting.

'And where my parents lived when they first got married,' Harry had explained to Jemma in a voice that kept stalling. 'In Kirk Bride. Where the parcel was posted.'

Kirk Bride was a hamlet on the northern tip of the island, away from the towns, set in rolling farmland that melded into a heather-covered coastline. They'd been there two days and had knocked on every door they could find. They had tea with the vicar, interrogated the local postmistress, who also ran the tearooms. 'We get lots of tourists,' the postmistress had explained, shrugging off any knowledge of the parcel that Harry waved at her. No one could help, which was perhaps not surprising, since Harry and Jemma had precious little idea of what they were looking for. Not a soul could remember tell of anyone called Jones who had lived in these parts, even after Harry had tracked down his parents' entry in the church's marriage register. Their spirits began to flag. This was the sad time of year with summer gone and the harvest in, after the tourists had fled and when doors were closed. Kirk Bride was battening down for the winter, which could be long in these parts.

'Why did they choose this spot?' Jemma asked, on their third morning when they had taken the road out to the lighthouse on the point. It was a clear, sharp morning with a testing breeze and a view that stretched across the sea to the Solway Firth and the distant purple-brown mounds of land that was Cumbria.

'Money, I guess. This is bandit country, or used to be, and you know what my father was like. They moved to London when I came along.'

'For you.'

'For me? I hadn't thought about it in that way. I'd assumed it was more for the buzz, the social life, Harrods. When they'd grown tired of being alone with themselves.'

She remembered what McQuarrel had told her about Jessie: perhaps she'd had other needs, needs she would never satisfy here, on the empty heath.

The breeze was stiffening, building white caps on the water, wrestling with the faded summer heather and gorse that had burst into brilliant yellow flower. Jemma retreated inside her coat.

'I hate this bloody place,' Harry muttered forlornly. 'Come on, Jem, let's go home.' His words were filled with frustration and confusion, and more than a little anger.

He took her hand and they turned. As they did so another couple came into view. The pair had parked their car a little way down the track, by the red-and-white-striped lighthouse, and it was evident they were taking the air rather than planning a long walk across the heath. The man was elderly, wrapped up inside an overcoat and muffler with a soft trilby pushed down on his head. He was bent into the breeze and leaning heavily on his walking stick. The woman at his side was much younger and had the practical appearance of a nurse. Harry guessed this was the daily outing for the old man, a gentle totter in the shelter of the lighthouse, a lungful of sea air and an eyeful of Scotland before the nurse returned him to his home and a blazing hearth. Their presence made Harry feel like an intruder; as the other couple drew close he took Jemma's hand more firmly and began heading back. The old man's stick tapped upon the ground, step after slow step, his free hand stuffed inside his overcoat pocket for warmth and to stifle the palsied tremor that ran through it. Despite his affliction, as they passed, the man raised his hat in silent greeting.

Harry stopped dead. The old man did the same.

'I knew you'd find me. Eventually,' he said. 'What took you so long, son?'

—✕—

The two men sat on a bench in a nearby windbreak, with Jemma in the middle, separating them. The nurse was dismissed to the car. Harry hadn't said a word. He sat with his head in his hands as though praying that his eyes were deceiving him.

'Mr Maltravers-Jones? I'm Jemma,' she said, deciding to break the tension.

'I know,' the old man said in a voice that came close to a wheeze. 'Tallon told me.'

'Forgive me for mentioning it but you're supposed to be dead.'

He nodded stiffly. 'Soon will be.' He tapped his chest, his breathlessness gave away the rest. 'Let's not hurry things, eh? And you can call me Johnnie.' The eyes were red, hollow, told of some incurable exhaustion, yet still they managed a little jig of pleasure as they gazed at Jemma.

'Silly question but ...?'

'What am I doing here?' He pulled out a handkerchief to wipe a dribble of spittle from his lips. 'I'm hiding, of course.'

'From whom? The taxman?'

Johnnie gave a dry laugh. 'No. It's never been about money.'

Suddenly Harry twitched into life, turning on his father as though he'd been bitten. 'It's always been about money. It's your life's work!'

The old man shook his head, didn't try to match his son's passion; perhaps he was no longer able. 'No, never that. Money's been more of a hobby. Some people collect stamps. I collected ideas. Gave them a little exercise.'

'So why did you disappear? Lie to everyone?'

'There were some very serious people who didn't

care for what I was doing. They intended to kill me. Just like they did with Ali.'

Harry jumped to his feet. He was no longer able to control the storm of emotion welling inside. 'I wish they ...' He didn't finish the sentence. Not even he was sure of what he might have said.

'If you sit down, son, I'll try to explain.'

Harry glared at his father in turmoil, the old resentment returned with all its fury, a scene that had been repeated many times but not for many years. Only reluctantly did he do as he was told.

'Ali was my closest friend, almost a brother. A bloody Arab, of course. Called me a Son of a Britsch, but that was nothing to what I called him. Like all Arabs he enjoyed making money but he was also an idealist. Wanted peace for his homeland, a respite from all the killing. Pathetic, I know, but ... a good man – yes, a very good man, was Ali. And a devoted friend. Shared what he had with us.'

'The Aunt Emmas.'

Johnnie nodded. 'But I was his best friend, you see, the very best. Loved his ugly face, his terrible jokes.' Johnnie paused, summoning memories. 'It was just before our annual get-together. He called from Riyadh in a state of great excitement. Said he'd discovered something that might be the most important piece of information we'd ever had.' He was staring at Harry, making sure he had his son's attention.

'He told me of a weekend he'd just spent with a Saudi prince, one of the lowlife types with sticky fingers. A man who loved to drink and to brag. Like all of us, eh, Jemma?'

He squeezed her hand and smiled, enjoying a little moment of mischief. She nodded in gentle agreement. Then the moment was gone and he returned to his tale of the darker side.

'One night the prince had finished with his whores and was off his head to the point of incoherence. Kept mumbling about an attack on the United States that was going to change the world. Something that was massive. And imminent. Ali thought it was no more than wild ramblings until in the morning the prince, now very sober, spent every hour shouting at his moneymen. Gambling everything he had. We're not talking just millions, but hundreds of them. That's when Ali knew he was serious. The prince was piling into gold and oil and defence stocks, getting out of things like the dollar, insurance. And airlines.'

'When was this?' Harry asked, his voice now cold.

'Early September 2001.'

'You can't be serious. Nine-eleven?' Harry gasped, incredulous.

'Was it? Perhaps. We had no way of knowing. It was a few days before. We thought it was simply a massive raid on the markets, some sheiks consortium selling everything short. So Ali and I did the same.'

'But how could the prince have known?' Jemma broke in.

'The nine-eleven hijackers,' Harry whispered, seeing through fog. 'Most of them were Saudis.'

'We had no idea what we were getting into; we made a monumental screw-up,' Johnnie continued, his breathing shallow, punctuating every thought. 'You remember what it was like after the Twin Towers: they were days of chaos and conspiracy. And revenge. I was appalled to think I might have got myself involved in some way. So I made a mistake. A terrible mistake. I talked to someone with connections to the intelligence services about it. Should never have trusted him. Never.'

'Why?' Jemma asked

'Because almost immediately afterwards the Saudi prince disappeared, not a trace. And within days Ali was murdered, very publicly, along with his family, as a warning.'

'Who would do that?'

'No idea. But you wouldn't have to look far for suspects, not with all that blood lust and retribution in the air. Could the Americans have done something like that? Of course they could if they'd become convinced we were mixed up in it. And they never took much convincing, did they. Jump in, bang bang, mission accomplished.But for my money – and there's still a deal of that', he said, eyeing Harry with an expression that was a mixture of both rebuke and pride – 'It was more likely some Middle Eastern government or a group of extremists who took fright. Something had gone wrong, the plan had leaked and we were a loose end that might lead right back to the source of it all. And whoever it was, they wouldn't have thought twice. Thousands had already died in the Towers, hundreds of thousands were soon to follow in the war. What did a few more matter? Ali's execution was a warning and I was next in line. So I started running.'

'But it wasn't just you,' Jemma said. 'What about the others? Finn, Susannah, McQuarrel? The bishop?'

'I hadn't mentioned any of them, hadn't needed to. They were all fine, until Finn started digging around for material to put in one of his wretched books. Made himself a target. That's why he tried to disappear.'

'He didn't do it too well.'

'I did it better. Took myself off the list. Spread a surprisingly modest amount of money around a Greek port and arranged a convenient heart attack.'

'Letting me think you were dead,' Harry said.

'Remember this. Whoever killed Ali also killed his family. That was deliberate. Cruel beyond words. A warning. I wasn't going to run the risk.'

He stared at Harry with piercing eyes; Harry glared back.

'Don't try to pretend you were protecting me!' Harry snapped, bitter.

'What are you complaining about? You didn't seem to care very much about whether I was alive or dead. You'd already cut me out of your life.'

'It was you – you who cut me. When I was eighteen.'

And all the years of hurt that had been locked away began flooding out once more.

'I didn't cut you. I made you,' the old man bit back. 'What would you have become if you'd arrived at your snotty university with your pockets stuffed full of my cash? You needed to learn. About knocks and bruises. I forced you to stand on your own feet. Best bloody lesson you learned at Cambridge.'

'You never took any interest, never made contact.'

'Now isn't that funny, son? I thought that's what I was supposed to accuse you of. How many times did I write? Did you ever reply?'

'Don't you turn this on me. What I became was because I got you out of my life.'

'Oh, really? It didn't seem that way when you got

your hands on half my fortune.' Johnnie was panting now, the colour creeping into his pale face suggesting he wouldn't stop, even if it killed him. 'Useful, wasn't it, the odd fifteen million or so, just as you got yourself into Parliament, became a bloody politician? I remember an interview you gave once, about how your money gave you independence, enabled you to be your own man. Very noble. Only bit you left out was that it wasn't your money at all, it was mine.'

Harry flinched.

'Tallon kept sending you money by the truckload. Took a while to unwind my affairs. He's still doing it. The Brazilian rainforest, I think he told you. That's bollocks. It's what I have left, squirreled away, what you'll get when I die. Don't lose it as quickly as you did the last lot.'

He paused, his eyes welling with an old man's sadness. He waved his stick in anger at a seagull that had grown inquisitive and come too near. It flew off, circling on the breeze, crying in disgust.

'Good man, Tallon. The only one who knew. I even had him arrange for an old friend to offer you a directorship, to see you through the rough patch. You didn't have the bloody sense to accept it.'

'You tried to own me!' Harry spat back.

'No!' But the effort had become too much. Johnnie

465

began spluttering, saliva trickling down his old chin. He wiped his mouth, struggled to regain his breath and with it his composure. When he spoke again it was no longer with venom, as if he no longer cared. 'I didn't try to own you, Harry. I simply tried to help you. As best a father could.'

He flapped a hand to summon the nurse. It was over. But Harry was on his feet once more, overwhelmed by old nightmares.

'You were never a father. And you were a pathetic excuse for a husband. I watched my mother die while you—'

His outburst was brought to a sudden halt. With surprising vigour Johnnie had raised his stick as if to strike him.

Harry stood his ground. 'You're not going to get away with that again.'

The words hit the old man as a storm hits an old ship and something broke inside Johnnie. He sagged, capsized, surrender flooding through his eyes. 'I remember,' he sobbed, wretched, hiding his face in his handkerchief. When he spoke again his voice was little more than a gasp. 'I did, didn't I? Just the once. I'm sorry, Harry, son, I was ashamed. And I lashed out to cover that shame because I didn't know what else to do. It was a time in my life when I wasn't doing so well. After your mother died.'

'I remember those years. The screaming matches. You storming out. The weeks you disappeared instead of being at home with us.'

'It wasn't like that.'

'You betrayed us.'

'Why do you hate me so?'

'You broke my mother to pieces!'

'Harry, you were young. You don't understand.'

'I can still see her in the bedroom where she died. You didn't even have the decency to bring me back from school to say goodbye to her.'

'You were thirteen. I was trying to protect you. When your mother died I didn't know what to do.' The breeze had picked up, scratching at his old eyes, making them watery, sending tears down his dry cheeks. 'Your mother . . .' He gasped in pain, then he raised his eyes in defiance, staring at his son. 'Jessie was a pearl. To me she was priceless. Not perfect, who is? But what does it matter if the woman you love has a few flaws? And I loved her so very much. But all she saw was the flaws in herself and the closer she looked, the larger they came to seem. It got too much for her, something inside telling her she was inadequate, unworthy. And it ate her away.' He groaned in misery. 'Past mistakes. Things she should have forgotten. Things I knew about and which ought to have been pushed to one side. But

467

instead she pushed me aside. Said I reminded her of all her guilt.'

'You left us!'

Johnnie shook his head. 'That was her choice, not mine. Never mine.'

'There were so many other women.'

'Only after Jessie had died and none that mattered. That's why when I staged my own death it didn't really matter to me. There was no one else. Even you had forgotten me. So I came back here, to my old world, this Elba in the Irish Sea. No one would find me here. And it was where I spent the happiest years of my life, with Jessie.'

'You bastard, I don't believe a word of it!' Harry cried, but Jemma was in his arms, her fingers to his lips, silencing him.

'It's true, Harry, believe me,' she whispered.

'How the hell do you know?'

'McQuarrel told me much of it.'

'McQuarrel!' Harry scoffed in dismissal.

'He thought I was dying at the time. He had no reason to lie.'

A fog of confusion settled on Harry. It was too much. He couldn't rewrite his entire life in five minutes. 'I still don't believe you,' he said.

'Perhaps you were too young to remember the good times, Harry, when we were in London, when your mother was in better health. Why, we had so much fun, Jessie and me, watching you grow.'

Harry was trembling. Jemma held him in her arms, then led him back to the bench where his father sat. She settled between them once more, took Harry's hand, then that of his father, joining the three of them.

'McQuarrel told me many things, Harry.'

Johnnie tensed in concern, she squeezed his hand in reassurance as she continued. 'How your father would come to their reunions bubbling with stories. About you. What you had done. How proud he was of you.'

The old man was nodding, a teardrop dancing down the ridge of his nose that he didn't bother to hide.

'McQuarrel also told me about how much your father loved your mother, through the thick and the thin, and for all the mistakes she made. You Jones boys, father, son – to hell with it, Harry, you two are so much alike.'

They fell to silence, each in the grip of their different thoughts, all three of them in pain. The sun stood high in the sky, warming the breeze that rippled through the heather on its way to the sea. The old man's nurse was standing at a respectful distance, waiting to take him back.

'That is a lovely ring,' Johnnie said, gazing down at Jemma's hand, which was still tightly locked around his own.

'He does well, your son. At times.'

'Dad?'

A single word. The old man looked up. It was the first time he had heard that word since a time so long ago it had almost disappeared.

'Dad, why don't you come home with us?'

ACKNOWLEDGEMENTS

So Johnnie was alive and had even become a grandfather. The Joneses are full of surprises. I hope the reader will forgive me for making the Jones family such an untidy unit but it has opened up all sorts of adventures for them. If you would like to find out more about Ruari, Harry's fascinating son, you will need to read *Old Enemies*.

A Ghost at the Door is Harry's sixth adventure and for anyone familiar with his escapades I have the usual list of suspects to thank. Ian Patterson has been an inspiration from the start of the series, as has Andrei Vandoros, and they continue to be a huge source of strength, humour and knowledge. As he was with *A Sentimental Traitor*, Sean Cunningham has been extraordinarily patient and supportive on the many occasions I have pestered him about police procedure.

A friend of many years standing – although she remains everlastingly young – is Sarah Maltby, with whom I used to work at Saatchi & Saatchi before we both went our different ways. Sarah ended up in Bermuda and has helped refresh many of my memories about that lovely island.

Another destination that featured heavily in the research and writing of this book is the Ionian island of Meganissi. It is small but wonderfully hospitable and I wanted to show my gratitude by naming one of the characters after Iro Kottikas, who has patiently provided so many of the Greek details.

Professor John Dodds is another friend from that part of the world who appears yet again on the list of thanks. He helped me with much of the background for the city of Trieste that featured prominently in *Old Enemies*. Evidently he didn't find the process too painful because he has continued to provide guidance about consular procedures.

Mrs Stephanie Harwood was a delightful host when I wanted to research houseboats on the Thames at Chelsea, while Dr Ian Plummer of Balliol College was very helpful with his unparalleled experience of the sport of croquet at Oxford. I only wish I could have used more than a tiny fraction of the fascinating information he made available to me. Also at Oxford I must thank those at my old college of Christ Church, and in particular Helen Camunas-

Lopez in the Steward's Office, who tolerated my frivolous enquiries with a cheerfulness I probably didn't deserve.

I owe several debts of gratitude to those who have helped me on Church matters. My long-standing friend Sir Tony Baldry is a Church Estates Commissioner who shares no resemblance whatsoever with the character of Cyrus Harefield MP. This may be at Tony's insistence rather than mine. Archdeacon Emeritus Peter Delaney allowed me to wander around the Wren church of St Stephen Walbrook and to clamber up its somewhat precarious tower. St Stephen's is a place of breathtaking beauty and peace; if you don't know it, I recommend a visit. My old Christ Church friend Alastair Redfern helped steer me around some of the ecclesiastical rocks – although in the case of Bishop Randall I fear I may have got myself firmly stuck on them. Alastair and I used to row together at Christ Church; he sat higher up the boat than me. He still does. Nowadays he is better known as the Bishop of Derby and is a colleague in the House of Lords.

Mary Hamilton provided a delightful evening at the Henley Festival on which I relied for one of the opening scenes, and Kevin Hughes was always willing to respond to my questions about the City of London. My colleague of far too many years, John Ranelagh, will, I hope, forgive me for stealing his family name.

Another dear friend was Shukri Ghanem. We met more than forty years ago at the Fetcher School of Law and Diplomacy. I helped type his doctoral thesis on oil pricing. We went our separate ways and he eventually became a controversial prime minister of Libya. He died recently under mysterious circumstances. I used his inspiring memory for the character of Ali Abu al-Masri.

I have taken creative liberties with so much of the advice and information I have been given. I hope those who provided it will forgive me.

A Ghost at the Door is a story of fathers and sons, and the unavoidable impact they have on each other. Inevitably I have mined the relationship I had with my own father for ideas and I found the process therapeutic. He lived at Bride in the Isle of Man for the last and happiest years of his life. I hope much the same can be said for Johnnie.

And as this is a book about family, my own family – Rachel and the boys – as always have earned the biggest round of applause. I do it all for them, just as they do everything for me.

Michael Dobbs
Wylye, June 2013
www.michaeldobbs.com
@dobbs_michael